the MARKET

the MARKET

J. M. STEELE

Disney · HYPERION BOOKS
NEW YORK

First Disney · Hyperion paperback edition, 2009
10 9 8 7 6 5 4 3 2 1
Printed in the United States of America
Library of Congress Cataloging-in-Publication Data on file.
ISBN: 978-1-4231-0016-4
Visit www.hyperionteens.com

For those whom I love
(You know who you are)

BOOK ONE

· · · · · · ·

AN INITIAL PUBLIC OFFERING

CHAPTER

$$\boxed{1}$$

SOMEWHERE IN THE DISTANCE I heard a cell phone ringing, and I slipped in unnoticed through the side door. Gretchen's kitchen was crammed shoulder-to-shoulder with kids from Millbank, and the smell of sweat hung in the air. By the window a pony keg filled the sink, the tap hose snaking up into some meathead's slurping mouth. As two of his friends lifted him upside down for a keg stand, I pushed my way toward the living room, which—if possible—appeared even more packed. Everybody was dancing to pounding hip-hop, and the room was vibrating; shaking, in fact. As I took another step, I felt heat and sweat rise up like a wall in front of me.

I'm so out of my league.

Was I a social pariah at Millbank High School? No. But

I wasn't the "I" or the "T" of the It Crowd, either. For four long and safe years, I had been comfortable moving with the herd of the forgettable, but standing in the midst of this truly unforgettable party made me realize how lame my life at Millbank High School had been. Gretchen Tanner was *that* popular girl with the rich dad who gave her everything she wanted: a brand new Mercedes convertible, an AMEX black card so she could shop till she literally dropped, and unchaperoned parties on the weekends when her parents went out of town. Oh, and she was gorgeous. She basically lived a fairy-tale life. To those mere mortals—like yours truly—it was enough to make you want to barf. Yes, Gretchen and I were from two different worlds. The fact that over the past four years we'd said maybe two words to each other only made the invitation that I'd discovered stuck in the grille of my locker all the more baffling. No one else I knew had been invited to Gretchen's party. Not Dev. Not Callie.

So why me?

Already regretting the pink sweater set from Ann Taylor that my mother had talked me into wearing, I grabbed a Diet Coke from a cooler and positioned myself by the door to the patio. The party was divided into what I liked to call the Three Rings of Popularity, and I was definitely the only person from the third ring—i.e., the outer reaches of this particular social galaxy. Camped out in the living room were the solid members of the second ring, which was comprised tonight of Mike Talbot and the rest of the zero-and-fourteen soccer players who thought they had the world by the balls, the field hockey girls who were never cute enough to be super cool but had amazing bodies and liked to party, and a group of annoying sophomore cheerleaders still in uniform popping out yet another version of some lame-ass line dance, like the lemmings they were. Out on the patio, securely forming the first ring, was Gretchen's inner circle, aka The Proud Crowd: Jodi Letz, Elisa Estrada, and Carrie Bell. Their silver "P"s (the Proud Crowd's trademark emblem) glittered on chains around their necks, while JV wannabes mooned around them, hoping to gain access to this rarified world. Gretchen Tanner, the epicenter, the force around which everyone at Millbank High orbited, was nowhere in sight.

After a few minutes of wall-flowering, silently wondering how long I needed to stay before I could make a face-saving exit via the back door, I noticed Will Bochnowski walk in with Jack Clayton following close behind. If Gretchen had a male counterpart at Millbank High, it was Will B. I'd had a major crush on him for, like, two years— and let's be honest, *every* girl had a crush on Will B.— because, don't let the name fool you, he was a hottie of the highest order. Shaggy brown hair that hung down almost to his shoulders, eyes so blue that you could swim in them, and a body that was to die for; he was, in a word, *it*. Will was on his way to Vassar next year, and he fronted a band called Jane Austen's Secret Lover, which—rumor had it—had just signed a deal with an indie record label.

Jack Clayton, who I'd never actually seen without Will B., was the guitarist in the band and widely regarded as Will's sidekick (or his "Boy Wonder," as some less charitable people put it). Dressed conservatively—new jeans, a perfectly ironed dress shirt, and a baseball hat pulled low—he hardly cut the same figure as Will and pretty much traipsed in his shadow. As they passed by, neither one of them noticed me, and I found myself staring into the crowd blankly.

So how does a girl busy herself for an hour when she has no one to talk to at a party? Well . . .

She makes no fewer than three trips to the bathroom, where she leans against the sink and waits until someone knocks.

She studies the tomes on the bookshelves with an intensity bordering on religious.

She keeps moving and makes at least three "laps" around the house, wearing a perplexed expression that suggests she's searching for someone specific who just *has* to be in the next room.

She steps outside for an important call on her cell— at which point others in the vicinity may overhear phrases such as, *Oh my God!* or *Shut up!* or *That's soooo awesome!*

In short, she does anything not to look like a complete and total LOSER.

But after my fourth trip to the bathroom (the max, lest someone thinks you have some sort of problem—bladder, drug, or otherwise) and more than a handful of sideways glances cast my direction courtesy of the Proud Crowd, I decided I had to mix it up. Dying of thirst anyway, I wandered out to the pool, where another keg sat in a plastic garbage can. Despite the fact that I usually walked the straight-and-narrow path, I decided I needed a drink. In fact, I reasoned, I *deserved* a drink. Besides, I wasn't driving. My car was getting inspected, so, much to my chagrin, my mother had ferried me to Gretchen's house and I was supposed to call her when I was ready to leave.

I grabbed a plastic cup from the table and picked up the hose, but when I pressed the button on the nozzle, nothing came out. I tried shaking the keg to see if it was empty, but its weight revealed that it was very much still full. I tried the button again, and nothing but foam spurted out.

"Let me help you with that," I heard a voice say.

I looked up just in time to see Will Bochnowski approach.

My knees—no joke—buckled.

"You have to pump it first," he explained, and he grabbed the knob on top of the tap and lifted it.

"Oh, right," I mumbled, feeling like the biggest moron ever. "Of course."

He must have been dancing because in the cool night air, steam rose off his sweat-drenched head. He filled two cups—one for each of us—and leaned against a pillar.

"Kate Winthrop," he said.

"Yup, that's me."

That's me? I couldn't think of anything less retarded to say? What about "the one and only"? Or "in the flesh"? Or "the girl you've always wanted to date"?

"So how's it going?"

"Oh, you know," I replied. "Just doing my thing."

I noticed then that his eyes were a little glassy—like maybe he'd had too much to drink—and his head lolled a little to the side. It was sexy, whatever it was, and he exuded a level of confidence that was paralyzing. Maybe that explained why I seemed to have lost the power of speech.

"Good times, huh?" he said.

For the love of God, I just couldn't respond. I stood there starry-eyed, just watching his mouth open and shut. Finally I blurted out, "Uh-huh."

"Sounds like it."

"It's true," I laughed.

I can't believe I'm talking to Will B.

"This isn't your scene," he observed, and I felt my spirits dip. It was a sobering reminder. No, I wasn't of this world.

I said nothing.

"That's a good thing," he said, looking around with distaste in his eye.

From within the screened patio, Jack Clayton shouted out to Will. When I turned, I saw that Jack was staring directly at me—in a sort of weird way—like my talking to Will had irked him somehow.

"Let's go, B.!" Jack shouted again.

"Comin'!" Will yelled back.

I noticed then that there was a girl lurking behind Jack, peering out at us as well. Was it Gretchen? Or just one of her groupies? It was impossible to tell through the screen door.

Will drained his beer and tossed the cup in the garbage. "Well, that's my ride. Shine on, little sister."

I nodded and gave him a little smile (I think the fly on the wall would have said it was my pathetic attempt at flirting). Just as he passed me, he stopped and turned. He was close enough that I could smell his cologne—piney and masculine.

"You know, Kate," he said, "you were always the one I couldn't see."

I just stared back at him. I couldn't speak. After a beat, he shrugged his shoulders like he didn't have time to wait for somebody as slow-witted as me and then turned and walked away into the crowd.

What the hell did that mean?

It wasn't long after my talk with Will that I realized it was officially time to leave.

I'd nursed about a third of my lukewarm beer and wandered around the front of the house when I noticed that quiet music had replaced the heavy dance beats. The party was evolving into one of those intimate, core-group-only moments, and I suddenly felt alone. I had to leave. But how? My house was a good thirty minutes away, and I surely didn't have money to call a cab. Needless to say, if I wanted to leave this party with a minuscule sense of coolness, the good-ol' mom taxi service was out of the question.

I was standing on the front lawn, lamely staring out at Manhattan in the distance, when I heard the front door unlatch behind me. If there were part of me that was hoping to see Will standing there, offering to give me a ride home, it was quickly crushed. It wasn't Will.

It was Gretchen Tanner.

With a wiggle of her fingers that passed for a wave, she closed the door behind her and sauntered over to where I stood.

"Cute outfit," she remarked, gesturing toward my sweater set, and I felt myself go red. She could deliver a backhanded compliment better than Maria Sharapova. I knew how I looked: like a soccer mom.

Whatever you thought of Gretchen Tanner—she wielded her Queen Bee status like a mace—you had to hand it to her.

Even at the very end of the night, when the average girl looked a little worn-out and worse for wear, Gretchen was still a veritable vision of beauty. Dressed in a slinky white shift that must have cost a gajillion dollars, with a huge strand of what-I-could-only-presume-to-be real pearls wrapped casually around her wrist, she looked ridiculously beautiful. Next to her I felt like a cow . . . a tall, pink cow. I wondered in that split second what it must be like to be that rich, that beautiful, and that popular.

"So how's it going, Kate?"

"Great. Awesome party."

"Yeah," she said, looking bored. "It was okay."

I shifted my weight and watched her. For some reason Gretchen had always intimidated me, and the fact that she intimidated me annoyed me. Still, I summoned all my social decorum.

"Thanks so much for having me."

"Sorry?" Her head cocked to the side, and she squinted.

"You know, for inviting me."

"What made you think you were invited?"

"Um, um," I stammered. "Didn't you put an invitation in my—"

"Invitation?" She laughed as she cut me off. "Does this look like a party for sixth graders?"

I studied the ground, too humiliated to look her in the eye.

"But you wouldn't know, I guess," she continued. "No worries, Katie. Somebody must've played a little joke on you. Or me. I just hope it wasn't too boring for you."

"It was fine," I said, wanting at this point to evaporate into the ether. "I had a nice chat with Will."

As soon as his name came out of my mouth, Gretchen's face changed, tightening up like a sixty-year-old on her third face lift.

"Will likes to slum, Seventy-one."

I blinked.

"Seventy-one?"

"Forget it," she said, all her poise returning.

Behind her, the front door opened again, and out stepped Gretchen's number-one protégée, Jodi Letz. Spotting me, she exhaled, looking exasperated and bored. What Jodi may have lacked in looks comparable to the rest of the Proud Crowd—she was a little thick around the waist, and her nose was oddly turned up—she made up for in bitchiness. Dev said she was overcompensating for her insecurities, but whatever the motivations for her mean streak were didn't matter—I feared I was in for a heavy dose.

"Katie," Jodi whispered, as she slid up next to Gretchen, "listen, I don't want to sound rude, but the party is PC-only now, so maybe your mom can pick you up. I saw her earlier in the PT Cruiser, right?"

I felt the heat rise in my cheeks. PC was an acronym for

Proud Crowd. My mouth opened, but nothing came out. Besides, what could I have said? It was a one-punch knock-out for Jodi. Her victim: me.

Gretchen let out a little laugh and then turned on her four-inch heels and headed back to the house. As soon as she crossed inside, she looked back my way and mouthed, "Bye."

I gritted my teeth and gave her my best fake smile.

Jodi closed the door behind her, leaving me standing alone in the dark. From within the house I heard Gretchen say it again . . . *seventy-one* . . . and then everyone laughed.

It was going to be a long walk home.

CHAPTER

2

UNLIKE GRETCHEN'S veritable castle, Chez Winthrop was a bungalow-style, two-story house in West Millbank. You could drive by the aging, yellow clapboard siding and wraparound porch without giving it a second look— but hey, it was home. Pretty much the cliché of the absent-minded college professor (he taught Literary Theory at NYU), Dad wasn't one for home improvements; but a few years back, Mom had convinced him to renovate the first floor. While the upstairs is still a bit of a rabbit warren of bedrooms and closets, the redesigned downstairs has an open layout—the humongo kitchen flowing into the requisite family room with oversized sofas, all of which lead to the porch via newly installed French doors. It's a great place to hang out when you have friends over—but if you're looking for privacy, you're out of luck.

By 9:30 a.m., I was sitting downstairs at the breakfast table and desperate for the Sunday morning cup of coffee my mom usually brewed for me. Unfortunately I was still empty-handed because my mother was on the phone and preoccupied with the star of her life, my sister, Melissa. A model of impossibly perky, preppie perfection, back in her day at Millbank High, Mel had been the junior-class president (opted out of the running her senior year), dated the captain of the soccer team (please, no comments), and now, just like Mom had, was running for president of her sorority (sororities—gag!) at Wake Forest. So when my sister calls, whether it's 9:00 a.m. on a Sunday or 3:00 a.m. on a Tuesday, the world stops. I could be on the side of the highway with a flat tire in a blizzard at midnight, but if my sister's number came up on the caller ID, my parents would drop me like yesterday's news.

"Wow, honey, he sounds great," Mom said into the phone as she glanced over at me. "And he's going to Harvard Business School next year?"

I got up to make my own coffee, but she waved at me to sit down. I rolled my eyes in annoyance.

"No sugar, right?" she mouthed as she nodded her head, listening to my sister blather on.

"One big one, please," I said, louder than necessary.

She sighed and placed my coffee in front of me. While she walked around the kitchen, checking for dust (she was a little OCD about cleaning) and yacking with my sister, I cradled the warm mug and stared at the wall, feeling lousy about myself. Lying wide awake in my bed, I'd spent the better part of the wee hours of the morning replaying my conversation with Will in my head—*why had I acted like such a retard?!*—and trying to make sense of what Gretchen said—*what the hell did "seventy-one" mean anyway?* And then there was the big question: If Gretchen hadn't invited me to the party, who had?

"So how was the party last night?" my mom asked. Lost in my own thoughts, I hadn't noticed that she'd hung up the phone.

"Fine," I said, now putting my nose in the Sunday Style section of the *New York Times.*

"Did you and Gretchen talk?"

Now, your average mom would've asked if I'd met any boys, how I'd gotten home, if anyone was drinking, etc., but it had been clear from the moment I mentioned the invitation to Gretchen's party that my mom had her own interests at heart. She was hoping for a bridge to Gretchen's mom, Abby Tanner—the one feat of social maneuvering that even Mel the Magnificent hadn't managed to accomplish. Abby Tanner is *the* Abby Tanner, the jewelry designer, whose earrings were most recently seen on Alicia Keys at the

Grammy Awards. Mr. Tanner's no slouch, either; he was a big Wall Street money guy and was the one who'd financed the start-up of Abby's company. Yeah, the Tanners, like their daughter, are what you'd call "big" in town. Long story short, for Mom, this party represented our family's first invitation to be included in the exclusive circle of Tanner friends.

"So did you talk to her?" she repeated.

She was trying to sound casual, like she didn't really care, but needless to say, I knew better. I decided to spare her my not-actually-invited-to-the-party humiliation. Trust me, it would've been worse for her than me.

"Not really," I said. "It was kind of loud."

She gave me a hard little look, as if to say, "Spill the beans."

"She said 'Hi' and 'Bye,'" I snipped. "We're not suddenly BFF if that's what you're hoping."

"What's BFF?"

Oh, c'mon.

"Never mind."

"Did you at least make an effort to talk to her?" she pressed. "You know we have our interview for the club coming up, and her parents—"

The Millbank Country Club. *Well, of course.* That's all my mother had been able to talk about for the last year, and despite the fact that Dad and I thought it was all really stupid, she had applied for membership. There were a million hoops you had to jump through—references, nominations, and some big-deal interview—but, like some desperate freshman boy, my mother was falling all over herself to get in. Gretchen's dad was on the board and Abby Tanner ran the selection committee, so you get the picture.

"—her parents would be really helpful for making things go smoothly."

"Mom, please leave me out of it."

"We're applying as a family. Our meeting with the club manager is in two weeks."

God, the woman is relentless.

I rolled my eyes, got up, and crossed to the island, where I grabbed half a bagel from the basket. Out of the corner of my eye, I could feel my mother watching me, holding her breath, so I took a glob of cheese and put it directly into my mouth. I could sense her blood pressure ticking up a few points, but this morning she deserved it.

Not that she ever would've admitted it, but I knew my mom wanted me to be more like Mel. I'm sure she stayed up late at night wondering how her daughters could've been so different. I mean, I wasn't a complete zero, but I didn't go out of my way to climb the social ladder at Millbank, either.

"Are you going shopping with the girls today?" Mom asked, changing the subject, probably in a desperate attempt to lessen my calorie intake.

"Maybe."

"You're just full of information, Katie."

The sarcasm noted, it was my turn to give her a hard little look. I made mine extra hard because she was being extra obnoxious.

"You don't want to buy anything you're not going to fit in," she noted.

Did I mention she was passive-aggressive also?

"If it doesn't fit, I'll throw on some of those shoulder pads you wore in the eighties—they made you look thin, right?"

It bugged her when I trashed the eighties, but let's be honest, there has never been a decade more ripe for trashing than the decade that brought us A Flock of Seagulls and *Porky's*.

"I just always hoped you'd get to go to the Black & White—like Melissa," she said, getting up and pouring the last of her coffee into the sink. She just had to bring up the Black & White thing, didn't she? The Black & White, for those of you from outside the greater Millbank area, was this huge yearly gala, but more on this later.

"Can we just drop it, please?!"

My mother pursed her lips and brought her hand to her forehead. She said nothing for a moment. "You know I'm only concerned because I love you, honey, right?"

"Totally understand, Mom," I answered, suddenly feeling guilty that I'd yelled at her. I knew deep down that she probably meant well. "But you know there are worse things in the world than my not going to the B & W."

Not that I foresaw that happening . . . even if there were no prospects yet.

"I know, sweetie. And if I can help in any way—"

"Mom!" I walked behind her and squeezed her shoulder. "Everything's going to be okay."

At least that's what I was hoping.

CHAPTER

```
┌ ┄ ┄ ┄ ┐
┊   3   ┊
└ ┄ ┄ ┄ ┘
```

EVERY SUNDAY, Dev, Callie, and I had brunch at Cozy Corner in what passed for downtown in East Millbank. Our brunch had become a ritual ever since Callie passed her driver's test two years before. She was actually a year older than me and Dev, because her parents had taken her to India for a year when they did Doctors Without Borders. Her mom was a big deal in the medical world—she was one of the first African American women to perform open-heart surgery—and she was always traveling to developing countries to train local doctors in the latest methods and treatments. Our brunch was really just an excuse to pore over everything that had gone down during the week: whether it was school gossip, parental drama, or anything boy-related. Although the geriatric crowd was often bumbling around, slurping prune juice, and waddling to the restrooms, we mostly had the place to ourselves, so we felt comfortable unpacking what needed to be unpacked.

When I walked in, Callie and Dev were already there, chatting away.

"Kate, sit down here," Callie said, patting the seat next to her. "So what happened last night?"

"Spill it." Dev grinned.

Callie, Dev, and I were different in our own ways, but we were close as close could be. If I had to choose two people in the world to count on—for like the rest of my life—I'd pick Dev and Cal. We'd been through it all together: first kisses, the SAT, college applications, even Dev's parents' divorce. Nothing meant more to me than our friendship. My invitation to Gretchen's party had mystified the three of us, and while it was clear Dev was a little jealous, they'd both pushed me to go.

"So what happened?" Dev pressed again.

"Nada."

"It's never nada with you," Callie said.

I winced and looked out the window. "Can't we talk about something else first?"

The girls glanced at each other, and a moment later, Callie reached out and grabbed my hand, clutching it between her palms. Of the three of us, Callie was the natural mother. At nearly six feet tall with an Afro that made her appear six-three, Callie was bigger than life. Beautiful, ethereal, and blessed with a natural instinct for fashion, she had earned her nickname "Miss Fabulous" ten times over. Let me put it this way: Callie probably could've been part of Gretchen's clique, but her moral compass was too strong to be involved in the evil one's silly games.

"C'mon. It couldn't have been that bad," she whispered, like I was her little baby. "But tell me everything, otherwise I'm heading home, because I didn't get up before noon on a Sunday just to listen to you say 'nada.'"

"Okay," I relented. "Turns out I wasn't really invited."

"WHAT?" Dev shrieked.

I leaned on the wood veneer table and proceeded to give them the blow-by-blow on what initially had happened (or for that matter, did not happen) at the party: wandering the house, studying the books, and desperately trying to blend in. Then I told them about my convo with Gretchen on the front lawn. Their eyes went wide.

"Omigod, that's harsh. Do you think she was lying?" Callie asked.

"Why would she lie?"

They both were silent for a beat.

"Either way," Dev observed, "the girl's a grade-A bitch. She didn't have to rub your face in it."

Dev and I had been friends since the seventh grade, but if you saw us side by side you never would have pegged us as such. For starters, we looked nothing alike. She was short, had dirty-blond hair, and was kind of *academic* looking (in middle school, she'd been voted most likely to be a bookworm by a bunch of mean boys, and I don't think she'd ever recovered socially or psychologically). I was a tall brunette, without any obviously definable drawbacks or advantages, if you catch my drift. But it was our personalities where we really diverged. I was somewhat quiet and prone to thinking too long before I spoke, whereas she was a neurotic attack dog high on NoDoz. Despite it all, we had an unbreakable bond, and Callie, always the one to dabble in Eastern philosophy, said Dev was the yin to my yang.

"And then, what was even more bizarre," I continued, forging on to the bitter end, "is that Gretchen called me 'Seventy-one.'"

"What's that?" Callie frowned.

"Gretchen said, 'Will likes to slum, Seventy-one.'"

Dev sat straight up. "Hold on a second. Did you talk to Will B.?!"

A smile crept across my face.

"Will B.!" Dev yelled.

"Now, that's why I got up this morning!" Callie chimed in.

"What did he say?"

I grinned and leaned back into my seat. It wasn't every day that you get to say that you were hanging out with Will

B. "Okay, so I was getting beer from the keg, and he sort of rolled up."

"At the keg." Callie smiled. "A classic guy move."

But Dev didn't flinch. Where Dev and I *were* similar was in our lack of success with boys. I think our combined record was four for thirty-one, and that—though I'm loath to admit this—included the occasional date with an underclassman. Totally on the down low, I don't think she'd ever even kissed a boy. Virgin lips were rare these days, but Dev had them. Some day when she met a boy as smart as she was, I knew the rockets would go off, but until then she had me and Callie.

"So he had this wild look in his eyes, like maybe he was on something. It was so sexy. He took my cup and started pumping the keg up, and then he sort of mumbled something extraordinary."

"What?!!" they shouted in unison.

I cracked up. I'd never seen the two them so worked up over a little boy story. Tears started to roll down my cheeks and my stomach was cramping from laughing so hard. Callie and Dev started laughing too, and eventually the waitress had to come over and offer us water.

"Okay, okay," I finished. "He said: 'You were always the one I couldn't see.'"

"Wow," Callie breathed.

Dev's eyes lit up.

"What?" I said, turning to Dev.

"Nothing," she said. "But it was only a matter of time."

Callie seemed to catch her vibe, because suddenly she nodded, too. "That's right."

"What's right?" I asked. I had no idea what Dev was talking about, but it was weirding me out.

"Anyway, he took off and then, like, the party emptied out in two seconds. Will practically evaporated before my eyes. That's when the whole Gretchen thing went down."

"Well, no wonder she was bitchy to you," Dev concluded. "She was pissed that you were talking to Will. You know she's always had a thing for him. "

"They dated," Callie said. "For like a millisecond—I heard he dumped her after they did the deed."

"Couldn't have happened to a more evil creature," Dev said.

The thought of Will B. getting down with Gretchen silenced everyone, and then our food came, and the subject drifted to Mexico and our senior summer trip. As the three of us started talking about where we were going to stay, the flight down, and whether there'd be time to visit the Mayan ruins, I felt a wave of nostalgia wash over me. How many more brunches were the three of us going to have together? How many more late-night hangouts before I was in Rhode Island (early admission to Brown, thank you very much),

Dev was in New York, and Callie was all the way out at Berkeley? The more I thought about the future, the more I thought about the past. Things I might have done differently. How high school was, once and for all, truly coming to an end.

Before I knew it, an hour had passed and Callie had to take off for her yoga class. While we waited for change from the waitress, Dev got up and went to the powder room.

Deep down, I knew I should just let it go, but something wouldn't let me.

"Cal," I said, "what did Dev mean before when she said it was only a matter of time?"

Callie stared at me for a few seconds. "You don't know, do you? If I hadn't known you this long, I wouldn't believe it."

"What?" I said, starting to feel self-conscious, like there was something wrong with me.

Callie got up from the booth and flung her yoga mat over her back. She kissed me on the cheek and let her beautiful, long, elegant fingers rest against my cheek.

"You're beautiful, inside and out," she said.

"Thanks." I blushed, not knowing what else to do.

"I mean it, K," she said. "The only difference between you and Gretchen is that she believes she is."

"Right."

"I'm serious." And then she pinched my cheek, like a

grandmother would. She walked away with a smile so big that it held all that was right in the world.

I wanted to *believe* what she just told me—that soon my Friday nights wouldn't only be spent with my girlfriends or alone with my dog—but I couldn't. In the mirror across the room I was still that little girl who always thought of herself as too boring, too brainy, and too wrong for any boy to like, never mind love.

CHAPTER

$$4$$

AFTER SCHOOL on Mondays and Wednesdays, and every other Sunday, I worked at The Millbank BookStop. When you walk through the door of the BookStop, the store's owner, Mrs. Sawyer, is always waiting to greet you so she can place the book she knows you'd want to read right in your hands. Sure, the place was a little unique—what with its oddball customers, dusty shelves, and quirky manager, Howie (Mrs. Sawyer's freaky-but-cool, forty-four-year-old son), who always sat perched on his stool by the door reading a dog-eared copy of Marx's *Communist Manifesto*—but despite it all, the four-foot-eleven turbocharged granny, who was born during the Depression, had a thriving business because the people of Millbank consider her and her little store a town treasure.

When I woke up that morning, I imagined finishing brunch and coming to the BookStop and working on the graduation window. Unlike stores that just put the stacks of bestsellers in the window, the BookStop windows are thematic. You might see one filled with a beach towel, a sand pail, and a bunch of books about boats, cruises, summertime, and a pile of thrillers, mysteries, and romantic "beach reads." Or a battered stockpot might be surrounded by wooden spoons and two hundred cookbooks. The themes are sometimes seasonal, but not always, and Mrs. Sawyer prefers not to repeat.

I hadn't always been such a fan of Mrs. Sawyer—she could be a bit of a tough cookie—but back in February of my junior year, after I'd spent nine months shelving books, Mrs. Sawyer asked me if I'd design a window for Valentine's Day. As much of an honor as it was to be asked to design a window, I wasn't dating anybody at the time—how shocking!—and to be honest, I was feeling like a little, bitter Miss Lonelyhearts.

"I don't think I'd make a very nice window, Mrs. Sawyer," I said. "I hate Valentine's Day."

"Here's an idea," she growled. "Make it for all the broken hearts in Millbank." She paused for a few moments, then said, "Use black hearts and make sure *Anna Karenina* is front and center."

And just like that, she disappeared into the back office,

leaving me with a window to design. I'd tried to sulk my way out of doing it, but she'd turned the tables on me. I ended up putting together an outrageous display with hanging black hearts surrounded by books about the worst breakups in the history of literature. *Madame Bovary. The Great Gatsby. Romeo and Juliet.*

From that day on, I knew Mrs. Sawyer was a go-to gal. We all have them—our "work mom" or "school mom"—the older woman who has some wisdom about the world, kind of like your own mom but minus all the baggage.

That afternoon, as I sat there trying to create a graduation window, I didn't need a listener. What I wanted was some peace and quiet, some time to think. In six short weeks, I'd be gliding by Mom and Dad in cap and gown as Mr. Johnson read the lyrics to "Turn the Page" by Bob Seger (it was an insane Millbank tradition started in the seventies and kept up for some inexplicable reason), and then none of this would matter. Not Gretchen, not my mother's harping, not my pathetic life.

I glanced out the window and watched a Hummer pull to a stop on the other side of the street. All four doors popped open, and a gaggle of Proud Crowd members— Elisa, Jodi, Carrie, and others—gaily poured out, heads bobbing, eyes sparkling. I watched them for a few moments and tried to imagine what their lives were like. I couldn't imagine that the smell of old books permeated their clothes or that they ever spent a Saturday night alone.

"Where are you today, Miss Kate?" Mrs. Sawyer suddenly said, standing behind me.

I turned around to see her staring at me over her glasses.

"Sorry, Mrs. Sawyer," I said. "I'm a little out of it today. I've got a lot going on."

"Something you want to talk about?" she asked. Her voice was like gravel from sixty years of smoking.

"No, just tired from studying late."

"On Saturday night, in April?" she questioned. "The rest of your friends stopped studying a couple of months ago."

I looked at her and wondered how she kept so sharp. Clearly her bullshit radar was finely tuned to my bull.

"Can I change the window on Wednesday? I just don't feel inspired today. The idea of graduating, leaving my friends, has me down," I sort of lied.

"All right. You do what you have to do. Wednesday is fine with me." She looked at her watch. "Howie hired somebody new. You can show him the ropes—Howie's no good at that."

I was more than happy to take her up on the offer, because I actually liked training new people. Besides, maybe walking someone through the store would get my mind off my problems.

"So who's the new victim?" I asked.

Howie was sitting on his bar stool, his nose practically

touching the book he was reading. When standing, which wasn't often when on the job, he was about six feet three, weighed no less than three hundred pounds, and had a bright red Afro. Mrs. Sawyer was African American and her late husband was Jewish, so I guess that's just how the genes blended. He looked up and pointed behind me.

I turned around to see who he was pointing at, and my eyes narrowed ever so slightly in surprise. It was Jack Clayton. Out of instinct, my eyes darted about looking for Will B., but the Boy Wonder was without Batman. I'd never really taken Jack Clayton in before. He had dirty-blond hair, a strong chin, and dark chocolate eyes flecked with green. He stood about six feet tall with a gentle slouch that bordered on awkward. From what I'd heard, he wasn't much of a talker.

"Jack."

"Hey," he said. "Good throwdown last night."

I nodded.

"You work here, huh," he mumbled. "Is it cool?"

I looked over at Howie and smiled. "Yeah, it is."

"All right, then."

We stood there for a few moments not saying anything. I mean, what was I supposed to do—boss Jack Clayton around?

"Anyway, I'm going to train you," I blurted out.

"Train me," he said. "Like Shamu."

"No, not like Shamu," I said, flustered. "They train Shamu with fish—I'm going to train you with free books."

"Free books," he said. "Right—I could get used to that."

"All employees get one free book a month and fifty percent discount on all others."

"Nice," he said. So Jack Clayton was a reader—a nice little surprise.

"Best part of the job," I continued. "So why are you taking a job with a month of school left?"

"To be close to you," he said, and his face was stone serious. My heart stopped beating for all of a second, and then a smile crossed his face. "Just kidding. Dad said I needed to kick in some money for college—you know, I'm learning the value of a dollar and all that."

"I see," I said. *Get out the violins—another rich kid sent to the salt mines.*

I spent the next hour giving Jack a tour of the BookStop and showing him "the ropes." The store was long and had three floors. On the first floor we kept all the new releases along with mysteries, thrillers, graphic novels, and comic books. On the top floor we kept our academic sections, stuff like philosophy, lit crit, and history. In the basement we had our more risqué section for women—romance and erotica. I was kind of skeezed out by it all, but it sure did sell. As I walked Jack around, he nodded mostly and occasionally asked a question, so it was a little hard to tell if he was picking everything up or if he was just planning on quitting the moment his first shift ended.

By the end of my shift I was so bushed from talking that I grabbed the largest cart of unstacked books I could find and started to show him how to shelve them by subject and author.

"How's the band?" I said, offhand. I was fishing for Will scoop, but I tried to make the question seem casual.

"Good. We're playing the Electric next Saturday—you should come."

"Uh—sure."

Just the thought of Will B. all sweaty and on stage made my heart swoon.

"Cool," he said. Jack picked up a copy of some poems by Allen Ginsberg and showed it to me. "Have you read the Beats?"

"No. Are they good?"

"*Were* good, but I mean out-of-their-friggin'-minds good," he said. "Don't tell me you haven't read 'Howl'?"

I shook my head and bit down on my lower lip. I took pride in having read books nobody else had, and now here was this boy making me feel like a reading lightweight. "No, I haven't."

Jack smiled and looked down at the book in his hand. "Here, take this—I'm giving you my first free book of the month."

"Thanks," I said, trying to sound normal. *Is Jack Clayton flirting with me?*

Just then Howie called my name over the PA system. I told Jack to finish stacking, and I tucked the book under my arm and walked to the front of the store.

"What do you think of the poem 'Howl'?" I asked Howie as I waited for him to give me another cart of books to stack.

"Brilliant poem," he replied, "but Ginsberg played the same note for too long."

"Fidel," I began—Howie and I liked to joke that I was Che Guevara and he was Fidel Castro at the beginning of the revolution—"our new comrade . . . he's a big fan of the Beats and he's donating his first free book to me." I held it up.

Howie scratched his goatee. It was a mixture of white, gray, and red, and it made him look like an old-time sixties radical.

"Is this comrade going to stack books or give them away?" he asked. "Because the revolution doesn't need a hero—it needs a good book stacker."

I looked back and Jack was reading—I guessed his head and mind were in another universe, and for a moment I envied him. There was nothing I would've liked more than to drop away into another world right then.

"I think he'll be a good, slow stacker, Fidel."

"Revolutions," Howie mused, "don't happen overnight. We'll give him a chance."

CHAPTER

5

BY TEN O'CLOCK, the Sunday-night blues set in. The bleak wasteland of an entire week of stupefyingly boring school stretched ahead of me like an endless desert highway.

In the hopes of staving off a trip to the freezer for a bowl of Chunky Monkey ice cream (this monk needed no more chunk!), I changed into my comfy sweats, donned the cheesy pink cowboy hat I'd won at Six Flags a few years back, and hopped online to check the status of a bunch of things I was auctioning.

I'd built a little business selling things out of my parents' attic. My mom was a pack rat, and Dad had been after her to get rid of some stuff forever, so when I suggested the idea, he was more than happy for me to turn her old Thighmaster, their ABBA records (who even owns a record player anymore?), and even his red lava lamp (this I actually kept for myself) into some cold, hard cash. Don't get me wrong, I wasn't making big bucks or anything . . . twenty bucks here, fifty bucks there . . . but it was enough to pay my monthly iTunes bill and, in a good month, fund a few trips to the mall.

I was just about to call Dev for a chat when my IM window popped up. I clicked over to it.

MikeMilken: *Do you want to know?*

Okay . . . that's creepy.

Who was Mike Milken? I searched my mind, trying to place the name, but I was drawing a total blank. School? The BookStop? Somebody I'd met online? Mystified, I grabbed the Millbank school directory, but there were no Milkens in it.

I sat back down. Two could play at that game.

KK: *Know what?*

MikeMilken: *What the Market is? You're number seventy-one.*

I literally froze at my computer, just staring at the words.

Seventy-one. Yes, I desperately wanted to know, but I also wasn't so sure I wanted anything to do with this freak who was IMing me so late at night.

Just as I was about to respond, there was a knock at my door, and I hid the IM window on my desktop. My dad poked his head in.

"Ice cream?" he said.

Try as I might, the world was conspiring against me.

"Sure."

He came in and put the bowl on my dresser. "What're you doing?"

Ever since my dad read an article about online predators, he liked to periodically drop in during the "dangerous times," e.g., IMing after ten p.m. Generally speaking, I appreciated the gesture, but tonight I was actually about to communicate with one of those weirdos and I wanted to be left alone.

"Busy talking to Dev."

"Oh, what's she up to?"

I turned around from my desk and gave him the I-love-you-but-please-leave-me-alone face. He was pretty sensitive to that expression and shuffled out with a little wave. I grabbed the ice cream and returned to my computer.

The IM signal dinged again:

MikeMilken: *theMillbankmarket.com/*
password: hedgefund

In a flash, I scribbled the address and password down on a Post-it, and a moment later, Mike Milken (whoever he was) logged off. By now, my hands were trembling a little, and I struggled to type the new address into Explorer. Once I did, I hit return, and sure enough the password screen came up.

What the hell was this?

I typed in "hedgefund" and pushed ENTER. The screen went blank for a few moments, and a fear that I'd just down-loaded the worst virus of all time swept over me; but a few seconds later, a new window opened.

THE MILLBANK SOCIAL STOCK MARKET

My eyes went wide and I took a big scoop of ice cream.

It certainly wasn't the most elaborate Web site I'd ever been on—it was pretty basic, actually. Blue background, white writing . . . that was it. The person who built the site was obviously no computer genius, and I mentally crossed off the mathletes as possible suspects.

I scrolled down from the top of the page, and there was a message.

WELCOME TO THE MARKET
Below are the valuations as of 4/19

I didn't get it.

I scrolled down some more, still trying to figure out what it was exactly. It looked like a page from the Stock Index of the *Wall Street Journal*. There was a long ranking of what I assumed to be stock symbols and their end-of-day trading value. Next to each symbol was a one-line analysis. The first twenty stocks were in a bracket that said BLUE CHIPS.

Why would someone be giving me stock advice? I mean, what was wrong with the world that people in high school were suddenly trading stock tips?

But the more I studied it, the more the oddities started to jump out at me. First of all, there weren't any companies I recognized. To be sure, I'm no money guru, and I've never really studied the stock market, but I certainly know what a blue-chip stock is—it's a stock everyone wants to own. GE, Microsoft, and Google, these were classic Blue Chippers, but none of them were anywhere to be found. As I began looking at the sheet more closely, I noticed some of the lingo seemed very unprofessional and young. Things like, "This stock's brain-to-body ratio is way off," or "Investment high, her return is low." Since when are companies referred to as her? Isn't that only for boats?

Gradually I focused on the number-one-ranked stock. It was called GRT Inc. and next to it was written: "Deep pockets needed, but the package is everything you dreamed of." That's when it dawned on me. G-R-T. This wasn't an acronym for a publicly traded company, they were initials. GRT stood for Gretchen Rachel Tanner.

What I was looking at was a ranking.

The ranking of every girl in the senior class!

Holy sh——!

Quickly I scanned the rest of the list. Number two: ETE.

Elisa Estrada, of course.

Not much of a surprise there, either.

Three through six were pretty much what I would've expected—more members of the Proud Crowd—and I began scrolling down through the names, looking for mine. Different sets of numbers had different subheadings: 20–40: Preferred Stock, 41–60: Penny Stock, 61–140: Junk Bonds.

I scrolled down.

And down.

And down. I suddenly wondered if I was even listed.

Until I finally saw my initials. I was right above Hester Schultz.

71. KCW—currently valued at $1.75 a share.
Change since last week: -3

Oh. My. God.

I didn't exactly know what the change part was, but I definitely knew what it meant to be ranked seventy-first out of the 140 girls in my class. I was just on the wrong side of the great divide. Was I that much of a loser?! Tears formed in the corners of my eyes, and I took another big bite of ice cream; and just when I thought it couldn't get any worse, I noticed that there was an icon of a bear flashing next to my name. Moving the cursor over, I clicked on it. A new window opened. And if the list part was horrifying, this new page was truly mortifying.

It was a whole dossier.

About me.

My photograph from last year's yearbook was posted in the top right corner—did I really look that bad?—and listed next to it were all my activities: my job at the BookStop, what courses I was taking, where I was going to college, how I got to school in the morning. It was crazy! To the left of my picture, there was a chart that tracked my ranking week by week (it was pretty much flat). Underneath my photo, there was a box titled INSIDER INFORMATION. It looked like a blog for market players where they could randomly contribute commentary on what individual girls were doing.

4/18 Seen at GT's shindig—who invited her?!
4/15 Stuffing
4/15 Is her chest getting bigger or is she stuffing?
4/11 Wiped out in the cafeteria—lol!

This was bad. Really bad. Had I wiped out in the cafeteria? Yes. Was I stuffing my bra? NO! I took my last spoonful of ice cream, and then, as I was thinking there couldn't be anything worse, I scrolled down to a box at the very bottom of the screen where there was a flashing star.

KCW LLC.

MARKET RANKING: 71

TODAY'S CHANGE: ↓3

SHARE PRICE: $1.75

CHANGE: ↓0.06 (-0.09%)

L/B RATIO: 2.3

3-MONTH RANGE: $1.23 – $1.81

STATUS: JUNK BOND

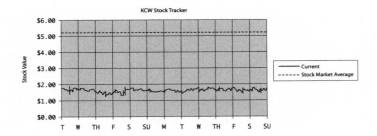

ANALYST RECOMMENDATION: has promise, but continues to show no interest in improving her l/b (looks-to-brains) ratio. A date night would probably yield a low R.O.I. (Return on Investment). The smart investor stays away.

DEFINITE SELL

CHAPTER

6

IT WAS A dark night.

I spent hours poking around the Market, checking out other girls' dossiers, poring over the rankings, and looking at my page over and over. Eventually I found Dev (she was worse off than me, No. 121) and Callie (she probably couldn't care less, but was No. 11), and much as I tried to brush the whole thing off and chock it up to a bad joke, I couldn't let it go. I mean, there it was—in black and white. It was undeniable. If what the Market said was true, I was what somebody with tact might call "below average." Don't get me wrong, I'd never had any illusions of being the It Girl, but to have it laid out for you before your very eyes is a whole other matter.

So what did I do when I discovered I was two notches

above chopped liver? Hide in my closet and skip the last six weeks of school?

No.

Hell, no.

I was a Winthrop, and my dad always told me that a Winthrop takes life head on.

For the first time in about two years, I woke up before my alarm went off. As I pushed myself out of bed at 5:30 a.m., Remington (my cocker spaniel) looked up at me from the corner like I was crazy, but I was feeling uncommonly energized. There were so many things to do and so little time to do them. Reaching deep into my closet, I pulled out a cute J. Crew dress that I'd accidentally put in the dryer a few years back and had shrunk. It was now a little too short and a little too tight, but tight in the right places, I hoped. After a quick trip to the laundry room to iron out a wrinkle, I hit the shower, dried my hair, and dug out the curling iron from underneath my bathroom sink. By eight o'clock my hair was looking as good as it ever had, and I'd managed to hide the big circles under my eyes from two sleepless nights with some heavy-duty concealer I'd snagged from my mom's vanity. After a few final touches—some Mac lip gloss and my jean jacket—I checked everything in the mirror one last time, and—if I may say so myself—I was looking pretty damn good.

It was going to be a good day. I just knew it.

* * *

But as soon as I set foot in school, my newfound grit disappeared. I'm not sure what triggered it, but by the end of first period I started feeling like my old self. The self that was seventy-first on the Market. Whether it was nearly breaking an ankle in my three-inch heels on my way to homeroom; or that the dress I was wearing *was* in fact way too small and I was pretty sure I looked fat; or simply a Pavlovian response to being back in the building where I had drowned in anonymity for four years, I don't know for sure, but my quick fix to popularity was turning into a quick trip to Depressionville. I felt more like a seventy-one than ever before.

How could I have thought that two hours of primping was going to change anything? I mean, who was I kidding? I was Kate Winthrop—smart girl, a little geeky, with a good heart. That's all I'd ever be, at least while I was still at Millbank. Who's to say how many people logged on to the Market every day? How many people were judging me on a daily basis—breaking down what I was wearing, who I was talking to, how I was behaving? It didn't matter really. There was no escaping it. Maybe once I got to Brown I could change into someone different, someone cool, someone sought after, someone different. Perhaps once I got to a place where my history as a social nonentity wasn't so well documented, I could shed my old skin, but until then, it was simply better to lay low. Blend in. Stay with the pack. What's that old saying? It's the tall blade of grass that gets cut? Well I didn't need—or want—any more wounds.

By the middle of seventh period, I was thinking about one thing: get through Econ Class, go home, and disappear into the old Katie Winthrop. While Dev stood in the front of the room giving her final presentation—something to do with the big bang theory of branding—I found myself gazing across the room at Gretchen and her coterie of It Friends, silently wondering to myself what made them cool, and me not. Elisa Estrada was Number Two on the Market. She was blessed with wavy brown hair, beautiful blue eyes, and a genuine warmth that won everyone over, including the ice princess Gretchen. Jodi Letz—Number Six—hardly a natural beauty, and known in parts of the county as Jodi "Lets-me," was ranked high purely by her association with the Proud Crowd. And then there was Gretchen. Sure, there were the obvious things that marked her for Number One: she was beautiful, her dad was a big wheel and all that, and rumor had it she wasn't too shy when it came to a late-night tango with the boys . . . but there had to be something else.

While my analytical mind (2180 on my SAT) worked overtime on the alchemy of popularity, I still couldn't make the math add up. There must have been some variable, some innate quality she possessed that lesser lights of the social universe like me did not. Was it something she learned from her mom—if so, why hadn't *my* mom taught me the secret handshake—or was it simply something that she'd been blessed with by the genetic lottery? Was there some regimen that I could undergo to transform me from a toadette into a princess?

Get it together, Kate!!

I took a deep breath and tried to clear my mind. This isn't who you are, I told myself. You don't care about empty things like popularity. You're above it all. You are your own person.

Right?

But no matter what I said to myself, no matter how many of those corny platitudes I managed to summon to my mind, the Market was still there. I couldn't get it out of my head. Seemingly overnight, I'd been transformed from a girl who felt like she knew her place in the world to a shivering bag of nerves.

"Kate? Are you with us?"

Blood rushed to my cheeks. Mr. Walsh was standing over my desk, and the whole class was staring at me.

"Sorry?" I whispered. Behind me, some guy chortled.

"Please pay attention, Kate," Mr. Walsh said, shaking his head.

Mr. Walsh was a Millbank alum who had come back to teach after making a lot of dough on Wall Street. Why he left Wall Street was beyond me, but he said he wanted to give something back to the community. My mom said he was noble, but Dad said he was perhaps a little foolish, too. We all considered ourselves pretty lucky to have him, because he was probably the best teacher in the school. He was tough and demanding, and though we complained, we knew he was pushing us to be as good as we could be. And that's priceless in my book.

"I was asking you what you thought of Dev's conclusion that the marketing of a product is more important than the quality of the product itself," he said. "Care to comment?"

"I think she's right," I mumbled. Mr. Walsh stared at me, and I searched my mind for something more appropriate to say, but he quickly turned to Gretchen.

"A dud's a dud," she tossed out. "Like when Coke tried to launch New Coke. You can't fake quality. It's like being beautiful—I mean, you either are or you aren't, right? You can't convince people that something is true just by telling them it is."

She looked really impressed with herself after she finished what I suspected was the first real thought she'd ever had. I glanced up at Dev, who was now beaming at me to counter.

"What about President Bush?" I said.

"What about him?" Mr. Walsh inquired.

"Didn't he have us all believing that they had WMDs

in Iraq?" I said, and then looked directly at Gretchen. "And his brain, didn't we believe he had one?"

The class erupted into laughter.

Mr. Walsh motioned for the class to settle down, and he walked back toward Dev, who looked very pleased by my challenge to Gretchen's argument.

"I think Miss Tanner and Miss Winthrop, in their own unique ways, are both correct. If you examine . . ."

But as Mr. Walsh waxed on about focus groups, case studies, and polling, I found the Market intruding on my mind once more, and one question kept popping up:

Who was behind it?

The person orchestrating the Market could be *anyone*. It could be a student or a teacher, or it could be a hundred students working together. He, she, them—whoever it was could be sitting in this very room. Suddenly the room was filled with perps, so I started eliminating suspects one by one. Jason Sanders was too lazy, Jeff Briggs was too stupid, the posse of skateboard dudes didn't give a crap. But I had a few clues, too: whoever kept the dossier was probably at Gretchen's party and possibly a member of this class, because we all filtered in from sixth period lunch (the scene of my aforementioned wipeout). Given that Gretchen had been the one to mention it all in the first place, I made a mental note: when class ended, I would watch her and her minions. If they were behind the Market—or at least the people contributing to my dossier—I was sure they'd be keeping close tabs on me.

When the bell rang, I lingered in my chair fiddling with my backpack zipper. It wasn't broken, but I needed camouflage while I observed others.

"Need some help?" said a now familiar voice. I looked up into the dreamy blue eyes of Will B., and next to him my new work buddy, Jack Clayton.

"Yeah, it's stuck," I lied.

Will took my bag and with a quick yank he opened it up.

"Oh, thanks," I said. "I must have been doing it wrong."

"I mastered the zipper in first grade," he said.

Great, now he's mocking me.

For the second time in my life I was talking to Will B., and for the second time in two days I was making a complete fool of myself. With Will and Jack standing side by side, you realized it was no accident that Will was the lead singer. You know how they say that movie stars have this quality where you can't help but want to look at them? Well, Will had it—and Jack didn't.

"Did you read Ginsberg?" Jack asked.

Will looked at Jack and then at me. That Jack and I had had a relationship of which he wasn't part seemed to throw Will for a loop.

"Yeah," I lied. Truth was, I'd brought the book home and intended to read some of it before I saw Jack again at work that coming Wednesday.

"Wow," said Will, as he punched Jack in the arm. "Dude, you push that wounded-poet game on every girl you meet?"

It was perhaps the single greatest exhibition of "blocking" I'd ever witnessed. "Blocking" (and that's a nice term for it) is when one boy "blocks" another from talking to a girl. There were two important facts to note in this particular case: first, a boy will only block another boy when they are both interested in a girl (me??). Second, it's often deeply painful to watch the "blocking" victim try to recover his rap after being bludgeoned the way Jack had been by Will's nifty workmanship.

Jack blushed and his mouth opened like he was about to say something, but then he looked down at his shoes.

"I'll catch you two later," Will said. "Jack—jamming at my house tonight?"

Jack chinned an "Okay."

"Bye," I said, but I wasn't even sure Will heard me.

"That wasn't true," Jack said, "what he said."

"What wasn't true?" I said, picking my bag from the desk. I was so consumed with watching Will disappear down the hall, I forgot that he had just shattered poor Jack's confidence in a single death blow.

"Never mind," Jack murmured. "I'll see you around."

I hurried down the east hall en route to my locker so I could grab my books for American Lit, but as soon as I turned the corner, I knew something was up.

A handful of guys from the soccer team were leaning against the wall snickering, and as I neared, one of the guys motioned to the others that they should take off. My pace slowed, wondering if I was missing the joke, but when I arrived at my locker, I discovered that the joke was on me.

Oh, no.

My locker number—156—had been crossed out with what looked like red lipstick. Scribbled above it, in big red letters, someone had written:

7!

Rage, horror, devastation—it all coursed through my blood. I leaped forward and started manically wiping away at the number with the arm of my jacket, trying to get it to come off. But it was useless.

It wasn't lipstick. It was permanent marker.

What had I done?! Why was I suddenly a target? Why had I been picked out to be humiliated?!

It was right then, in my most vulnerable moment—

spastically scrubbing metal, tears running down my cheeks, hair falling in my eyes—that Gretchen Tanner strolled past. She looked at me and a sly, knowing smile crept onto her face.

A hitherto unknown girl took hold of me, and I dropped my bag and stalked up to her, blocking her escape.

"Who are *you*? Who are *you*?" I stammered. "To rate people!"

"What are you talking about?" She smiled as she guided a lock of hair behind her ear.

"The numbers, the rankings. Do me a big favor and leave me out of it!" I yelled.

This time she laughed, and I think that's what pushed me over the edge. The blood drained from my face, and my fist rolled up into a ball.

"You know what?" I snapped. "I can't wait to tell everyone what you've done, because then . . . then . . . then . . . you're toast!"

Toast? Toast was my big threat? I deserved to be seventy-one if that was the best I could do.

"I'm lost here, Kate," she said.

"The Market!"

Her expression changed, slightly—softened perhaps—and she shifted her weight before adjusting her Hermès bag on her shoulder. She glanced down at her manicured nails and sighed.

"Let me give you a little piece of advice, Kate," she said.

"Don't worry about the Market, because there's nothing you can do about it."

"You can do something about it—like take me off it!"

"Me?" She squinted. "I don't have anything to do with it. I don't control it. And to be perfectly frank, I don't even know who does."

"Bull."

She shrugged her shoulders, then stared hard into my eyes. She was fierce, and I felt a chill go down my spine. "Get a clue. You think I want to be dissected on a daily basis?"

That's when I knew she wasn't lying.

I looked down at the ground, suddenly embarrassed.

"But you're Number One," I said.

She smiled condescendingly as if to communicate *Of course I am, you idiot.* Then she put her hand on my shoulder for a moment and said, "Just forget about it, Kate. It's stupid."

She paused, searching for the right words.

"You are what you are . . . and that'll never change."

CHAPTER

```
┌ · · · · · · ┐
·            ·
·     7      ·
·            ·
└ · · · · · · ┘
```

As I WALKED toward the parking lot, I felt dizzy. The hallway was spinning and suddenly every face, every set of eyes,
was on me. Checking me out. Evaluating. Judging. Scoring.
Every boy in the school was a potential buyer, and what I
wore, what I thought, what music I listened to, mattered. I
suppose every teenager felt the same anxieties at one time or
another, but with the Market, my worst fears were quanti-
fied and made real and very public. I couldn't delude myself
anymore by saying I was on the right side of the "pretty"
fault line. No, I now knew exactly where I stood: Number
Seventy-one out of 140.

In a moment of true unhappiness, I did what any red-
blooded American girl in my situation would have done: I
bolted. I ran straight to North Adams Street (where I parked

my car for easy exiting), jumped in, and gunned it. I didn't know where I was going, but anywhere was better than MHS. Tears flowed freely, and my chest heaved with overwhelming sobs, and I felt out of control as I headed away from town.

I finally came to a stop at the Springs Reservation parking lot, overlooking all of Millbank. I'd dreamed of coming here with a boy after some mythical date, the two of us gazing at the burning lights of New York City just a few miles away. I imagined it being the most romantic night of my life, but instead I was staring at the midday smog as it slowly burned away from the hazy city skyline.

Just then my cell vibrated. Text message:

DEV: Where r u???
KATE: In hell.

Dev was the perfect person to drop some drama on. Of the two of us, I was normally even-keeled and—as I already explained—she was the neurotic psycho (her phrase, not mine), but today it was my turn to be the drama queen.

DEV: Meet me at Bucks

Starbucks was one of the few brand-name stores in the whole town of Millbank. There was a McDonald's, but it was banished to the highway and was practically inaccessible from the town itself. There was a Quiznos sub shop, a

Gap, and one or two others, but that was really it. Of the hundred or so restaurants and other merchants in town, almost all were homegrown and local. In my mind, that's what made the town great.

When I walked in, Dev had already landed us a couple of comfy chairs and two double tall skim lattes. Her laptop was open on the table, and she was reading a book, so she didn't notice me. I slowed down for a second, trying to decide what I should tell Dev. Would she understand why I was so upset? I was pretty sure she would. But then again, she was even further down the list than I was. Shouldn't I have been more concerned about her than I was about myself? Was I being a bad friend?

"Dev."

"Hey," she said, closing some book called *Freakonomics*. I looked into her eyes and immediately began to sob.

"What's wrong?" she whispered as she rubbed my back. "It's okay, Katie. Talk to me."

When I tried to speak, my throat constricted. She handed me the latte and I took a few sips, drying my eyes with the sleeve of my jean jacket.

"I'm Number Seventy-one on the Market," I said.

. She got a strange look on her face. "What's the Market?"

"Somebody ranked all the girls in the senior class—it's called the Millbank Social Stock Market . . . the MSSM is what they call it."

"Yeah, so who cares?" She laughed. "It sounds goofy."

"You don't get it," I huffed. "It's online—everyone is ranked from top to bottom! It's really sophisticated."

This time Dev said nothing.

"You want to see for yourself?"

"No—it's just nonsense." She seemed annoyed, perhaps a little distracted.

"Look at it for me?"

She nodded, and I gave her the address and password. She pulled up the site in a matter of seconds, and the blue hue of the computer screen beamed off her eyes. She could read faster than anyone I knew, and scarily, she retained more, too. Her pupils ticked back and forth, like a pendulum on a clock. She seemed to be devouring the Web site. She clicked on individual girls, read the comments beneath their names, occasionally laughing or mouthing the word "Ouch," and whenever I tried to interrupt, she put her hand up and said, "Wait—one more minute."

After ten minutes, my melancholia receded, and I just became plain bored waiting for her to respond.

"So?" I said. "What do you think?"

"Honestly," she said, looking directly into my eyes. "It's totally awesome—I mean, I wish I'd thought of it."

This was so *not* the response I was expecting—or frankly wanted. Where was the outraged feminist? I wanted her to rise up like an army of Smith College undergrads ready to take back the night and tear down the chauvinist super-structure guiding these misguided pigs. I needed someone to back up my own anger, but it didn't seem to be forthcoming.

"How can you say that?"

She must have felt my disappointment, because she backtracked a little bit.

"I mean, it's total guy garbage, but you have to admit, you can't jump off once you're on. Do you know how much money we could make if we marketed this software to high schools across the nation? We'd trounce MySpace in, like, a millisecond."

Let me take a brief detour and explain Dev's response. Dev's dad is Mark Rayner, as in the founder of Dreamscape. He's worth more money than Daddy Warbucks, but don't be misled; if you met him you'd never know it. He's just one of those computer guys who made truckloads of cash, but really only ever cared about the science of it all. Ever since I've known her, Dev has been on a search for the next big thing. What drove her was hard to say, but secretly I always thought that she wanted her dad's attention, and that she thought being an entrepreneur of her own was the only way to do that. Maybe her parents' divorce had something to do with it, as well.

"Great," I said. "I can't wait to see my pathetic social status splashed all over the country."

She laughed. She actually laughed! I meant it to be funny, but not to be laughed at, if you know what I mean.

"*Your* social status!" she shouted. "What about mine? Number 121, with comments like 'I once saw her face when she actually put a book down, and it wasn't pretty.'"

Now it was my turn to laugh at something that wasn't quite as funny as she intended.

After a few minutes, we were cracking up as we pored over the commentaries on our fellow classmates. (Schadenfreude is indeed a cure for self-loathing!) Dev showed me how the stocks were traded and how values were compiled. Without boring you with too much financial mumbo jumbo, the Market was essentially an online game based around girls' popularity. Dev and I couldn't trade, see, because we weren't "traders." To be a trader, you had to have a "brokerage license," which, according to the Web site, cost five hundred dollars. Let me repeat that: just to play, you had to throw down five hundred dollars!! Once you got your license, you were given a password, a portfolio, and one-million-dollars' worth of "market money." It was a bit like Monopoly—except with stocks—and the only way a trader could increase his overall earnings was to buy stocks and hope their values rose.

"So how do you win?" I asked.

"Whoever's portfolio is worth the most come graduation takes the whole pot. With"—and she counted something on the screen—"fifty-odd portfolios, the winner stands to take away over twenty-five thousand dollars."

It was totally crazy.

"But I could win that game easily," I realized. "Why doesn't everyone just buy Gretchen's stock—her value is off the charts!"

A little smile crept across Dev's face. "It doesn't work that way. Gretchen is actually a conservative bet. Let me explain: let's say you invested all your money in Gretchen. Her stock is so high already that it's unlikely to increase in value, and frankly, it's more likely to decrease. I mean, she's gorgeous, but she's not quite Google, now is she?"

"You mean buying Gretchen is just playing it too safe?" I said.

"Right! You'll never win. The greater the risk, the greater the gain."

I was actually getting into it—I guess my econ class helped—even though I was being treated like your common pork-bellies commodity; the idea of the Market itself, I now realized, was kind of cool.

If only there were a site about the boys, I thought.

"Actually," Dev said with a smile spreading across her face, "in a perfect world, the ideal stock would be somebody just like you: pretty, totally untapped potential, and a low trading value."

"So I'm the living embodiment of the phrase, 'Buy low,

sell high.' That's great!" I said sarcastically. "I can't wait to tell Mr. Walsh."

She laughed. "Yeah, sort of, but without the high part, yet."

"Yet?"

A second, more devious, smile danced on her lips, and a dark light sparkled in her eye. "As in . . . we should play the market. We should enter."

"No way—I wouldn't bet five hundred on me."

"I would."

I cocked my head to the side and realized that Dev was already hatching a plan in her mind.

Ten minutes later, we were in Dev's attic.

Unlike her room, where her younger brother could pop in at any second—or worse, be listening in through some high-tech device (he was the true tech geek of the family)—the attic was basically impenetrable. You had to open two doors just to get to the staircase, and back in middle school, Dev had put long noisy beads midway up so it was virtually impossible to approach without us knowing. In the middle of the space there was an old-fashioned desk and a couple of antique wicker chairs. It was like going back in time, and somehow that made us feel safe.

When we first got there, Dev was like a whirling dervish. Jumping from one carton to the next, pulling out every yearbook their family had ever collected. Between her and her sister, it basically covered the last seven years at MHS, dating back to the class of 2001. I had no idea what she was looking for, but she eventually laid out all the books, opening each to a single page, dropping Post-its under the pictures of girls I only vaguely remembered.

"Beth Zupan," Dev said.

"Yeah, what about her?" I said, searching my memory banks for a little 4-1-1. "Yearbook editor when we were freshmen, right? She was a junior, I think."

"Exactly," she said. "What else do you remember about her?"

"Dark hair, green eyes, cute, but nothing to write home about. . . ."

"Right," she said. "I mean, mostly right." She turned the yearbook in my direction, and sure enough there was a picture of Beth Zupan with the Yearbook Club. I might have even used the description "dowdy."

She closed the 2003 yearbook and opened the 2004 yearbook. She turned to the back, and there was a collage of pictures titled "Spring Fling." She snapped off a Post-it and neatly placed it below the picture of a girl in a group photo with the caption, HOTTIES.

"Here," she said, sliding the book in front of me.

"What?"

"That's Beth Zupan."

I was stunned. I grabbed the old yearbook and compared the two girls. It was like an alien had inhabited the body of a yearbook editor and turned her into a Maxim swimsuit model. The conservative brown hair had been replaced by a mane of sassy blond hair, and her pasty "I stay indoors and read a lot" skin had been tanned golden. But it was more than that—she seemed to positively glow.

"This is amazing."

"That's not the half of it," Dev shouted. She grabbed the other yearbooks and showed me a series of before-and-after photos. It seemed that every year there was another girl who had come out of nowhere. Dev had even created a term for the type: the Latebloomer.

I was speechless. After an hour of looking at girls who had risen from the middle of the pack to top dog in the span of a year, Dev hit me with her theory:

"In every school, there's a girl who wallows in anonymity for three and a half years. Then, suddenly, she explodes into the consciousness of her peers," she explained. "One week she's a no one, then she goes on spring break and comes back a different girl, or suddenly one month her body changes, or the right boy notices her, and then bang, she's it and the world she'd watched from afar instantly becomes her oyster."

I said nothing for a moment. "I'm not that girl, Dev."

If I were, then anybody in school could be.

"You could be, Kate," Dev said. "And I know how to make you that girl."

"You can't tell me a tan or a haircut or a dye job is going to change my life," I snapped. "That's just make-believe."

"No, it's just good business."

"What the hell does that mean?" I said, getting more annoyed with every statement she made.

"Remember when Britney had her babies, and the world thought she was so over? And then suddenly she started showing up with Paris Hilton at nightclubs and forgetting to wear her panties? That was all just PR—she wanted to be the bad girl again because everyone just saw her as a mom, and there is nothing more deadly boring than being a mom."

"Oh, really? I thought she just forgot them," I huffed as I rolled my eyes. "I'm not an idiot, Dev. I understand how the celebrity game works. I mean, I read *US Weekly*."

"But that's just it," she said. "We're playing the same game at old Millbank High. It's just in a really, really small pond."

She paused for a second to gather her thoughts, and for some reason I kept seeing my super-popular, wonder-woman of a sister shaking her head at me and saying, "Kate, you'll never be that girl. . . ." Even with her away at college, I was still haunted by her popularity.

"But it's more than just PR," Dev continued. "That's only part of running a business."

"A business," I said deadpan.

"Sure. They're treating you like a commodity, so why not act like one? C'mon, I'm great at business stuff. We can totally transform you."

Her confidence made it seem so easy, like if I just followed her plan—whatever it was—I could go from nobody to somebody in a couple of weeks. It couldn't be that easy, I thought, or everyone would do it.

"I've studied these girls," she continued, as her tone changed—a sadness inflecting her voice. "Do you think I just pulled this all out of a hat? Are you that blind? I've been trying to think of a way to go from 'mouse' to 'maven' for four years. And while I see the right steps, I can't do it, but *you* can."

I was dumbfounded. Dev had just confessed to me her innermost anxieties and fears, albeit in a rather odd way. She wanted to be this so-called Latebloomer—I mean, I guess we all do—and that's why she knew about these girls already. Dev was like every one of us; she wanted to be somebody. Even with all her brains and the protection they granted her, she was as desperate and as vulnerable as the rest of us. I suddenly felt ashamed for not recognizing the obvious before me, for not recognizing how badly she wanted to be somebody other than who she was.

"But why me?" I questioned, staring down.

"First, you're beautiful, and you don't even know it.

You're intelligent and have just enough artistic brilliance that you can imagine a new you. To become *that* girl, you have to imagine yourself as *that* girl."

I just sat there. The whole idea sounded like science fiction, but then I thought about being Number Seventy-one and how awful that had made me feel. I thought of Will and how much I wanted him to want me. And I thought of Gretchen and how wonderful it would be to knock her off her pedestal. But most of all I could imagine in my mind's eye my mother telling my sister how popular her little sister had become, more popular than she had ever been.

"What about the money—I don't have five hundred dollars to blow on a lottery ticket," I said.

"A Megabucks lottery ticket is about one hundred forty-eight million to one," she said. "Given that you're already Seventy-one—our odds are a helluva lot better. I'm willing to make that bet."

"I'm lost here."

"I'll front it," she said. "If we win, I'll split it with you and Callie."

"Callie?" I said.

She looked me up and down, and then smiled. "Oh yeah, we can't do this alone. You need an intervention!"

BOOK TWO

· · · · · · ·

PENNY STOCK

BUSINESS PLAN FOR KATE WINTHROP
Formulated by Devlin Rayner

OBJECTIVE:

To take Kate Winthrop from junk bond on The Millbank
Social Stock Market to a Blue Chip in the next four
weeks.

COMPETITIVE ANALYSIS:

Your competitors in the Market are girls we already
know well: Gretchen Tanner, Elisa Estrada, Jodi Letz,
etc. But rather than worrying about their stock, we're
simply going to focus on taking your stock from
good . . . to great!

DEVELOPMENT PLAN & MILESTONES:

1. **Reinvent the Brand**—bottom line, Kate, you need a
   major makeover. This is Business 101. Hair, nails,
   clothes . . . everything (sorry, but it's true!). We have
   to have an improved product to sell.

2. **The Big Bang Theory**—we will introduce the new
   you in an explosive way that blows everyone away.
   You can't just walk into school and hope somebody
   notices you. We have to create an EVENT to launch
   your brand.

3. **Establish Brand Loyalty**—to be honest, I haven't
   quite figured this one out yet (maybe you could bake
   free cupcakes? offer people rides to school?), but the
   goal is to get everyone to want to be part of your life.

4. **Co-Branding**—often by associating yourself with another super-successful brand, you can capture some of its heat and improve your own business. Just look at big partnerships—Nike and Tiger Woods, Beyoncé and L'Oréal . . . Nick Lachey and Jessica Simpson (sure, it didn't work out, but hey, look what it did for their careers!). Who can we co-brand with? Will B.? The Proud Crowd? An unknown mystery man?

5. **Paradigm Shift**—just when people think they have a handle on what you are, you will reposition yourself in a new radical act. Bottom line: a little act of rebellion.

6. **Merger & Acquisition**—this is a big one. Often an upstart business needs to merge with a competitor, or . . . if it has enough cash flow . . . acquire it (i.e., AOL and Time Warner, Paramount and DreamWorks). In your case, you're going to co-opt the biggest brand there is at Millbank: Gretchen Tanner.

*****Intangible Alchemy**—now, this isn't exactly a business term, but in business—like life—you need a little good, old-fashioned luck. Hopefully, there'll be some moment that allows the other six steps to come together in a way that's more than simply the sum of the parts. You can't plan this one—you can only prepare for it; and then strike!

CHAPTER

8

THE REST OF the week passed while Dev finished what she called her "business plan." I was a little surprised by how seriously she was taking this—did we really need a big proposal?—but it was classic Dev: methodical, precise, and fixated. While I waited for the saga to begin, with each day I found myself getting more excited. Could we really do what Dev claimed? Could I bail myself out from the social dregs of Millbank High and suddenly become an It Girl? Could I actually be more popular than my sister ever was? To be totally honest, I wasn't so sure. But the way I saw it, what was the worst thing that could happen? If I didn't move at all, and I stayed there stuck at seventy-one, no one would even notice.

So why not give it a shot?

On Friday night, Dev picked me up and drove me over to Callie's house for our "board meeting" all-nighter. On the way, she dropped the bomb on me.

"Okay. Here it is."

"What?"

She reached into her bag, pulled out a leather folder, and removed a sheaf of papers. "Here's what we'll cover for our first board meeting."

I snatched it from her hands and scanned the pages. It was elaborate, to say the least, and I was only able to make it through the first page. Basically, it was made up of seven steps, and most of them didn't make a whole lot of sense to me. It was a lot of business jargon, but the first step a two-year-old could've understood. *Makeover.* Dev's term for it was "reinvent the brand," but I understood what it really meant.

"What's wrong with how I am now?" I asked.

"I just know the necessary steps," Dev answered. "I leave the analysis and judgment to the experts. Let's see what Callie has to say."

Earlier in the week, she had called Callie to rope her in on what she had jokingly titled Project Re-eduKate. While Dev may have been a genius with business and computers, she was hardly a fashion plate, so she called Callie and told her about our plan for total transformation. Callie's sense of style was a wild mix: part fashionista, part rock star, all amazing. But when Dev explained everything to Callie and asked for her help, there was just silence at the other end of the speaker phone.

"Are you kidding me?" she answered. "Not a chance."

We were speechless. I looked at Dev, and she raised hands as if to say, "I have no idea what she's all worked up about." Dev had already e-mailed her the link to the MSSM, and while Callie reveled briefly in her own status as Number Eleven, she was very down on the idea of playing the market, so to speak.

"Don't you realize how offensive this game is to women?" she began. "It's classic male bull—objectifying women— and assigning values to them. You really want to be part of this?"

"Don't start with that feminist crud," Dev said.

"It isn't feminism—and even if it were, hello, there's nothing wrong with that. It's just common sense, which the two of you have apparently lost."

There was a long pause on the phone while none of us said anything.

"You two think playing the popularity game is fun," Callie said finally. "But trust me—it's an obsession like any other. And it'll ruin you and your friendship. So I'm out."

With that, she hung up, and Dev and I stared at each other, apparently thwarted at the very beginning of our journey.

But fifteen minutes later, right when Dev and I were

combing through the *Teen Vogue* Web site, pathetically searching for fashion ideas, Callie called back.

"All right. I'm in," she sulked. "But only because I love you and want you to look good. But don't come crying to me when it's all over."

Dev and I arrived at her house still squabbling over my fashion sense. Callie was sitting in her kitchen with a mug of chamomile tea, sporting a T-shirt that read, ORDINARY.

I laughed when I saw it, knowing how ironic it truly was.

"Ladies," she said with a grin, "welcome to the fashion dome."

Dev sat next to Callie, and they pointed to an uncomfortable chair that had been conspicuously placed across the room.

Was this a makeover or an inquisition?

"Why are we here, Kate?" Callie asked. She started tapping her pencil against a sketch pad on her lap.

"Ummm . . . because I need a makeover," I said. "But can I just say first that I think I have a pretty good style all my own? I'm pretty cool, right?"

Hello, it's true. Sure, I wasn't fabulous like Callie, but my cute little jean-jacket thing worked okay.

Apparently Callie and Dev didn't agree. They exchanged a look.

"I told you," Dev said low to Callie.

Told her what?

"Kate, you know how much I love you, right?" Callie said, as she turned back to me. "Then I'm only going to tell you this out of love and because there's no time to waste. You're a fashion *disaster*."

I'm so going to live to regret all this.

"And to make things worse, you suffer from what I like to call schizo-fashion-phrenia. It's a disease, and it affects young girls who think putting on the right color top to go with a jean jacket is 'a look.'"

"Harsh," Dev said. "But oh so true."

Callie turned and pursed her lips.

"If I were *you*," she said, looking at Dev, "I'd reserve any commentary you may have, because you're just as bad with your smart-girl glasses and your half-goth-half-just-pasty-because-you-don't-get-enough-sun look."

Dev cowered into her chair and zipped it. I tried to suppress the smile that crept across my face. It felt good to have somebody else's fashion sense destroyed in a single sentence.

"Okay, fine. Maybe I could try harder," I relented. "But I do have a style all my own."

"What's your style, Kate?" Callie said, putting up her hand. "When in doubt, throw on J. Crew and look like everybody else? You know what I call that? Mutt Fashion. Do you know what a mutt is?"

Did I look like an idiot *and* a fashion disaster?

"It's a dog," she continued. "Occasionally cute like you, but defined mostly by its lack of definition. It isn't a collie or Lab or dachshund. It's a little bit of everything, but it adds up to a whole lot of nothing."

By now I'm sure I must've looked pretty shell-shocked, because Callie took it down a notch.

"I'm sorry, honey. Dev told me this was a fashion intervention, so I'm laying it on a bit thick. Believe me, you've got everything you need, you just need to put it together the right way. The hair, the nails, and then clothes—we'll make it work for you. But you have to have faith. Are you with me?"

"I guess so, but can I keep my jean jacket?" I said.

She put her finger to her lips. "Hush, little girl. You don't need your safety blanket anymore," she said. "You're in my hands now."

Millbank isn't known as the fashion capital of the world, but it has a few good spots, so come Saturday morning we decided to stay local. Callie said she wanted to avoid what she called the obvious styles and create something new and bold for me.

"You can't shop at the mall," she said. "That's for the common herd only."

We were walking toward a vintage shop called Lucky's.

It was on North Adams just after it crosses River Road, by the Ice Cream Palace. We'd ditched Dev, who had to go home and do some research and development (or "R&D" in business lingo) for our other six steps.

"There are two types of people, Kate: sheep and wolves," Callie mused. "Sheep wait to see what everybody else is wearing, and then they run out to the mall and buy it. That's fine if you want to blend in. But wolves eat sheep."

"What are you?" I asked, thinking I was being coy. "Sheep or wolf?"

"Me," Callie mused. "I eat wolves."

Okay. This girl, a girl whom I'd been best friends with for eons, was starting to scare me.

We walked into Lucky's, and while Callie looked through the racks, I checked myself out in a mirror. Was she really right about my look? I'd worn this jean jacket with some form of J. Crew wear for three years now. Had I really been that blind? I realized that there was nothing wrong with it per se, but there was nothing special there either. If you put a paper bag over my head, I probably could've been any one of a hundred girls in the halls of Millbank High School.

"All right," Callie shouted from across the room. "Come check this out."

She was holding a very old Lacoste shirt, bright green, circa 1986. I'm pretty sure the color is chartreuse, and it was probably two sizes two small. She started rifling through the racks and tossing clothes into a basket. Short shorts. A vintage von Furstenberg wrap dress. An old GUNS N' ROSES T-shirt. A blue blazer. A pleated skirt like Catholic school girls wear. Cut-off denim shorts.

"What's all this?"

"The new Kate," she said. "And FYI, let's change your name while were at it. We're going to call you Kat, like a sexy, smart little kitten." She giggled like she'd hit upon something clever.

I wasn't sure about the whole name thing or the clothes, and frankly, I couldn't make sense of them either. In some ways they were within the realm of what I was wearing already, but they were pure vintage, and tighter and sexier, to boot. As Callie's vision started to jell in my mind, I started imagining outfits I could put together, and I wasn't entirely sure that my mother wouldn't have a complete and total heart attack.

"You're going for prep," I said cautiously. "But . . ."

"But sexy prep. Lacoste with a drop of Paris," she explained. "The tart, not the city."

"Right," I replied. "Not more than a drop or two, though—I mean, she's a skank."

Callie laughed. "Indeed. A skank who's worshipped because she was an original, although a skanky original."

We both cracked up.

"By the time I'm done"—she grinned—"nobody's even going to recognize you."

Four hours later, Dev joined us and we were all sitting in Images, waiting for Carlo. I was halfway done with my makeover, and a new hair style was part two. My new wardrobe—although mostly thrift store—had ended up costing some serious change, but Dev had offered to front most of the cost. What can I tell you? It's pretty helpful to have friends with gobs of money when you're doing a total makeover, and Dev was generous like that.

Now that I was face-to-face with actually going forward with this insane plan, however—i.e. cutting, straightening, and dyeing my hair—I was more than a little hesitant.

Clothes you could always throw away.

A new hairstyle was permanent.

I looked at Dev. "Remind me why I'm doing this again?"

"Because of the Market?" she said, looking less than convinced by her own rhetoric.

"There has to be some other reason. Am I really that shallow?" I said.

"You're so beautiful, Kat," Callie piped in. "You are just showing the world what I've known—that you are a star. There's nothing wrong with shining."

But what was my mother going to say when I got home, and it looked like a diva had commandeered the body of her hitherto super-conventional daughter? On the other hand, I *did* like the way I looked in the new clothes that Callie had found for me. A little older, a little more daring, a little over the edge. For the first time, I felt like I'd been given permission to show a little more leg, let loose, and nudge a little closer to a wilder side. But truth be told, I still wasn't sure I was ready to make that leap.

"Katie," Carlo called in his thick Peruvian accent as he approached, "Devie here tells me you want to be wild. Tell me it's true."

I looked skeptically at Dev, who made a face that said, "Don't disappoint Carlo." I turned to him and laid some puppy-dog eyes on him.

"I'm not sure."

"You are not sure about what?" he quizzed. In a whirl he ushered me to a chair, and before I could answer, he'd already spritzed my hair with water and was gently massaging my scalp.

Carlo was flamboyant, gay, and a force with which to be reckoned. We all loved how over-the-top he was. He'd moved to Millbank from the West Village about five years ago and quickly became the rage among the under-twenty crowd. There was a little boutique salon around the corner, but that was for the rich and the old (with kids). Images and Carlo, they were for the hip and the young. No toddlers allowed.

"Let me tell you, Katie, the truth about women," he started in.

And this was the other thing about Carlo: he loved to hear himself talk. Once he got started, there was no stopping him. He was the king of pontification; you give him a subject, he had an opinion. I would say he was right only fifty percent of the time, but he was so damn sure of himself, you just couldn't help but listen.

"Every day," he continued, "women come to Carlo and ninety-nine out of a hundred stay just like before. *Boring.* But once a month there's a woman who says, 'Carlo, I want to be a star . . . Carlo, make me a star,' they say. And you know what?"

"What?"

"Carlo does!"

"Maybe I don't want to be a star."

"No!" Carlo shouted. "*Everyone* wants to be a star."

I closed my eyes. So the moment of decision was truly at hand.

I could hear Callie and Dev mmm-hmming and nodding, but I didn't say a word. I opened my eyes and looked into the mirror in front of me. I'd always wondered what life would be like as a blonde. Did they really have more fun? I looked at the clothes I was wearing, the old jean jacket and the maroon L.L. Bean button-down.

Was Callie right? Was this jacket my blankie? Did I carry

around this piece of cloth because it made me feel safe? Was Carlo right? Was my fear holding me back from what I truly wanted?

In a flash I stood up. I could see Callie and Dev were nervous, thinking I was about to walk out, but instead I whipped off my jean jacket and tossed it to Dev.

"Take this and hide it till school is over. Callie, could you shorten those skirts we bought just a bit—a little more leg? And Carlo, I want to go blond. And make it as sexy as you can."

"Whooooo-HOOOOO!" is all I heard from the three of them.

Carlo did a little mambo—or some South American dance—and then took out the coloring bottles and asked me to choose which color blond I wanted to be. Misty Dawn? Honey Blond? Corn Straw? I never realized there were so many choices.

Callie pulled out the plaid skirt and held it up. "Now, how short do you want this?" she asked.

"Where the mystery begins," I replied.

Dev and Callie nearly fell on the floor with laughter.

"Where did you hear that line?" Dev asked after she composed herself.

I shrugged, smiling. I had no idea where it came from, but I made a note to ramp it down. I was quickly realizing that once you let your inner Paris out, it was hard to keep her in check.

Three and a half hours later, I was within a single shade of platinum blond. Yeah, I'd gone all out. And maybe, just maybe, I'd gone a little too far. But as any girl knows, when you sit for two and a half hours watching the "paint" dry on your hair, you have more than a little time to contemplate life's big questions. Looking in the mirror and watching my curly brown hair turn straight and blond, the question of why I was doing this was impossible to avoid.

I thought of Mom and Mel's close relationship and how desperately I wanted to be part of what they had; of always being the six or seventh or whatever number picked for anything (never the first and never the last, which I always thought must have had its own charms); of never being the "-est" girl in anything, and by that I mean never the prettyest, smart-est, sexy-est, tall-est, fast-est. Everyone of us, old or young, smart or dumb, ugly or beautiful, wants to be somebody. It's why people read *Us Weekly* and think they are reading about friends. It's why in England people follow the trials and tribulations of British royalty. We all have a never-ending thirst to be more "important" than we are. "I want to be somebody," I felt like shouting over the hum of hair dryers and electric buzz cutters. I wanted everyone to know me, to remember me, to be on the lips of strangers who told stories about me like they knew me . . . as if I were their friend. If changing my hair, coloring it blond, and jettisoning every piece of clothing that screamed of the old, invisible me was what I needed to do, then I was more than willing to do it.

When Carlo removed the towel from my head, blew out my hair, and I saw the new me, I was sure I'd made the right move.

I got up from my chair and, at the prompting of Callie, did a short catwalk for the girls. Carlo and the girls applauded, and Stephania (Carlo's station mate) gave me the thumbs-up. Yup, this was going to be the start of a whole new life.

The life of Kat.

But when I turned around and started walking back toward the chair, I stopped dead in my tracks. It wasn't the new me in the mirror, or the ghost of the old me standing there in disbelief. No, it was worse.

It was my mother—and her jaw was on the floor.

I'd forgotten that the third Saturday of every month was re-coloring day. She liked coming to Images, she said, because it made her feel young. (Hey, moms, that makes the rest of us feel old!) With her hands gripping a swivel chair she'd apparently grabbed to prevent her from fainting, she looked like she was about to kill somebody. Me. Carlo. Callie. Dev. I'm not exactly sure who, but she had murder in her eyes. Callie and Dev—veterans of my mother's anger— wilted like two week-old flowers and grabbed their stuff before bolting for the door. Dev gave me the "Call me" sign, and Callie shrunk her six-foot frame and skittered out like a mouse. I nodded to them and then slinked back into Carlo's chair, hoping for some protection, but he just raised his eyebrows nervously and straightened up his station.

My mother strode up to me and spun the chair around. She stood there for what felt like an eternity.

"Hey, Mom," I said.

When in serious trouble, pretend nothing is wrong.

"What were you thinking?" she hissed.

Yes, there's nothing quite like a parent to rain on your parade.

"I'd like an answer. Now!"

I was silent. I mean, I couldn't tell her the truth. What? That there was a list going around school and that I was on the bottom of it? That only would've confirmed all her criticism over the years.

"I wanted to do something special," I replied. "Something different."

"Different? Different?" she stammered. "Different is ironing your sweater for a change. Not deciding you want to look like Suzanne Somers."

I looked at Carlo and said, "Who?" He put his hands up and made an I-don't-know-either face.

"I think she looks beautiful," Carlo chimed.

My mother gave him the evil eye, and he shuffled to the other side of the room.

"Let's go."

I gathered my bags and gave a hidden wave to Carlo, who blew me a kiss. Right when I reached the door, he motioned subtly and mouthed something to me. At first I didn't get it, but when he said it the second time, I couldn't help but smile.

"You're a star."

CHAPTER

9

ON ALMOST ANY other night in my high school career, you'd have found me studying, but as graduation loomed ever closer, I relaxed. I'd already been accepted to Brown and I knew I could coast to the end without seriously jeopardizing my grades. Most teachers understood the need to kick back a little as we approached June, so allowances were made and grades were inflated. It was a little game we all consciously took part in, but of which we never spoke.

So there I was, supine on the sofa in the basement. TNT had a teen movie marathon and I was watching *Can't Buy Me Love*—a classic—with Remington curled on the pillow at my feet. Upstairs, my parents were hanging out, no doubt discussing what had happened to their curly-brown-haired daughter. The ride home from Images with Mom was oh-so-pleasant—she laid into me for a good fifteen minutes about the damage I'd done to my hair between the dye and the straightening, and demanded to know if I was on drugs. Yeah, she was a little prone to hysterics. Silently I figured that she was actually just freaked because the interview for the Millbank Country Club was coming up, and she was worried how it would seem to the committee if her daughter looked like Christina Aguilera in her glam days, but I didn't call her on it. I've found over time that it's best just to let parents blow all their steam out, and then respond later. Engaging them in their moments of rage only stokes the fire.

As the show went to commercial break, I heard the buzz of my cell phone and my first thought was to just ignore it. Then the ridiculous thought that perhaps Will B. might be calling—hey, we all like to fantasize—literally pulled me right off the couch. When I glanced at the caller ID, I sighed.

"Hey, Cal," I said.

"What are you doing right now?" she asked.

There was an urgency in her voice, like the world was about to come to an end.

"Lying down and dreaming about McDreamy," I answered.

"Well, wake up and start dreaming about boys your own age," she shouted. "Meet me at the Café Electric at ten p.m."

"I already told my parents I was staying in for the night. You know how they are."

What I didn't bother adding was that my mother was probably still really pissed at me and that it was best to let sleeping dogs lie.

"Did you forget that Will B. and his band are playing at open mike, and everybody who's anybody is going to be there? So you've got to get there, too. It's time to introduce Kat to the world."

I said nothing. Truth is, the thought of trotting out the new me was terrifying. Prancing around in front of Carlo and my friends was one thing, but out in public? That was altogether different. What if everyone thought I looked ridiculous? What if everyone laughed? What if this whole transformation thing had been a big mistake?

"I don't know," I hedged.

"Sheep or wolf?" Callie shot back. "Do you want to explode like the big bang or whimper like a mutt in the rain?"

Dev had obviously gotten into her brain, too.

"Okay," I said, without thinking. "I'll meet you out front."

"By the Cuban place," she said.

I hung up and ran to my room. I dug through all my new outfits and considered what would be best for the occasion. I pulled out a little white pleated skirt Callie had picked out and a sexy yoga tank that made me look more full-figured than I really was, but that was the point, after all. My hair was still perfect—maybe a little flat in the back from lying on the sofa—but there was no need to fuss with it. I grabbed the highest heels I could walk in, the little Kate Spade bag Callie had loaned me, and threw in my keys and a couple of twenties.

But as I reached for the door, it hit me: if I walked out into my living room dressed like this, my parents would flip. Like Superman—or Supergirl, I suppose—I quickly undressed and threw everything into a little gym bag, including my purse. Instead, I put on an old ratty pair of jeans, flip-flops, and my Mack Trucks baseball cap.

Now there are any number of excuses you can give your parents when you're trying to get out of the house, but here's the problem: almost none of them work. If it were my dad, I'd probably have used the tried-and-true "I'm going to get tampons." With Mom sitting there, however, that was out the window, so I opted for the classic intimate-talk trick.

"Mom, could I talk to you for a minute, *alone?*" I whispered from the doorway.

Adding the "alone" part is key. We moved to the kitchen, where I lied and explained that Dev had just been dumped by a boy she hardly knew but was hoping might ask her to the Black & White (note how I played on my mother's own anxiety about me—the Black & White and that damn club?). While things weren't exactly hunky-dory between us since the whole Images drama, she nodded as if she understood and told me to call if I was going to be late or sleeping over.

Flawless.

I was out the door and in my car in a matter of seconds. I had to get re-dressed, but the question was, where? The passenger seat of my incredibly glamorous 1996 two-door Honda Civic was far from spacious, and Millbank wasn't one of those rural towns with lots of empty spaces where you could ditch your car in the woods and feel pretty safe that nobody was going to come along and see you. So I pulled into the community parking lot and drove to the very top, where there were no cars, and parked in the darkness of a corner spot. It took me a few minutes to wrangle out of my jeans into my skirt, but like Superman in a phone booth, when I emerged, I was ready to fly.

River Road was always hopping (at least by suburban standards), but tonight it seemed especially busy. There were probably twenty restaurants on the main drag and more than a handful of bars. People from all over the area came to Millbank to party, some to see hip indie films, some to get a bite at restaurants like Violet or Lex that served New York–quality food in New Jersey. The media-savvy citizens of Millbank, many of them in the "biz" (as they like to refer to anything entertainment-related), thought of their little town as the "sixth" borough. Others, less generous, liked to call it the Upper West Side of New Jersey. I, like any other American kid, called it home . . . and I couldn't wait to get as far away as possible.

As I walked down River, in the distance I could see Callie standing in front of Café Electric, playing with her big hoop earrings. She looked cool in wide-wale cords and her purple Crocs, but it was hardly the outfit for a night at Café Electric.

Why would she wear that?

"Hey, Cal." I waved and gave her a light look up and down, as if to say, "Really?"

"You look delicious, Kat. I could eat you up."

"Thanks," I said. I glanced down at my heels, saw a trace of mud that I whisked off with my pinky finger.

"Here's the plan," she whispered into my ear. "I'll hang out here. You go in and do your stuff."

"What?" I snapped. "I'm not going in by myself."

For starters, I'd never been in Café Electric in my life. Second, I was supposed to roll in there, sporting a whole new wardrobe, a whole new hairstyle, without a wing girl? I shook my head again, but Callie smiled her comforting, wide grin. She put her arm around my shoulder and walked me to the alley beside Electric.

"Listen up," she said calmly. "You need to go in there and be bigger than life. If I'm there—well—that's going to be tough. We'll end up sucking each other's energy right out of the room."

"No way."

First Gretchen's party, now Café Electric. Since when did I have to face the world alone?

"So it's the same old Katie, but with different clothes," Callie sighed. "I get it."

I could see the remarks on the Market already: "Looks like someone dropped a bottle of peroxide on her head!" or "Fashion Disaster 101" or "Who would've thought that she could look lamer than before?" But whatever, I thought. If I didn't do it, it would probably read: "Didn't see her out; must have stayed home with cats on Saturday night."

"Fine, tell me what I have to do."

I walked to the door of Electric and paid the ten-dollar cover charge to see the open-mikers. Pushing my way through the crowd, I made my way down the hall to the back of the club where the stage was, and as soon as I set foot in the room, I felt my body tense up. Millbank students packed the place, and nearly every table was taken. Callie was right—anyone who was anyone was here. In the very back in the corner—no doubt weaving her black widow's web—was Gretchen surrounded by the Proud Crowd posse. There were others I knew—some seniors, some recent grads who went to nearby colleges—but Callie had given me very specific instructions: I wasn't allowed to talk to anyone I knew. There was no safety in familiarity. I was to be bold. I was supposed to walk right to the edge of the stage, sit down, and just stare into Will's eyes as he sang. Callie's theory was that if Will noticed me, everyone else would notice me, hence launching my new look—or "brand" as Dev would say— into the stratosphere. That's the big bang model, anyway.

In theory? Easy.

In reality? Terrifying.

Let's all remember that exactly one week ago I was the girl wandering around Gretchen's party unable to work the tap at the keg.

Well, that doesn't matter now, I reminded myself. I checked the mirrored wall across the room to see if there was any trace of the little girl who was frightened of everything, of everyone, and for the first time . . . I didn't see her. Not totally, at least. Maybe I didn't see Kat either, but I saw somebody different, striving however awkwardly to be something else.

I took a deep breath, held my head high, and took my first step across the room.

I was going to do it. It was time to show the world the new me.

Say hello to Kat!

And right then, the whole mirage came crashing down around me.

My right heel slipped on something—a wet napkin . . . a crack in the floor?—and for a pregnant moment that seemed like forever, I felt myself falling sideways. It's safe to say that "graceful" has never been an adjective used to describe me, and images of me eating it into a table—cups of soda and coffee drenching my new outfit, and people hysterically laughing over me as I lay on the floor, perhaps even bleeding from a fresh gash in my forehead—flashed through my mind like a bad movie. This was it. Just when I thought I might be making my jump to super cool, I was about to become super loser!

But in an instant—and with agility I'd never realized I had—I threw my right hand out onto an empty chair and miraculously caught my balance. I shot a quick look around, and—thank God!—I could tell nobody noticed. Adjusting myself once more, I shook it off and began taking long catwalk-like strides across the room. I kept my eyes focused on a spot in the distance, and zeroed in on an empty chair.

Don't fall, Kate.

Please, please, please don't fall.

And as I walked down the center aisle toward the stage, praying that I wasn't going to make a total ass of myself, the strangest thing happened. I could see the shadows of boys' heads turn my way and the heavy eyes of girls fall upon me.

As I passed tables, a hush trailed behind me. I glanced back once, just to make sure that it wasn't Gretchen making the room stand still. And it wasn't.

It was me.

I was making it happen!

I sat down at the first table just to the left of the stage, but—and forgive the cliché—I was floating on air. The whole thing had been so intoxicating—almost how I imagined the strongest of drugs. In the wings, I spotted Will B. working with his drummer, Dee Brown, trying to get his kit ready for their song. A waiter strolled up, gave me a wink, and took my order. (I could get used to this!)

After a few minutes the lights dimmed and Jane Austen's Secret Lover was introduced. The band came out led by Jack, who tuned his guitar and strummed a few notes. After a moment of settling, Will B. stalked to the middle of the stage and straddled the microphone stand. It was like a slow dance with a girl he loved. Jack started a hard guitar riff—intently focusing down—and gradually the music began to build, like the best of The Shins or the Yeah Yeah Yeahs. About two thirds of the way through their song, while the drummer ripped off a solo, Will came out of his performance-inspired coma and looked around, searching the crowd, it seemed, for familiar faces. Suddenly, his eyes met mine, and I gave my gaze all the intensity I could muster.

But nothing happened. His eyes fell away as if I weren't there.

For a moment I felt crestfallen—crushed is probably the better word—but then, like an electromagnet whose power is delayed, he came back to me with a fierce look, and howled a few more bars. I kept my cool, but I knew for whom he was singing. Me!! My stomach flip-flopped around and my legs wobbled, but on the outside, I'm pretty sure I kept my cool.

As the mini-set ended, I checked my watch; it was three minutes before midnight. Deep down, I hoped that Will would come and talk to me—perhaps he was wondering who the blonde in the front row was—but I was going to leave at twelve. This was the last thing Callie had told me. As soon as midnight rolled around, no matter what was happening, I was supposed to get up and walk out.

"Arrive late, leave early," she'd advised.

A few moments later, Will and Jack and the rest of the band disappeared behind the stage, and I was sure that would be the last I'd see of him. I went to grab my purse from the table, but an instant later he entered the room from the EMPLOYEES ONLY door on the opposite side. Will sauntered right up to my table with Jack in tow, and I could swear he gave a soft wave to Gretchen as if to say, "What up." What I definitely saw was her sit back in disgust.

"Kate!" He grinned. "You look awesome."

"Thanks," I said. "You were wonderful. You too, Jack." Jack gave me a little nod and then continued to stare at the ground. Just then, Dee Brown—the drummer and a boy I had known since fifth grade—bounced up and introduced himself.

"Hey, I'm Dee."

"Dude, don't be an idiot," Will said, hitting him playfully. "It's Kate Winthrop."

Dee's mouth fell open ever so slightly in disbelief. "Holy acts of total makeover."

Will grabbed a chair and swung it around so he was sitting backward on it and leaning over the back in a relaxed, I-don't-care-what-the-world-thinks way. Frankly, I didn't care either. He was the dreamiest thing I'd ever seen.

Jack stood directly behind Will, and he looked up from his shoes and stared at me. His unwavering gaze would have made me feel awkward in any other situation, but my entire focus was easily placed on Will.

"Hey, Will," Jack said. "We need to break down the gear so the next band can set up."

"Sure, sure," Will waved him off, keeping his eyes on me. "I'll be right there."

Jack sighed and headed back toward the stage.

"Are you hanging here?" Will asked.

"Not sure," I said. I looked at my watch and it read midnight on the dot. *Crap.* I gave myself a little more rope and told myself to be out by 12:05a.m.

"We're getting together at my house," he said.

I nodded and asked who "we" was.

"You know, just some peeps, the usual suspects," he answered.

I nodded again, though I had no idea who he was talking about.

Just then I heard my cell go off and picked it out of my purse. I looked at the caller; it was a text from Callie:

CAL: Leave the glass slipper on the table, princess.

I laughed a little and looked at Will.

"Who's that?" he asked.

"Oh, nobody," I answered, with the coolest of shrugs. With every waking second, I could feel my confidence growing. "But I have to go."

I stood up. In my heels I was a good inch or so taller than Will, and he looked up at me. I could see he was a little starry-eyed, and for the first time in my life, I knew what the word "power" meant.

"Later, Jack," I said as he waved from the stage. Then with a knowing touch on the back of Will's hand, I whispered, "Bye, Will—maybe next time."

KCW LLC.

SHARE PRICE: $3.75
    CHANGE: ↑1.90 (+102%)
L/B RATIO: 5.3
3-MONTH RANGE: $1.23 – $3.77
STATUS: PENNY STOCK

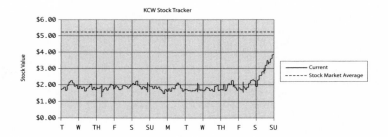

KCW Stock Tracker

ANALYST RECOMMENDATION: a significant repackaging has this analyst taking a closer look. Tongues were wagging at Café Electric, but it remains to be seen if new management will stay the course and do what needs to be done to truly transform this stock into a buy.

HOLD

CHAPTER

10

WHEN I WOKE UP Sunday morning, I had a hangover. Not from booze, mind you, but from the euphoria of the night before that had settled to the back of my brain and morphed into something new and heavy. There were now two of me living in one body. On one side of the bed, the little girl in the jean jacket—still thinking of herself as the wallflower. Beside her, awakened for the first time by a kiss from destiny, was a radiant young woman who was just opening her eyes and seeing for the first time a big wide world.

Sadly, the old me looked at her clock radio and knew there wasn't even enough time to roll out of bed and get to the BookStop before opening. Thus, a mere sixty seconds later, I was in my standard BookStop uniform: jeans and a Che T-shirt (courtesy of Howie). But as I grabbed my purse and headed for the door, I caught a glimpse of myself in the mirror.

I paused.

Although I'd always thought the look was original, it dawned on me that maybe I just looked like every other little faux radical in Millbank. We wore our T-shirts protesting this or that, or we sported clever shirts formerly owned by real gas-station attendants and thought we were cool. But were we? I looked over at the closet and I knew behind the doors was a new outfit—something original and mind blowing. Whatever lurked there was probably totally inappropriate for the BookStop, but I realized that if I wanted to change myself, I had to go whole hog or else the old me would keep seeping into the picture.

I tossed my purse on the bed and started peeling off my clothes.

It took me a few minutes to put together a somewhat fabulous outfit (it's not as easy as it looks) that wouldn't send Howie into total shock. The BookStop was a left-wing bookstore, after all. So here's what I did: I took that Che T-shirt and did a quick nip and tuck, threw on some hip-hugging, navel-blazing jeans, a pair of wedge-heeled boots, and added some jewelry that conveniently dropped pearls right over old Che's beard. For good measure I tied a cool scarf around my neck, and as I finished getting dressed, I even came up with a name for the look: Sexy Che. I'm sure

Señor Guevara rolled over in his grave, but no doubt he admired my audacity.

Twenty minutes later, I pulled open the door to the BookStop, and Howie was already sitting on his stool perched way above me. He did a double take as I walked in, and made a face somewhere between a smirk and a laugh. I was late, to boot, so I'm sure that added to his general disgust.

"Britney Guevara," he observed. "A clever response to the suffocating pressure of a bourgeois middle-class existence."

I breezed by him with the simple joust, "Fidel, fatigues were so yesterday—it's a new world out there." Whether he was caught without a response or just quietly amused by my barb, he didn't respond.

I walked into the employee room, dropped my stuff, and knocked on Mrs. Sawyer's door. She was doing the books—she didn't believe in Microsoft Excel; she literally did all her accounting by hand—and was talking on the phone to someone she apparently didn't like very much.

I nodded and then picked up a box of stuff she had set aside for the graduation window. *A Short Guide to a Happy Life* by Anna Quindlen was sitting on top, followed by a whole host of other stuff about going to college, how to avoid the Freshman Ten, etc.

"I'm going to work on the window for a bit, if that's okay."

She waved me on, and I took the box and slipped back

out into the store. In the comic book section I noticed two stoner types—both sporting those pathetic white-boy cornrows—thumbing through some of the older issues. As I passed by, one of them, who was distinguishable from the other only by an eyebrow pierce, glanced over and gave me a wink.

"What up, *mamacita*?" he cooed.

Needless to say, this was not the sort of attention I was looking for.

I faked a smile and walked to the front of the store. When I opened the hatch that led to the front window, I was greeted by Jack Clayton's mug—it was unshaven and his eyes were a little bloodshot, like he had been up all night.

"Um, what are you doing?"

He pushed himself up off his hands and knees and brushed the dust off his pants. Clearly, my tone caught him off guard. "Hey, Kate."

"*Kat.*"

"Oh, okay," he said. He was distracted and looking around the bay of the front window.

"What are you doing?" I asked again.

"Howie asked me to clean up the window, before we put in the graduation display."

"That's *my* job," I snapped.

Who did he think he was? New people shelve and stack—I do the creative work. Just because he ran with Will didn't mean he could run roughshod over my turf, even if he'd been told to do so. I turned around to go track down Howie, but as I looked across the store, something caught my eye. It was the stoner guys.

They were stealing some of the comic books.

I motioned to Jack with a wave of my hand and then put my finger to my lips.

"What?" he whispered.

"Look." I gestured with my head. "They're shoving comic books down their pants."

"And you want them to put them back?" he quipped.

Nothing like having a clown by your side in a moment of crisis, I thought. Where was Will when I needed him?

I rolled my eyes. Unfortunately, Howie—the usual enforcer—was nowhere to be seen. What should I do? Call the police? No, these guys would have been long gone by then. Confront them myself? Somehow I couldn't quite imagine that I would make a formidable opponent to either in a confrontation. But ignoring them didn't exactly seem like the right thing to do either. Maybe it was my years of working with Howie that roused my righteous indignation, because a moment later I was striding across the store toward them.

Kids, don't try this at home.

"Wait," I heard Jack whisper-shout from behind me, but it was too late.

I snuck up behind them and tapped the pierced one on

the shoulder. When they turned I realized how big these guys were—my head only came to their shoulders—and how much they stank of booze.

"What's that?" I demanded, pointing at the book-size bulge in his crotch.

"You like it?" the piercer said, throwing up his hands in mock innocence.

"Put them back."

"Take 'em back yourself, Lolita," the other joked.

"I'm going to call the po—"

Before I could finish my sentence, eyebrow pierce took off for the back exit, and when I went to grab the other guy—honestly, I don't know what I was thinking—he shoved me into a shelf of self-help books.

"Help!" I yelled as an avalanche of advice fell on me.

In a flash, Jack jumped out from the front window as the book-lifter tried to bolt through the door. He grabbed the dude by the throat and yanked him off his feet and against the wall. *Wow!* Jack was a good three inches shorter and twenty pounds lighter than this guy, but you wouldn't have guessed it by the way he had him pinned against the wall. For the first time, I noticed the size of Jack's hands and forearms—they were weirdly out of proportion to the rest of his body, which I gathered came from thousands of hours of guitar playing. What would've happened if Jack had to hold him for more than a few seconds, I have no idea, but it didn't matter because Howie walked back into the store with a cup of coffee.

"What up?" he asked in perfect teenage speak.

I pointed to the lump in the front of the guy's trousers.

"Glad to see me, huh?" he drawled, but a split second later his face grew dark and threatening. "The merchandise. Now!"

The stoner dropped five or six comic books on the floor before Howie spun him around and yanked out the guy's wallet. He glanced at the driver's license before tossing it back to him.

"Larry Goff? Tell you what, young man, I won't call the cops on you."

The stoner smiled with relief.

"What's your buddy's name?"

"I don't know."

Wrong answer—definitely the wrong answer. A strange grin bordering on psychotic grew on Howie's face.

"Kate, get the police on the phone. Tell them I have somebody here trying to steal this classic pre-film version of *Hell Boy* worth about two thousand dollars—that's grand larceny."

"Mark Altiere—his name is Mark Altiere."

"Thanks, Larry. I'll be calling your parents, and Mark's. And if you come in here again, I'll just break your hands in the back room—got it?"

Larry's face went white, and then he took off out of the store at a full sprint.

"I can't believe they had them down their pants," Howie said, staring down at the comic books. "Now I'm going to have to get rubber gloves and make new cover protectors."

Howie gathered the comics and walked toward the back. When he was gone, I gave Jack a high five.

"Dude, that was awesome. Where'd you learn that?"

He shrugged his shoulders diffidently.

"Listen," I started, "you want to help on the window?"

"The graduation window?" he asked. "Isn't that your thing?"

"Yeah, but I need help. Mrs. Sawyer is too old to spend a couple of hours stooped in the window, and Howie would find a way to offend the entire population of Millbank."

"No doubt," he said. "I can see the Christmas window now, 'A No-Logo Christmas: How to make your own gifts and bomb the System.'"

Observant lad, I thought. He got Howie and, I could tell, still liked him.

"Okay, then," I said, "I like to start with the theme and then find a new way into it. If you do what everyone else is doing, then nobody will stop and notice."

"It's a noisy world," he said.

How true, I thought.

We ended up working steadily for an hour and cleared the bay window, packed the books into boxes, and swept the floor. We took the portable and temporary window stand and put it in place (in between themed windows and holidays, we always put a rack of the rare classics we owned). We hardly said a word the whole time, but by then I was starting to get a good vibe from Jack. When he liked doing something, like playing guitar or, in this case, taking down the window, he was supremely focused. You could tell by looking at his face that he was serious, more serious than most kids in high school. Considering his scene at Millbank, I expected something far different, and part of me wondered if he didn't hang with the Proud Crowd more from circumstance than want. As the day wound down, we traded a few ideas about what the window should be, but none were really sparking.

"Why don't we put this on ice?" he said eventually.

"Really? Graduation's like a month from now."

"I think better when eating. How 'bout we hit Dickey Dogs on Saturday? You in?"

Was Jack asking me out on a date? Two weeks before I would've been over the moon to be asked out by him, but for some reason, I hesitated. Was it because I was hoping Will might ask me out, too? Then, a much tougher calculus problem flashed into my mind: what would going out with Jack mean in terms of the Market? Would it have an impact on Will being interested in me—assuming he might be? In about a millisecond, I computed all the possibilities and concluded that in the end it could only be a positive. In the school's eyes it would definitely be perceived as a big step up for me—easily done after dwelling in Anonymityville for four years—and would certainly give me a bounce in my numbers.

"In," I declared. "I'll meet you here."

And as soon as I said it, something warmed in my heart.

BOOK THREE

ON THE BIG BOARD

CHAPTER

11

WEARING MY NEW clothes to Café Electric was one thing. Wearing them to school was another.

Sure, I was starting to feel more confident—especially with my Market ranking on the rise—but it was still a bit of an adjustment. When I wore my Catholic schoolgirl outfit—with extra short skirt courtesy of Callie—more than a few disapproving eyebrows were raised by teachers I'd known since I was a freshman, but it was all worth it when I noticed later that week that at least two underclassman had copied my look. How cool is that? Even better was that Will actually started to say "hi" to me whenever I passed him in the halls.

Kate Winthrop, previously a nonentity, was suddenly a legitimate presence at Millbank High School.

Despite it all, I still had some reservations about Dev's master plan. Now that I'd had some time to review it in depth, there were a few things I needed to hash out with her. Yes, I wanted to climb the Market, but I wasn't going to do it at all costs—I had my pride. So Wednesday after school, Dev, Callie, and I called our second "board meeting"—it was sort of ridiculous calling it a board meeting considering it was just the *three* of us, but it was entertaining all the same—and we met up at Bella's, our stalwart pizzeria where Callie worked three days a week.

We sat in the back room and Dev ordered our favorite, the mushroom ravioli *ala famiglia*, with a grande green salad. As we settled in and sipped our waters and devoured old man Giovachinni's fresh bread, Dev took out her business plan.

"So steps one and two have been a success. We've rebranded you and then created a big bang at Café Electric."

"What's next?" Callie said.

She flipped to a page with the words Step Three written in large block letters.

"A month before Kathy Parker went big in '04, she had a car accident. The doctors thought she might be braindead, but miraculously, she recovered. Shortly after she returned to school, Eric Benson asked her out. And the rest, as they say, was history."

"And?" I asked, waiting for the punch line.

"Remember I was struggling with a way to establish brand loyalty? Well here's my plan. Read." I swung her notebook around and scanned a paragraph written in Dev's Unibomber-like script.

If she wasn't my best friend and partner in crime, I would have turned her in right there. I pushed the notebook over to Callie, who read it quickly.

"It's pure insanity," I said. "And the answer is N-O."

"You've lost your mind, Dev," Callie seconded.

"What's wrong with faking a car accident?" she asked without an ounce of irony. "We'll bang my car into a tree out by the estate section and nobody will be the wiser! It's the perfect way to get people emotionally invested in you."

She's lost it. Completely and totally.

"I've got a better idea," Callie replied. "We'll cut off her left hand with my dad's power saw—that'll create sympathy . . . and who needs two hands anyway?"

I guess Dev started to see the light, because she spat out her food as she convulsed into laughter.

"No, wait," I countered. "Let's cut off both my arms— then I can be the girl in that documentary who had to do everything with her feet."

"Don't laugh—I actually considered that!" Dev shouted.

I know, I know. Laughing at disabilities is horrible— and, yes, we're going to go straight to hell—but at that moment, it was the most hilarious thing we'd ever heard.

"Okay, that's fair," Dev conceded. "Let's table Number Three for now—I mean, we'll come up with something else, right?"

Callie and I nodded, and Callie scanned the rest of the steps.

"So you think this will work?" Callie asked.

"I've never been more convinced of something in my life," Dev replied with a devilish grin on her face. "Every girl we looked at in those yearbooks last week took one, two, or even three of these steps during her senior year. I'm not saying they did it consciously, but they took them nonetheless. We just have to do them all to cover all the bases."

A bemused look must have shadowed my face because Dev frowned at me. Was she becoming Dr. Frankenstein and I her experimental monster?

"A few steps might be okay," I said. "But seven? People will think I'm a freak."

"I agree," Callie chimed in. "I mean, people might think she's trying too hard. It could backfire in a big way."

"They won't even know," Dev said. "Only we will."

She may have been right, but for the first time, I worried that I might be manipulating people. Manipulating how they felt about me. Sure, no one else would know what we were up to—but I would know. Somehow that began to feel bad enough.

"It seems a little wrong, like I'm tricking people

into liking me," I heard myself say.

"Why?" Dev shot back. "People manipulate each other all day long. They wear clothes that supposedly say something about themselves, or they color their hair, or they pretend to like you so you'll help them on a test, or so you'll give them a ride somewhere. Wake up—the whole world is one big sleight of hand," she said. Dev had an edge in her voice, like she was tired of being a victim of that world herself, and this was her chance to strike back.

"But this feels . . . extreme," I countered.

"It *is* extreme," she pressed. "But that Market is even more extreme. If the boys, or the Proud Crowd, or whoever it is, are going to play rough, then we need to play the game rougher. If they're going to judge a book by its cover, then let's give them the hottest damn cover in the world."

She was twisting the old proverb, but I knew she was right on some level. School, life, however you organized it, was one big game, and the only way you were certain to lose was by sitting out. But if you were in, you might as well go all out.

"Cool," I said. "I'll do them all, except Number Three. I don't want sympathy, and I don't want to fake it to get it, even for the Market. I mean, that would make me lower than them, and that's not the point of this. Or is it?"

Dev shook her head and said, "We'll work on the next two, then."

She seemed disappointed, but I'd made a stand, and I felt a little better about things. Could I "co-brand" myself with a cutie like Will B.? Definitely. Could I stand winning that witch Gretchen over? I didn't see it happening in a million years, but I'd certainly give it a shot. And as far as a little rebellion went, well, I hadn't broken a rule in four years, and no one should go through high school without breaking at least one rule, right?

"Okay, then," I said. "Thanks. I really do want to do this, Dev. For all of us, but Number Three is off the table."

She nodded like she understood.

"You saw that nod, right, Callie?" I said.

"Affirmative on the nod."

We all laughed, but as much as I wanted that to come off as a joke, there was a piece of me that was becoming paranoid about Dev's ambitions and how far she was willing to take this little project.

The rest of the night we ate and talked about how to co-opt Gretchen and how dreamy it would be to win over Will . . . even for a day. Briefly we got sidetracked into fantasizing about what we'd do with the money if we won— new cars? a crazy shopping spree?—but Dev steered us back on track and made us focus on how we were going to win. We didn't come up with anything concrete per se, but I felt happier about the whole experiment. For the first time in my life, I felt like I was taking control of the world around me, and all those forces that seemingly worked against me in high school faded away for a few moments. It made me smile, as I drove home, to know I was heading in a direction that, right or wrong, I had chosen.

When I walked in the door, it looked like an Ann Taylor store had exploded in our living room. Half-empty bags littered the floor, and outfits of varying colors and styles were draped over almost every surface. Purses and hats were hung from door handles and the backs of chairs. I would've guessed that Mom was spring cleaning except there were tags on all the clothing.

"Kate, thank God you're home," my mother said as she stood up from behind the sofa. She had a slightly crazed look in her eye and was wearing a dark purple skirt and jacket with a green hat that made her look like an emaciated eggplant.

"Mom, what's going on?"

"Well, I thought I should get a new outfit for our interview at the country club on Friday."

Oh, yeah, our interview.

"So you bought the whole store?"

"It's not the whole store," she chuckled. "I just thought it would be a good idea to have options."

She called it options. I called it mania.

"Besides," she continued, "I'll just return whatever I don't end up wearing."

"As long as you don't make me return it," I laughed.

"And you better not wear one of your 'new' outfits," she said, making exaggerated quotation signs. I took it as an olive branch of sorts.

"Got it . . . they don't wear super-minis at the club."

"Exactly!" She nodded perfunctorily. "So what do you think: pants are more professional, but skirts are more feminine," she noted as she grabbed a floral outfit.

I shrugged my shoulders impotently. "Um . . . do you think it really matters?"

"Of course it matters. Can I show you a few things?"

I should've said no, of course. I should've said I had homework to do. I should've said I had a brain-splitting migraine and that I desperately needed to lie down before my head exploded. But I didn't. Ever trying to be as good as my big sister was . . . I said yes. And so I spent the rest of the evening with my mother, looking at different tops, pants, skirts, blouses, hats, scarves, and combinations— discussing ad nauseum the advantages and disadvantages of each outfit, and whether it was now culturally acceptable to wear white before Memorial Day. We made *Project Runway* look like amateur hour.

By the end, my eyes had glazed over and I silently wondered why my mother was so invested in getting into the club. I mean, who cared? None of her tennis buddies were members, and it wasn't like she needed the pool—we had one in our backyard. Besides, Dad wasn't really into the idea, so why was she?

Thankfully, when my dad arrived home, he put an end to my misery. Seeing my mother in the middle of the living room, surrounded by piles of discarded clothes, with a scarf wrapped around her head like she was Jackie Kennedy, he calmly put down his briefcase and put his hands together in front of his chest.

"Ladies, can I ask a question?"

Mom and I nodded.

"Who are you, and what have you done with my family?"

CHAPTER

12

FRIDAY BROUGHT THE first really warm day of the year, and come lunchtime, most of the senior class was out on the back lawn. Callie, Dev, and I snagged the bench under the old maple and shared a barbecue chicken pizza that Callie had zipped out and picked up from Bella's. Random students lay on the grass around us—heads propped on bags— eager to soak up some rays, while Gretchen and the Proud Crowd were situated around one of the patio tables, apparently sharing the most hilarious joke ever because they couldn't stop laughing. Out by the baseball field, some boys on the Millbank lacrosse team had started an impromptu game of Ultimate, and every now and then an errant Frisbee would land in someone's lunch.

"Did you see our graduation gowns?" Callie asked as

she finished her second slice. "They're hideous. I'm going to talk to Principal Johnson."

We'd all been measured for our gowns earlier that morning, and a sample had hung stiffly behind the disturbingly hairy woman from the company that did the rentals. Callie was right. They *were* hideous. Royal blue, with yellow piping, it was less a graduation gown and more of a carnival outfit. What was wrong with just the standard black?

"Nobody looks good in those things anyway," Dev mumbled as she whipped out her Sidekick. "We'll wear them for three hours and then never see them again."

"Have you *been* to my house?" Callie asked. "My mother already has a spot on the bookshelf for a photo of me at graduation. I'll be seeing that outfit for the rest of my life."

"Maybe you can ask for a close-up," I joked.

It was right then that someone yelled "heads!" before a pink Frisbee whizzed in and nearly decapitated Dev. For once, being short was a plus, because it flew just over her head and ricocheted harmlessly off the tree trunk.

"Watch it!" Callie yelled.

One of the cuter lacrosstitutes broke out from the game and ran toward us. "Sorry 'bout that!"

As the guy neared, he noticed something and his pace slowed. Reaching the Frisbee, he bent over and picked it up.

He didn't leave.

"Hey, Kat," he said with a little lift of his head.

The guy stood there awkwardly waiting for me to respond. Next to me I could feel Callie and Dev look my way, probably wondering the same thing I was.

"Hey," I said, not knowing his name.

"Chris, my name's Chris," he said, as if he could read my mind. (I hoped not, because he was a total hottie!)

"Hey."

"Hey," he replied. A beat later, a couple of his teammates yelled for him to come back. "See ya."

Amused, I smiled and nodded, and he took off.

"Look at you!" Callie giggled. "Just slaying boys left and right."

"I don't know what you're talking about," I managed to reply with a straight face.

"Junior lacrosse players?" Dev said. "C'mon, guys. Big picture. Think Will!"

Granted, Chris Whatever-his-name-was didn't hold a candle to Will, but what was wrong with enjoying a little attention? Or acknowledging that I was in fact becoming more popular?

Suddenly, Dev's Sidekick beeped in her hand, and immediately she checked the message. Grinning, she pumped her fist in the air.

"What?"

"The next step. It's all lined up for three o'clock."

"We're doing a step today?"

She nodded. "It's perfect!"

"I can't do anything today—I have the country club meeting with my parents tonight."

"It'll take thirty minutes," Dev said.

"You should've warned me."

"Why?"

"Dev, you can't just spring these things on me out of the blue," I snapped. "I'm not a trained monkey."

"C'mon. It's easy and fun. We're going to co-brand you with a really cute boy."

"Oh," I said. Cute boy is really the only motivation a girl in high school needs.

"Look, it's really simple," Dev replied. "The guy will pick you up after school in his car. He's a friend of my sister's from Princeton."

"A college man—I like that," Callie cooed.

"That's exactly the reaction I'm hoping to get from the whole school," Dev answered, her eyes now beginning to sparkle. "And since he's from out of town, no one can ask him if it's for real or not. Perfect, right?"

Credit to Dev—she'd really thought it through. But I didn't like that she'd planned the whole thing without talking to me about it.

"Just trust me on this," Dev said. "When the bell rings after eighth period, make sure you're out front and across from the pick-up lane. Stand under the flag."

"Stand under the American flag?"

"Yeah. Subconsciously people will read it as . . . patri-otic."

Callie raised a skeptical eyebrow.

"Okay, maybe not," Dev said, "but it's still the best place to be seen."

She took out a hand-drawn map from her book bag and spread it out on the ground.

"See here?" She pointed. "This is the optimal position. Between the buses lining up over here and the lacrosse team coming out for practice here. And don't forget Will and his boys head out to the parking lot from these doors. So does Gretchen. Standing beneath the flagpole will ensure that just about everyone who needs to notice you being picked up by the incredible college hottie, will."

"I see," I said. It would be nice to give Will a little shove, and even nicer to give Gretchen a little run for her money. Still—this was going to be *way* public.

Sensing that I was feeling skittish, Dev put her hand on mine.

"I promise I'll keep you more in the loop next time," she whispered. "Besides, you can't back out on me."

"Why?"

"I paid the guy three hundred bucks."

When the bell rang at 2:55 p.m., I dashed from my locker

and headed out the west wing, which would deposit me right beside the flagpole and bus line. I had my head down and was making good progress, when a hand grabbed my shoulder.

"Kate," a deep voice said.

I turned around to find Mr. Walsh standing in front of me.

"Oh. Hi, Mr. Walsh."

"I didn't get a chance to talk to you after class the other day," he explained. "I wanted to see how your final paper was coming along."

My final paper. *Right.* Ever since Dev and I had embarked on our little adventure, basic things like homework had totally gone out the window. Granted, we were all skating through senior spring, but there were a few things that did need to get done, like said Econ paper.

"I'm . . . um . . . getting there," I mumbled.

What was I writing it on again?

"I'm glad to hear that. Remember you're giving your oral-presentation portion next week."

"I'm on it—no worries."

"There was actually an interesting article in the *Wall Street Jo*—"

I glanced at my watch—the minutes were ticking away.

"I'm sorry, Mr. Walsh, I gotta bolt." And I took off.

Two weeks ago, I never would've dreamed of cutting

off a teacher mid-sentence, particularly the likes of Mr. Walsh. After all, he had written one of my college recommendations—but these were desperate times.

It was now 3:01 p.m.

When I got to the doors I banged them open and rushed across the street to the flagpole. There was no one there yet, and as I waited, catching my breath, I watched a sea of kids start filing out the east and west wing doors. I glanced up the road, but so far there was only a long line of school buses and a few parents in minivans picking up students. Where was this guy?

It was right then that—just as Dev had predicted—Gretchen Tanner exited via the side door, trailed by Elisa Estrada. Instead of lingering by the curb, where Carrie usually picked them up in her BMW convertible, Gretchen stood by the doors and then glanced over my way, whispering something to Elisa. A second later, she handed Elisa her bag and cruised across the road toward me.

Uh-oh.

"Kate," Gretchen called as she approached, her diamond-encrusted Proud Crowd "P" swinging from its silver chain.

"Hey." I smiled in an attempt to channel someone much calmer and cooler than I.

"I wanted to tell you how much I love your hair."

I studied her for a beat. *Was she for real or was she just messing with me?* My spider senses didn't detect any sarcasm.

"Um . . . thanks."

"Where did you go? Salon Noir?"

"Images."

Gretchen reached out and touched my shoulder. "Carlo is the best!" she cooed. "Don't you love him?"

Okay, this was really weird. Since when had Gretchen decided to get all girlie-girl with me? I glanced around to make sure that I wasn't being filmed or something, but there weren't any cameras; at least any that were visible.

"Yeah, he's awesome."

A squeal of tires pierced the silence, and before I knew what was happening, a black Porsche peeled down the road and screeched to a halt in front of us. A moment later, a cute boy of about nineteen or twenty, sporting a Princeton T-shirt, popped out of the driver's seat and walked over to us. He stared for a few moments, and it took me more than a second to realize he didn't know which one of us was Kat.

"Hey, you're a little late," I said. I thought I detected disappointment in his face when he realized he was picking up the non-bombshell of the two, but he quickly recovered.

"I got held up after class."

Gretchen gave him the once-over, and I could tell she was totally impressed. She looked at me for a second, and then a light went off in her eyes. Maybe she smelled a fake or maybe she had something else in mind, but whatever it was, she wasn't going to accept this at face value.

"Hi, I'm Gretchen," she said, and flipped her hair like we were still in eighth grade. "What dorm are you in at Princeton? Rockefeller? Forbes?"

My pretend boyfriend turned toward Gretchen and all but forgot I was there.

"Wilson, actually," he said, as he held out his hand and she took it. He might as well have been drooling. "I'm Rick Sasson. Are you an alum's daughter or have you come up for a 'fun' college weekend before?"

This was turning out to be gross and humiliating all at the same time. If Dev had actually paid this guy three hundred dollars to be my pretend boyfriend, I was about to demand a full refund. He actually took a step toward her, and you could see the smile spread across her face. Gretchen Tanner was about to steal my boyfriend, albeit my pretend one, in front of the whole school.

I cleared my throat as loud as I could. "Rick, we need to get to that thing?"

"What thing?" he said, not even bothering to look away from Gretchen.

Was this idiot really attending Princeton? I mean, was he on a sports scholarship?

"That three-hundred-dollar thing. Remember that?"

His head snapped toward me, and he had a little fire in his eyes. "Oh yeah, that *desperate* thing we're taking care of together."

"Yeah, that one," I said.

He turned toward Gretchen and gave her a pregnant stare, like he was telekinetically sending his phone number to her. Little did he know Gretchen's brain couldn't hold more than six digits at a time. Then he turned away and handed me the keys.

"You drive," he said.

I got in the front seat—musing that Dev must've put him up to the "you drive" line—and put the key in the ignition and turned it over. The engine roared, and as I looked down to my right, I was immediately thankful that my dad had taught me how to drive a stick shift. I rolled down the passenger window, revealing Gretchen's long legs.

"Gretchen," I shouted. She bent over, bringing her head on level with mine.

"Yeah?"

"See ya around," I said. I slammed the gear shift into first and hit the gas. The tires spun, rocketing us forward, and as I pulled away I looked into my rearview mirror and saw Gretchen standing there dumbfounded in a haze of dust and smoke.

CHAPTER

13

THREE HOURS LATER, Mom, Dad, and I—the very portraits of perfectly coifed suburban happiness—were standing in the parking lot of the Millbank Country Club. No joke, if Norman Rockwell were alive today, he would've painted us for the *Saturday Evening Post* or whatever it was called. We looked *that* annoying. My dad was in a blue Brooks Brothers blazer, pink button-down, and perfectly pressed khakis, while my mom was in pearls and an aqua skirt and blouse. Me? All I can say is that when I caught a glimpse of myself in the window of the Mercedes next to us, I realized that I could've passed for Country Club Barbie.

My sister would've been oh so proud.

"Tuck in the back of your shirt," my mother whispered to Dad.

He sighed and did as he was told. As I said before, Dad (like me) was against this whole thing. Sure, he was a golfer, but he said he enjoyed the public courses and felt no need to join a club. In fact, he was opposed to country clubs in general. The way he put it—just five minutes ago in the car on our way up—they were filled with "limousine liberals" and "created an elitist environment." Had he not been sitting in the front seat, I would've given him a high five, but instead I nodded to myself and stared out the window.

The Millbank Country Club was situated on the top of Ryland Mountain and had views of both the valley below and New York City in the distance. The main clubhouse was surrounded by towering trees, and a huge lawn rolled all the way down the hill to the stone and wrought-iron gates.

"Can I help you?" the boy behind the reception desk said as we entered the vaulted foyer. A precocious master of the snotty how-must-I-help-you voice, he couldn't have been a day over sixteen, but he acted as if he had the keys to the universe. I will admit, however, that he was cute in that ultra-preppy way, so he kind of got away with it.

"We're here to see Mr. Biddle," Mom said with a smile.

Cute Snobby Guy opened a black leather-bound book and ran his finger down the page. "Yes, the Winthrops," he noted. "Would you wait in the tea room?"

He didn't look up at us, mind you—just pointed to a

room off to the side—and like cows being herded to slaughter, we wandered over.

The "tea room"—as it was so incongruously named—was about the size of a basketball court. At the far end of the room, a few families were having drinks, and a waiter cruised by with a silver tray full of food. Mahogany paneling covered the walls and ornate chandeliers dangled from the ceiling, giving the room a warm, yellowish glow. Hanging throughout the room were series of framed reprints by Manet and various other Impressionists. Over the stone fireplace was a five-foot-tall portrait of Taylor Millbank, the grandson of the town's founder and the first president of the club in 1896, and next to it hung a large photograph of Dan Tanner—the current president of the club.

Barely able to contain her excitement, my mother sat down primly in one of the overstuffed leathers and positioned herself on the edge of the seat with her hands on her knees. I'm telling you, it was like she'd teleported in a version of herself from the 1950s. For my own part, I dropped into the sofa with my father and fiddled with the burgundy matchbooks emblazoned with the MCC logo.

I couldn't wait to get out of there.

Fifteen minutes later I was still fiddling with the matchbooks because we were still waiting for Mr. Biddle. Cute Snobby Guy from the reception desk poked his head in and announced that Mr. Biddle was delayed and it would be yet another fifteen minutes, but my mother smiled as if nothing were wrong and told the boy that would be "totally fine."

A few minutes later, the fireworks began.

"This is exactly the sort of nonsense I hate," my father hissed.

"What are you talking about?" my mother asked without breaking her smile, like she was worried there were surveillance cameras watching us or something.

"The elitism. The 'we're better than you' attitude," he started. "You know, all these people who are members here moved to Millbank presumably for its diversity of people, cultures, and activities. And what do they do? They cloister themselves up here on the mountain."

"Don't be ridiculous," she answered.

She was still smiling.

"I don't have all night to wait around for these people. Frankly, I'd like to watch the Yankees game at seven."

"Yeah, and I have to be at work soon," I chimed in.

Mom fidgeted in her seat, but refused to respond to either of us.

Taking her cue, I pulled out my cell phone and called information for the number of the Millbank Taxi and Limousine service.

"If you make that call, Kate," Mom whispered, "you'll regret it." She had a sharp little look in her eye that said she meant business.

I hung up and hit the speed dial for the BookStop. Howie answered after fifteen rings.

"Fidel," I said. "It's Che. I'm in the den of the enemy and running late."

"Where are you, Kate?" he asked.

"The Millbank Country Club."

There was a long pause on the phone and then a loaded sigh. A beat later there was a click. He actually hung up in my face. Well . . . I'd deal with that later.

"What did he say?" Mom said.

"He felt sick at the mere mention of the Millbank Club and hung up," I said.

"Kate! Someone might hear you!"

"I don't care, Mom! I hate this club."

"Well, then," Mr. Biddle said, walking into the room.

I couldn't tell if he'd heard me, but Mom gave me a death-ray stare, and I slumped back into the sofa.

"Sorry to keep you waiting. My sincerest apologies."

My mother, who had apparently been doing research among her female friends, told me in advance that not only was Mr. Biddle the club manager, he was also quite the hit with the ladies of the club. Now I understood what she meant. Dark hair with a sprinkle of white, slate gray eyes that were bright against his tanned skin, and a muscular body—I could see why bored housewives would go for him.

He opened a file that was labeled WINTHROPS and began the interview by prattling on about the club, its history, the type of members who joined, blah, blah, blah. He asked us what members we knew (although I'm sure that had been on the ten-page application my father had filled out), if either Mom or Dad were four-o's (tennis lingo, I think), and inquired if we belonged to any other clubs and organizations. Mom and Dad volleyed back answers, and I have to say it seemed to start off smoothly.

"Excellent," Mr. Biddle said. "Now, tell me. Why do you think you would make good members for the club?"

I could feel my father tense up next to me, but my mother jumped in, talking about her community service, my father's job in New York, and—I *never* would've guessed it—my sister, who was sorority president.

"So you have two daughters. Of course," Mr. Biddle remarked. "You must be Kate?"

I perked up and nodded.

"What year are you in?"

"I'm a senior, sir."

"Ah, our little Gretchen is a senior, too," he said.

Little Gretchen? To hear him say it, you would've thought she was some poor defenseless soul—like one of those "sponsor a child" kids from Africa.

He scrawled something on his paper, which no doubt was "ask Gretchen about Kate," and Mom started to fidget.

She looked down at me, her eyes widening ever so slightly in an urgent prompting for me to say something.

"Gretchen . . . *Tanner?*" I queried like someone in Special Ed. Biddle nodded. "Yes, I know her."

"Gretchen's the daughter of our current president."

No kidding. Like I missed the billboard over the fireplace.

"She's delightful," I said out of desperation. "We're in Econ together. She's *very* bright."

Mr. Biddle nodded, and I couldn't tell if he believed my lie. "Now, Mr. Winthrop, can you tell me a little more about your line of work?"

It was right then that I saw Will. He walked in through one of the French doors and was a little sweaty and wearing tennis whites, like he'd just finished a game. In that moment, I couldn't decide if I wanted him to see me or not, but as he walked across the room, he spotted me and smiled. He was cruising right over to us.

Omigod.

"Mr. Biddle," Will said as he arrived. "You wanted me?"

"Will!" Mr. Biddle beamed. "Yes, while I'm talking with the Winthrops, would you mind showing their daughter around the club?"

Did Will work here?

"Of course," Will said. "I actually know Kate from school. She's friends with Gretchen and me."

"Really? How terrific," Mr. Biddle replied with a grin.

He jotted something else down on his paper—this time, no doubt, something good.

While I felt myself growing faint from excitement, across from me, my mother lit up like a neon sign. I'm sure she thought having me as far away from Mr. Biddle was a good thing.

I rose to my feet, and Will winked before gesturing toward the hall. "Right this way, Miss Winthrop."

Maybe this country club thing wasn't so bad after all.

"Your parents are thinking of joining the club?" Will asked as he walked me down the stairs to the game room. It had a low ceiling and was filled with pool, Ping-Pong, and foosball tables.

"Yeah," I said. "It seems kind of cool." The words just slipped out, like another person inside of me was speaking.

Hadn't I just said to Howie how much I despised this club?

"My mom's really into it," I added, not sure how the MCC fit in with my new "Kat" persona. "And . . . well . . . you know."

As evidence has shown, when it came to talking to Will, I basically reverted to a third-grade idiot. Granted, I was pretty smooth that night at Café Electric, but there I felt like I'd been playing a role—everything had been scripted for me by Callie—and, of course . . . it was dark. Here in the bright lights of the country club, I felt exposed, and worse, that cotton-mouth feeling returned. Still, I forced myself to keep talking.

"So you work here?"

He shrugged his shoulders. "Part time during the school year. Full time in the summers. . . I mean, it's better than paying the $10,000 initiation fee."

"Wow."

I must have looked surprised, because he quickly added, "It's more for adults and families, like $25,000."

No wonder my dad was against the whole idea.

I looked up at Will, who was now racking the loose balls on the pool table. It kind of hit me again, like a sting seconds after a slap, but he worked here. It must have been awkward for him among the Proud Crowd, who were all members. Did he serve them drinks? Did he get them towels at the pool? Every day seemed to bring me a new revelation about the *famous* Will B.

I followed Will back upstairs and we walked through a marble foyer past the patio, which was lit up blue from the lights in the pool. It was still a little cold for swimming, but a thin steam rose off the water, where a few diehards were doing laps. We turned left down a long hallway that finally opened onto a gigantic ballroom. A huge crystal chandelier hung from the middle of the ceiling, and through the glass windows that lined the back wall, you could see Manhattan beginning to twinkle in the distance. Will flicked on a switch, and the chandelier glowed to life.

"And this"—Will motioned to the room—"is where the Black & White Ball is held."

The Black & White Ball. He said it like he was talking to a foreigner. Everybody knew it was held here. It was *the* biggest social event in Millbank; bigger than homecoming, bigger than your birthday, bigger than Christmas. The true origins of the Black & White Ball stretched back to before Truman Capote (the guy who wrote *Breakfast at Tiffany's*) threw his big party in New York in the 1960s. MCC legend had it, in fact, that Capote stole the idea from *them*. Basically it was a masquerade where everyone wore either—yes, you guessed it—black or white, and let me tell you, people in Millbank went all out. The night of the ball, you'd always see people walking to their cars dressed to the nines, while others were chauffeured to the top of the hill. For seniors at Millbank, on the first Saturday of June, it was the only place to be. Assuming, of course, you were invited. It was for members only and their guests.

"Have you been to it?" I asked.

"What?"

"The ball."

"Totally," Will answered as he turned off the light. "It's cool. But it's also not the big thing that everyone makes it out to be."

"How do you mean?"

He shook his head and didn't meet my eye. "It just isn't exactly my scene."

I can't tell you why exactly, but there was something in his answer that made him seem . . . well . . . human for the first time. Up until that point Will had always been, you know, *Will B.*, dream guy. And now that I was seeing him tread upon the earth—metaphorically speaking, of course—what had just been an infatuation shifted into something more. I could feel my heart in my throat.

"I'm surprised you've never been," he added.

"My sister went. All four years in high school," I revealed stupidly. I hated being compared to her in any way, and here I'd just lined it up. I looked away and stared down at the carpet.

"Melissa, right?" Will asked, and I nodded. "Yeah, I remember her. She was really cute."

I said nothing. Like I hadn't heard that from every guy to whom I had ever spoken.

"But you've got something she doesn't."

Stop. The. Press. Did Will just tell me what I think he told me?

I'm sure I went bright red, but I kept looking down at the floor.

"You don't have to say that."

He reached out and lifted my chin. "But it's true."

Someone catch me when I fall!

"But I'm sure your boyfriend has told you that before."

"Boyfriend?"

"You know," he said, "that guy who picked you up this afternoon."

Oh, yeah, that boyfriend!

"He's not my boyfriend," I confessed. "I mean, we've gone out a couple times, but it's not, like, serious or anything."

Will cocked his head to the side. "This is probably going to sound weird, but I'm glad to hear that."

I smiled, despite myself, and Will kept staring at me.

"Will." I heard a man's voice call. I looked down the hall, and Mr. Biddle was approaching with my parents. Truthfully, it was probably a good thing, because I had no idea what I would've done next.

"How was your tour, Kate?" my mother asked as she entered the room.

"It was great." I glanced over at Will. "Will's a wonderful guide."

Mr. Biddle nodded with appreciation, and Will ran his hand through his hair. "Think about what I said," he said with a little grin.

And I did—the whole rest of the night. I was so over the moon about my conversation with Will that I totally forgot to go to my shift at the BookStop. Instead, I sat at my desk in my room, staring out the window across the tops of the maple trees, and never fell asleep.

KCW LLC.

MARKET RANKING: 43
TODAY'S CHANGE: ↑7

SHARE PRICE: $6.95
    CHANGE: ↑.20 (+2.9%)
L/B RATIO: 5.3
3-MONTH RANGE: $1.23 – $7.01
STATUS: COMMON STOCK

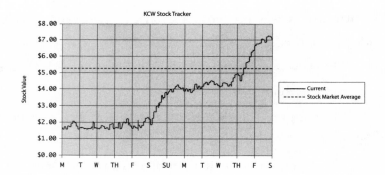

ANALYST RECOMMENDATION: This stock is taking off faster than a Porsche. Well-heeled investors are apparently already getting in on this—you should, too.

BUY

CHAPTER

14

SATURDAY NIGHT, I was due to meet Jack for our Dickey Dogs outing. I'd actually been looking forward to my chow-down with Jack, but with the turn of events at the country club with Will, I felt a little less certain. Part of me considered canceling, but I couldn't bring myself to do it, so we agreed to meet at the BookStop at seven p.m. I needed to pick up my paycheck anyway.

"So lovely of you to grace us with your presence today," Howie drawled as I walked in.

Even though I'd called Mrs. Sawyer earlier in the day to apologize for missing work, I knew that Howie's anger wouldn't dissipate so simply.

"I know, I'm sorry," I said, and made a face like I was the biggest idiot ever.

"What-*ever*," he answered. "Clearly a girl who's going to be joining the Millbank Country Club doesn't need a job."

"Mea culpa. It won't happen again."

"That's what you say now, but there have been more than a handful of radicals who sold out when a better opportunity came along. I'm starting to worry that you'll soon be joining their ranks."

"C'mon, Howie. Do I look like a sellout?"

As soon as I said it, I realized that in the vintage von Furstenberg wrap dress and leather boots that Callie had picked out for me, I didn't exactly look like one of Chairman Mao's foot soldiers. He was silent.

"Fine. Fine. Point taken," I acknowledged. "But it was my mother's idea, remember? She's the one who insisted that I go there. What could I do?"

He picked up his pen and pointed down at me. "The Nuremberg defense only goes so far."

I didn't know what the Nuremberg defense was exactly—was it some chess move?—and I stood there for a few moments blinking. After a beat, Howie waved me away.

"Never mind, I'll just start calling you Eva Braun from now on," he sulked. "Your check is in the back."

I didn't want to push the argument too far, but it wasn't lost on me that Howie wears Air Jordans when he plays hoops at the Y. They are the male equivalent of

Blahniks, after all (I know all the utilitarian arguments—sorry, they don't fly!), so I wasn't sure that he was entirely in the right. As I wandered to the back, I found I was actually a little surprised by how hard Howie had come down on me.

"You ready?" I called to Jack, who had his back to me and was digging through a box of books.

"Hey," he said as he stood up, and a totally cute alarm went off in my head. He was wearing well-worn khakis, a dress shirt, and his hair was perfectly messy—I was certain it must've taken him an hour to get it so ratty.

"So," I said, a little nervous now.

"Let's roll."

Dickey Dogs was the type of place that in another era would've probably been called "a joint." On the border of Belleville and Newark, it had originally been an old North Ward Italian mainstay until some kids discovered it, embraced its kitchiness, and turned it into a hangout. It certainly wasn't the coolest place to be, but for a certain set it had become a must-visit destination on any night out.

What was the appeal, you might ask? For some, it was the photographs of old-school Italian dudes on the wall, but for most it was the Dickey Dog—which actually was a bit of a misnomer. A Dickey (as it was called) was not one, but two hot dogs, deep-fried in oil, smothered in fried peppers and onions, and then topped with fried potatoes and stuffed into a hollowed-out hoagie roll (which was the sole part of the sandwich that *wasn't* fried). Nasty as it may sound, it was, in fact, totally tasty, but you could never dream of eating more than one.

The evening with Jack thus far had been . . . well . . . uneventful. Sweet he was, and he certainly was a gentleman of the highest order—opening every door, even pulling out my chair at the table—but he also wasn't exactly what you'd call thrilling. He always seemed a little tense, like there was something percolating deep down that he just couldn't quite get out.

"So that's where you were? The Millbank Country Club?"

As Jack seemed trustworthy enough, I'd confided in him about the reason for my no-show at work.

"It's okay," he noted as he took a sip from his soda. "But it's kind of a scene."

"You're a member?" I asked, surprised.

"Yeah, sort of. My dad joined for business reasons; we never really go, though. It's not my thing."

"Oh, that's what Will said."

"He isn't a member," Jack replied, his eyebrow nudging up.

"No, I know—I mean that it wasn't his thing. Actually, he said the Black & White wasn't his thing."

Jack looked up at me and squinted. "Huh."

Something told me that I was wading into deep waters, so I steered things back toward the shore. "Well, I always heard it was really great."

"You could totally come with me, if you wanted," Jack suddenly offered in his trademark earnest way. "I've never taken anyone."

I couldn't believe it. Three weeks before, I would've jumped at the offer—like bounced off the ceiling to get an invite—but something within me checked my excitement. Much as I didn't want to admit it, I guess I was hoping Will might figure out a way to take me, as far-fetched as that might be.

"Sure, uh, maybe," I mused as I fiddled with my straw.

Jack seemed unfazed by my hedge. "No worries. Think about it."

No commitment, no foul; that was my philosophy. And since I couldn't think of a clever response, I changed the subject. "So what's the background on Jack Clayton? You're a bit of a cipher."

Jack shrugged his shoulders. "What do you want to know?"

"Let's start with the guitar."

"My parents had me take piano lessons growing up. I taught myself to play guitar."

"Impressive."

"Not really," he said, but something in his eyes made me think he was being very modest. "It's really not that hard."

"For me it would be. I'm tone deaf," I joked. "I think I got it from my mother. She always jokes that people used to make fun of her when she tried to sing me lullabies."

"Actually, there's no such thing as being tone deaf," Jack noted. "It's just a myth."

"I'm happy to prove that it's a reality."

He laughed. "And then Will and I started jamming together in seventh grade, and you know the rest."

Trying to act as casual as possible, I adjusted my bracelet.

"So that must be cool, playing in the band."

"Yeah, I really like what we do. Music has always been a refuge. . . ." Jack trailed off and gazed down at his food.

"Will's a good songwriter."

Jack's eyes flashed my way. "He doesn't write."

"Oh," I said. When I was watching them play last week, Will made it seem like he owned the songs, like they had to be his. "Sorry, I just assumed."

"Whatever," he said. "I'm playing by myself on Friday. I don't have the pipes Will does, but I'm okay."

"Oh, I'll come," I said spontaneously.

"Really?"

I thought for a beat. There was something about Jack that

intrigued me. What was that saying? *Still waters run deep?*

"Absolutely."

"Cool." His mouth creaked into a smile for all of a second.

I glanced away and surveyed the room while he finished eating. The place was packed mostly with kids our age, and there were more people than I could count from Millbank. Peppered among the crowd were some old Italians—people who had clearly come here long before it had become a trendy spot for hipsters—and they eyed the younger crowd with a palpable disgust. I'm sure they were less than pleased that their local spot had become overrun. Even the owner practically snarled at you when you ordered, but I guess he wasn't complaining when he went to the bank.

"So can I ask *you* a question?" he said.

I raised my eyebrows as if to say, Well, go ahead.

"What's with 'Kat'?"

The question threw me, and for a moment I struggled for a response. His directness was unsettling.

"I guess I just felt like a change," I answered and popped a French fry into my mouth.

"Tired of being you, then?"

"That sounds right."

"Were you unhappy?"

"What gives, Sigmund?" I laughed.

"Sorry."

I took a deep breath and stared down at the manicure I'd gotten the week before. The polish was chipping away, like my self-confidence. *Why was I getting wound up?* His questions were simple enough—not even remotely offensive—but for some reason they were striking a raw nerve. Something about Jack was challenging, like he was pushing me. I kind of liked it, but at the same time, I wanted to push him away.

"Sorry," I said. "We all have ten selves for ten different situations."

"I understand," Jack replied. "I'm totally different onstage. But for the record, I like *this* you best."

I blushed, or at least I felt the heat in my cheeks. I knew he meant he liked me and not Kat, or the previous mute Katie, and for some reason that made my heart swell more. He was so sincere, so guileless.

"All this won't make you happy—only you can make you happy," he said.

"Jack," I began, unable to meet his gaze. "You're so sweet."

As soon as I said it, I knew it came out the wrong way; like I was being patronizing.

He shook his head. "Weird how a nice word can mean such a bad thing."

"No," I whispered. "It . . . I like the things you say."

He stared at me for a moment, and for the first time I

didn't break away. A beat later—calmly and gently—he leaned over the table and kissed me on the lips. We parted, faces still close, and my heart fluttered, and . . . I kissed him again.

And then something happened that was both unexpected, and now, looking back, so deeply sad. I was kissing Jack Clayton in Dickey Dogs, my heart was pounding, my face flushing, and all I could think of was one thing:

My Market rating is going to go through the roof.

CHAPTER

15

ON MONDAY, no mention of the kiss fest at Dickey Dogs appeared on the Market, but there was another bounce in my numbers. It seemed that nothing could stunt my ascension. Not even Jodi Letz trying to spread rumors about me becoming bulimic (she was inadvertently named as a "source" for one of the INSIDER INFORMATION tips). Nope, according to Callie—who was our "portfolio manager"—our little enterprise was taking off, and one by one, we were surpassing the other portfolios on the Market. Sure, we still had a ways to go, but the three of us had already figured out how we were going to spend the $25,000. There was only one other portfolio (TKWP Enterprises) that was doing as well as us, but we weren't worried because we had Dev's plan to fall back on.

With the bit officially between her teeth—and dollar signs in her eyes—Dev was like a girl possessed. It was a little disturbing, actually. Aside from her usual plotting and constantly calling me with Market updates—"they loved the pigtail look!"—Dev arrived at my house one afternoon and plopped down a stack of highlighted business books that I was supposed to review (yeah, right!) as part of my business education. *Good to Great*, *The Art of the Deal*, *The Art of War*, *Winning*, bios of Donald Trump, Warren Buffet, and Steve Jobs—it was a big stack. She said that if I wanted to make it to the top, I needed to learn how the masters of the universe had done it.

Despite my intense focus on climbing the Market, I couldn't shake the image of Jack and me kissing. There wasn't any shift in our relationship—we weren't suddenly dating or anything like that—but what he'd said really stuck with me. Was he right? Was the "normal" me better? Not according to the Market. Still, a little voice inside my head tried to sound a warning cry about the road Dev and I had chosen, but I told myself over and over that the proof was in the numbers.

The topic in Econ class that Thursday was ethics in the business world. The list of disgraced businessmen—as you might imagine—is a long one, and Mr. Walsh trotted out a cavalcade of names and companies to demonstrate how bad bad can be. Charles Ponzi (he's the guy who invented the

Pyramid Scheme), Ken Lay (he drove that company Enron into the ground by lying about profits), oil companies that ran private militias in Africa to advance their interests, General Electric dumping waste into the Hudson River in the 1970s, businesses that outsourced manufacturing to Southeast Asia so they could hire cheap child labor—it went on and on. The greed for a dollar seemingly knew no boundaries, and the lengths to which people would go for a few more, extreme. By the middle of class, we'd gotten to the stock market and, specifically, insider trading.

"While it's the Securities and Exchange Commission's job to monitor suspicious trading, the eighties were a period rife with illegal stock market activity," Mr. Walsh explained.

"Isn't that what Martha Stewart did?" Elisa Estrada asked.

"Accused of," Mr. Walsh corrected. "She was only ever convicted of lying to authorities. But, yes, the idea behind insider trading is that someone has privileged information about a company and buys or sells stock based on that."

Gretchen snorted and rolled her eyes. "Isn't that just called being connected?"

"It's called breaking the law," Mr. Walsh answered without missing a beat. "And many people have gone to jail for it. Ivan Boesky, Michael Milken, David—"

"Michael Milken?" I exclaimed.

That was the screen name of the person who first IMed me about the Market!

"You've heard of him before, Kate?"

"I guess I read about him," I covered, when I realized that half the class was staring at me. "What did he do exactly?"

Mr. Walsh leaned back on his desk and folded his arms. "It's complicated, but basically he made his fortune in the junk bond market. He'd invest in poorly rated securities, drive their value up, and then sell them at a huge profit. He made billions."

A junk bond. *Wasn't that what I was first rated on the Market?*

"Is he still in business?"

"No, he does philanthropy or something now," Mr. Walsh replied with a chuckle. "So moving on, if we look at—"

Obviously the person who IMed me wasn't the real Michael Milken—like he'd care about Millbank High School—so it must've been someone who identified with him somehow. And what did it mean in terms of me and the Market?

It was right then that there was a quick knock at the door and a moment later, much to my surprise, Dev walked in. Her face looked sad, her eyes a little puffy, and she crossed to Mr. Walsh and handed him a note. They

161

conferred for a moment, and he opened the piece of paper.

His expression fell, and he nodded grimly.

"Ms. Winthrop," he said, "please go with Ms. Rayner."

What happened?

Concern coursed through me, and I quickly packed up my stuff and walked to the front of the room. Dev put her arm around my back and whispered loudly into my ear.

"I'm so sorry. Your grandfather died."

There was a palpable inhale from the students in the front row, who'd heard it all, and I just stared at her. I'm certain that my face must've looked like a truck had just run me over, and after a beat, I glanced over at Mr. Walsh, who reached over and patted my back a few times.

"I'm so sorry," he said.

I didn't know what to do, and I felt my chest convulse a few times—a vague feeling of nausea overtook me. I covered my mouth. I could feel the eyes of the class on me, so I ran out and across the hallway and into the bathroom. Dev rushed after me. When the door closed and we were alone, I turned toward her.

"How could you?" I hissed.

"It was perfect!" Dev grinned back.

Let me explain: I never knew my grandfather. Both my parents' parents had passed away long before I was born. Despite the conversation we'd had, Dev had blatantly gone against my wishes and invented a tragedy for "brand loyalty" or whatever. Never, ever, ever would I have gone along with it, but with Mr. Walsh looking at me so sympathetically and the whole class staring straight at me, what could I do? Expose Dev and have her get in trouble for falsely conveying info to get me out of class? No, I wasn't going to rat out my friend, but she had crossed the line.

"I told you I didn't want to do Step Three," I said angrily. "We didn't need it."

Just then the door to the girls' bathroom creaked open, and Dev shoved me into one of the stalls and shut it.

"Hey," I heard a voice. "How is she?"

"She's really upset," Dev replied. "But she'll be fine— I'm going to take her home."

I heard the door open again, and while somebody left, the sound of heels clicking indicated a few others coming in.

"Omigod, is she okay?" I heard Gretchen Tanner ask, followed by a barrage of queries from her posse of chicks, who'd obviously followed like sheep to inquire about my emotional well-being.

Standing there in the stall, staring at the scrawl on the back of the door, I felt sick about the whole thing, but I stayed silent. If I said anything now, I'd only look like a complete and total liar. In those next ten minutes, while word was seemingly passed throughout the school and more and more people came to check on me, all my concerns and anxiety about what we had been doing came back to roost deep in my chest. If I'd been able to justify what we'd been doing up until now, I couldn't anymore.

It was going too far. It had to stop.

Shortly, the bell for next class rang, and finally the bathroom emptied. I walked out of the stall and snatched my bag from the tile floor where it lay.

"Let's get out of here," Dev whispered.

"Don't talk to me!"

I stormed out of the bathroom, and we headed to the car. I kept my head down, and I'm sure people thought I was crying, but I was really just trying to avoid eye contact. The thought of people feeling sympathy for me because Dev had faked a tragedy made me feel sick to my stomach.

When we got outside to the parking lot, Callie was waiting for us at Dev's car. Seeing me so clearly pissed, she shook her head.

"I knew she'd be upset!" she shouted as I approached. "I knew you two would regret this!"

"I'm out," I said as I wheeled around on Dev. "I'm out of this crazy game. No more clothes, no more new Kate, no more Market."

"What are you talking about?"

"When I said I didn't want to fake a tragedy, I meant it. I don't want to be a fraud! How could you?!"

Her faced dropped. She had no real response. She just stared at me with big teary eyes that slowly overflowed.

"I didn't think," she said. "I didn't. I'm sorry."

"Pathetic," I said.

Irony of all ironies, I thought as I slipped into my car and gunned the engine to life. Dev stages a fake tragedy to help me, but the only real victim was our friendship.

······························

KCW LLC.

MARKET RANKING: 32

TODAY'S CHANGE: ↑7

SHARE PRICE: $11.56

CHANGE: ↑ 4.31 (+62.7%)

L/B RATIO: 5.3

3-MONTH RANGE: $1.23 – $11.62

STATUS: PREFERRED STOCK

KCW Stock Tracker

ANALYST RECOMMENDATION: Tragedy may have struck, but investors are more exuberant than ever. Blue Chip status is within reach for this stunning mover.

STRONG BUY

······························

CHAPTER

16

No MATTER HOW I may have felt about what Dev and Callie had done, one thing was for sure: it worked.

When I checked my e-mail that night, I had about fifty messages from people saying how sorry they were to hear about the death in my family, wanting to know if I was okay, and if there was anything they could do. It was unbelievable! Half the people I barely even knew. Was I less unpopular than I thought, or had Dev dialed into what made people tick? I'm still not sure, but either way, Callie later told me that word spread like wildfire through the school. Students and teachers had come up to her and Dev the whole rest of the day, asking about what had happened and wanting to get the whole story. Needless to say, they didn't exactly give anyone a straight answer, but that only baited people more. The less information she gave them, the more they wanted to know about it.

But as I scanned through the e-mails and listened to the *dings* of incoming sympathy, I couldn't help it: I felt dirty. For starters—and I'm not a superstitious person—it seemed like really bad karma to go around lying about death. But more importantly, it just felt wrong. It was manipulation of the worst kind, and although I remembered all of Dev's justifications, I didn't want any part of it.

There was a quick knock at my door, and as I spun around in my desk chair, my dad poked his head in the room.

"You have a sec?" he asked.

I nodded before shooting a glance around my room, and I noticed that it was only 6:30 p.m., about an hour earlier than my father usually got home. Not a good sign, but truthfully, I already had an idea what this was going to be about.

"What's up?" I asked.

He put his hands in his pockets and glanced up at the ceiling for a moment—his telltale sign for "We're going to have a serious conversation."

"I got the strangest call from Principal Johnson this afternoon," he began. "Do you have any idea what it might have been about?"

It was that classic moment when you know you're about

to get busted by your parents, and you're faced with the unenviable choice of either copping to it, or issuing the bald-faced lie of a flat-out denial. I chose the former.

"I'm sorry. It wasn't even my idea—"

Before I could get started, he put up his hand. "I'm sure it's a very long and convoluted story, and frankly, I don't have time to hear it. I have to take your mother to buy a new vacuum cleaner."

"What?"

"Don't ask," he silenced me. "Anyway . . . I didn't say anything to Johnson, because I don't want to put your academic status in jeopardy."

"Thank you!"

"But I do suspect that this stunt you and your friends pulled has something to do with this new . . . 'persona' you've adopted."

I stared down at my carpeting on the floor. Obviously he was right on the money.

"I want it to stop. *Now.* Are we clear?"

I nodded. "I'd already decided that anyway."

"Good."

Before my father could say anything more, the doorbell rang, and we looked at each other quizzically.

"You want to go see who that is?" he asked.

I shrugged my shoulders, and with Remington trailing at my heels, I padded my way down the steps to the front hall and opened the door. Oddly, there was no one there. Down the street, I could hear the whine of an engine zooming away, and it wasn't until I glanced down at my feet that I discovered there was a modestly wrapped gift leaning against the doorjamb. I picked it up, and as I held it in my hands, I realized almost immediately it was a book.

I closed the door and made my way into the kitchen, where I unwrapped the present. It was a copy of *A Grief Observed* by C. S. Lewis.

C. S. Lewis? The guy who wrote *The Chronicles of Narnia*?

I thumbed to the title page and saw that there was an inscription.

> I was really sorry to hear about your grandfather today. I never know what to say in these situations, but someone gave me this book when my mom died—maybe it'll make you feel better.
> Best,
> Jack

I just sat there for a few moments, staring at what Jack had written. Once again the master of understatement, his gesture was incredibly touching—and it only made me feel worse about everything that had gone down.

Yes, it was official. Kat was off the Market.

CHAPTER

```
..........
:        :
:   17   :
:        :
..........
```

I DIDN'T HAVE too much time to rehash my decision, because Friday I was due to give the oral presentation portion of my final project for Econ. My paper was on Horatio Alger—he wrote a series of rags-to-riches novels in the 1900s—and how the idea of what constitutes success has changed in America over the last century. It used to be that all you needed was some middle-class security and a good reputation. Obviously, we all know it isn't that way anymore. Anyway, Thursday night mainly consisted of going over my notes, making charts, and even drawing a graph depicting the relationship between GDP and wealth on a piece of poster board. (What can I say, I'm a fan of visual aids.)

Before I went to bed, I felt the need to reclaim a little

of the old Kate, so I woke up my computer and hopped online. There were a bunch of IMs from Dev, apologizing for the day, but I still wasn't quite up for dealing with her, so I didn't reply, and instead I logged on to my Gmail account. I shot Jack an e-mail thanking him for the book and told him that I'd definitely be there for his solo show tomorrow night. There was also a note from Callie, claiming, and I believed her, that she tried to talk Dev out of the fake tragedy. At least I didn't have to feel betrayed by two friends.

I arrived at school the next day, happily resigned to wherever I was on the Market—not that I had any intention of ever looking at it again. Nope, I'd put it in the ground for good, kind of like what you'd do with an obnoxious ex-boyfriend who called you fat.

To be honest, it was a relief to be done with Dev's master plan. While I had no intention of symbolically burning my new wardrobe beneath the flagpole (a girl can be contrite and still look good), the knowledge that there wasn't another task around the corner was a load off my mind. Yes, there was part of me that still wondered what it would've been like to be a Blue Chip. And yes, I found it hard to let go of the fantasy of every boy in the school swooning when I passed. And yes, it pained me to finally get a taste of the popular life and have that snatched away, but something my father was fond of saying hung in my mind like a banner: "Character requires sacrifice." So if I had to sacrifice Kat in order to hold my head high, that was the way it was going to be.

It was after third period that I was standing at my locker, trying to slip my poster in without crushing it under the load of books and boots and magazines and makeup that filled my measly six-inch by forty-eight-inch box, when I felt a tap on my shoulder. A second later, a droopy-eyed Will leaned against the locker next to mine.

"Hey."

"Hi," I replied, catching a glimpse of myself in the mirror I'd taped to the inside of my locker door. Thank God I hadn't done anything crazy that day like swearing off makeup.

"I'm really sorry," he whispered.

I smiled. "About what?"

"Your grandfather."

Oh.

Right.

I allowed my gaze to drop to the floor and I nodded. "Thanks. It was a real . . . shock."

For the first time in my life I appreciated President Clinton's mastery of the evasive response that neither confirmed nor denied.

"Things like that can be really hard," he continued. "It sucks. There's not much else to say about it."

A gaggle of cute sophomore girls bounced by—pert and carefree—with the requisite "Hi, Will," and he waved back at them.

"Listen," he said as the hall began to clear, "I know this is going to sound a little weird, but do you want to get out of here?"

"And go where?" I asked.

This is strange.

"Get out—blow off the day."

I laughed. "Cut? Why?"

"I don't know . . . sometimes it's 'why not?'" he said as a mischievous grin crept across his face. "It's Kat—not Katie, right?"

By now my mind was beginning to race. The Kat versus Katie button was the one to push. Add that I was struggling with this small question: was Will asking me to hang?

"That's sweet, but . . ." I paused, somehow summoning the courage for the truth. "The grandfather thing was a—"

Will cut me off before I could spill the beans.

"I bet you've been here four years and never cut just for the hell of it."

It wasn't every day that someone like Will asked me to blow off school and hang out. In fact, no one had ever asked me. It also wasn't every day that I was supposed to do an oral presentation in Econ.

"I can't," I answered like the true geek that I was

beneath the blond hair and the cool clothes. "Besides, I'm sure one of your friends will be up for it."

"They will," he said. "But I'm only up for you."

That was a knee-buckler!

Still hesitating, I leaned against my locker and coyly gazed at him. "Until two weeks ago, we'd said maybe three words to each other. What's up with the mad rush?"

His eyes sparkled and he backed away with a playful shrug. Apparently, he wasn't accustomed to girls calling him out, but he recovered faster than I expected.

"Are you taking a pass?" he said. He was throwing down the gauntlet—it was now or never. Forever Katie? Or did this Kat have a few more lives to live?

I shot a look into my locker—at my poster and the presentation I was supposed to give—and knew that if I bailed on Econ the fallout could be big, but not world-ending; after all, I was a senior in my final three weeks of school. The familiar part of me that had guided my high school career to a 3.8 GPA and admission to Brown hammered away at my conscience, reminding me that under no circumstances could I cut out on school. At the same time, another part of me pointed out that this modus operandi also had led me to many dateless Friday nights, a junk-bond status on the Market, and a severe jean jacket dependency.

Going with Will, I thought. Definitely going with Will!

* * *

Unlike most of the Proud Crowd, Will did not own a brand-new, German-engineered, ultimate driving machine. Instead, he piloted our way east in a rattling and rusting, but impossibly cool 1974 Triumph Spitfire convertible. More rocket sled than automobile, the Spitfire lacked the basics—a roof of any sort, air conditioning, non-splitting seats—and the feel of certain death clawed my chest whenever Will took a turn too fast. Yet on the straighter roads with the wind roaring in my ears and my hair unwillingly crafting itself into a bird's nest, I couldn't help but feel like I was being squired by a movie star.

When you're cutting school, staying in your hometown is obviously out of the question, and come one o'clock, as the speedometer dropped below forty-five, we zoomed out of the Lincoln Tunnel and headed to downtown Manhattan. With a confident familiarity, he zipped down Ninth Avenue and then over to Soho and parked the car on a cobblestone side street.

We spent the next few hours walking around. First we walked uptown and grabbed a falafel at Mamoun's in the West Village, then over to Gear, a cool skateboarding store on Houston, and we even contemplated seeing the new Wes Anderson film at the Angelika Film Center. Ultimately, we bailed when we realized we'd be out at seven-fifteen, but a little part of me likes to think that we skipped it because we were having so much fun just talking to each other.

Contrary to my previous experiences with Will, where I always lost the capacity to speak, as the hours wore on I found myself growing more and more comfortable around him. Maybe it was being in a totally different context where I felt on equal footing, and he felt like he could just be himself and not "Will B.," but for the first time I was able to see him more as a boy than as the near demigod he was in the halls of Millbank High School.

I extracted tidbits of information about Will that I'd never known before. They didn't always jibe with the person I'd presumed him to be, but this opening of closed doors only made him all the more captivating. It ranged from the humorous—as a boy he'd been fat—to the weird—he ate peanut butter sandwiches with thinly sliced apples on toast almost every night—to the enigmatic—he'd been writing poetry since he was in sixth grade.

"Why don't you write songs, then?" I asked, thinking of what Jack had said.

"I do—Jack and I do," he countered. He looked at me strangely, like perhaps this question had come up before.

"Oh, right," I said.

Why would Jack lie about the songs? Or was Will lying?

He quickly changed subject, so I made a note to myself never to bring up their creative relationship again—definitely a tender spot. But that's artists for you.

Regardless, the day had a dreamlike quality. There was

one perfect moment as we walked up lower Broadway toward the Strand Bookstore. The wind was blowing and the reddening sun was just lounging over the shorter buildings of southern Manhattan, and I realized I'd never before been enthralled in the rapture of a perfect day. I owed it to Will. For the first time in my life, I felt like an adult, but oddly free of all the obligations that supposedly came with being one.

En route back to Millbank, Will asked if I wanted to grab something to eat, and we decided on burgers at Gifford's, a small joint in Roseville, the town next to Millbank. Just outside of town, Will's cell phone rang, and he slipped the phone from his pocket and checked the caller ID.

"What up, J?"

Oh, no.

I immediately knew who it was: Jack. I was supposed to be going to his show tonight! This was bad . . . *really* bad. I checked my watch. It was already 6:30 p.m. and the show started at 7:00 p.m.. Even if I came up with a clever excuse to cut short my day with Will, I'd never make it to Jack's show in time. I'd completely blown it. As Will and Jack talked, I came up with various stories I could tell Jack, but none of them seemed viable. And then disaster struck.

"Listen, dude, I'm MIA tonight—I'm gonna grab some chow with Kat."

My heart fell to my toes. There was an obvious pause.

"Yo, Jack, you there? Jack?" Will looked over to me. "Must've lost him—he'll be cool about it."

Then his phone started buzzing again. I braced myself for the worst—the two of them figuring out I was hanging out with both them (what was I becoming?!), but when Will looked at the caller ID, his face drained. He was obviously upset.

Did Jack send him a text?

He answered rather briskly: "Yeah?"

The conversation that ensued was brief, but in those two or three minutes of mostly one-sentence responses, it escalated from "No" to "I can't right now" to "Can I do it after?"

Was he talking to Gretchen?

It was impossible to say, because the howl of the engine drowned out any sound below seventy decibels. In the end, Will hung up with a terse "Fine" and glanced my way.

I had the sinking feeling that our day was coming to an end.

"Sorry, but I have to go to my dad's shop."

"No worries," I answered. "Do you want to skip?"

"No," he said. "It'll take a minute."

Will turned off the highway and headed toward Roseville. It was what you'd call a working-class town, I suppose—the yards were smaller, American cars trumped European—and their football team had a habit of mauling ours every year when we faced off. The score last year was 55–0. It was hardly foreign soil for me because my mother always went to the Roseville Costco (other than her Ann Taylor binge, she was actually quite thrifty), and there was a broad selection of big chain stores like Bed Bath & Beyond and Target that Millbank just didn't have.

On the edge of town, Will slowed and pulled into a gas station cum auto-body repair shop. "I'll just be a minute," he said, hopping out of the car.

A few minutes passed, and as I waited, I realized Will had never even mentioned his father to me. I knew only that he lived alone with his mom in a small house over in the Fairlawn section of town. When Will walked out from the garage seconds later, he was flanked by a tall, burly man who looked like he'd spent his entire life working—and not in an office, mind you. *That's Will's dad?* His hair was greased straight back, and his hands were large and rugged.

They both walked directly to my side of the car.

"Hi," I said. "I'm Kate."

"I'm Will's father," he said in a soft-spoken voice that caught me by surprise.

"Satisfied?" Will said rudely, walking around to the driver's side of the car.

"My son doesn't like to bring his friends around— Dad doesn't strike the right note, if you know what I mean."

I just nodded, a little thrown by the palpable tension between the two.

"The principal called me, so I wanted to see what was worth skipping school over," he said, looking at his son, who was now sitting next to me and staring straight ahead.

"Oh," I responded as the air shot from my lungs. "I've never done this before, I swear."

"I'm sure you haven't, but Will here likes to be a bad boy, like his old man."

"Can we go now?" Will asked through his teeth.

"Your mother is expecting you—no detours," his dad said, and then slapped the back of the car with two quick strokes. Will quickly fired the engine and took off down Woodmont Avenue.

We didn't speak for a few minutes. Anger overflowed from his eyes, and if I were a betting girl, I'd say he was holding back tears. I didn't want to say anything to embarrass him further, but on the other hand, all of us have been there when a parent just makes us look and feel like crap in front of our friends. I had empathy galore, but how to broach the subject with him, I did not know. Mercifully, he broke the ice at a stoplight.

"He left us when I was seven," Will said. "He hates me because I hate him."

"That's brutal," I said. "You never talk about him."

"He isn't worthy."

I nodded, not ever expecting to be tied into such an intimate moment with Will.

"With that friggin' neo-Nazi, fifties greaser hair—who'd want to introduce him to anybody?"

It wasn't a pretty thing to say. Let's face it, we all have aunts and uncles and cousins who don't dress or live or act the way we want them to, but it doesn't mean they're bad people. Maybe his dad was an ass (though it appeared he was at least a concerned one), but his hair and his clothes and his job didn't seem to be the problem.

"Introducing one's parent in general is always like war of the worlds."

He nodded, like he knew what I meant. I'd seen Will's mom from afar once—she sold real estate in town—and she was petite, blond, and wore preppy clothes. My mother told me that she had come from an old-line WASP family in Greenfield that had once been wealthy (but subsequently fell on hard times), and in my mind's eye, I could see her as a young woman running off with Will's dad and causing quite a stir among the royalty of Greenfield.

"Don't tell anyone that you met him, okay?" Will said low without looking at me as we crested a hill.

I glanced over at him and nodded—not really under-standing his shame, but knowing it was a secret that would stay between us.

* * *

Gifford's was busy, and a handful of MHS students sat at the counter, but we snagged a booth by the window and munched down on cheeseburgers, fries, and black-and-white milk shakes. Simply to die for.

"So when do your parents have their interview with the committee?" Will asked.

By the end of the evening, the episode with his father was forgotten, and our conversation had rambled over to the Millbank Country Club.

"Week after next, I think," I replied. "My mother—God—she's like frothing at the bit to get in."

Will chuckled and took a sip of his soda.

"And you? What do you think of it?"

"I don't really care either way. I mean, it doesn't affect me. I'm leaving for college in what, four months?"

He nodded.

"But maybe I'm wrong," I continued, not wanting to seem too anti-anything Will was part of. "The summers could be cool."

"I don't think so," he said, not looking up. "It's sort of tired."

"Really? Isn't it basically the Proud Crowd's meeting lodge?"

I meant it as a joke, but he frowned.

"They're all ridiculous."

"But they're your friends," I pointed out delicately. "I

mean, that's your scene. You and Gretchen—you're on the top of the food chain."

"Maybe it looks that way from the outside . . ." He trailed off and shifted in his seat. "Do you ever feel like you've outgrown people?"

I'd never felt that way until Dev pulled her stunt earlier in the week, but I now knew exactly what he meant. "Yeah, I kind of feel that way about high school in general."

"The Proud Crowd thing—it makes me a little ill to even think I hang with people who refer to themselves like that."

I laughed out loud. "I know, it's kind of pathetic when you think about it."

"But you'd be part of it, if you could, right?" He asked it in a strange way—almost as if it were posed to me, but also to himself. We were silent, because I think we both knew he was right. But if he knew how pathetic I'd acted over the past three weeks in a vain attempt to climb the Millbank Market, I think he would have left me right there in Gifford's with my half-eaten burger and shake.

"Lately I've been trying to avoid that crowd," he added, his eyes now meeting mine. "I'm tired of Gretchen and her minions."

But like some evil spirit that you summon merely by saying her name, none other than Gretchen Tanner herself walked into Gifford's. I couldn't freakin' believe it. With

Jodi Letz and Elisa Estrada in tow, it took all of ten seconds for Gretchen to notice us by the window. Jodi and Elisa fell into close whispering, but Gretchen appeared unfazed and tilted her head to the side, as if in thought. I glanced over at Will, who'd already noticed them as well, but if he was remotely concerned about getting discovered with yours truly, his face didn't betray even the slightest worry.

"Hey," Gretchen shouted as she walked up to the table. "You two were conspicuously missing from class this afternoon."

Econ—*great*. Up until now I'd managed to put it totally out of my head, and her reminder caused an immediate knot in my stomach.

"Bold move, Kat, and admirable for the sheer audacity." She nodded. "Should I ask where you two were?"

In Gretchen's presence, the Will of old—the Proud Crowd acolyte Will, the BMOC Will—returned like a seasoned actor who knows his cue.

"The city, hanging," he parried. "Wassup?"

Gretchen smiled thinly—well, I guess you could call it a smile. It was more like she drew the corners of her mouth toward her ears.

"Are we on for tonight?" she said, looking at Will.

Will nodded and Gretchen turned to me. "We should hang sometime."

I didn't quite know how to respond, and I managed to

get out a "Sure," but she didn't follow up with any invitation and she departed. It must've only been show for Will.

"Funny timing," Will observed, once she was out of earshot, our intimacy of minutes before now gone. "We have a project for English—that's what that was about."

"You don't owe me explanations, Will."

He blinked a few times as he registered my reaction to the whole situation.

"What's the deal with you two?" I asked.

"We're friends," he quickly answered. "I mean, we had a thing but it didn't work."

"For whom?"

He yawned nervously, trying to imply it was casual and cool. "For me."

"That explains the dagger eyes, I guess."

"I think you'd get those with or without me," he replied. "You're a threat to her."

I just squinted at him.

"C'mon, you know what I mean," he pressed with a glint in his eye.

It was like having cold water splashed in my face . . . on a really hot day.

"You don't have to say that. I know I'm not in her league."

"You're right. She's not smart enough to play in your league," he said as he leaned forward and took my hand.

This all seemed too impossible to be true. The day. Everything he was saying.

"I'm not interested in Gretchen's throne," I lied.

"Then what *do* you want?"

He couldn't have been more clear. I knew what he was asking—and offering.

KCW LLC.

MARKET RANKING: 25
TODAY'S CHANGE: ↑5

SHARE PRICE: $18.56
CHANGE: ↑6.06 (+51.7%)
L/B RATIO: 6.1
3-MONTH RANGE: $1.23 – $18.72
STATUS: PREFERRED STOCK

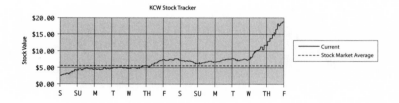

KCW Stock Tracker

ANALYST RECOMMENDATION: Not only did this company show that it's willing to take chances in the marketplace by risking the ire of regulators, but a major player has demonstrated serious interest in this commodity. This one is about to go stratospheric.

STRONG BUY

BOOK FOUR

. . . .

AMONG THE DEN OF THIEVES

CHAPTER

18

HISTORY IS MARKED with turning points—some seen, some unseen—that represent a profound shift in the course of future events. The Boston Tea Party. The Allies invading Normandy. Bill Clinton deciding that a little one-on-one time with Monica Lewinsky would be a good idea. Surely at their inciting moments, it was unclear if these choices would result in triumph or calamity, but the decision was made nonetheless. And so it was for me after my date with Will. My righteous indignation and intrepid moralizing of just twenty-four hours previous melted away into a renewed flood of gusto and determination to rise to the top of the Market. If I needed to drive my stock price a little higher to capture Will's heart, so be it.

Was it a noble fight? Well . . . not in the Abraham

Lincoln framing of the term, but it's amazing what a little love—or at least a huge crush—will prompt you to do. C'mon! Will—for all intents and purposes—had essentially said he wanted to go out with me! Thus, my mission for the last two weeks at school now couldn't have been clearer, and within an hour of my arrival home, I'd called Dev, buried the hatchet, and was plotting how to execute the next two steps of the business plan.

My numbers got an unbelievable surge from the grandfather incident, but an even bigger boost for my stock was the revelation that I'd cut a day of school to go out with Will. Truthfully, it couldn't have been better if Dev and I had planned it. I guess it was basically a combination of co-branding and a paradigm shift—no one ever had me pegged for the type of girl to bail on school, let alone with Will—and suddenly I found myself knocking on the door to the Blue Chipdom. I was trading at eighteen dollars a share and was twenty-fifth on the Market. Dev and I spent the next week solidifying my position on the Market for the final assault on the Blue Chips, which basically consisted of me doing various small but public acts. Dev called it "raising capital." I started some cheers in the stands at the lacrosse game. I brought a case of beer that Dev snagged to Elisa Estrada's party. I even helped Nina Licht with her calc problems. As it was impossible to say who was buying in the Market, I had to cater to everyone.

Now more than ever, Dev and I were in constant communication—her texting me when opportunities presented themselves, constantly giving me directives—and everything else began to fall by the wayside. To be honest, it got to be a bit much, but I hung in there with her. Once school was over, I reasoned, I'd ride out the summer and by September I'd be at college, riding down to Poughkeepsie on the weekends to visit my boyfriend Will Bochnowski.

But not everyone was so impressed with me. The Tuesday after my date with Will, I was running out to watch the lacrosse game after school—an event that anyone who was socially conscious at Millbank would never dream of missing—when I spotted Jack at his locker, his guitar case leaning diagonally next to him. Although I'd e-mailed him a few times apologizing for missing his show, he'd never written back. In retrospect, I probably should've called him over the weekend to set the record straight, but a mix of guilt (about Will) and giddiness (about Will) had stopped me from doing the right thing.

I almost turned around to take the west exit to the field—thereby avoiding him yet again—but something forced me forward.

"Jack."

He looked my way, but when he saw who it was, his expression darkened ever so slightly. He turned back to whatever he was doing in his locker.

"How's it going?" I asked.

"Fine."

"So how was your solo show?"

"Fine."

He still wouldn't look at me. The fact that the hallway was almost entirely empty only made the situation more uncomfortable. Sometimes you want privacy for a serious convo, but sometimes it helps to have other people around to minimize the awkwardness.

"Listen," I began, "I'm sorry about missing your show."

"I heard you were out with Will. No worries."

It was clear from his delivery of "no worries" that it was anything but.

"I really wanted to be there," I offered.

Jack just nodded and said nothing.

"Can we talk about it?"

"What's to talk about?" he said directly. "Just be honest: you prefer him over me. That's totally fine."

Rational as I'd been about my friendship with Jack, face to face with what I'd done to him now, something dormant and repressed shuddered deep in my chest.

"No, it's not that," I stuttered.

"Don't lie," he snorted. "Something better came along and you took it. I just wish you'd been honest instead of playing me. 'Cause that's what you did. You played me."

"That's not fair, Jack," I pleaded.

"Get used to it." He picked up his guitar case and slung the strap over his shoulder. "I hope you're happy."

Before I could say anything, he turned and walked away. I stood there alone, watching his figure disappear, the jubilant cheers for our lacrosse team echoing softly in my ears.

When I woke up the next day, a dull, relentless ache hammered at my head, and as I dressed for school—feeling more like I was suiting up for warfare than getting ready for classes—I couldn't shake a simmering anger invading every crevice of my being. Like some borderline lunatic, I even found myself muttering furiously under my breath. It was the Market. All night I'd been awake, thinking about what had happened with Jack—about our conversation in the hallway—about how I'd bailed on him. But as much as I knew that I should just forget about the Market, to stop playing these stupid games, I couldn't. The rational voices in my head were drowned out by the all-consuming need to make it to the top.

I didn't see Dev until Econ class, and because Mr. Walsh was such a rule freak, we barely got to say hello before he started speaking. In a move of expert manipulation pulled right from the Gretchen Tanner playbook, I'd managed to smooth over my cutting class the previous week—I played the depressed-about-grandpa's-death card—but I knew I had to watch my step. That day it was Gretchen's turn to give her presentation, and Mr. Walsh gave her a little introduction. She was focusing on the 1980s, a time, Mr. Walsh said, when Wall Street was king in terms of its cultural influence. Gretchen walked a little nervously to the front of the room and shuffled her papers before beginning to speak.

"'Greed is good,'" she started. "This is the most important line of movie dialogue, in my mind, from any movie made in the eighties. In that one line, the entire mindset of the eighties, the Wall Street decade, is summed up."

I could see a bunch of kids immediately slump in their chairs, but Mr. Walsh's ears perked up. Unlike most of my classmates, I knew what movie it came from: the appropriately named *Wall Street*, directed by Oliver Stone and starring Charlie Sheen as Bud Fox and Michael Douglas as the infamous Gordon Gekko. It was a morality tale about money, friendship, and how far one should go to earn the almighty dollar. My dad made me watch it with him one summer night, and besides being drawn to a very hot and sexy younger version of Charlie Sheen (a total freak now), the story was weirdly compelling. Gretchen wove in and out of discussing the movie by ducking into real-life stories of corporate greed from the book *Den of Thieves* by James Stewart, which, intriguingly, was about Michael Milken.

(*Was that a connection?*) By the end, Gretchen wound down her report by recounting the final scene between Charlie Sheen and Michael Douglas when Bud Fox confronts Gordon Gekko in Central Park.

"Is greed good?" Gretchen asked to end her report. "*Wall Street* tries to tell us the moral dangers of greed, but I don't know if it is convincing—something in it tells me the moralizing champion, Charlie Sheen, isn't the real hero— Michael Douglas is."

The class broke into a lackluster round of applause. Several boys in the back row woke up and made some lame catcalls. Gretchen walked back to her seat, and a few of the Proud Crowd patted her on the back. Mr. Walsh said nothing, but I noted he did not join the class in applause. He rose from his desk, grabbed a piece of chalk, and turned to the blackboard. He wrote: IS GREED GOOD?

"How many people believe greed is good?"

A few hands went up, mostly comprised of Gretchen's friends.

"And how many think greed is bad?"

Most of the class raised their hands.

I didn't vote.

"Gretchen," Mr. Walsh said, "it appears most of the class disagrees with you—that Michael Douglas is not a hero and what he represents is not heroic. What do you have to say to them?"

Gretchen looked pained. She probably thought she'd breeze through this report like most of the class had, but she'd picked a subject that was dear to Mr. Walsh. In fact, because he left the Street and came to teach, one would suspect he wasn't on the "greed is good" side of the fight at all. He was a do-gooder by nature, and I'm sure his run on Wall Street (by all accounts a successful one) brought him face-to-face with what greed could do, even to good men and women.

"Winners win, and losers lose," she responded. "I didn't make the movie, I just watched it, and that's what I felt."

"Yeah. Don't hate the player, hate the game," some meathead chimed in from the back.

"But the ending clearly showed what Michael Douglas truly was: a cold, heartless man with a soul rotted out by greed. He's no hero, and the director clearly wanted you to believe that Charlie Sheen was the man we're meant to follow. It's about right and wrong. It's too easy to say 'hate the game, not the player.' In that world, no one's responsible for anything."

I'd long admired him for his moral high ground, but there was something about his tone that day—perhaps it was an attitude of utter certainty, his confident assurance of his moral position—that made me crazy.

I couldn't help myself.

"I actually think Gretchen is right," I jumped in.

Everyone turned toward me like I had smashed a bottle on the ground.

Mr. Walsh glanced over at me and raised an eyebrow. "Unexpected support from our little leftist."

"Just because the screenwriter tried to make Charlie Sheen the hero doesn't mean he was, no matter how you want to construe it."

A big "Oooooohhhh" erupted from the boys in the last row. Mr. Walsh turned red, and I assumed at this point he was a little angry, but I wasn't about to hedge my position. I was tired of teachers and parents trying to pretend that the world was fair and that good things happened to good people. The meek did not inherit the earth. They ended up Seventy-one on the Market—anonymous and forgotten.

"I think you're being simplistic," he said.

"That's funny—I thought you were."

Another burst of giggles and shouts filled the classroom, and as much as I knew that I needed to back down, to give up this fight that wasn't my own, I only felt emboldened. Across the room, Gretchen and her posse watched me wide-eyed and grinning, impressed by the battle I was waging.

"Why don't you explain to the class your 'complex' theory, then?" he said.

"Fine," I started. "Take Michael Douglas and Charlie Sheen—which one do you remember more from the movie, Mr. Walsh?"

He sat down on his desk. The hardened gleam disappeared from his eyes, and his thirst to skewer a student faded. "Well, I would say Douglas is the more memorable char-acter."

"And what piece of dialogue spoken by any character in the movie is the most memorable?"

" 'Greed is good,' " he said.

"By Douglas," I added. "And do you remember any single piece of dialogue spoken by your so-called hero, Charlie Sheen?"

He shook his head no.

"That's because even though he's supposed to be our moral hero, he's a wimp. The movie is supposed to be anti-greed, but all too tellingly, Douglas is the only thing we remember. Greed is our hero, our romance. Financial success, or say, in high school, popularity—at any cost—is the American dream. Its victors are heroes."

It was as if someone else had taken over my body.

"Well, that's certainly one way of looking at it," he said evenly.

"It's the real way, the American way," I sneered.

"If you—"

"No—all that nice guy stuff is bull."

"Ms. Winthrop," he breathed, "you've always been bright, but you used to also be humble."

"I could have said the same of you."

Jaws hit the floor. The class was dead silent—I don't think anyone was even breathing.

Did that really come out of my mouth?

Mr. Walsh looked at me carefully and then down at his desk.

"Why don't we discuss this further," he began as he pulled out his pen. "In detention."

Right then the bell rang. I put my books in my bag and didn't even look up at Mr. Walsh as I exited the room and headed to my locker. I was wrong to be so harsh, but something about finally saying something back to a teacher, even a great one like Mr. Walsh, felt right.

"Kat!"

I slammed my last book into my locker and turned around to discover Gretchen and her crew walking up behind me. She was smiling, clearly amused by my standing up for her paper.

"Thanks—for today in class."

"No worries, you were right," I said, trying to impart that it wasn't for her that I stood up to him. As I looked Gretchen in the eyes, I suddenly wondered if part of the reason I'd gone after Mr. Walsh so hard wasn't simply to impress her. Had I somehow internalized Step Five of Dev's plan—"a merger with Gretchen Tanner"? Was that what had made me go so overboard?

"Listen," Gretchen said. "I'm having some people over tonight—you should come."

"I've got plans," I said. I'm not sure how I pulled it off, but I managed to be nonchalant about her advances. It helped that I wasn't lying. The week before, Dev and I had made a date to sack out at her house and rent old John Hughes movies—you know, *The Breakfast Club* and *Sixteen Candles*. "But thanks for the offer."

Gretchen touched my arm.

"C'mon, Will's going to be there," she pressed.

Yeah, she wasn't the Queen Bee for nothing. The fact that Gretchen implied there was something between Will and me made my pulse race, and despite my better judgment, I found myself getting drawn into her vortex. Could I legitimately pass up a chance to spend an evening with Gretchen and her crew, if our plan was to work?

It was right then that Dev spotted us across the hall and scurried right up between Gretchen and me.

"Weren't you Miss Ballsy today," she said.

Right away I saw what she was up to; she was trying to capitalize on the whole Walsh episode to make me appear cooler than I was—a rebel questioning authority. I looked at her sharply, trying to silently communicate that she needed to stay away from this situation.

"So are we still on for tonight?" Dev asked, clearly not getting my communiqué.

Out of the corner of my eyes, I could feel Gretchen look at me in mocking disbelief, as if to say—*She's why you were turning us down?*

"Huh?" I grunted in the poorest of concealed non-answers.

"Movie night?" Dev prompted.

Behind her, Jodi and Carrie smirked at each other and then rolled their eyes.

I mean, if she was trying to puff me up in front of Gretchen, revealing that I spent my Friday nights watching movies at home wasn't a well thought out idea. It didn't occur to me that perhaps, subconsciously, Dev didn't want me to fall under Gretchen's spell.

I realized then that this was a decisive moment—not a personal choice, but a business decision. I struggled to distance myself from the situation . . . to look at it objectively . . . but with Gretchen and her friends surrounding me, and dreams of blue-chip status swirling in my head, my deductive skills were clumsy and imprecise. Wouldn't being seen hanging out with Gretchen and the Proud Crowd send my Market number skyrocketing?

Of course it would.

I knew immediately what I had to do—and if Dev had the full picture of what was unfolding, she would've told me to do the same thing. I know it. If I passed on Gretchen and the Proud Crowd now, our plan would fail. This was my big chance to both merge with Gretchen and create that little bit of alchemy every great plan needs to succeed. Dev would just have to sit tight until I could fill her in later on what I was doing.

"Actually, I'm hanging with Gretchen tonight," I replied.

Gretchen's head snapped back, and her eyelids lowered ever so slightly—a pleased smile on her face.

"Come again?" Dev said.

"Yeah," I continued, now settling comfortably into my role, "she's having a party—Will's going to be there."

Dev just stared at me, clearly unwilling to accept what she was hearing.

"We had plans," she hissed through clenched teeth.

"Movie night?" Carrie Bell asked with a little mocking laugh.

"Puh-lease," Jodi seconded, apparently tasting blood in the water. "So you could make hot chocolate and knit friendship bracelets?"

The girls all laughed—their snickers like little knives—and Dev's cheeks burned red. I tried winking to let her know what I was up to, but she was clueless. Momentarily, I debated coming to her defense, suggesting that she come too, but that would've only ruined things. No, I had to hold firm, no matter how horrible it was to see Dev twisting in the wind. Besides, she *had* to understand the hand I was playing. There were always losses accumulated during an M&A—movie night would be one of them.

"Kat's ready to play with the big girls now," Gretchen drawled after a moment, and she slipped her arm through mine. "Aren't you Kit-Kat?"

I looked over at her, and Gretchen stared at me, apparently waiting for me to affirm what she'd just said. It was that classic moment in any initiation when you had to show your allegiance to the new order—be it the Mafia, the military, or the Proud Crowd. Awful as it was, I swallowed and took a deep breath.

"Yeah, I am."

"I see," Dev whispered. "I see."

Her face was inscrutable as she turned and walked away. As she did, Gretchen and the girls drew closer—whispering and smiling—and our bodies formed a circle, blocking out everyone else. For a second, I thought Dev might turn and give me a knowing wink, but she just disappeared into the sea of other students flowing down the hallway.

CHAPTER

19

THE DOOR SWUNG open and Gretchen handed me a glass of bubbling champagne.

"What's this for?"

"We're celebrating." She grinned.

Through all of detention and my whole drive over to Gretchen's house I tried to imagine what the evening would hold, and this was certainly never how I'd imagined it beginning. Not three and a half weeks before, I was practically ridiculed off the property, and now here I was being welcomed with open arms.

I took the glass and Gretchen motioned for me to follow her back through the house. Her parents didn't seem to be home, and except for the low rumble of a techno beat thumping from a room somewhere in the house, there were no signs of life. As we snaked our way through the darkened spaces, the music gradually grew louder until finally we arrived in a large open room that overlooked the tennis court. Candles, burning smoky and red, peppered the surfaces, and once my eyes adjusted to the dim, flickering light, I discovered Elisa, Jodi, and Carrie—champagne flutes in hand—lounging casually on silk pillows on the floor. It seemed we were in a game room of sorts—a shuffleboard table lined one wall, a pool table stood unused at the far end, and MTV played silently on the largest flat-screen television I'd ever seen.

The girls nodded to me, and Gretchen picked up a bottle of Veuve Clicquot from a felt-covered table and passed it around for everyone to refill their glasses.

"Take a seat," she said as she gestured toward an open space.

"What are we celebrating?" I asked. Gretchen looked at Elisa, who giggled and sipped her drink. Jodi pursed her lips and studied her shoes, which I estimated at three hundred plus.

"You," Carrie said.

"To Kat," Gretchen announced, holding her champagne up. "Better late than never."

They all laughed, and I couldn't help but join them. I took a seat on the floor next to Elisa and sipped the champagne. I wasn't much of a drinker, but I could handle a glass of champagne . . . or two. I drank it slowly, and gradually I merged into the scene.

Decadent as the night was—raiding Gretchen's mother's closet and trying on all her Harry Winston jewelry, opening more bottles of champagne, and taking a quick dip in the bubbling hot tub—fundamentally, it wasn't any different from a hundred other nights Dev, Callie, and I had spent together. We talked about boys, and then we talked about boys some more. We did some catty chatting about girls, the ones we hated and the underclassmen we admired, and we talked about Walsh and the other teachers. We talked about how annoying our moms were, and how much we were going to miss them once we got to college. We talked about going to college and never coming back to Millbank, though we all knew that was a lie and that we would see each other at the homecoming game next fall.

As I sat there, I have to admit there were moments when the whole scene made me a little melancholy. A quiet part of me missed my true friends, and I wondered what Dev was doing right then. I'd tried to call her the moment I got in my car after detention, but her cell went straight to voice mail. I'd tried again at home, but still straight to voice mail. By dinnertime, I started to worry that perhaps the two of us weren't on the same page about the M&A of Gretchen and her crew, but I told myself that, given the circumstances, I should just put the whole situation in the back of my mind until we could clear the air, if it needed clearing.

But maybe I should try her one more time . . .

The doorbell snapped me out of my worrying, and when my eyes looked down the long hallway that separated the game room from the front of the house, I could see Will's blue eyes glowing. By his side were two of his band members, Dee Brown and Walter Pond . . . and Jack.

Oh no.

As the boys sauntered into the family room, Will looked directly at me. There was definitely an element of surprise written on his face, and while Gretchen had told me that Will was coming, it was now clear she hadn't informed Will that I would be here. Jack wouldn't even meet my gaze, and it was also clear that he was holding to the same tactic he used when he saw me at the BookStop: pretend I wasn't there.

While Jack awkwardly went over and looked through Gretchen's DVDs, Will effortlessly joined the party and pecked all the girls on the cheek. When he got to me, he simply said, "Hey," and sat down next to me on the couch. Once the conversation started up, he turned to me and whispered, "Meet me on the porch out back," and a moment later, he got up and announced he had to make a call. He walked out of the room like he knew the place intimately, and it unexpectedly stirred a little pang of jealousy. I quickly remembered, however, who he had just asked to meet for a rendezvous.

I waited a good five minutes before excusing myself, eventually asking where the powder room was located. There were two, one by the foyer and the other just off the kitchen, and I quickly deduced that Will had known this and thus suggested the back porch, which was accessible from the kitchen only.

Through the darkness, I could see a cigarette ember glowing outside. I quietly slid open the glass door and moved toward Will, who was silhouetted in the moonlight.

"Can you see me?" I joked, half hoping he'd remember the words he spoke to me the first night.

"I have to admit something to you," he said, staring off into the dark.

"Go ahead," I whispered, half of me scared to listen and the other half thrilled with anticipation.

"Those were Jack's words—that first night."

It was like a little jab to my belly. The eight words that changed my life—"You were always the one I couldn't see"—were falsely spoken. Will had stolen them from Jack Clayton.

"Why are you telling me that?" The tone of my voice was more cross than I had intended, but Will was unfazed.

"Because they were his words and you were his observation, but I've been falling for you ever since."

That line was more than a jab—it was a full body shot.

"Falling is a slippery word," I warned. Perhaps he feared

that Jack would sell him out, or perhaps it was just a simple desire to come clean; either way I appreciated the honesty. "I guess we all play parts we haven't written."

"Yeah, but I don't want to play a part with you—that's why I'm telling you." He turned and tossed his cigarette off the porch before cupping my face in his hands. He kissed me on the lips once, and hard. "Don't trust her," he breathed into my ear.

"Who?"

"Gretchen," he whispered. "She doesn't want you to succeed."

"Succeed at what?"

He was very quiet for a few moments, like he was considering his words carefully. "I meant us," he finally said. "She doesn't want us to succeed."

"I don't care what she thinks."

"Good," he breathed. And he kissed me again.

Just then the light in the kitchen popped on, and the porch light followed shortly thereafter. We quickly separated, and by the time the sliding glass door opened, revealing Gretchen flanked by Jodi, we were on opposite sides of the porch and Will had managed to light another cigarette.

"You two can't get enough of each other," Gretchen said. "It's so cute."

I fidgeted nervously and I heard Will exhale loudly, like he was letting go of a little anxiety.

"Will," Gretchen continued. "I'm glad you're here because I had something important to share with Kat."

Will turned toward Gretchen with suspicion in his eyes, and for a second I could swear he was terrified of what she might say. I looked down at my shoes, almost feeling like I had interrupted her and Will, and not the other way around.

Was Gretchen about to call me out?

"It's about the Black & White," she said like she was singing a song. "I'm putting Kat at my table!"

I couldn't believe it—I was speechless.

"But there's no room for her," Jodi complained. "The table's totally full."

Clearly, Jodi hadn't reconciled herself to my newfound status and still had it out for me.

Gretchen shrugged her shoulders with nonchalance. "Well, you wouldn't mind sitting at Jack's table, right?"

"What?"

"Kat can have your seat."

If I hadn't known how cruel Jodi was, I might have felt sorry for her. Betrayed by the girl who was no doubt her idol, she looked destroyed.

"Well, if that's what you want," she mumbled pathetically.

"Perfect," Gretchen concluded before turning back to me. "What do you say?"

I walked over and threw my arms around her and gave her a light kiss on the cheek. "Thank you! Thank you!"

"It's nothing, really."

Listlessly, Jodi wandered back inside, and Will just stood there, mute. His eyes were telling me he didn't trust a word Gretchen was saying, but I was too thrilled to care. Finally, as if nothing had been said of any interest to him, he mumbled that he had to take off.

Making his exit, he gave Gretchen a little kiss on the cheek and then turned to me with a weak smile. "You keep falling up." And with a wink, he left.

An hour or so later, Gretchen followed me to the front door. It was past my curfew for a school night, but when I'd called my mother and told her where I was, naturally she said it was fine. Standing on the front steps now, I looked up at the stars. They were blazing in a way that you rarely see under the canopy of the suburban lights.

"Beautiful night," I said.

"Yes," Gretchen answered. "Thanks for coming."

"I'll see you tomorrow," I said. "And thanks again for the Black & White."

"It's nothing."

Not that I had been on many by then, but strangely, it felt like the end of a date—like Gretchen and I had passed a threshold. I waved and made my way to my car. As I looked over my shoulder back up at her house, I pictured Will kissing me on the porch, and it made my heart flutter to even think about it. Gretchen stood at the door, smiling, and she kept the light on until I started the engine. Finally she nodded and went back in to her small party that I suspected would go on late into the night.

As I crept slowly down the steep hill, I could feel my tires slipping on the gravel.

KCW LLC.

MARKET RANKING: 19
TODAY'S CHANGE: ↑5

SHARE PRICE: $29.16
CHANGE: ↑10.06 (+43%)
L/B RATIO: 9.7
3-MONTH RANGE: $1.23 – $30.13
STATUS: BLUE CHIP

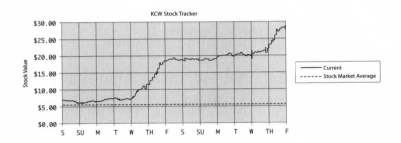

ANALYST RECOMMENDATION: A merger with GRT?
Could it get any better for this stock? This CEO is
making all the right moves.

STRONG BUY

CHAPTER

....
: 20 :
....

HAD I TURNED TO the Dark Side?

I'd be lying if I didn't admit that I enjoyed hanging out with Gretchen and the Proud Crowd, but that didn't mean I was going to become one of her brainless clones. No way. In the light of day, I took the party for what it was: an unexpected entry to the Black & White and an opportunity to deepen my relationship with Will. Dev would have been proud of my cold-hearted approach to Gretchen. Machiavellian? Mata Hari-esque? Perhaps. But by this point I was savvy enough to know that the key to climbing to the top of the Market was keeping Gretchen close enough to add luster to my shares, but far enough away that I could shine on my own.

When I woke up and checked the Market the next

morning—there it was: I was officially . . . a Blue Chip!! Granted, ranked at number 19, I'd just barely cracked it, but I was certified nonetheless. I could barely restrain myself from doing a little victory dance as I snatched my phone from the cradle and called Dev. When she answered, I launched right in.

"Did you see? We did it!" I yelled. "I'm a Blue Chip!"

Right when I was expecting Dev to be at her giddiest, there was dead silence on the other end of the line.

"Hello?"

"I'm here," she said. "How could you?"

"How could I what?"

"Don't play dumb," she snapped. "You totally humiliated me in front of Gretchen."

"Dev, I left you messages last night to explain, but you never called me back. I was doing it for the Market—for the final step of your business plan—and it totally worked! They were practically eating out of my hand last night."

"You're full of it. You walked all over me to get what you wanted."

"Why are you overreacting?"

"Overreacting?!"

"You're not listening to me," I cried as I felt things spiraling out of control. "It was just business—part of your plan. *Really.* It was that moment of alchemy you went on and on about. It's not a big deal."

"Not a big deal? Not a big deal?" her voice quivered. "You were a total bitch to me. And maybe, just maybe, it really was a step in the plan, but even if it was, it was still wrong. You got greedy. It was completely out of line."

So many thoughts collided in my head at once—the fact that she'd been driving me crazy with the Market, how it was seemingly okay for her to pop things on me out of the blue, like Princeton guy, but when I did it, it was wrong—that my mouth froze. I may not have been entirely in the right, but she wasn't exactly innocent either.

But before I could apologize, Dev launched back in.

"You're so full of it, it's disgusting," she said. "You ditched me so you could be one of them, plain and simple."

"But—"

"Since you're apparently too good for me now, do me a favor. Don't ever call me again!" She hung up on me.

I was so upset that it took every ounce of self-control not to hurl the phone against the wall and watch it shatter into a hundred pieces, so instead I slammed it down into my comforter. I walked over to my computer and refreshed the Market, my obsession apparently uninhibited by my falling out with Dev.

In one twenty-four-hour period, my life and my dreams became one, and together they were one big nightmare. As I watched my Market ranking jump from nineteen to sixteen in less time than it took Dev and me to implode, I wondered how I'd save our friendship. I fell onto my bed and buried my head in my pillows as my chest shuddered with deep, painful sobs. For what or who, I couldn't exactly tell you, but I knew somehow it was all shackled to the Market.

With Gretchen's tacit stamp of approval and (for those in the know) my newly minted Blue Chip status, my life was transformed overnight. Suddenly Gretchen was extending invitations to go swimming at the Millbank Country Club, and I was even offered my very own seat at the Proud Crowd table in the cafeteria. In a lot of ways, it was still pretty baffling, but I wasn't complaining. With less than two weeks left of high school, the world was my proverbial oyster *(why hadn't this happened sooner?)*, and life took on an almost surreal quality: my walk more confident, my smile more seductive. Every day there was somewhere to be—trips to the mall with Elisa, late-night convos with Nina, a private party at Café Electric—and I reveled in this new, though foreign, life. I'd become someone new, someone sought after. In many ways, it made me think back to that afternoon when Dev and I hatched our plan, and we pored over pictures of girls Dev referred to as Latebloomers. Suddenly, I was that girl, and I was reaping all the rewards. Glamorous as my life was on the surface, however, I was feeling torn apart inside—torn apart by what had happened with Dev.

A week after that fateful day, I took a gamble that Callie might be working at Bella's, and I turned down River Road. Sure enough, when I walked in, Callie was on break, sitting in the back room reading a stack of magazines and sipping an espresso.

"Hey," I said as I gave her a smooch on the cheek and plopped down in the chair opposite.

"Where've you been?" she asked.

"You know."

"Mmm-hmmm, too busy for Cal," she observed, and looked back down at her magazine.

"I know, I'm sorry."

Callie fixed me with a stare before dropping her magazine on the table. I noticed she didn't have that bouncy smile I so loved. "Kate, when are you going to get tired of this game?"

"What do you mean? What game?"

"A month ago you came to me with a sob story about being Number Seventy-one, about being a 'nobody.' And I warned you not to care what other people thought, but you and Dev had a plan, so I played along because you said you needed me. And now you don't seem to need anyone."

"What are you talking about?"

"You haven't been to a brunch with Dev and me in two weeks, you bailed on helping me with the graduation decorations, and you haven't called once in over a week."

"I've been—"

"So you come in here with the 'you know' excuse?" she finished without missing a beat. "And it's not just me— now you and Dev are in this huge fight."

"She told you about that?"

"Of course she did."

"You have to help me. She won't talk to me. She either doesn't take my calls, or when I go up to her in person she just walks away."

Callie shook her head, obviously concerned.

"I don't want to say it, but I told you so."

I was silent for a moment, desperately wanting a confidante.

"Can I tell you something?" I asked.

She raised an eyebrow and cocked her head.

"Do you ever think the reason why Dev's all upset is because she's not getting to be the Latebloomer? Because she's still stuck where she is?"

Callie's face was like concrete. I'm not sure she was convinced of my analysis of Dev. After a few moments of silence, she sighed.

"Free pass," she said. "I'm giving you a free pass."

"What for?"

"You're all kinds of twisted around—you don't even know who your real friends are," Callie continued. "The three of us need to sit down—you, me, and Dev, no excuses—

because, to be honest, you've both been whack ever since this stupid Market thing started, and we need to fix it."

I studied her for a few moments and then glanced out the window. A tractor trailer filled with brand-new BMWs rumbled by beneath a sky pink-hued from the setting sun. I wondered then, darkly and only for a fleeting instant, if my friendship with Dev had come and gone.

"This Saturday," she declared. "Are we on?"

The morning of the Black & White?

"I don't know," I said.

"What do you mean?" Callie snapped. "Don't you want things to go back to how they used to be?"

I looked at her and shrugged my shoulders and said, "Yes." It was true. I definitely wanted to reconcile with Dev—I couldn't imagine my life without her—but did I want to go back to being Seventy-one? Did I want to go back to movie night every Friday? Or did I want Will and the Black & White and parties at Gretchen's?

Why couldn't I have both?

CHAPTER

21

THAT NIGHT WAS the big moment, the main event, the evening to end all evenings—for my mother.

"Where have you been?" she fumed, rollers in her hair, an eyelash curler clutched in her hand, when I cruised into the house fresh from a spruce-up at Images (I needed something to make me feel better after my convo with Callie). "We're supposed to meet the Tanners at the club in thirty minutes!"

Yes, it was time for my parents' all-important one-on-one meeting with the Tanners. Strictly speaking, this was not the final step in their application process, but as Abby Tanner was chairwoman of the New Membership Committee, it was well known that if she approved of the applicant, it was basically a done deal. Hence the fate-of-the-world-hangs-in-the-balance level of anxiety for my mom.

"Don't stress. I'll be ready before Dad."

And this was true, too. If we had to be anywhere by a certain time, Dad would inevitably snooze away on the couch in his study until fifteen minutes before we were supposed to leave, while my mother fluttered about, admonishing him to get ready, until it escalated into a full-blown diplomatic crisis. It was a routine I'd witnessed a thousand times. He'd wander into the hall, they'd bicker, and he'd shave and prep while the hemming and hawing continued until finally they got out the door, only to discover a smear of white shaving cream hanging off his ear that, at that very instant, would drip down and stain his shirt. At that point, there'd be either a family laugh . . . or a family breakdown. One time, my mother walked back into the house and refused to come out, but more often than not, it ended in laughter. It was no accident that my parents had been married as long as they had. Yes, they got into it from time to time, but at the end of it all, they worked well together.

I hoped I would be so lucky one day.

"No, you won't," I heard my father yell, as he suddenly appeared in the hallway, the back of his hair disheveled, no doubt from the pillow he was napping on. Nothing got Dad going like a little competition, and I watched him hurry into the bathroom and heard the spigots squeak on. He barked out an outfit request to my mom.

With my hair and nails already done, all I had to do was slip into my dress—an appropriately conservative Ralph Lauren scoop-neck number—and grab some jewelry, so I knew there was no way he was going to beat me. It took me all of two minutes and thirty-eight seconds, and after zipping down the stairs, I ended up beating Dad by more than three minutes.

When he did sheepishly arrive, however—thankfully, because my mother was wearing out the new linoleum floor with her pacing—disaster had struck. A steady stream of blood was inching down his chin. This was cause for alarm, because whenever Dad cut himself shaving, it was like he'd opened an artery. He's what you'd call a real bleeder.

"Frank! Didn't I tell you to shave last night?" she started.

Mom was always encouraging Dad to shave the day before a big meeting or event because his face was so sensitive, but like most middle-aged men (or so I've observed with my friends' fathers) he never paid any attention to her warnings.

My dad grumbled something inaudible, and she expertly pulled a Kleenex from the box on the counter, ripped a corner off, and pressed it to the open wound. After a few minutes, the tissue shred just stayed on by itself, the blood acting as an adhesive.

"Let's go. It'll stop by the time we get there," Mom announced like a general about to take the field of battle. "At least it better."

And with that, we were off.

Cute Snobby Guy who ran the front desk at the club showed us into the private dining room behind the library. Minutes before in the parking lot, Mom had pulled the Kleenex from my father's face, and much to our relief, his chin seemed to be holding up.

As I circled around the wood-paneled room, I counted six place settings at the table, and I silently wondered who the sixth person was who would be joining us.

"Kat, do you and your parents want anything while you're waiting?" Cute Snobby Guy offered.

Out of the corner of my eye, I saw my mother look over at me, confused.

After coming to the club a bunch of times with the Proud Crowd, I'd actually gotten to know Cute Snobby Guy (his name was Max, in fact). Elisa admitted to me that she had a huge crush on him, but while all the girls agreed he was a total cutie, I'd been informed there was an unspoken rule of no smooching the staff, Will being the exception of course. . . .

"We're fine, Max, thanks."

Max nodded officially and turned to leave, and just as

he got to the door, in walked the Tanners. I'd never met Abby Tanner before, but I'd certainly seen her on television. Here was the crazy thing: she was more beautiful in person. Long brown hair that was naturally wavy, and blue eyes flecked with violet—she looked like Elizabeth Taylor in her prime. For his part, Mr. Tanner appeared even bigger than in his portrait, and his slow gait and easy drawl suggested a Texan replanted in the soil of Jersey. My mom had once described him as a tall drink of water (I have no idea where she'd seen him, in town?), and now I grasped what she meant. He was graceful and manly. Each step flowed contin-uously into the next until he was upon you, and then you felt like you were swimming in emerald ponds.

After the usual greetings, and nice-to-meet-you's, Mrs. Tanner squinted and then gestured at my father's chin.

"What happened there?"

I shot a look over at my mom, and no joke, I thought she might split in half and transform—like a werewolf, or the Incredible Hulk—into some crazy beast. Whether she'd eat Mrs. Tanner for obnoxiously pointing out my father's chin, or Dad himself for not shaving a day in advance, I just couldn't quite tell.

"Razor," Dad answered with a bashful smile.

Mr. Tanner stepped up and put a firm hand on my dad's back. "Happens to me all the time."

That was cool, I thought to myself.

"Kit-Kat," I heard a familiar call from the doorway, and from the nickname, I knew right away who it was.

Gretchen.

"Hey!"

She was wearing a sexy, empire-waist dress with diamond drop earrings, and yet again, she proved herself to be the most gorgeous person in the room. Gretchen came over and gave me a big hug, and for the second time in two minutes, I noticed my mother's head jerk in my direction. I guess she was wondering how it was that I suddenly knew everyone so well.

"When my parents said they were having dinner with your family, I just had to come," Gretchen explained before going on to introduce herself to my parents. Beaming, my mother shook her hand.

"It's always nice to meet one of Kate's friends," my mother gushed as Mrs. Tanner looked on.

"She's the best," Gretchen answered.

I have to admit, I was somewhat perplexed by her appearance, but I just smiled. Mrs. Tanner delicately took a glass of wine from the full tray a waiter had just delivered. "So you're a senior as well, Kate. And where are you off to next fall?"

"Brown."

"Very impressive." She swiveled her head toward Gretchen and nodded. "We always thought Gretchen was going to go to an Ivy League school, but she proved us wrong."

A brief silence filled the room, and my father cleared his throat uncomfortably. Gretchen, the master of poise, appeared unfazed by her mother's slam, but I had to imagine that part of her was shriveling up inside. Hard as it is to believe, I felt bad for her.

"Well, there are so many good schools," my mother interjected.

"Definitely," my father chimed.

Mrs. Tanner just tapped her perfectly manicured nail against her glass and stared at her daughter with barely veiled disappointment.

"That's enough, Ab," Mr. Tanner said in a low voice before turning to my parents and smiling. "Shall we sit down and order?"

Desperate for a safe exit from this outrageously awkward exchange, we all nodded eagerly and moved toward the table.

As it turned out, my parents really got along with the Tanners. I wouldn't say that they were on their way to sending each other Christmas cards and going on family vacations, but the conversation flowed easily, and when my mom and Mrs. Tanner discovered they both had a passion for antiquing in Bucks County, they were off to the races. Dad even got in on the lovefest, because Mr. Tanner started talking football (seems he was a Texas Longhorn guy), and like most men, my dad could shoot the bull ad infinitum about anything sports related. They jawed on about running backs and the BCS, and before I knew it they were making plans to play golf together.

"Looks like it's going well," I whispered to Gretchen.

She grinned slyly and nodded. "I gave your family good pre-rap. Just remember who had your back."

It was textbook Gretchen: simultaneously ingratiating herself, but also letting you know that she was the string-puller, the playmaker, the Svengali behind the scenes. And what was given could also be taken away.

Despite the fact that I constantly had to be on my guard around her, it was actually great that Gretchen had come, because we all know how boring it is to have to sit through a long dinner with your parents and another couple. Sure, I needed to be there to say my lines whenever the Tanners had a question about MHS or college, but for the most part, Gretchen and I were able just to chat between ourselves, and there were few people as entertaining as she.

"Meanwhile, I had the best idea last night," she whispered.

"What?"

"You know how I usually have a party after graduation every year? Well this year I was thinking maybe you wanted to do it at your house. I'll help you plan it."

"Really?"

I was shocked. Gretchen's party had become an annual event since we were freshman—and from what I'd been told, it made that little shindig I went to last month look like a middle-school cookie party.

"But that's your night."

She shook her head. "I totally wouldn't care if you did it. Besides, it would be so much fun for us to do together. The whole school would come. We could call it 'Heaven'— you know, 'cause the 'Hell' of high school is over?"

A huge party? At my house? I wasn't so sure that my parents would be into it—I could just picture my dad's reaction when he found one of the football players booting in our bathroom. But wouldn't it be so cool to throw the final party of senior year? Wouldn't that once and for all cement my position as this year's Latebloomer? The ultimate coup de grace over my sister's previously superior reputation?

But another question flew into my mind: why was Gretchen offering to do this? Was there an agenda behind it?

"I don't think my parents would be into it."

She leaned forward. "Watch and learn."

I realized what she was going to do before she even opened her mouth.

"Mrs. Winthrop," she cooed as she inserted herself into

our parents' conversation, "Kate and I were talking and we just had a terrific idea. We want to plan a graduation-night party together. Would you and Mr. Winthrop be okay if we had it at your house?"

I'll give her this; it was a masterful move. There was no way my mother could say no. I'm sure the idea of Gretchen Tanner and her daughter cohosting a party together was right up there with me marrying a prince, anyway, but even if my mother had wanted to refuse, there was no way she could in front of Mr. and Mrs. Tanner. Not with club membership on the line.

And neither could I.

My father wrinkled his brow, but my mother jumped in before he could say anything. "That sounds wonderful. Assuming of course that Abby and Bill are okay with it."

The Tanners nodded.

"I'll give you my caterer's number," Mrs. Tanner reassured my mother. "And a good party rental person, so it's not too much work for you. Just ring me tomorrow."

While my father was surely calculating how much this party was going to cost him, my mother's eyes glimmered with excitement. No doubt she couldn't wait to call Mrs. Tanner.

"See?" Gretchen said as our parents fell back into their own conversation.

"I'm impressed."

She took a sip of her mineral water before touching my knee. "So, you have to tell me. What's the deal with you and Will?"

That was out of left field.

"What do you mean?"

"You have been spending a ton of time together. Are you guys hooking up?"

In the Tanner-Winthrop merger, Will Bochnowski was the one deal point that had never been closed. No matter what she claimed, I suspected she still had a thing for him, and I knew this was a subject that needed to be handled with extreme caution. Like a vial of nitroglycerine, one fumble and the whole thing would blow up in my face.

"I can never tell what guys are thinking," I answered.

Gretchen reached across the table and grabbed a roll from the basket. "That's not what I asked," she pressed. "Are you guys hooking up?"

Thankfully, before I could answer, Mrs. Tanner put her hand on Gretchen's arm. "You're not having more bread, are you?"

Gretchen's tongue darted across her teeth. She put the roll down. "Of course not."

"That's what I thought." Mrs. Tanner nodded, turned back to my mother, and picked right back up with their conversation.

Gretchen said nothing for a few moments, and I picked

my purse up from the floor and feigned looking for something to spare her the extra humiliation.

It was pretty disturbing to see Gretchen interact with her parents. Although my relationship with my family could be a little bonkers sometimes, I never doubted the fact that they loved me. Look, I'm not saying Mrs. Tanner didn't love Gretchen; I'm sure she did. But it seemed that she treated her more like a possession than a daughter. There was a cold distance to their interaction, and Mrs. Tanner was constantly watching her like a hawk, criticizing things she did, and ordering her around.

"All I'm saying, Kat," I heard Gretchen start up again, "is that you need to be careful with him. He's a player."

I glanced up at her and nodded.

"It's for your own good," she added. "I wouldn't want to see you get hurt. Do you trust me on this?"

"Totally."

I don't have to tell you that I trusted her about as far as I could throw her, but I also knew there might be more than an ounce of truth to what she was saying. But hadn't Will warned me about Gretchen, as well? Were they both lying or was one the true deceiver? I realized then how isolated I was from people I could rely on—I was now on this road alone.

We didn't talk about Will again for the rest of the night, and after my parents shared a second bottle of wine with the Tanners, everyone air-kissed good-bye, and I drove my family home. When we pulled into the driveway, and before I got out of the car, my mother turned to me gave me a kiss on the cheek.

"Thank you," she said.

"For what?"

"You just made my dream come true."

CHAPTER

22

SO, YEAH, Mom was on cloud nine.

Much as I have should've been right there with her, however, I had a nagging, nervous feeling which I couldn't quite shake. It was about the party. By the time I had checked my e-mail that night, Gretchen had already sent a "save-the-date" Evite to—yes, it's true—the *entire* senior class announcing our party. Now I was locked in and there was no backing out. I should've been thrilled about throwing a blowout with Gretchen—and part of me was—but it just seemed wildly uncharacteristic. And therefore suspicious. Gretchen Tanner was never one to share the limelight. So why now?

I also worried how Dev would react when she heard this latest piece of news. I was sick with the feeling that she would only see this as further evidence, however unfounded, that I'd turned away from her and toward Gretchen. But a way out was nowhere in sight.

Troubled, and knowing that my mother was still up, I wandered downstairs, hoping that maybe if I laid some of my cards on the table, perhaps she could help see me through this. I've always been a little cagey about sharing things with my mother, but what can I say? Sometimes you need your mom. When I reached the foot of the steps, I discovered that she was on the phone with my sister.

"A huge success, Mel. Huge!" I heard my mother say in the family room.

I lingered in the hall.

"Uh-huh . . . uh-huh. . . . and it's all thanks to Katie. The Tanners love her . . . What? I told you, she's totally changed. It's unbelievable!"

I closed my eyes and waited a few more moments.

"You wouldn't even recognize her, Mel. She's totally taken off. It's like . . . Cinderella."

Outside, a gentle breeze blew, rustling the leaves in the trees and rattling our screen door. While my mother continued to sing my praises to my sister, I silently backed away and climbed the steps back to my room.

In the middle of the night, I awoke to the sound of my cell buzzing with a text. Was it Dev? Gretchen? Callie? Groggily, I flipped it open.

WILL: Are u ^

Well, I was now.

KAT: Y—Y R U?

WILL: Need 2 talk

KAT: go ;-)

WILL: In person

I sat straight up. Will wanted to get together . . . now? Why? What was so important that it had to be said in person at three in the morning? I'm not going to lie and say I'd never snuck out before. My junior year Dev and I got caught climbing out my window on our way to see a Blind Bastard concert in New York City. My parents grounded me for a month and told me that if I ever did it again, they would ground me for three months. Even with the success of the dinner with the Tanners, I still couldn't risk it.

KAT: Can't—Rents r crazy

WILL: K. I'll come to u

That shifted my brain into overdrive. The following disjointed thoughts all popped into my head at the same time:

1. *I'm not wearing a bra.*
2. *Are orange pajamas sexy?*
3. *Should I call Callie?*
4. *Pinch yourself and see if you wake up.*

I sprang from bed and ran into my bathroom. It took me a minute to adjust to the light, but I realized soon enough that I looked like a complete and utter disaster. I took a deep breath and put my head under the faucet and drenched my hair straight, and then combed it into a ponytail. I wanted to look a little bit sexy, so I ditched the pj's and changed into a tank top and some boxer shorts. Sitting by my window, I turned on my small bedside lamp and waited. And waited some more.

Ten minutes.

Then fifteen minutes.

Twenty minutes.

When the clock read four a.m., I dozed off, but some time later I heard the sound of a car coming down my street. Craning my neck, I watched as it went by my house, and I thought it must have been somebody else, but then it turned around and slowly came back down the street. The driver shut off the engine maybe fifty feet before reaching my yard and glided up, like a cat on the hunt.

A figure popped out of the car, and sure enough, it was Will. He was wearing frayed khakis, flip-flops, and a white T-shirt.

"Hey," I whispered from my window.

He waved for me to come down.

I put out my index finger and mouthed, "One minute."
He nodded and sat down on the porch steps. Thankfully,
Remington was about the furthest thing there was from a
watchdog, and my parents' room was in the back of the
house on the second floor, so I figured we'd be okay. When
I opened the front door open, it creaked—in retrospect,
probably no louder than usual, but on that night, in that
moment, it sounded like a sonic boom. My heart started
racing and my hands shook, but somehow I managed to
silently close the door behind me

I stepped outside, and the night air cooled my feet and
slid up my uncovered legs. I shivered a little as I walked
down the steps to where he was sitting.

"Hi," I said. "We have to whisper. My parents would
kill me."

"I know," he said. "I'm sorry, but I really wanted to see
you."

Every beat of my heart reverberated throughout my
body. Every nerve tingled, from my feet to my hair follicles.
I think my brain stopped working, and the words that came
out of my mouth were formed by some unknown force that
keeps a girl's thoughts in order when the rest of her is falling
apart.

"Hey," he said, with a tiny smile. "I'm glad I'm here."

"At my house?"

Apparently this "unknown" force couldn't stop me from being retarded.

He moved closer and put his arm around me. He was warm.

"Thanks," I said. "Why are you up?"

He looked at the stars and didn't say anything for a few moments. His eyes were tired, dark half-moons sagging below them, and while I couldn't say for sure, it seemed like something was weighing on him. Like he was holding a secret he no longer wished to carry.

"I wanted to see you, because I have something I need to tell you. It's important," he said.

"What is it?"

He nodded, and then became silent again.

"I don't believe in promises," he started. I was waiting for the "but" that followed that statement, but again he fell silent. In his eyes I could see a struggle going on. Gretchen's warning slithered through my mind, but I pushed it away.

He took my hands in his, and my heart fluttered.

"I hate the Proud Crowd," he said. "I hate everything about them. Gretchen and her crew. The Black & White Ball. It's all so stupid."

These were not the romantic words I expected.

"But they're your friends, Will. Why are you telling me this?"

He sighed.

"What I'm trying to say is that I like you. A lot. You're so different from them. Whatever you do—don't become one of them."

I wasn't sure how to reply.

"Listen, I have to tell you something more, something that's hard." His voice was trembling a bit.

"What?"

He brought his hands to his head and pulled his hair. For a beat, it seemed like he was going to say something dramatic, but suddenly he smiled.

"Do you want to go to the Black & White Ball with me?"

Has your mind ever short-circuited? I mean, has something a boy said to you ever caused you to momentarily go schizo?

"I'd love to." I grinned. "But aren't we all sitting with Gretchen?"

"Sure. But that doesn't mean that we can't go together. As a couple."

"Are you serious?" I said with a smile. "If you think Gretchen will be okay with it."

He gritted his teeth, and I could see the muscles tense in his jaw, but a beat later he smiled. "Don't worry about her," he said. "I'll take care of it."

In those next moments he gazed into my eyes more deeply than any boy ever had. I felt as though he was stealing my soul. There were no words for what I was feeling, and I knew that was exactly what he was feeling, too. Our hearts were alive together.

Then he leaned in, wrapped his hand around the base of my neck, and kissed me softly on the side of my neck . . . then my ear . . . then my lips . . . then my throat . . . and then he scooped me up and carried me to the hammock just off the porch in the dark. We dropped down into the netting. His lips were soft and his hands were a little rough, but that made me feel oddly safe. I won't lie to you, we got heavy quickly, but being near the porch, and it being my parents' house, and them being but thirty feet away, we kept it under control, for the most part. My heart was pounding and I could feel the blood rushing to my head, to the point where I felt dizzy.

"Let's stop," he said.

"Don't go yet."

"I don't want to, but the sun is coming up, and my mom gets up early."

I looked and, indeed, the first rays of the sun were shining through the tree line.

"Okay."

Suddenly I felt a little weird, like I wanted some confirmation that this night had happened. That he had actually said all those things to me. That we were, I hate to say this, a *couple*.

"No words," he said, putting his finger to my lips and kissing me on the forehead. "No words."

He pulled me up off the hammock and we walked toward the side yard, stopping at the corner of my house. He looked into my eyes for a few moments and held me. His right hand caressed my cheek, and then he turned and walked to the Spitfire. He got in and nodded for me to go inside before he fired it up. And I did, walking backward up the porch stairs, watching him the entire way. After I closed the door, I tiptoed up the stairs to my bedroom window and watched him drive west toward the disappearing moon.

I'd done it. I was going to the Black & White Ball with Will. I'd gotten exactly what I'd wanted. I had an urge to call Dev right then and tell her everything that had happened and find a way to patch things up with her; but somehow it didn't feel right. Will? The Black & White? It was all real now, but it felt nothing like I imagined it would. It felt empty and thrilling all at once, and it left me feeling jittery and unsure and alive in a way I'd never felt before.

BOOK FIVE
. . . .

THE CRASH

CHAPTER

23

THE THING ABOUT the Market was that even when you thought you should get out, there was something sucking you right back in. In the business world they call it Golden Handcuffs. You may know that you should quit, but the high life becomes so addictive that you're essentially imprisoned by it—and so it was with me. I became more and more obsessed with making it to the top of the Market. Soon after making Blue Chip status, the bloom was off the rose and Nine (my ranking as of 5/15) seemed incredibly low. It was like I'd hit a glass ceiling. Carrie Bell was still above me? Nina Licht? C'mon! Now that I'd had a taste of being ranked high, I wanted to be at the very top. Number One. Remarkably, the portfolio Dev, Callie, and I opened was right near the top in the rankings—our only real competitor was the same one Callie had pointed out to me weeks before: TKWP. It had moved in lock step with ours.

But after four weeks of ups and downs on the Market, and more than a handful of sleepless nights, I was worn out. On paper I may have been living the dream, but inside, I could feel something twisting—torquing my very being. Was this what it felt like to finally come out of one's cocoon, or was my soul getting perverted into something I never wanted it to be?

On the Wednesday before the Black & White, I was due to have my going-away dinner with Mrs. Sawyer. While I'd been feeling a bit reclusive most of the day, I decided I was going to put on a happy face and deal, because this was one date on which I could not bail.

We met at Louise Morel's, a little French bistro on North Adams Street. Before coming back home to Millbank to open the BookStop, Mrs. Sawyer lived in Paris for four years. She loved all things Parisian. I think outside of Howie and the store, her romance with the City of Light was the most meaningful relationship of her life. She was already sipping on a glass of wine when I arrived, and I ordered a wineglass of cranberry juice and pretended we were on the Left Bank. We easily fell into conversation, mostly memories of my time at the BookStop, Howie stories (a topic we often bonded over), and my plans for college. It wasn't until dessert was served that she surprised me with a question I expected more from my mother than from my boss.

"Are you happy, Kate?" she asked. "With the new you?"

I hadn't been aware of it, but Mrs. Sawyer had obviously been keeping tabs on me.

"What do you mean?" I asked. "I really haven't changed. It's just some new clothes."

"That's true," she said. "How's your mom's quest to get into the club?"

"Oh, ridiculous as ever," I quipped. "On Monday, we all had to get dressed up and have dinner with the Tanners."

"Oh, yes. He's nice. Mr. Tanner, that is."

"He is," I said. "But she sort of creeped me out."

"Why do you think your mom wants to get in the club so badly?" she asked.

It was a good question, one to which I'd never found a satisfactory answer.

"Maybe because she grew up in this town. Maybe she's proving something to herself?"

Mrs. Sawyer took a sip of wine and then she looked over toward the old high school building across the street that was now used as a YMCA. "I went to school when it was over there," she said, pointing with her free hand. "The Black & White Ball was the thing then, suppose it still is."

"Did you go?"

"Me, no. We were too poor. And they didn't let

blacks go to the dance—or in the club."

She took another sip. I felt foolish for not knowing that and even more foolish for my mother for trying to get into the club.

"I'm sorry," I said, not knowing what else to say. "I didn't know."

"Why would you?" she said. "They let everyone in now . . . if you have the money. They've come a long way—it doesn't matter if you're black or white or yellow or stupid or smart or one-eyed or two," she said, and then whispered, "As long as you're the right *kind* of person." And then she started laughing. I couldn't help but laugh with her—I'd never seen her so amused.

"Right." I smiled. "I imagine all the women are just like Gretchen and Mrs. Tanner."

"I imagine so," said Mrs. Sawyer. "Is that who you're trying to be?"

That's when the laughing stopped. At least, my laughing. Somehow Mrs. Sawyer had tricked me into her little trap.

"No," I said. "I don't want to be her."

I looked down at what remained of my dessert and suddenly felt like I couldn't eat another bite. A few moments passed before either of us said anything.

"I didn't mean to upset you, Kate," she said.

"I know, but it wasn't like that. Dev and I just wanted to beat the Market."

"The Market?"

"Some people—boys, I guess—in school started a Web site that rated all the girls. It's like a stock market, but girls are traded. It's disgusting, really."

"It sounds it," she said. "And you were low, I assume, and wanted to be higher, is that right?"

"Yes," I said. "It sounds worse having you say it."

Then she surprised me. "I think you did the right thing," she concluded, not meeting my eye. "Sometimes you have to work within the system before you can change it." Then she took her last swallow of wine. "And you beat it, I suppose?"

"Yeah, pretty much," I said, kind of giddy now that I had her approval.

"Mm-hmm," she said. "That's good. So tell me now, what is it you are going to do to change it?"

I didn't have an answer. I had been so busy climbing the ladder that by the time I got to the top I had simply forgotten how—and why—I'd gotten here.

"There's no time left—graduation is next week. There's really no time to change anything," I said.

I knew it was lame as soon as it came out of my mouth. More importantly, I knew she wouldn't believe me.

She sort of nodded, and a beat later asked the waiter for another glass of wine. We sat there for another half hour, chatting about unimportant things, but what she'd said echoed in my head and in my heart: what was I going to do to change things? Sadly, I had no answer. I didn't even know if I had the desire.

I drove south across River Road and headed in a direction that was the opposite of my home. In the past few days I'd taken up a little habit that I hadn't told anyone about. I liked to drive by Will's house, hoping to catch a glimpse of him in his bedroom window. It was sort of childish, I know, but this is what a huge crush will do to you. It was a dark, moonless night, so I had my high beams on as I drove down South Adams and took a right onto West Main. He lived on a little street called Soos Circle, and as I turned, I cut off my beams and coasted toward the end of the cul de sac. His light was on, and I could see his silhouette behind a shade. He was sitting with his feet up and if I had to guess, he was typing on his computer. There in our separate worlds, divided maybe by fifty feet, I wondered if that person, the boy, had been worth everything I'd done.

When I arrived home, my father was sitting on the front porch, nursing a bottle of Stella Artois—his favorite beer. In that form of silent communication you have with a parent, I didn't even wave as I approached. I just walked up the steps and sat down next to him on the retro 1950s glider that had stood underneath the picture window off the dining room for as long as I can remember. It was rusting on the edges, squeaked a bit when you moved, but there was a comfortable familiarity in it.

We sat there quietly for a few moments, and without looking over, he offered me a sip of his beer. Dad had offered me "swigs"—as he put it—of his beer since I was a little girl. It used to drive Mom crazy, and she told him to stop, but he always argued that if he let me have a little alcohol now, it wouldn't be such a forbidden fruit later. He'd been right.

Gently, I took the bottle from his hand and took a sip. A beat later, I handed it back to him and he nodded.

"I don't want to join Mom's club," he said.

"Did you tell her that?"

"No," he answered. "I don't really have the heart."

"It means a lot to her."

"Sadly, it means a lot to a fair amount of people," he remarked. "I never understood it."

"I do," I said. "I do."

He looked over at me quizzically, waiting for more, but I didn't answer his gaze. It was too much for me to explain, and I wasn't sure he'd get it, even if I did.

"Well, I prefer this club right here," he said, and he put his arm around me.

Across the street, a television snapped on in an otherwise black room, and I reached over for another sip.

CHAPTER

24

CLAD IN OUR BIKINIS, Gretchen and I were lying out on the balcony off her bedroom soaking in the Thursday afternoon sun. Ostensibly I was there to work on planning the graduation party with her, but after an hour our will had waned and we decided that a little tan would be a good idea. Memorial Day was right around the corner, after all, and as Gretchen was quick to point out, nothing looked worse than pasty skin against a white dress.

"It's *so* white trash," she'd declared.

Half an hour later, Art (the Tanners' cook) brought us some fresh beef teriyaki lettuce wraps, along with a few bottles of San Pellegrino and dessert. Supposedly, the masseuse was coming over at seven p.m. so the Tanners could get their massages, and Mrs. Tanner invited me to get one as well.

Yeah, I could get used to this.

"So I'm thinking the invitations should be blue and gold—sort of like our graduation gowns," Gretchen mused, eyes closed against the sun. "We'll get them rush printed at Kate's Paperie. We only have ten days."

"I thought you said that invitations are only for sixth graders."

Wasn't that the critique she'd leveled me with that time I came to her party?

"Hel-lo," she replied as she grabbed the Evian mister and sprayed herself. "For a get-together, yes. But this is a *real* party. You have to take it seriously."

"Got it," I answered and sat up.

Art had also baked us some fudge brownies that— though melting in the sun—were tempting me just a few feet away. Gretchen, however, hadn't touched them, so I figured I shouldn't either. I snagged a piece of celery and swirled it around in the ranch dressing before munching down. I may have come a long way, but sitting side by side with Gretchen in a bikini was a pretty sobering reality check. My midsection was a little soft; hers had been ab-blasted and was chiseled.

"Besides, you have to tell people what to wear," she continued. "We don't want people showing up like slobs. We'll call for 'casual chic.'"

"Good idea."

"And we have to get the DJ who played at Elisa's sweet sixteen. He was the best."

A cool breeze blew in from the west, and the tops of the trees on the edge of the Tanners' property swayed, leaves fluttering up and down. Feeling a chill, I pulled up my towel from the lounge and wrapped it around my shoulders.

"Thanks for doing all this," I said.

"Please, it's nothing," she answered, rolling onto her side. "What we really have to do is find you a cool dress. You have a reputation to live up to now."

"How do you mean?"

Gretchen stared at me for a beat and then smiled. Pushing herself to her feet, she disappeared into her room before returning shortly with a small velvet box. She handed it to me.

"What is it?"

"Just open it."

When I did, I felt my eyes go wide. Inside the box was a silver "P"—the same one that all the girls in the Proud Crowd wore. I couldn't quite believe what I was seeing.

"Is this . . . for me?"

Gretchen nodded. "You're one of us now."

I slipped the "P" from the box and guided its silver chain around my neck. The metal was cold against my skin, and I was at a complete and total loss for words. I was now officially one of the Proud Crowd.

"Wow," I mumbled in shock.

"You're a Blue Chipper, babe."

The mention of the Market smashed through my revelry, and try as I did to blink away my thoughts, the moment was tainted.

"Do you ever worry about it?" I finally asked, looking up at her. "Does it bother you?"

"What? The Market? I don't really think about it."

"C'mon," I challenged back. "I know you're Number One and all that, but it has to have an effect on you. You're telling me you never look at it?"

She pursed her lips and considered what I was saying.

"Sure, I look at it," she confessed. "But things like that aren't, like, isolated. You think it's any different from *People* magazine or Page Six or any of those blogs tracking stars? It's all the same."

"We're not celebrities, Gretchen."

"We are in this pond, Kate. No matter who you are, somebody's judging you."

"Like your mom?"

I actually hadn't even considered the full import of what I was saying before I spoke, and immediately I wanted to kick myself—assuming, of course, that I could've gotten my foot out of my mouth.

But just when I was expecting Gretchen to rip me in two, her expression cracked ever so slightly and I caught a glimpse, however fleeting, of the little girl beneath the It Girl. She looked away and wrinkled her nose. I wondered then, that cocooned as she was by her ass-kissing friends, if anyone ever had the nerve to point things out to her as they really were.

As if wary of revealing too much, she pulled the rubber band from her ponytail and flipped her hair behind her shoulders. "Just get used to it, Kate," she breathed. "The sooner you do, the better off you'll be."

I wanted to contradict her, to tell her that I knew, in fact, that it didn't have to be that way. Don't ask me why I was suddenly on a mission to save Gretchen Tanner; I was probably the one who needed saving, after all. But before I could say anything, Gretchen's cell rang. In an instant, her all-knowing smile returned, and she flipped open her phone.

"Hey, Pip!" she gushed. Then she mouthed to me: "It's Will."

I felt my jaw clench. Was "Pip" her pet name for him?

"You don't mind if I take this, right?" she asked as she covered the mouthpiece.

I shook my head, and Gretchen retreated into her bedroom, leaving me alone on the balcony. It's no news flash to report that it made me crazy that Will was calling Gretchen, but my rational side, which I'll fully acknowledge was waging an uphill battle, kept reminding me there was nothing strange about Will talking with Gretchen. They were good friends, had been long before I ever entered the picture, so what was my issue?

Well, I'll tell you exactly what my issue was.

It was Gretchen laughing a little too loudly at everything Will said. It was Gretchen calling him "hon" every third sentence. It was Gretchen telling him that she'd "swing by his house later" when she was "alone" so they could "chitty-chat." I was pretty sure she was playing it all up for my sake—I was no dummy—but regardless, jealousy constricted my body, and I grabbed my jeans from the balustrade and slipped them over my bathing suit. If I was about to wage war, I'd also better be ready to flee.

A few seconds later, Gretchen said 'bye to Will and although fuming, I forced a smile. "How's Will?"

"Just Will being Will," she answered, and tossed her cell on the lounge. "He's so sweet, though."

"It's true." I nodded as I started lining up my shot.

I knew I was playing with fire, but I just couldn't help myself.

After a carefully calculated few seconds, I inhaled sharply and allowed my mouth to fall open ever so slightly. "Omigod, I totally meant to tell you. The strangest thing happened the other night."

"What?"

"Will came over to my house—really late. And he asked me if I'd go to the Black & White with him."

"What are you talking about? You're both sitting at my table."

"I know, but he said he wanted to go together. You know"—I paused here for effect—"he wants to go as a couple."

Now, Einstein tells us that the passage of time is relative to the observer, and I swear in that moment, it was as if time stood still. Gretchen was frozen, immobile, not flinching, not even blinking as she processed the news. I don't know how long we both remained like that, eye to eye, but it felt like an eternity.

"Good for you," she cooed. "That's *sooooo* great."

"I know you warned me about him," I continued. "But I figured it's just one night. What's the harm, right?"

Gretchen picked up a brownie and took a bite. "Totally. But you're still going to hang with me and the girls, right?"

"Duh." I smiled and put my hand on her shoulder. "You're my girl."

"Remember it," she answered, and looked out at her pool thoughtfully. "I'm just going to get changed and then we need to finish planning things. Okay?"

I nodded, and Gretchen grabbed her towel and left. Standing alone on the balcony, I suddenly worried if it had been a mistake to tell Gretchen. Well, I would've had to at some point anyway. She was going to see me there with Will, so it wasn't going to stay a secret forever.

No, I was right to have done what I did. Gretchen and I may have been becoming "friends," but she needed to know who she was dealing with. Slipping my T-shirt back on, I took one last look at the now-setting sun, and walked back into Gretchen's darkening room.

KCW LLC.

MARKET RANKING: 4

TODAY'S CHANGE: ⬆1

SHARE PRICE: $35.06

CHANGE: ⬆4.06 (+12%)

L/B RATIO: 10.2

3-MONTH RANGE: $1.23–$35.18

STATUS: BLUE CHIP

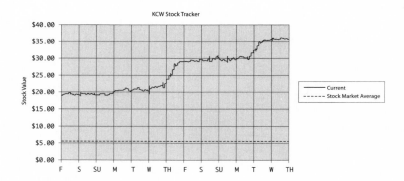

KCW Stock Tracker

ANALYST RECOMMENDATION: The only question that needs answering is how long it will be until this performer is #1.

DEFINITE BUY

CHAPTER

25

THE NEXT THIRTY-SIX hours passed in a blur of preparations for the Black & White. Having my hair blown out at Images, a manicure from Nailtiques downtown, even a facial in New York at this spa, Cornelia—I was on a whirlwind beauty tour, this time courtesy of my mother. Mom was so fired up about the Black & White that she even wrote me a note so I could get out of school early on Friday, and we drove into the city (a *second* time) to check out a dress by Michael Kors. Apparently, the one we'd already picked out from Nordstrom wasn't good enough. The latest dress was a stunning white number, which is the color all the women wore, that Mom discovered online. Tiered with a lace border, it did a lot for my body, but when I looked at the price tag, I thought I was going to have a heart attack. True to character, Mom was adamant that her daughter look her best for what basically amounted to my coming out, and with a confident nod, she calmly reached into her purse and plunked down her credit card next to the cash register.

When I wasn't transforming myself into a mannequin for the Black & White, I was planning the big graduation party with Gretchen. To be honest, she was doing most of the planning—I performed more of a "yes, ma'am" role—but kids at school kept coming up to me asking if they should bring anything and whether Gretchen and I were going to let juniors or kids from any other schools come. Word had traveled far and wide. While I enjoyed all the attention, it also wasn't lost on me that up until four weeks ago, I'd had barely a passing acquaintance with ninety-nine percent of these people. My true friends, or at least those who had been so before the Market began, had said nothing about the party. I'd sent e-mails and texts, and left voice mails for Dev, but she'd never replied. I prayed that when the three of us sat down on Saturday, we'd be able to set everything right. If I could just look her in the eye, and she could see how sincere my intentions were and also how honest my apology was, she'd forgive me.

Through it all, there was the Market. I was constantly checking it, poring over the analyst's recommendations, obsessed with my ranking, and even when I had no access to a computer, Gretchen would gleefully call me with updates.

Hour by hour my stock value kept climbing, ultimately passing Carrie and Elisa. By now, these incremental steps barely registered, determined as I was to make it to the top, and when I logged on to the Market Friday night and discovered I was now ranked Number Two—with only Gretchen above me—I didn't even bat an eye.

I awoke Saturday to a spring morning. My room was filled with crisp cool air, and bright light filtered in through my shades.

"I'm going to the Black & White with Will," I heard myself say. It was a veritable fairy tale end to my high school career.

I was still in a sleepy daze, but I soon recognized my mother's voice calling my name.

"Kate! Callie's on the phone!"

I looked over at my clock, and in an instant, I realized that I'd overslept. I was supposed to meet Dev and Callie at the Cozy Corner at 9:00 a.m. for the dreaded powwow. It was already 9:30 a.m.

Sh—!

"Tell her I already left," I shouted. I threw on some old sweats, splashed some water on my face, and grabbed my keys and ran downstairs. I could see my mom was still talking to her on the phone, so I tiptoed by and zipped out to my car.

By the time I got into town and had parked, it was nearly ten. As I hurried down the sidewalk, through the plate glass window I could see Dev and Callie holding court in our corner booth, and neither looked too happy.

"Hey," I said as I slipped into the booth. "Sorry I got a late start. My alarm never went off."

That much was true.

"Right," Callie said. "We ordered you coffee and toast."

"Thanks."

Callie took a sip of her coffee, but her eyes never left me. Dev, on the other hand, wouldn't even look my way, and her stare remained glued to her hands that were folded in her lap.

"So," I opened, as I shredded the corner of my napkin.

Callie glanced over at Dev for support. "We're concerned about you."

"Concerned?" I frowned. "Why?"

Dev sighed and looked up. "I think this experiment—this quest to beat the Market—has gone to your head."

I took a deep breath to collect myself.

"Look, I understand that you felt blindsided by what happened with Gretchen. And I apologize for that. I really hope you can forgive me. It wasn't cool."

"That's one way of putting it."

"Dev," I said as I touched her hand. "I'm really *sorry*. Honestly."

If I was hoping that she'd smile, and we'd have a make-up laugh about it, nothing of the sort was forthcoming.

"I hate to say it, but you've gotten so wrapped up in the Market, that you can't see what's going on," Dev finally said. "You're in too deep."

The tone of this conversation was less like reconciliation, and more like confrontation. I felt myself mentally backpedaling in confusion. My toast and coffee arrived, and there was a welcome pause in the conversation.

"I got in too deep?" I asked as delicately as I could. "Dev, whose idea was the experiment in the first place? Who was the person who thought we could beat the system? Who pulled me out of class and pretended my grandfather died? Who e-mailed my rising and falling numbers almost hourly until I became so neurotic about it I couldn't sleep at night?"

"Is that true?" Callie asked, looking at Dev in disgust. "I knew this thing would make you two crazy."

"Okay, I got a little excited," Dev said, waving me off. "But we're getting off topic here."

"Fine," I snorted as I started to become frustrated. "What is the topic exactly?"

Dev put her face in her hands, and Callie looked out at the street nervously.

"It's about the TKWP portfolio," Dev began.

So here it was. Dev was finally going to admit that she

was the one behind it from the very beginning. Well, it was better that we get everything out on the table.

"TKWP, you see . . ." Dev hesitated. "It think it's Gretchen and Will."

I laughed.

"Kate, really. Dev explained it to me last night. It sounds legit," Callie seconded.

Dev leaned forward. "They've been using you the whole time."

I read in AP Bio once that when the human body switches into fight-or-flight mode, there's a literal narrowing of the field of vision, almost as if you're looking through a tube. Well, that's how I felt right then, and I was totally targeted in on Dev; and I was in fight mode.

"You've got to be kidding—"

"Kate, it's true!" Dev said.

"No, it isn't!" I fired back as rage, like a snake, spiraled up inside me. All my goodwill disintegrated in an instant. "You're just jealous that I'm going to the Black & White with Will. You wish you were me. Why can't you be happy instead of trying to tear me down?"

"Because it's all a front!" Dev shouted.

"Will's in love with me!"

Dev grew quiet for a moment and looked down at the table. "No, he isn't."

There aren't words to express the fury I was feeling. Just

because I'd moved past Dev, here she was trying to tear me down. Yes, that's exactly what it was.

"Let's all try to be cool here," Callie calmed us. "Just think, Kate. Their portfolio has gone up equally with ours."

"Do you think that it's an accident that you ended up at Gretchen's party?" Dev asked, still hot. "That Will asked you out? That Gretchen's suddenly your new best friend? They've been playing you."

"No, it's no accident. It's because people finally saw the real me."

"What they saw was the perfect mark, or in this case, the perfect stock," Dev fired back. "You were beautiful but untapped, hidden from the world of Millbank High. At Seventy-one your value was well below what it should've been. That's totally true. But you were just a racehorse to them—a long shot that had good odds of coming in."

Doubt crept into my mind for the first time, but I pushed it away.

"Let me tell you what I think," I spat. "Maybe *you're* TKWP."

Dev looked like somebody had hit her with a baseball bat. Next to her, Callie put her face in her hands.

"Why else would you have been so obsessed with my popularity?" I continued. "Goading me on like a lunatic. Maybe—"

"Are you serious?!" Dev said. "You've gone off your friggin' rocker! TKWP—think about it! The Kate Winthrop Project!"

Suddenly, it all seemed too real. I fell silent.

Across from me, Dev's face went blotchy, and tears began to form in the corners of her big brown eyes. "You're an idiot, Kate," she whispered as her lips quivered. "Do you know what it's like to be me? Five feet two with a squat ass and a plain face? Do you?"

I couldn't say anything. My mouth was frozen and my head spun wildly with emotion—both enraged at what she'd said and saddened to see her so upset.

"You were always one step from beautiful, from having it all," Dev explained. "I'm miles away, and for a couple of weeks I wanted to be you, to be climbing the ladder with you, I suppose. And this is what I get."

Dev burst into tears before Callie put an arm around her and gave her a hug as she sobbed.

Guilt. Well, that's a word that doesn't quite describe the hollow feeling that was in my gut. If I could take back the last fifteen minutes, I would have given everything up, even Will and the Black & White. Everything.

Confusion swept through me, and suddenly the only thing I did know for certain was that I had to get out of there. Without another word, I got up, threw five dollars on the table, and walked right out of the restaurant. Tears now began to pour from my eyes, and as I got to my car, I couldn't catch my breath.

Could it be?

The Gretchen stuff—well, that much seemed plausible. I'd had my suspicions about her right from the beginning. And hadn't she done her paper on Michael Milken? But Will? Had everything we'd done together—every word he'd whispered in my ear, every caress of his hand—been a total lie? It was unfathomable, but if true, the single cruelest thing ever done to me. I sat there for a half hour, unable to drive, unable to move, feeling nothing but nausea rising in my throat. In nine hours I was supposed to be on the arm of Will, waltzing into the Black & White with my new friends. Tonight had had the promise of being everything I had ever imagined high school could be, and now it was becoming everything that high school actually was: heart-breaking and cruel.

I looked up from my car window and saw Callie, like the bighearted mother she was, walking Dev out of the Cozy Corner. Her arm was around Dev, who was still sobbing, and she was saying something to her. As they disappeared around the corner, I knew I was truly alone, and I under-stood then that sitting on top of the world just meant you were all by yourself.

CHAPTER

26

IT WAS SEVEN O'CLOCK and I was sitting on my bed, staring at my white dress hanging beneath its clear plastic sheeting. Mom had knocked no less than five times in the last hour to see if I needed any help, but with my door locked I was hidden from everyone, desperately trying to figure out what to do.

The intervening hours since the big scene with the girls had done nothing to soothe my aching heart and tortured mind. With dark suspicion planted, right when I should've been in some state of breathless anticipation for the big night ahead, I was instead looking backward, replaying everything that had happened to me, starting at Gretchen's party. And much as I didn't want to believe any of it, when I really broke down every step that Gretchen took, it began to become more and more clear that reasonable doubt was not in her favor. The episodes flashed through my mind like a prosecutor's slide show before a jury: the invitation to her party where she first mentioned the Market, the late-night IM taunting me to look at the Web site, the number scrawled on my locker, inviting me to hang with her and the girls, planning the big end-of-the-year party together—Gretchen had crafted it all meticulously. Worse, I'd allowed myself to be hypnotized into believing it was all real.

The question that still loomed was why? For money? Gretchen was totally loaded; she didn't need to win the game. For pride? To show that she was the ultimate social manipulator?

But the biggest question I couldn't answer for myself—and undoubtedly the most important—was Will himself. Let's say he was involved, let's say he'd been in on it with Gretchen from the beginning. I guess I could make sense of all the moves he'd made except one: the night he came to my house and asked me to the Black & White. If he weren't truly in love with me, why would he bother? I clung to that night as evidence of his love for me. Otherwise I was lost.

I walked toward my closet, tossed the white dress aside, and took out a black one that Callie had loaned me ages ago. Silk with spaghetti straps and a plunging back that dropped just to the tip of my tailbone, it was just the dress for the evening. If I were going, then I was going to make a statement, and not wearing white was the only way I could think of reclaiming a little bit of myself. I didn't know how I was going to do it exactly, but I had to find out for sure if Will was really behind the portfolio. Obviously, I couldn't come straight out and ask him, because if he wasn't involved, I'd look like the fool. But if he was, I wanted to look him in the eyes when he confessed.

Come 7:30 p.m. when the doorbell rang announcing Will's arrival, I was dressed head to toe in black. The two exceptions were my mother's beautiful string of pearls and the little silver "P" Gretchen had given me. I knew my mom would go crazy when she saw me not wearing white, but I was banking on the fact that she wouldn't say anything once Will was there.

I opened the door to my room and slowly walked across the hallway and stopped at the stairwell. I could hear my mother talking to Will in that way mothers talk to their daughter's boyfriends—somewhere between flirty and complimentary—and I walked down the stairs as quietly as I could. I didn't capture their attention until I hit the landing, when Will's eyes lit up and gave me that up-and-down that all boys give girls. Shock at the black was quickly followed by an approving grin, and it was clear that he liked what he was seeing.

But when my mother turned and gave me the up-and-down, unlike Will, she was less than pleased.

"Kate," she snapped. "In the kitchen for a second, please."

I looked at Will and then back at my mom. My dad was standing behind her, totally oblivious to what was going on.

"Mom, we're late."

She shot me an icy stare, and I felt the hairs on the back of my neck tingle.

"It'll just take a second."

I really couldn't get around it, so I relented and followed her to the kitchen, but I wasn't going to fold, either. My entire identity had been destroyed earlier in the day, and this mild protest was all I had left of my self-esteem. I wasn't going to let my mother take it away.

"You can't wear that," she fumed once we were out of earshot. "You have to wear white."

"Says who? That dumb club?"

I thought her eyeballs were going to pop out of her head.

"You're going to go change—right now! We spent a lot of money on that white dress."

"I know. So now you can return it."

Her fists clenched at her side. "It's the tradition, Kate—what will Gretchen say?"

"I don't care what Gretchen or you or anybody else says!"

"Why do you always have to make things difficult?" my mother shot back.

"Difficult—you mean difficult for you, right?"

"I'm not the one going to the ball."

"No. You're just worried about getting in this stupid club that no one else wants to be part of. Not me. Not Dad. It's all about you and your stupid insecurities!"

"That's enough!" she shouted, and in a flash, her hand flew up and slapped me across the face. She had never hit me before. Tears formed in my eyes, but I willed myself not to give her the satisfaction. Not that she got any. I could see her eyes go from angry to sad in about a millisecond, and she stepped back, not quite comprehending what she had just done.

Without a word, I turned and pushed through the swinging kitchen door and went straight for the foyer. When I reached the front door, I snatched my purse from the table and pushed by Will. Behind me, I heard him offer polite good-byes to my parents before following me like a puppy dog to the car.

When he got in, he looked over at me. "You cool?"

"Let's go."

I sat in silence the entire drive to the dance. Will tried a few questions at first, but when he got no response, not even eye contact, he barreled ahead, the Spitfire growling beneath us.

At a red light, where Forest Avenue crosses Piedmont, he pulled to a stop, and for a few moments there was relative calm. Around us I could hear crickets sawing away in the trees. Turning in his seat, Will reached over and touched my welted cheek with the outside of his hand. I didn't respond—didn't smile, didn't recoil—but inside, the pieces of my heart were shattering a little bit more. I wanted to believe that he loved me or was at least falling in love with me, but every gesture, no matter how tender, was met with the continuing echo of Dev's words: *he's using you*.

The light turned green, and his hand dropped to the gearshift. For a split second there was the gunning of the engine before we lurched forward, my back pressed into the seat.

We pulled in front of the club and were met by an army of valets, who scooped us from our car and set us on the black-and-white carpet. It felt like we were walking into the Academy Awards. Flashes popped, photographers shouted, and guests greeted each other with air kisses as a parade of beauty and wealth glided down the carpet toward the entrance of the club. My black dress raised eyebrows on a few of the old biddies, but I shook it off and held my head high.

Peppered among the crowd—heads constantly rotating, nervously sizing up other people's outfits—were a handful of my mom's friends. Even though they were all members of the club, I couldn't help but notice how they were com-paring themselves to other people—the clothing they were wearing, the jewelry that dangled from their wrists and necks. I realized then that my mom and I weren't really that different. We were both chasing popularity, that elusive circle of status that doesn't really exist. It's always one circle away, unattainable. It struck me that there's only a two-letter difference between "exclusive" and "elusive." I shuddered for a moment with guilt, realizing that I had made accusations at Mom that I should have been leveling at myself.

The ballroom, cavernous and barren when Will had given me the tour of the club, now overflowed with guests. Tables of hors d'oeuvres with ice-sculpture centerpieces flanked the dance floor, and tuxedo-clad waiters, balancing silver trays of champagne, wine, and daiquiris, skated through the crowd. On a stage, a twenty-piece band cranked out an odd assortment of songs, and while no one had ventured as yet to dance, guests young and old swayed to the rhythm among the safety of tables. The whole scene had an otherworldly quality to it, like we'd just entered a time warp, and I thought to myself that this was no different than a ball at Versailles in the eighteenth century, a reception at the Taj Mahal in the seventeenth, or no doubt what was happening tonight in some club in Kansas or Oregon. The history of man was one long repetition.

As Will and I wove our way through the revelers, I spotted Jack on the other side of the room. Impeccably dressed, he leaned against the wall, chatting amiably with a bevy of girls. For a split second, our eyes met—I'm sure of it—but he showed no trace of a reaction and continued on with his conversation.

At last, Will and I arrived at our table. Gretchen, her girls, and the elite of the Proud Crowd were already there, laughing and enjoying the scene. My black dress caught the eye of every girl, but I nodded to everyone and silently took my seat.

It was Gretchen who finally acknowledged what they were all thinking.

"Didn't Will tell you, Kat?" Gretchen grinned. "The ladies wear white."

I didn't respond. I gave her a calm stare, one I suspect an assassin develops over a career. It was pure indifference and I could tell it bothered her.

"What's wrong?" she said. "I was just teasing you."

My face remained flat. I looked into her eyes for a moment, but with a deadness that disarmed her even more.

I turned to Will.

"I feel like dancing," I announced. He looked around, a little surprised. The dance floor was entirely empty, and the band was playing a very slow instrumental, but I stood up and grabbed his hand, leading him to the dance floor. As we crossed the parquet, I could feel eyes on my bare back, my blond hair coiffed to perfection; but my pulse didn't flicker. I felt cold as ice.

I pulled Will close to me, and we rocked back and forth together. As we spun there on the wood floor, the chandelier glowing softly above, I noticed that most of the room was watching us. I suppose on the surface we looked like the perfect couple. Men nodded. Women smiled. The little girl inside me who'd always dreamed of a fantastical night like this wanted everything to be right, everything to be a storybook ending; but my now-tired soul told me that it was going to be something far different. Something within me kept whispering the truth, and by now it seemed unavoidable. I suppose Will must've known that something was up, because for all his cool, I could feel his hands trembling and his heart pounding. I pulled him to me as tight as two humans could be on a dance floor.

As we turned, I looked up and caught Gretchen's eyes following us. She was as furious as I've ever seen her. It was then that I started nibbling on his ear, in a cute sexy way, and Gretchen averted her gaze, the veins in her forehead showing.

I whispered in his ear, "Gretchen's watching us."

His back tightened.

"Ignore her."

"I will, if you can."

He stopped dancing and pulled away from me just enough to look me in the eyes. There was sadness there, and he fumbled over some words before he was able to put together something coherent.

"What are you doing?" he asked.

"Just making sure I'm not upsetting anything between the two of you."

"We're done, Gretchen and I. I've told you that before."

"But you're a team?" I said.

He looked at me funny. And then a glimmer of recognition lit his eyes.

"What do you mean, team?"

"I think you know what I mean, Will."

"No I don't—what'd she say?"

"Nothing, she said nothing. It was you, remember? I was the girl you couldn't see. But you really could see me— I was Number Seventy-one and a perfect mark for the little game you and Gretchen were playing. TKWP—The Kate Winthrop Project—how clever. Did you come up with that name yourself or do you just take credit for it, like Jack's songs?"

His face froze. He tried to speak but nothing came out. His eyes looked all around, but couldn't hold mine.

If there had been a drop of hope that this all might end right, it evaporated.

"You don't understand," he said. "I really fell for you. I think I love you."

My right hand came up like a flash, and it smacked against his face harder than I expected, and the Black & White suddenly became the quiet and stupefied. It was like all the oxygen in the room had been sucked right out. Hands went to mouths, and then mouths went to ears, and the place buzzed.

I turned and walked toward the table to get my purse.

"Kate!" Will called, but I didn't stop.

Gretchen stood up and blocked the walkway between the two tables.

"What the hell are you doing?"

"Drop the bullshit, Gretchen. I know about TKWP."

Unfazed as ever, she smirked and shot a look over at her friends. "This is a good lesson, guys. If something's cheap—there's always a reason."

I looked at her and then at the table of her sycophants. It made me sick to think that I had spent even one night with them. Just then a waiter walked by with a tray of virgin strawberry daiquiris—thick and red and icy. I reached over and grabbed one off the tray.

"Tasty," I observed after taking the tiniest of sips. "Why don't you try some."

And in one fluid motion, I tossed the contents of the entire glass on the front of her pure white dress. All of her friends screamed before she could. Like someone who'd just been shot—by a very big gun, mind you—she stared down at the front of her dress, soaked bloodred, completely slack jawed and speechless.

My hands shaking, I plunked the glass down on the

table, grabbed my clutch, and ran out of the room. Careening down the black-and-white carpet, there were no pictures being taken of me this time, and as I reached the front door of the club, a hand grabbed my arm. I turned with a balled-up fist, thinking it was either Gretchen or one of her friends . . . but it was Will.

"Wait."

Tears were swamping his eyes, and his face was contorted in pain.

"Wait," he repeated.

"For you? I'd rather die."

I tore my arm free and raced out into the pitch-black night.

Ten minutes later, I stumbled along the shoulder of the road, black mascara-laden tears running down my cheeks and my broken heels in my hands. A thin drizzle spitted down from the sky, and every now and then a car would pass, tires shushing on the wet pavement. In between sobs, I cursed Will and Gretchen and the day I met them both, and wondered how I'd ever allowed myself to fall for their deception.

Illuminated by the headlights of a car approaching from behind, my dark shadow stretched out far ahead of me, and I veered to the right, away from the road. As the car neared, however, the sound of the engine quieted, and as it pulled alongside me, it drew to a stop. The driver beeped his horn.

Nervously, I glanced over. The windows were tinted and I didn't recognize the car, so instead of trying to figure out who it was—one of Gretchen's girls? some freak?—I picked up my pace. The car glided forward and pulled up beside me again. Against my better judgment, which was telling me to run, my emotions got the better of me, and I turned toward the driver and screamed.

"What do you want?!"

There was no response, but a beat later the window lowered and my fear-cum-anger melted.

It was Jack.

"Get in," he said simply.

Embarrassed, horrified, wrong—none of it mattered anymore, and after glancing down the pitch-black road, I opened the door and dropped into the passenger seat. I closed the door, which shut with a reassuring *clump*, and put my face in my hands. We didn't say anything to each other the whole way back to my house. He drove silently; I continued to cry. When we reached my driveway, I wiped my tears away and found Jack looking at me, concern in his eyes.

"Did you know?" I asked.

"About the Market?" He nodded. "But about them?" He shook his head.

I looked down.

"I'm sorry," he said.

I nodded, and after a barely audible "Thank you," my throat choked with emotion, and I staggered into my house.

BOOK SIX
· · · · · · ·

DIVIDENDS

CHAPTER

27

I DIDN'T GET UP for nearly an entire day. Not the phone ringing, not my mother's vacuuming, not my heart's rending could rouse me. When the sun had come and gone, and the darkness of night returned, I finally staggered out of bed. When I bumped into my desk as I made my way to the bathroom, my computer woke from sleep mode and the Market flashed up on the screen. For a split second, I considered looking at my ranking, just to see how far I'd fallen, but an instant later I yanked the cord from the outlet, and the monitor went black.

First things first (as my mom is fond of saying)—if I wanted to get back on the right path, I needed to make up with Dev. Despite everything that had happened at the club and everything that was surely to happen Monday morning at school, courtesy of the Proud Crowd and their JV minions, what I cared most about repairing was my friendship with Dev. We had both taken a turn toward the dark side, seduced by the siren call of popularity. We wanted to be remembered for being more than just average, and now we would both always remember, perhaps more than anything else, how we destroyed our senior spring and possibly our friendship. We were both guilty, I knew that much, but I also knew that we had both been driven blind by the Market.

I snuck downstairs, trying not to stir my parents. I could hear the late Sunday football game in the living room and Dad's snoring. A perfect cover for a late-night departure. I tiptoed into the family room and then through the mudroom door, and slipped out into the night. It was nearly summer, but the air still had a cool bite, and I took a big gulp of air and felt my lungs expand. With each breath I took, a bit of hope filled me, and like a newborn free from its mother for the first time, I couldn't take in enough oxygen. A torrent of emotion welled up inside, but I pushed it down.

I'm not going to cry anymore, I told myself.

When I pulled on the door handle of my car, I discovered it was locked, so I reached into my purse and fished around for my keys. That's when I heard the front door open and saw my mom step outside. I searched her face to see what emotion it held—anger, sorrow, disappointment—but the porch light created a halo around her head and obscured her expression. I turned and faced her head-on. I was ready to tell her everything. To tell her how her daughter had sunk to new lows just to be popular. How her daughter had really just mimicked her mother's own desires to be "in the club."

"Need these?" she said, dangling the keys.

I could see her eyes now. They were sad and the moon shadow made them only sadder.

"I do."

"I heard about what happened last night. All of it."

Yeah. I wager the whole town had.

I said nothing, awaiting my certain death sentence. Would it be by firing squad or lethal injection?

"How did you get home?" she asked.

Not the next question I was expecting.

"I walked, part of the way. Jack Clayton from the bookstore drove me the rest of the way."

"Mrs. Sawyer called me last night," she said simply. "She told me . . . what you've been going through. I didn't realize."

"I was a fool."

She didn't say anything. She just walked up to me and put her arms around me and let me have a long hug. My chest heaved a few times, but I didn't let a tear fall. I could hear her sniffle, and her voice kept catching as she tried to speak. Even in the thick swirl of emotion, I knew I'd never forget this moment. I gripped her hard for another few seconds and then released.

"Sorry," I said. The word tumbled from my lips unexpectedly, without an ounce of reluctance. For years, since middle school, perhaps, we had been sparring with each other over every inch of territory. But tonight we each ceded some ground for what I knew would be a new friendship. It felt good, natural, like it was something that had always been on the horizon but we were just unable to see it.

"Me, too," she said.

"About the club, I'm sorry. I guess I really screwed it up for you."

She played with my hair and shook her head.

"I wouldn't want to be somewhere with people who'd treat my daughter like that." After a moment, she laughed a little. "Besides, I think your dad is happy."

She handed me the keys, and I smiled. "I guess so."

"Let me know how late you'll be, so I don't worry?"

I nodded.

That much I could certainly do.

I took the long way over to Dev's house. I needed time to sort out what I was going to say to her. Somehow, the simple "sorry" my mom and I had made up with a few minutes earlier wouldn't be nearly enough. I thought about telling her why we should never have started with the Market, of explaining how her obsession with my popularity drove me bananas, of asking her how long she knew Gretchen and Will had been conspiring against me, but I knew she'd have her own tale to tell. How I had forgotten our pact to expose and takedown the Market, how I had forgotten about her and Callie in my quest to become popular and be part of the Proud Crowd, and it would all be true, sadly. We were guilty of abusing our friendship, and I wasn't sure how to get it back.

I pulled up to the curb in front of her house and watched as a young family arrived home across the street, the father hoisting his little girl up onto his shoulders. I sat in my car for a few minutes and thought about being a child and that innocent period when you're unaware of anything outside of your own little world. Not wealth, not boys, not popularity.

After a few moments, I pulled out my phone and hit Dev's number on my speed dial. She picked up on the third ring.

"Yeah," she said. Her voice had a coldness I had never encountered before, and it struck me that it was pretty much how hate sounded.

"Come down. I'm out front."

There was a click and the line went dead. She drew the curtains back in her room, a triangle of light framing her small form, and then she let them go. For a few moments I worried she might not come, but then her front porch light went off and the door opened. I guess she didn't want her parents to see us.

When she got in the car—the hood on her gray sweatshirt pulled up—she stared out the windshield, refusing to look at me. I did the same, unwilling to yield the high ground. If I did, I knew we'd never be friends again. We needed to understand that what happened was a team effort, that we had brought this plight upon ourselves.

"What do your parents know?" I asked.

"Nothing," she said. "Except what your mom told my mom. They spoke last night."

"Good, that's good," I said. "So I guess you know what happened last night?"

A little grin caught her by surprise, but she quickly suppressed it.

"I'm sorry, Dev."

"Me too," she said. "But I can't even look at you right now. I can't think about you."

"We let ourselves get carried away. It wasn't me or you talking yesterday. Whoever we were disappeared a few weeks ago."

She nodded, and tears filled her eyes and then poured down her cheeks. I held mine in place, though inside I was drowning.

"I don't trust you anymore," she said, and I felt myself pull back in surprise. "I could never trust you again."

"Why? Because I took our dream too far? And you didn't?"

"You bit the apple . . ."

I was trying to process what she was saying. It was true, I suppose; I had tasted the popular life, and truth be told, I didn't want to go back. I couldn't, I guess. No matter what happened tomorrow at school—and total social pariah was the most likely outcome—I'd never go back to being the old Katie Winthrop. That was the price I'd pay for flying too high.

But did that mean we couldn't be friends anymore?

"You're being dramatic, Dev. It's not like I passed through a door that can't be opened again."

"It is, actually," she said. Her voice was tiny, mouselike. "It is. You made me feel unworthy of you. Your eyes, these past few weeks, told me I wasn't good enough. I can't look at you now and think that isn't what you still believe."

"C'mon, Dev."

Without a word, Dev opened the door and stepped out. She shut the door quietly, as if she were being careful not to break something, and shuffled her way back toward her house. On her front steps, she glanced over at me one last time; but just when I thought she might say something, she shook her head and disappeared into her house, and the lights in the foyer clicked off.

CHAPTER

28

THE MONDAY FOLLOWING the Black & White fiasco was supposed to be the beginning of the most fun and memorable week of any we had had as a class. Senior Week at Millbank High was a euphemism for doing absolutely nothing. Sure, it was anything but a party for the juniors, who were taking finals and desperately hoping to improve their GPAs before applying to colleges that fall, but for the seniors, the week translated to day after day of no classes, no worries, and a whole lot of letting loose, both in and out of school.

That morning, however, I was surely the only senior at MHS who was dreading the week. As I drove up North Adams toward my parking spot for the last year, I braced myself for what lay ahead, and it definitely wasn't going to be pretty. Slyly working your way up the Market was one thing. Leading a crazy one-person public attack on the most popular girl in school . . . well, that was something else all together.

The festivities began as soon as I set foot in school. Walking down the hallway toward my locker, I could feel people looking at me askance—suspicious, smirking—and behind me as I passed, I could hear whispers and giggles. Like some death-row inmate taking that final trip toward the chair, with all her fellow prisoners eyeing her as she passed, I walked, eyes focused on the floor, hoping just to make it to my locker without breaking down. *Dead girl walking.*

When I got to my locker, I got my first taste of what was sure to come. The door had been keyed. *140* had been permanently etched into the cheap green paint.

I knew what it meant, of course, but a month ago, when I agonized about being labeled Seventy-one, I had completely ignored the fact that there was a Seventy-two, and Seventy-three, and worse, a One hundred forty. How was it that I could agonize so deeply about my own plight, but fail to imagine the utter pain of being One hundred forty? But then here was a stranger thing—I couldn't even remember who One hundred forty was. Wasn't that the ultimate irony of the Market? It was a ranking of everyone, but all we (or maybe I) thought of was ourselves.

I opened my locker to find ten or twelve invitations for Heaven laying haphazardly on the bottom. People had slid them through the small vents on the top of my locker. I opened the top one and written in red lipstick were the words, "Die Bitch."

Look, ma, I'm on top of the world.

I picked the others off the floor and stuffed them into my book bag. There was no point in reading them—I was sure they all said the same thing. I closed my locker, leaned on the cold metal, and took a deep breath. I knew the moment I sat down in my homeroom seat, the real chaos would begin. Now that I was no longer a moving target, someone was bound to get the courage to actually ask me what happened Saturday night, and I really didn't know what I was going to say—I mean, I couldn't tell them the truth, about the Market, about Gretchen and Will, about how messed up the world of MHS had become, about how crazed I myself had become in effort to be considered "good enough" for some invisible group of tastemakers, about—

"Ms. Winthrop?" said a deep voice from behind me. I turned and looked up into the eyes of Francis Johnson, the principal of MHS.

"Yes?"

"Come with me."

We walked toward his office in what felt like superslow motion. If all eyes were on me before, it's hard to describe the heaviness of the attention I was now receiving. Teachers, administrators, rent-a-cops, students from every class—they all watched as Principal Johnson escorted me down the hall.

When we reached the waiting room outside his office, he turned.

"Sit. Wait. Don't speak until I come for you."

I gulped and nodded. There were two couches, and one was filled with boxes and files. I felt rattled and I looked down at my hands; they were shaking like I'd had twenty espressos at Starbucks before coming to school. I clasped them together in an effort to look cool under pressure. Never having been to the principal's office in my entire career, except to pick up the certificate for being a National Merit Scholar—ah, how far I'd fallen—I was scared to death. Was he going to call my parents? Would he suspend me from graduation?

I could feel my heart racing and my ears ringing from the rise in my blood pressure. Then Vice Principal Taylor, as if on cue, delivered his version of a massive sedative: he marched Gretchen Tanner in and seated her right beside me. My heart screeched to a halt, and my nerves suddenly went steely. If Johnson was going to drag us both in, I wasn't going to hold back. I'd take her, her crew, and the damn Market down for good. Gretchen stared directly at the wall and made no sign of actually acknowledging that I was sitting next to her. As always, her skin was beautiful, but beneath the makeup, I could see dark rings under her eyes. She probably hadn't slept since Saturday.

"Ms. Winthrop," said Principal Johnson. "Come in."

I stood up and walked by Gretchen, and for the first time that morning, our eyes met in an intimate way. She was trying to say something, but what, I had no idea. A plea for mercy, perhaps? Well, as I walked into Principal Johnson's office, I didn't feel an ounce of guilt for what I was about to do. If I was going to get busted for what happened at the Black & White, then Gretchen was going down with me. I'd tell them everything.

It was the usual school executive's office—small book-shelf of teaching-and-administrative philosophy books, a few framed degrees, and a large oak-veneer desk cluttered with papers and family photos. Nothing fancy, but enough stuff to let you know he wasn't just a teacher. No doubt the politics of MHS on the teacher and administrator level suffered from its own version of "Us and Them."

Johnson sat heavily in a large, black leather swivel chair. He was a big man with dark-brown skin and a bushy black beard salted with white whiskers.

"Do you know why you're here?" he asked.

I did know why I was there, and though I'd never been in this kind of situation before, I knew enough from watching *Law & Order* not to give any information unless I was physically compelled to do so. I needed to see exactly what his agenda was.

"No," I answered innocently. "Not really."

"Do you think you can stonewall me, Ms. Winthrop?"

He was leaning over his desk now, and I could smell the stale coffee on his breath.

"Why don't you tell me why you and Gretchen had an altercation at the Black & White?"

"That's not a school event—why do you care?"

His eyes flared. He was sending a message via his mind: *Don't test me or I'll squash you.* How many times had a scared student come into these offices and been crushed under his power? He'd probably imagined that since I'd been such a Goody Two-shoes, I'd kowtow in a matter of seconds.

I guess he missed the memo that things had changed.

"There's more to this and we know it," he pushed.

"I'm not sure what you are talking about, sir."

He sat back and eyeballed me for a moment. Above us, the fluorescent lights hummed.

Spinning his chair around to a stack of files behind his desk, he picked up the lone red one from the pile. It had a white sticker on its tab section, and even from where I was sitting I could read the label: THE MARKET. He opened it up, pulled out a sheet of paper, and slid it across the desk so I could read it. It was a printout from the Market—the rankings as of May 24th.

They'd known about it all along?

"Why are you showing me this?"

"Surely you don't expect me to believe you've never seen this before?"

"No," I said. "I've seen it, but I had nothing to do with it."

What else was there to say, but the truth?

"Kate, I know how far you've come, so to speak."

How far I had come? Had he tracked my climb? Did he know that I went from Seventy-one to Blue Chip? Did he know about me and Dev? About my little fake tragedy? Did he know about Will and Gretchen and their plan to use me in their little stock scam? These questions, and many more, rocketed through my head, and I struggled to see where this was all leading.

"I'm not sure I follow," I said.

"We've been aware of the Market for a month or so now. We haven't closed it down for two reasons. First, it appears to have been accessible to only a very small group of students; and second, because we wanted to catch those who were behind it. I know, for whatever reason, you were somebody who caught the eye of the Market and became a success."

"Look, I don't know who was running the Market, and I don't know why they were interested in me."

He put his hands on his face and rubbed his eyes, and then he crossed them like a little boy might when about to begin prayer.

"Let's start over. We're fairly certain Gretchen Tanner was involved. It appears some group bet a lot of money on you, and your unlikely rise to the top certainly assured them of winning. So here's what I think: Gretchen, and whoever else, used you, Kate. You found out about it, and you took out your anger on Gretchen at the Black & White. Is that right?"

I sat still and didn't allow a single muscle to twitch. I didn't blink or scratch my wrist or rub my eyes. This was it—my chance to annihilate Gretchen, Will, and everyone else who'd wronged me in last few weeks.

"Care to elaborate?" He smiled. "We can make this all go away for you."

I won't lie: the words "used you" made my stomach twist in knots, and I wanted revenge. To rain destruction like hellfire down on that smug, confident little world that was inhabited by Gretchen Tanner and every other girl like her. And I was about to tell him everything I knew . . . the whole story from the very beginning . . . but something stopped me.

I thought of Mrs. Sawyer and how she questioned me the last time I'd seen her. And I kept coming back to my deepest feelings, which all revolved around one true fact: I'd wanted what they—what the Market—had to offer. If I'd been truly offended by the Market, even from the get-go, I would've walked away from the whole thing. Sure, I knew it was a kind of fantasy, that whatever the Market said was only one subjective view on "popularity," but it was a fantasy of which I wanted to be part. No one had forced me into it.

"There's no one to take down," I answered after a period of silence. "It's like the real world, Mr. Johnson. Nobody, not even Gretchen, creates popularity—it's just there. None of us knew who created the Market. We were just players, in one way or another."

Now it was his turn to be silent. He sat leaning back in his chair, the support creaking under his girth.

"The Market is dead—just leave it that way," I whispered. "We'd all be better off."

"I can't do that now. This was illegal gambling. Besides, your escapades on Saturday upset a lot of people, important people."

"Club people, you mean?" He didn't respond. "Are they your Proud Crowd, Mr. Johnson?"

"Watch it, young lady," he said. "This isn't going to die."

"No, you're right about that, but that's for next year's class to handle. For me, it died two days ago."

Just then his phone rang, and the secretary announced that the superintendent was on the line. Without excusing himself, he took the call, swiveling his chair around so he was staring out the window with his back was to me. He mumbled so softly that I couldn't make out what he was saying, but I knew it was about me and Gretchen.

A thought sprang into my mind, and I reached into my book bag and tore out a piece of paper. I quickly wrote the following note:

> Gretchen,
> I didn't say anything. Don't give yourself
> up no matter what he says to scare you.
> He knows nothing.
> K

Mr. Johnson hung up, and I quickly folded the note before he turned back to me.

"That was the superintendent. He's recommending suspension during Senior Week for you and Ms. Tanner. You'll be allowed to graduate, but will not be able to participate in any other activities planned by the school . . . unless you have something to share?"

It's called "hardball" because when it hits you, it hurts. I was mute for a moment, before choosing my course.

"I'll tell you what concerns *me*," I began.

He leaned forward with a pleased smile on his face.

"I'm concerned that you were aware of the Market and let it go on for so long. Some of us could have been deeply scarred over the past month. I think my parents would be concerned about that, too."

His eyes widened, and I could tell I had his attention. The words "law" and "suit" no doubt passed through his mind.

"I'm going to go now," I said as I rose. "As I said, I consider the Market a dead issue, and I couldn't care less about Senior Week and anything else related to this school. Call my parents if you want to. I suspect they will care—but in a way you wouldn't like."

I turned and walked out the door. I expected to hear him scream my name or for him to physically stop me, but my not-so-veiled threat must have left him tongue-tied.

From the couch, Gretchen looked up as I approached, and I could tell she had been crying.

"Hey," I said, and without missing a step, I thrust the note I'd written into her hand.

I had no idea if she was going to read it, but at that moment, I felt like I had finally found peace with everything that had happened.

Gretchen Tanner was not a good person, but she was part of the hundred and forty senior girls of Millbank just the same. Sure, I could've taken her down, but what good would that have done? I would have delivered some sad little comeuppance, courtesy of the principal's office, which in the end would just have been another example of a girl taking down a girl at the request of a man—albeit the principal. And wasn't that where all this began? When I allowed myself to be judged against another girl? Did I truly believe I was any better a person than Gretchen Tanner? In my heart, I wanted to believe I was; but knowing my sins, was I worthy of being her judge and jury? Had I grown up in her house, with her mother, her money, and her beauty, would I have come out any differently than she did?

I hoped I would've, but at that moment, after spending a month realizing how weak I could be, I wasn't sure. I just knew that I hadn't earned the right to sit in judgment of her, or anybody else.

CHAPTER

29

I WALKED OUT of MHS that day knowing I'd never again pass through those doors. Whatever fond memories I may have had prior to the Market had now disappeared like the Web site itself.

The next few days were a blur of depression. I left Dev several messages, hoping we could bring things back to normal, but I only got her voice mail and never a call back. Callie and I spoke once, but she was so busy with graduation (she was on the graduation committee—and needless to say, she wanted everyone, especially herself, to look just right), she didn't have time to see me.

The day before graduation, the only place I had to be was the BookStop. When I got there, I learned that Mrs. Sawyer, who was on vacation to see her sister in North

Carolina, had left a little graduation gift for me. No surprise here—it was a book. But she had taken the time to wrap it up and put a nice pink ribbon on it, and I took it to the back room so I could open it alone. I tore open the paper, and beneath I could see the worn cover of a used book: *The Wings of the Dove* by Henry James. I hadn't read any James, aside from the scrap excerpt here and there in class, and as I flipped through it I found a letter tucked inside the flap.

Dear Kate,

I'm so proud to know you. This is one of those stories James liked to write, about a girl named Millie, an American innocent. She falls prey to two Londoners who scheme to steal her fortune by wooing her heart. She teaches them something, though, about love and its power—for both good and bad. It is one of my favorites, and this is a first edition. Treasure it as I have treasured knowing you.

Always your friend,

B.

A tear came to my eye. I always knew that Mrs. Sawyer had had a soft spot for me, but I now realized how much I meant to her. I carefully turned the book over a few times and gently placed it in my bag. At least my relationship with Mrs. Sawyer had survived the Market. It was a small consolation, but the thought that I did have a true friend out there, somewhere, made me smile. She may have been fifty-eight years my elder, but she was my friend. And now, more than ever, I realized how dear true friends were, and how painful they were to lose.

Time flew by that day at the BookStop. With Mrs. Sawyer out, Howie ran the show. He was a little more hands-on and he liked to have all the books shelved at the end of each day, so there was never any downtime whatsoever, even between seven and nine p.m. when normally the store emptied out. At eight thirty p.m., I was manning the register and it looked like I might get out before closing, but then Hal Allen came in with four boxes of books to trade in for store credit. Normally, we ask people who are selling books to make an appointment, but Mr. Allen was an old friend of the store, and we did so much business with him (I think he worked in publishing) that Howie felt obligated.

As Howie reviewed each book, he placed them on different carts: one for the first floor (recently published fiction and nonfiction), one for the second (hardcover non-fiction), and one for the basement (paperbacks). I knew Howie wouldn't let me leave until all of Allen's new arrivals were shelved, so I grabbed the paperback cart as soon as Howie finished filling it up. I rode the freight elevator down and exited with the cart into the basement stacks. The first thing I did was alphabetize the books, which took a good fifteen minutes, and then I started to shelve. The cart was overloaded, so I knew I wouldn't be home until ten. Not that it mattered much—I had no friends and no plans.

At nine fifteen, Howie called down on the interoffice phone and said he was closing at nine thirty, to finish what I had on my cart, and he would handle the rest in the morning. I took the last fifteen paperbacks and carried them by hand to the "Romance" room, where we kept all of our novels for women of a certain age (apparently Mr. Allen's wife liked bodice rippers). Men like Fabio always graced the cover with shirts torn off and muscles flexing, and women fell faint in their presence. I quickly began stacking the books, but it was hard work because the shelves were overflowing, so in an effort to make room, I started plucking duplicate titles and making a stack of them that I'd bring to Howie for storage. As I rearranged the shelf, I became lost in my own thoughts about tomorrow. I couldn't believe it was graduation day. No more high school. No more Millbank. Tomorrow was going to be first day of the rest of my life, I told myself. It wouldn't be what I expected, but I was excited, nonetheless, to move on.

I heard the elevator kick into gear, and I took the last duplicate novel off the top shelf and walked back to the elevator to meet Howie. When the doors opened, my heart skipped a beat. There, standing before me, was Will B. His hair was its usual faux-messy style and he had two or three days' worth of stubble. A week ago, I would have been swooning, but tonight the sight of his face made me feel sick. As beautiful as it was, I could see nothing but the ugliness underneath.

"Hey," he said.

"Hey."

There was a long awkward pause.

"What are you reading?" he said finally, pointing to the book in my hand.

I looked at the book. It was *Eternity* by Daphne Dugan.

"Trash," I said. "I'm just shelving trash."

We stood there awkwardly, not knowing what to say to each other.

"I came by because I wanted to tell you something."

"More lies?" I snapped. "What do you want?"

He stared at me, and I think he whispered "You," or at least that's how I read his lips.

"Don't say 'me,' Will! Don't say 'me'!"

"I fell in love with you," he said. "I love you."

"Everything about you is a fraud."

He had tears in his eyes, and for a moment I felt a twinge of forgiveness flow through my veins. I wanted so badly to go back in time—to that first bloom of feelings between us, when I believed in his true feelings. But that would never happen. He was being sincere, there was no question about that, but how could I ever manage to trust him? Even as the phrase echoed in my head, I was conscious of the fact that those were the exact same words Dev had said to me a few days ago.

"I don't trust you, Will."

"You shouldn't, but let me explain."

"I'm going home, excuse me." I walked around him, hit the elevator button, and the doors slid open immediately. I stepped in, but he managed to jump in with me before the doors shut. The freight elevator was numbingly slow, and the sound of the old-fashioned motor made it difficult to have a conversation.

"Listen," he shouted. "What happened was out of control, but I did fall in love with you, and you fell in love with me . . . didn't you?"

I didn't have to think about that answer very long because I knew the answer was "yes."

"What difference does that make? I can never look at you again without thinking you used me to play some stupid game."

"I tried to tell you several times but I didn't know how, and then it snowballed and I thought, or maybe just naively hoped, it might all just blow over once we graduated. And you'd never know."

"But I do know, and 'we' will never be again." I stepped off the elevator and strode as quickly as I could toward the front door. Howie was standing there with his keys in the door, waiting to let me out.

"Everything all right?" he asked, casting a glance at Will.

"Nothing I can't handle," I answered.

He smiled like he knew that firsthand.

I walked out into the night air. It was warm and sweet, the way only an early summer night can be. Will followed me all the way out to my car.

"So there's nothing, then?" he said.

"No, there's nothing left."

We stood there staring at each other, and my heart was exploding beneath my chest, but I held back the tears. I would not cry for this boy ever again, I told myself.

"That night when you approached me at Gretchen's party—did you know then?"

He kicked the tire of my car gently and looked up to the sky and into the stars, searching for the right words.

"Jack had a thing for you. He'd been going on about you for weeks; about how great he thought you were—"

"Did you know?"

He sighed. "Yes."

"So you're the one who put the invitation in my locker?"

"I'd put five hundred dollars in the Market and I was in last place. I'd made stupid picks and I was screwed," he began. "I told Gretchen, and she offered to stake me more money if we played together. She said she'd help me make it back—and more."

"Why didn't she just invest herself?"

"She thought it would be a fun project—for 'us,'" he said as the edge of his lip curled. "You read between the lines."

Of course.

"I was just supposed to take you on a few dates. Make people notice you," he continued. "I didn't realize how right Jack was—that I'd fall for you so hard—until it was too late."

"How could you do that to me? To Jack?"

"I couldn't turn her down! I was desperate," he said, wild-eyed. "I needed to win—for the money!"

"Is that your pathetic excuse? Money?"

"You don't understand what it's like . . . hanging around Gretchen . . . the guys," he said as he looked off into the distance. "When you're around people with so much money all the time, you realize how little you have. With her I saw what it was like. And I just . . . I wanted to be like them. Me, but better."

I suddenly saw Will for who he was—someone who had once been good, but who over time had been corrupted, not by Gretchen, but by the promise of a life that wasn't his. Gazing at him, I saw he was being torn apart, the person who he truly was battling with an image of what he so desperately wanted to be. I thought then of the afternoon I'd met his father and realized that Will hated him because he reminded Will of who he actually was: not one of the Proud Crowd.

"Why would you need any of that?" I said quietly. "It's sad."

"What about you?" he whispered. "What about your plan to climb the Market? You and Dev. I have eyes, too, you know."

How did he know about Dev and me? Who could have told him? But he didn't wait for me to respond, and instead he turned around and started walking up River Road. I stood there watching his dark jacket and jeans disappear into the night. After a few moments, I could only see his shadow, and then nothing. Just like that, the boy of my dreams had come into my life, stirred passion in my heart, and now he had disappeared, like a faint memory.

I realized then that after four years with the same group of people, there are no secrets. My sins were his sins and his sins were my own. Yes, I believed his were the worse of the two, but mine no less tragic.

As I slid into my car, I was still holding *Eternity*. I looked at the cover again, at the man with the long flowing hair and ripped muscles, battling a tiger on top of a hill, and I wondered if the last woman who read this believed in him as deeply as I had believed in my own Prince Charming.

CHAPTER

30

HIGH SCHOOL was officially over.

When Principal Johnson handed me my diploma, he was gracious and politic. He guided me in close to him and whispered, "I'm sorry it ended the way it did—you were a model student and you'll be missed." Then, as with every other student who now clutched that piece of paper in their hand, he turned toward the photographer just offstage, who was there to commemorate the occasion. We both gave thousand-watt smiles, and if some student fifty years from now were to stumble upon that photograph in a dusty old yearbook, he or she would never know what lay beneath the surface.

I exited the stage, took in my class one last time, and a few moments later we all tossed our caps high, high into the air. Callie and I found each other in the crowd and hugged, and Dev and I managed cordial nods. By noon, families headed from Lafayette Park and made their way to afternoon parties. My parents invited our extended family over—aunts, uncles, cousins, etc.—and all in all, it was about thirty people. They stayed for a few hours, congratulating me on my success, asking about my future plans. As dusk settled in, they all departed, and I found myself standing alone in our garden.

I'd warned my mom that the party Gretchen and I had planned was off. After the Black & White, I knew nobody would come, especially if Gretchen decided it wasn't the thing to do. No doubt she'd organized her own bash and had drawn most of the senior class. I'm sure I could have coaxed a few stragglers in, but why? I didn't want a room full of strangers, and truthfully, I wasn't in the mood for a celebration anyway. What I really wanted was to spend the night with Callie and Dev. Callie promised to swing by at some point that night, but she couldn't commit to a time because her mom's family was in from out of state, and nothing had changed on the Dev front, so it looked like I was going to be spending the night on my own.

My parents had made plans to go into the city. When planning the party, I'd told them they had to be nowhere in sight, so Dad had surprised Mom with tickets to a Broadway show and a meal at the Palm afterward. Now that the party wasn't happening, they asked if I wanted to come, a pity move that I actually appreciated but declined, and they were off.

I shut the lights off around most of the house, lay down in bed, and took out the book Mrs. Sawyer had given me. The pages were old and brittle, and I was careful to turn them gently. I didn't get very far into the novel when the doorbell rang. I blew out the candle I'd lit by my bed and went downstairs. I took a peek out the window beside the front door before opening it, and there, standing stiffly, was Jack Clayton.

"Jack," I said. "Come in."

He looked around as he stepped into our foyer. "I'm the first, then," he said.

"And the last," I said with a smile.

"What's that?" he said. "Isn't there a party tonight?"

"No," I said. "I mean, Gretchen's throwing something, I think, but not here. I just assumed you'd be there, with everyone else."

He neither smiled nor frowned. He just mumbled something to himself and handed me his coat. Then he brandished a six-pack of beer and gave me his keys. "Hold these for me and don't let me leave plastered."

"Jack—there's no party. I mean, you can stay, but it would just be me and you."

"Sounds like a party to me," he quipped.

We both stood there for a moment—the truth of how I'd treated him between us.

"You don't have to stay, just because you came by mistake," I offered. "I know I let you down. I know how I screwed things up."

"You did."

"So why are you staying?" I asked meekly.

"Let's just say I'm big on second chances." He popped off a bottle cap. A beat later, he opened another and handed me a bottle. We tapped glass and took a big swallow of beer. I smiled at him for what felt like a full minute.

"What's so funny?"

"Nothing—I'm happy you're here, with me," I said. "Thank you."

I moved toward him and gave him a big hug. Nothing romantic, mind you, but a hug for being there. It was true that he was a recent friend, but I was thinking Dev needed to add a new theory to her Latebloomer model. The Latebloomer friend: it's a phenomenon that often occurs late in senior year when silly social guards are dropped, and a friendship that had been heretofore impossible to imagine blooms in the spring sun.

As we broke from our embrace, I couldn't help but think back to that night in Dickey Dogs when we kissed, and for a moment, I felt real passion. I knew now that I'd missed a chance with him. Happiness? True love? A one-month fling? I'd never know. But he had told me he liked me for me—for my natural self—and I took that sincere declaration for granted. Not for Kat or for the timid Katie. What he liked, I now realized, was the person I had mistakenly run from in my climb to the top of the Market. Simply put, he liked Kate.

I popped a bowl of popcorn, and we sat in my living room, drinking our brew and yucking it up about the BookStop. I told him about the gift Mrs. Sawyer had given me, and he looked over the volume. His hands caressed the cover, and when he opened the pages, he tenderly turned them over, careful not to fold any of the edges.

"It's beautiful, Kate."

I nodded.

By the time we got to our second beer, I was starting to feel the weight of the past week lift off my shoulders. We talked about the conversation Will and I had, and he told me that the two of them had had a throwdown as well. "We haven't spoken since," he said.

"I'm sorry, Jack."

"Don't be. We've been through a lot. We'll find a way back." He grabbed a handful of popcorn and sat back on the couch, looking up at the ceiling. The sadness of the situation enveloped the room, and I had no words to comfort him.

"Can I ask you one last thing, and then we don't ever have to talk about it again?"

He nodded.

"Did you ever invest in the Market?"

He said nothing for a moment, then smiled. "What do you think?"

I looked down at the floor sheepishly. Of course he hadn't.

A few minutes later, bizarrely, the doorbell rang again—no doubt a straggler who had heard a rumor I was throwing a party. I pulled the curtain back for the second time tonight, and the air jumped out of my lungs. Dev was standing on my stoop holding a six-pack of beer! I threw the door open and then wrapped my arms around her in uncontrollable joy.

"Don't squeeze too hard—the package is still fragile."

I stepped back and looked at her with a big smile on my face. No other person could have made me feel happier than Dev had just made me feel right then. She reached into her bag and pulled out my old jean jacket and handed it to me. I held it up, and a big smile crossed my face.

"Old blue," I said. "I missed you."

"I missed you in it," she said. "I mean, don't misunderstand me—you look a lot cuter now, but I liked the girl in the jean jacket a little bit better."

"Me too," I said. She laughed and then held out a copy of our business plan. "I want you to burn this tonight in honor of our friendship."

"I'm sorry," I said again. She looked at me and mouthed, "Me too," and then we hugged again, but for longer and with more meaning and less youthful exuberance.

From out of the darkness I heard a voice as familiar as my own, "Now that's the kind of loving I expect from the two of you."

It was Callie, and after she stepped up onto the porch, grinning from ear to ear, we circle-hugged like the high school girls we were. It was all like a dream, like the past month had never happened, though we all knew it had. We probably would never trust again, at least not in the naive way that we had, but perhaps we'd created a new level of trust, one earned rather than assumed. We all knew what it meant to have such great friends, and never again would I take that for granted.

After a few minutes of chitchat, we all moved to the back porch, and Jack entertained us with stories about playing music in dive bars and summer tours with Jane Austen's Secret Lover. Callie and Dev knew Jack, but they had never really spoken to him, and I could tell that Dev took an immediate shine to him, and he to her. And Callie, well it wasn't hard for any guy to fall under her spell.

It was about a half hour later that a stream of headlights started pouring down Woodside, my block. Dev noticed them first, and I looked out toward the street, bewildered. One by one the cars rumbled down my street and parked. In each car, two and sometimes four students from our class piled out, one after another. Jack stood up, walked through the house, and opened the front door. Within fifteen minutes, a waterfall of students fell in and moved out to my backyard. Paul Skibnewski and Kevin Healy from the football team lumbered out, kegs on their shoulders, and a very conscientious girl from the graduation committee collected keys from all the drivers. Warren Rabin pulled his SUV up to the end of the driveway, opened his lift gate—exposing huge speakers—and turned on the music. Within a matter of minutes, my quiet night with friends transformed itself into a rager with my entire senior class. It was surreal, I admit, but I couldn't help but smile.

As I looked around, I could scarcely keep count of the numbers. It was an eclectic mix ranging from the Proud Crowd, to the Goth kids, to the president of the Latin Club (who had stunned everyone by winning the schoolwide talent show, singing a Stevie Wonder song with a karaoke machine). In my twelve years in the Millbank school system, I had never once witnessed such a coming together. Had the euphoria of actually earning our degrees exploded all the imaginary social barriers we had placed between ourselves and our fellow classmates?

From the corner of my eye, I recognized the listless saunter of Will, entering the outer edges of the party. Frankly, I didn't know how to react, and I braced for an unpleasant scene when I saw Jack walk up to Will. For a few moments they stood there toe-to-toe, exchanging some words. Jack, who was a few inches taller than Will, opened his arms and embraced him in a man-hug. Then Jack turned in my direction and pointed, and I saw Will make his way through the crowd and up the stairs toward me. It gave me time to prepare, but nothing came to mind. What more was there to say than what we had said last night?

When Will reached the top step, he stood there until I gave him a nod that it was okay for him to approach. He hopped up and walked over to me, but not too close.

"I'm not staying," he said. "But I couldn't let this day pass without saying something: you were the best thing that happened to me."

"Are those *your* words?" I said. It was a smart-ass thing to say, but my heart was still raw.

"They all are now," he said with a weird little grin. "This is me."

"Okay," I said. "Thanks."

I didn't feel the same way. In fact, I pretty much felt the opposite, but by now we were past recriminations. We said nothing, and Will looked down at the gray planks of the deck.

"You should stay," I said, staring out into the sea of seniors occupying my backyard. "This isn't about us—it's bigger than us."

Then he said something I didn't expect at all.

"Gretchen did this."

My head snapped around and I stared at him hard. He didn't turn my way, but he knew I was looking at him.

"That was real . . . what you did for her the other day. The note, I wouldn't have done it."

"She told you?"

He nodded and then took a pull off his beer. "She told everyone that they should come here."

She did that? Really?

"Is she here?"

"Yeah. On your stoop chatting with a few friends."

Weaving between party-goers, I walked toward the sliding glass door off the deck. It was already open, and I pushed the curtains over, before looking back at Will. His eyes were still on me.

"You're staying," I called.

He nodded and walked over to me and put his arms around me. I embraced him. A little sob slipped and my chest shuddered, but I caught myself. He whispered something to me that I couldn't quite make out, but it didn't matter. We'd never be together again, and all his apologies would never mend my heart enough to trust him. But I suppose the sincerity in his voice, not the words themselves, felt honest and truthful.

I let go, and he disappeared behind the drapes. I walked

slowly to the front of the house and opened the door. Sure enough, Gretchen was sitting there on my stoop. We had come full circle from six weeks ago when I was stranded on *her* stoop, trying to figure out how I was going to get home. She looked up, and her little entourage—Jodi, Elisa, Carrie—all looked up, too.

"Can we talk?" I asked.

Gretchen chinned her posse away, and they stood up and walked around the side of the house. We waited a few moments to make sure we were alone.

"I'll leave," she said. "I just wanted to make sure everything was under control."

"Why did you do this?" I said, waving to the back of the house.

"Why did you give me that note?" she countered. I wasn't ready for that sharp of a response, but I guess I shouldn't have been surprised. We had ripped each other apart over the past week and there was no reason to hide behind niceties.

"I was tired," I said, taking a deep breath. "Just tired."

There was so much more to it, of course—I was tired of being at war, with Gretchen, with what people expected, believed, imagined—but sometimes things are best left unspoken.

"Yeah, me too," she said. A few moments of silence passed, and then she added, "It won't make you feel better, but it was innocent. It was a game, and then it became real."

"It was always real," I said. "It just made us feel better to pretend it was a game."

That was the thing I learned after four years. Popularity is *both* imagined and real. It's in my head as much as it's in Gretchen's or Dev's. But outside of us, outside the understanding of any one person, it existed as a very real thing. The Market, its valuations, were ridiculous and meaningless. Simply put, it represented the musings of a handful of kids who got their jollies judging others. But for those of us drawn into its world, it was as real and painful as anything could be.

Gretchen's eyes flickered. "No more games," she said with more sincerity than I believed she was capable of mustering.

"You can't say that and mean it forever," I said. "But I guess we can say it to each other. No more games between *us*."

"Between us," she echoed. "Yes. I meant just between us."

We sat there for a few minutes longer, looking into the night, not speaking. The stars twinkled like faraway stage lights. In the background, I could hear hundreds of voices colliding behind us, melting into one loud roar of relief.

Dr. Dyment

To my parents, Bill and Willa Dyment, who have always believed in me and who introduced me to a deep friendship with a creative, gracious God who operates far outside the realm of limits and excuses.

Dr. Dayhoff

To God, for blessing me with the gift of helping others. To Leticia, the love of my life; Ryan and Amanda, my pride and joy. To David and Janet, the greatest parents in the world, who would never let me make excuses. To Davis and Jairus, brothers and friends. To all my clients who have allowed me to help them in their moments of pain and suffering. You are my driving force.

IN MEMORY OF

Our friend and colleague Dr. Mark Sall. Our college mentor "Colonel" Lawson Saunders. You are greatly missed.

Don't let what you can't do keep you from doing what you can.
JOHN WOODEN

He that is good for making excuses is seldom good for anything else.
BENJAMIN FRANKLIN

CONTENTS

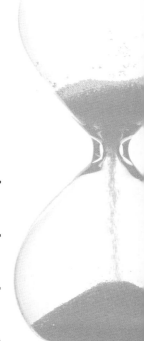

ACKNOWLEDGEMENTS

WE OWE MANY THANKS TO THE PEOPLE WHO HAVE HELPED US throughout the writing of this book. We are most grateful to our families who believed in us, prayed for us, and gave us the time to finish this project.

Dr. Dyment would like to thank his parents, Bill and Willa Dyment, his sisters, Beth, Amy and Wendy, and his brother-in-law, Eric, for their encouragement and hospitality, as he juggled writing, traveling, and speaking between Los Angeles and Boston. Dr. Dayhoff would like to thank his wife, Leticia, for her unending love, support, and patience from the beginning of this endeavor, and children, Mandy and Ryan, for their understanding.

We are also especially grateful to our colleagues, associates, and staff. Special thanks go out to Scott Sall of Dyment & Associates, Inc., who provided hands-on editorial and statistical help, and design insights along the way, and to Kim Denigan, who was there at the very beginning. A tireless encourager, she provided us with timely inspiration and marketing ideas at innumerable points over our writing adventure. A special thank you must also be extended to accomplished authors Dr. John Townsend, Dr. Bill Maier, Austin Hill, and Danae Dobson for their advice, enthusiasm, and introductions into the publishing world, but most of all for their encouragement.

We could not have completed this book without the help of our colleagues, mentors, and friends. Dr. Dayhoff wishes to first thank the corporate office staff at REACH Employee Assistance, Inc. as well as all REACH client organizations, past and present. Sincere thanks to former boss, mentor, and friend, Pierre Stolz, who has always been an encouragement and an inspiration. Thanks to Sylvia Livingston, Dr. Tomas and Christine Flores, and Paula Norris for giving him his respective starts in the EAP, mental health and addiction professions. Thanks also to Dr. Doug Matthews, Tim Scanlon, and Rudy Garcia, for their friendship, humor, and psychological and spiritual support.

Dr. Dyment wishes to thank his colleagues and friends at Cigna Behavioral Health, Cigna Heath, Disney Worldwide Studios, United Behavioral Health, Prive-Swiss, Sobel and Raciti Associates, Verizon Wireless, St. Vincent Medical Center, College Hospital, and South Coast Children's Society for their great partnerships over the years. Thanks also to his alma maters, Eastern Nazarene College and Rosemead Graduate School of Psychology at Biola University.

He also wishes to acknowledge his extended team of supporters and champions, past and present, for their encouragement, friendship, and advice: Scott and Danita Maxwell, Scott and Ellen McGuirk, Steve and Debbie Wolford, Carolyn and Benjamin Benjamin, Dave Coen, Aimee Wing, Michelle Garay, Barbara Danzi, Sandra Reyes, Bill and Marcie Seery, Steve and Kim Raynesford, John and Amber Taylorson, Jeff Happy, Richard Marymee, Annette Lange, Sharon Hannah, Stephanie Waters, Elizabeth Trevino, Yvonne Brack, and Dr. Kevin Narramore.

A heartfelt thanks goes to his late mentor, Charlie Cove, for inspiring him to pursue his doctoral studies; Dr. Phil Rountree, for introducing him to the world of speaking; his advisor, Dr. Doug Degelman, for encouraging him to apply for graduate school; and to the Gailey family, for forever "ruining" his U.S.-centric view of the world by hosting him in Africa for one unforgettable summer.

Finally, we owe a great debt of thanks to everyone who provided key logistical support. We are most grateful to Mark Byrne for developing our online presence and website, to Mark Hauchwitz for designing the layout of our online assessment, to Jim Stodd for his statistical work on the assessment, and to Karla Shippey for legal counsel and trademark support. Also, we would like to thank Terri Arredondo, Kate Etue and Anita Palmer for their editorial assistance, and Brett Burner and Lamp Post for their publishing services.

Marcus Dayhoff, Psy.D., Anaheim, California
Bill Dyment, Ph.D., Costa Mesa, California
April 2012

INTRODUCTION

WHAT HAPPENED TO US? WE ARE A NATION THAT HAS GROWN FOND of making excuses.

We have not always been this way. Those who grew up in what has been called the Greatest Generation—the children of the Great Depression and those who endured WWII—faced horrendous difficulties head on. They made whatever sacrifice was needed, regardless of cost, and overcame huge obstacles.

While we associate the generation that followed them with Woodstock and the questioning of authority, a different, subtler change was happening that was not as immediately apparent. We became a society that felt comfortable with denial, blame, and minimization. Living in an unprecedented time of prosperity and plenty, we have gotten away with these attitudes and values for more than four decades.

One does not need to be a physician or an economist to see that our recent way of living has become unsustainable. Consider the following facts that were true of us even before the recent economic downturn.

- Many Americans entered the 2008 recession already deeply in debt. According to the Federal Reserve, American consumers owed an average of $18,654 per household in October 2003, not including mortgage debt, a 41 percent increase from 1998.[1]

- In 1984, the average American saved 11.2 percent of his or her disposable income. By 2004, this percentage had fallen to 1.2 percent.[2]

- America has more obese residents than any other industrialized nation.[3] In 1990, ten states had an obesity rate of less than 10 percent and no state had a rate greater than 15 percent.[4] By 2010, at least 20 percent of the residents of every state, except Colorado, were obese and in a dozen states the obesity rate had risen above 30 percent.[5]

• According to the Bureau of Labor Statistics, in 2010, Americans spent nine times as much time watching television (2.73 hours/day) than they did engaging in sports, exercise, or recreational activities (0.31 hours/day.)[6]

To say "a change is needed" is only a token response to our current condition. Truly, we stand at a critical juncture, individually and as a nation. Are we ready to say "enough is enough"?

Why Now?

You may be reading these words because you resonated with the challenge of the title. Maybe you sensed that your excuses have cost you a lot already and are significantly limiting your success. Perhaps you can think of a friend or family member in the same position.

On some deep level, you know that this moment in life can no longer be viewed as "batting practice." This is it—"the big game," the one that will ultimately decide everything. You are ready to start the journey we call "walking the last mile of denial." It is time to *Fire Your Excuses!*

The tough news is that if you define change in terms of your newest resolution to "get more motivated," you will likely fail. Well-intended techniques and "willpower" just don't work. Instead, they ultimately leave us feeling demoralized and helpless. At worst, we eventually give up altogether, convincing ourselves that real change is not possible or even necessary.

You don't need another pep talk or self-help book. You need principles and a plan to follow that have been clinically proven to result in permanent change. You can no longer wait for your spouse, sister, or friends to get motivated with you, nor can you afford to wait for your country to get back on track. This type of change has to begin with you, regardless if anyone follows.

The great news is you won't be alone. The Fire Your Excuses Community is there to help. They, too, know *it's time.*

One of the most important therapy and coaching questions we ask is, "Why now?" What is happening at this moment that is causing you to seek assistance now, instead of a month from now or a year ago? What we are getting at is this: *What will* not *happen in your life if you don't make the necessary change today? And, where will you likely be in three to five years, given your past experience with this behavior or way of living?*

Fire Your Excuses is a powerful system of insight, accountability, and motivation based on principles and actions that lead to a new way of taking ownership of your life. This book is designed to help you put your excuses in their proper place—in the past—and remove them from any further mention in the script of your life.

> **Not all excuses are created equally. Some excuses hinder us, some hurt us, and some kill us.**
> **– Dr. Marcus Dayhoff**

Your first step is to take the online Fire Your Excuses (*FYE*) Self-Assessment. You will find instructions for doing so in the next section. You then will explore the eight life areas measured by the assessment where our excuses, destructive thoughts, and behaviors cripple us the most. Included are systematic strategies to help you make positive, lasting changes based on our research and clinical experience. The 30-Day Challenge, at the end of each chapter, has been created to get you started on your journey.

Not a Quick Fix

This is not a volume about gimmicky short-term change. It is a book about *accommodation*, not *assimilation*. Most likely you have heard these words used before. We would like to define them a little differently—as psychologists do[7] when they are speaking about change and growth. In psychology, the term *accommodate* means to "make room by breaking the mold." To permanently change long-term habits you will need to "knock down some walls." What is required will not fit into your existing lifestyle. Changing the way you view your situation and doing what you have never been willing to do in the past will take you far beyond your comfort zone.

To use another familiar metaphor, *accommodators* have decided that, like it or not, they will have to pull everything out of the garage to clean it properly; they can't just sort through a box or bin here or there. And, once they commit to the process, they feel a deep sense of exhilaration and hope, often for the first time in years.

It is our sincere goal that you become just that: a true accommodator, a person who is willing to do whatever it takes to change permanently. Accommodation is hard work! For this reason, most people who need to make a significant change avoid and dismiss this mold-breaking process as unnecessary. Many clients have walked out of our offices over the years, unwilling to pay the price of accommodation required to eradicate their negative behaviors.

All of us would like to believe that a pattern of behavior that has been in our lives for three or four decades will simply disappear with a new attitude, diet, video, or counselor. The truth is, any habit that has persisted for years enjoys that type of longevity for a reason—it is deeply entrenched. Make no mistake; it will require accommodation to remove it. Accommodation is disruptive, messy, and long-term, but also highly effective.

Assimilation, in contrast, promises a much easier route. It can be defined as a minor or short-term change to our current lifestyle that requires minimal investment. It is the stuff of late-night exercise infomercials and New Year's resolutions. It is a "surface-cleaning" approach—cheap, convenient, but minimally effective.

To return to our metaphor of cleaning out the garage, assimilators hope that sorting through a few shelves and rearranging some boxes here and there will do it. It won't. Accommodation, not assimilation, is needed. It is a process that takes more time but yields permanent benefits.

What the Fire Your Excuses Program Is Not

The Fire Your Excuses Program is not a substitute for therapy or other treatment. However, we occasionally find in our seminars that people are attracted to what they see as the positive nature of our programs but they actually need some preliminary or concurrent treatment. It is understandable that we all want to "move on" and "not dwell on the past." One of the biggest challenges we face professionally is telling someone who is eager to move forward that more healing is needed first.

It is also critical to underscore what excuses are "not." For some readers, this may be the most important distinction we can make. Please know that in our more than twenty-five years of clinical practice we have heard from scores of individuals struggling with ongoing congenital and other medical conditions that in no way fall into the category of an excuse. Anyone who has suffered with depression, anxiety, fibromyalgia, cancer, or arthritis, to name just a few disorders, knows how much courage it can sometimes take just to get out of bed and through the day.

At the same time, all of us, including those with the above challenges, are capable of falling into an excuse pattern. Having an illness is never an excuse in itself; not seeking ongoing treatment for it is.

The Fire Your Excuses (FYE) Excuse Cycle

Excuses are deadly to our dreams, health, emotions, and lifestyle because they rob us of the most important ally we have in our efforts to change—the truth about ourselves. Once we begin to live an excuse-free life, everything else changes dramatically. There is always plenty of blame to go around. We are not 100 percent responsible for everything that happens to us, but we are 100 percent responsible for how we react to it.

The simple graphic below illustrates the basis for our FYE excuse model:

The Excuse Cycle

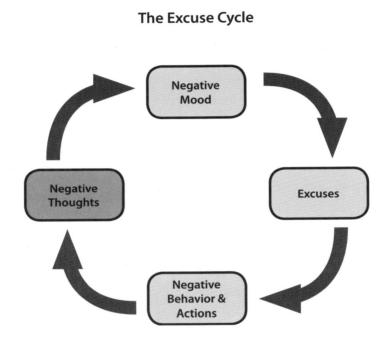

Copyright 2011, Dr. Bill Dyment & Dr. Marcus Dayhoff

It is easy to slip into a negative view of the world and one's own life. This may arise from our perceptions, upbringing, experiences, and even genetics. Left unchecked and unchallenged, these *negative thoughts* invariably lead to *negative feelings*. Insidiously, our mood begins to be distorted by shades of hopelessness and despair. Many who suffer from negative *feelings* about themselves and their ability to change do not realize that these feelings originate from their thoughts. Eventually, we begin to overlook the true options available to us and fall into denial and excuse-making. Finally, our *behaviors* reflect our excuses, in our actions or inactions, and the cycle repeats itself. *Excuses*, left unchallenged and in full operation, lead to poor choices indeed. Just as "the fish doesn't know the water is wet," excuse-makers have no idea how much their excuses are affecting their perception, feelings, and actions.

"It's Time!"

In the corporate setting, firing someone is serious business and not undertaken lightly. Its ramifications are far-reaching, and much thought and legal counsel precede it. It is nearly always also a permanent event. We would like you to think about the excuses in your life in similar business terms. After all, in a very real sense, you are the CEO of you!

When we are speaking about identifying the things in your life that are holding you back from excelling and being your best, it is equally serious business. It is easy to keep a part of your life that should have been fired years ago. You can be assured that if you do nothing, these issues will continue to "show up for work." In fact, one manager told us recently: "My employee retired three years ago. She just forgot to tell me!"

Just as we have met a number of well-meaning executives who did not have the skills, insight, or corporate backing to fire an employee who was consistently underperforming, individuals too can lack the skills, insight, or support to fire their own excuses. The following pages will provide you with the resources necessary to no longer permit your excuses to come back to work. *It's time!*

How to Get the Most from this Book

We recommend beginning your journey by taking the free Fire Your Excuses Self-Assessment available at *www.FireYourExcuses.com*. You are welcome to read the book first, but some of the key passages, especially the case studies contained in each chapter, will be more relevant and clear upon completion of your own assessment.

The core of the book is divided into eight chapters, which correspond to the eight excuse areas we commonly wrestle with on a day-to-day basis. Each chapter contains the following:

Excuse GameChanger: A key concept for defeating the excuse highlighted in each chapter. For example, the Finances chapter contains a financial Excuse GameChanger.

ExcuseStopper: A free extra resource, available by typing in a keyword at FireYourExcuses.com. Each ExcuseStopper has been designed to aid you in tackling a key excuse highlighted in the chapter.

30-Day Challenge: A coaching "dare" consisting of four action items, designed to be accomplished within a month. Each challenge has been carefully crafted to help you make significant progress toward the elimination of your excuses for that period of time. These items are quite similar to the type of goals we set for clients in our Fire Your Excuses (FYE) Coaching Program. Because they do take focused effort to achieve within one month, we recommend you only take on one 30-Day Challenge at a time. We encourage you to use the results of your assessment to determine which three challenges you wish to tackle over the course of ninety days. Then, take the assessment again to measure your progress.

We also hope that you will join our free online Fire Your Excuses Community to network with others who are taking positive steps in their lives, and read their inspiring stories. Here you will find kindred spirits, new ideas, encouragement, and inspiration. We wish you all the best and look forward to hearing your stories too. Please tell us about your journey at: *MyStory@FireYourExcuses.com.*

Your First Step:
Take the Fire Your Excuses Self-Assessment

The book you hold in your hands is designed to be a companion to the FYE Self-Assessment described above. Your friends and colleagues are welcome to take the free assessment as well. While not a psychological instrument, this assessment provides a snapshot indicating those life areas where your excuses keep you from making needed changes.

The FYE Self-Assessment is a confidential, 82-item, self-paced instrument designed to help you identify the impact of your excuses on eight key life areas. In addition, it measures three other important factors related to change. The first is your *Potential for Change*, which assesses the likelihood that you will take positive action in the areas where you tend to use excuses the most. The last two are your *Offense* and *Defense Scores.* Your *Offense Score* reflects your current level of *offensive*, career- and life-enhancing activities, while your *Defense Score* assesses how well you take care of equally important, *defensive* or maintenance tasks. Keep in mind, in this assessment high scores in both are ideal as they reflect positive and important activities.

In your assessment report, you will learn your *Total Excuse Score*, your eight individual excuse scores, and your scores for the three additional scales described above. You will also receive a detailed explanation of what your scores mean and information about the specific actions you can take to improve them.

Unlike an IQ or personality test, your assessment scores are not "genetically based," nor are they necessarily stable over time. If you work on the areas that have been identified as needing attention, your individual scores in these areas can and should improve rapidly. You will find a description of each of the 12 Fire Your Excuse scales in the *Appendix* at the back of this book.

Be sure to wait at least three months before you take the test a second time if you wish to do so to measure your progress. Taking the assessment too quickly after your first experience can affect your results, due to what is called "the memory effect"—the tendency to answer the way you previously did because you consciously or unconsciously remembered your earlier responses. Once you have finished your assessment and reviewed your results, set a reminder in your phone or calendar in three months to take the assessment again to see the changes that you've made. Also, a 90-day interval between assessments provides ample time to work on several identified excuse areas. For example, you might use the time to complete three 30-Day Challenges for the three excuse areas that received the lowest scores.

For further questions about the assessment or technical issues, please don't hesitate to contact us by email at our website.

FIRE YOUR EXCUSES

CHAPTER ONE:

BLIND SPOTS AND WEAKNESSES

CHAPTER 1

BLIND SPOTS AND
WEAKNESSES

The only thing worse than being blind is having sight but no vision.
HELEN KELLER

Once we know our weaknesses they cease to do us any harm.
GEORG C. LICHTENBERG

ON MAY 25, 2001, ERIK WEIHENMAYER BECAME THE FIRST BLIND man in history to reach the summit of Mount Everest. Seven years later, on August 20, 2008, Erik joined the elite ranks of those who have climbed the Seven Summits—the highest mountains on each of the seven continents. Fewer than 100 mountaineers, sighted or blind, can claim this honor.

"If disability is a matter of not being able to commit certain acts," writes James Burnett, "then Weihenmayer is arguably more able-bodied than most people with working eyes."[1]

Like Erik, each of us has a choice to make when faced with our "disabilities" and challenges, whether blindness or blind spots. Our weaknesses may be permanent or temporary, physical or emotional, plain to see or hidden even from us. Whatever they are, we probably make excuses for them. These are the challenges we will be examining.

Blind spots and weaknesses end lives, destroy families, sabotage careers, and derail dreams. In the last decade we have witnessed

3

a dramatic scandal involving an international golfing megastar, and a comeback by the King of Pop cut short by his shocking death. That's on top of the scandalous falls of numerous presidential hopefuls and high-ranking religious leaders. Our own struggles are rarely as dramatic or public but, if ignored, their limiting effects can be just as devastating. At the very least, they will prevent us from achieving our highest purpose in life and accomplishing the goals we know we were meant to achieve.

Case Studies Based on Real Life

In each chapter we will introduce you to a person or a couple whose behavior best illustrates the excuse we are discussing. While these individuals are fictional, the issues they are battling are not. In fact, the challenges highlighted have been selected precisely because they are so representative of real-life situations. Next to each case study we have also included their relevant scores on the Fire Your Excuses Self-Assessment. As you read their stories, keep in mind that these individuals are not without their strengths as well, just like you and me. We begin by introducing you to Scott.

Fire Your Excuses Self-Assessment Snapshot: Scott, Middle Management

Scale	Score	Range
Total Excuse Scale	274	Average
Potential for Change Scale	46	Average
Blind Spots and Weaknesses Scale	25	Below Average
Offense Scale	110	Average
Defense Scale	124	Above Average

Meet Scott, a mid-level manager for a large technology company. He is unquestionably bright and would very much like to move up into an executive role. Last year Scott was passed up for such a position, one that he had his eye on for over a year. The hard truth is this: The executive team will never invite Scott to join them. The way they see it, Scott is a decent manager who lacks some of the critical skills needed in someone who would function effectively at the highest level of the organization. Like a soldier so focused on the battle he doesn't yet realize he's mortally wounded, Scott's career is "terminal" and no one has the heart to tell him. Though caring, hard-working, and honest, Scott routinely misses the emotions of others and he avoids conflict at all costs. Instead, he offers shallow weekly pep talks to those he supervises.

At home, Scott's wife and children see and are upset by his disappointment at being passed over. Yet, if they were told the real reasons, they would have to reluctantly agree with his boss's assessment. Scott is unable to hear and respond to emotionally-charged concerns. He gets visibly uncomfortable and spouts reassuring platitudes. His wife might observe that it all makes sense: Scott grew up in a volatile home with an alcoholic father. He survived by staying in his room when things got ugly and signing up for every sport that was offered at his school.

Keeping his head down served Scott well in the battlefield of childhood, but it has hamstrung his relationships and career. He is very fortunate to have such an understanding wife, but his kids, still preteens, already tell him only what he wants to hear.

Good News and Bad News

Looking at Scott's FYE Self-Assessment Score Summary, we note that his Total Excuse Score is in the Average range. In a number of areas, he is, in fact, taking care of what needs to be done in his personal life and career. His problem is reflected in his Blind Spots and Weaknesses Score. Scott's score barely lands him in the Below Average range and is greatly impacting his career progression and his family.

The good news is Scott's Potential for Change Score and Offense Score are both in the Average range. This gives us some reason to believe that he may be able to make the needed adjustments if he grasps what is going on. Currently, however, he is very invested in a "maintaining" pattern, as confirmed by his Above Average Defense Score, and likely has been stuck for some time.

Quick question: What do you think the chances are that Scott will suddenly wake up one day and identify and address his blind spots on his own?

If you answered zero percent, you would be very close. Given his life-long tendency to shy away from conflict and strong displays of emotions, it is unlikely that Scott will see his deficits and their impact, and make a change on his own. He will need help. Help he doesn't even realize he needs and help he would most likely deflect as inaccurate or "not a big deal."

"It's the Ones You Don't Hear Coming that Kill You"

BLIND SPOT: NOUN

1a: The small circular area at the back of the retina where the optic nerve enters the eyeball and which is devoid of rods and cones and is not sensitive to light — called also optic disk.

1b: A portion of a field that cannot be seen or inspected with available equipment.

2: An area in which one fails to exercise judgment or discrimination.[3]

In World War II London, Nazi-led air raids were a near-daily occurrence that resulted in more than 40,000 deaths from September 1940 to May 1941.[2] There was a saying that arose during that time: "It's the ones you don't hear coming that kill you." In other words, whenever you heard the screech of a falling bomb you were generally safe. Death-dealing bombs, ones that fell directly over you, were another story—you could not hear them.

Blind spots can be equally deadly to our relationships and careers.

Blind spots, for our purposes,

are personal and occupational weaknesses that we don't see or bits of important feedback we don't hear. All of us have blind spots. Note that blind spots, as defined in the above dictionary entry, are dangerous for three distinct reasons:

First, we do not have the necessary equipment to see or inspect our blind spots. Only with the recent availability of rear-mounted cameras for vehicles can we see into the blind spots immediately behind our cars or trucks. This new technology has already saved the lives of countless young children. Standard side- and rear-view mirrors do not provide this view. In a similar fashion, there are personal and professional blind spots we cannot examine without "special equipment" in the form of extra outside feedback.

Second, blind spots are areas in which we fail to exercise judgment. Unable to see into the hidden zones of our personal and professional habits, we consistently make decisions based on inadequate or missing information. It is no wonder our blind spots do so much damage to our dreams and our relationships. Like the traveler who fails to consult a map before heading off into unknown regions, when it comes to our blind spots it is as if we are driving through life with our eyes closed.

Third, when we are blinded we cannot tell the difference between what is good or bad for us. We think we are making good personal and occupational choices, but we may be doing just the opposite.

Fortunately, not all blind spots remain so. Some eventually become known to us. In this case, they may still be a weakness, just not an unknown one. For the purpose of our discussion below, we will use both the terms "blind spots" and "weaknesses." Blind spots, as defined above, are weaknesses that we are in the dark about. Weaknesses, however, may or may not be known to us.

"Spot" Removal: How Top Performers Differ from the Rest of Us

People who continually grow professionally seek out more feedback about their blind spots and known weaknesses, not less. At the highest level of corporate life, top executives receive constant real-time feedback about their performance. This may range from criticism of their leadership style and its financial impact to their personal habits. Feedback can be quite comprehensive, including the use of "360-degree" reviews, a process where people at all strata of the organization provide feedback in stereo to the leader. In today's networked society, such feedback is increasingly public and global.

In marked contrast, the average or mediocre performer shies away from feedback. Lest we sound too harsh, we must admit that hearing honest feedback about our performance and behavior can, at times, be quite unpleasant. Still, our avoidance tendencies are self-defeating at best and catastrophic at worst. In essence, without feedback, we stop growing.

"Nancy, I told you if we got here early
there wouldn't be a line!"

Blind Spots and Our Emotional Intelligence

In 1995, psychologist Daniel Goleman ignited a firestorm of debate and research. He argued that while it was your IQ and technical ability that got you hired, it was your "Emotional IQ" that got you your promotion.[5] At a certain level in an organization, he explained, everyone was intelligent and knowledgeable enough; it was one's people skills that determined who would become the top performers. Think about it. You can probably recall a "genius" classmate who failed to live up to the anticipated greatness expected of him or her after graduation.

We're convinced Goleman was right. We've used the Reuven Bar-On's Emotional Quotient Inventory[6] to test hundreds of executives since 2003. Emotional intelligence has everything to do with rooting out our blind spots and shoring up our social weaknesses.

The Bar-On EQ-I highlights five major competency areas comprising emotional intelligence. How do you suppose you would do on a test of the Bar-On's five EQ skills listed below?

> **The range of what we think and do is limited by what we fail to notice. And because we fail to notice that we fail to notice there is little we can do to change until we notice how failing to notice shapes our thoughts and deeds.[4]**
> **—Daniel Goleman**

- **Interpersonal Skills:** Your empathy and general people skills

- **Intrapersonal Skills**: Your level of self-awareness

- **Adaptability Skills**: Your ability to be flexible, to change under pressure, and to see things realistically

- **Stress Management Skills:** Your patience, anger, and ability to handle stress

- **General Mood:** Your optimism and happiness levels

While our interpersonal skills are critical and the most obvious to others, intrapersonal skills have been shown to be the most foundational factor in predicting our career and life success.

Self-awareness, the core intrapersonal competency, can be our biggest area of blindness. And, when it comes to our weak areas, we can be the last to know. As the old saying goes: "If you are so happy, please inform your face." Self-awareness is essential in understanding and developing your emotional intelligence. Without it, we simply do not have the insight to see any of our weaknesses.

Which of the five areas above do you think presents the greatest challenge to what you hope to do in life? Would those closest to you agree?

Before we close out this section on our weaknesses and our emotional intelligence, here are two essential caveats:

1: *Truly irrelevant weaknesses can be ignored.*
First, as a general rule, weaknesses are only harmful if they fall in areas critical to your success. Being a below-average base-stealer may have little or no impact for Tim, a star major-league pitcher. If, however, arthritis develops in Tim's shoulder, that situation becomes a critical weakness indeed.

2: *There are other weaknesses that will eventually destroy your life and must be met head-on and with great courage.*
Second, in contrast to principle one, if your weaknesses are some type of addictive or compulsive behavior, there is a good chance that these behaviors will, over time, drag down every area of your life, including your work, health, spirituality, and relationships. Because these negative behaviors deeply impact our core character, they are not so easily contained and can become severe distractions to full engagement in seemingly unrelated areas.

The Stages of Awareness

When we are confronted with our blind spots, either through a flash of self-awareness or through feedback from another, we tend to respond in predictable ways. In fact, our responses to learning about areas of weakness are surprisingly uniform. Not surprising, however, is that weaknesses are far easier to identify in others than in ourselves.

Each of us passes through a series of emotional and behavioral responses as we grapple with our newfound weaknesses. Some stages we may skip (e.g., jumping from blindness to acceptance) but usually we follow the trajectory of the following six stages:

1. Blindness
2. Minimization
3. Shame
4. Grace
5. Acceptance
6. Healing

The Stages of Awareness

Stage One: Blindness

The blindness stage is that period of time where we have no understanding of a particular weakness. This phase can last months or decades. In some cases, we have always had a specific weakness. Other unknown weaknesses might have developed at a given point in our lives.

Blindness about our weaknesses can be conscious or unconscious. Conscious denial refers to that period of time when we have been confronted with evidence of our weakness but we still refuse to believe it. Unconscious blindness is that period of time where we have no awareness of our blind spot nor have we ever been confronted with it. Here is an example of each.

Conscious denial: Nicole is engaged to Mark, whom she adores. Mark is a great guy but he has a serious drinking problem. Her closest friends, having witnessed this on several occasions, have repeatedly expressed their concerns. Nicole has rebuffed every worry her friends have raised about Mark's drinking. Nicole is adamant that he doesn't have a problem. He just comes from a large family that "loves life." In the midst of wedding plans, she is just not ready to accept the reality of Mark's addiction.

Unconscious blindness: Ken thinks he is a great communicator. He even obtained a master's degree in communication from a prestigious school. While he would make a great instructor on the topic, no one would ever confuse the one-way conversations they have with Ken with true communication. Ken knows a lot and has done a lot, and you are sure to hear about both if you get within speaking range. If you go to Ken with a problem, he will interrupt you and start suggesting solutions, solicited or not, as soon as you pause for a breath. Because he is competent, verbal, and intelligent, no one at work will talk with him about it. If you have a debate with him about anything, you will lose. This is a fact his ex-wife would be the first to confirm.

All of us have dark areas in our lives that are hard to see and accept. Human beings are complex beings. We are blind about things big and small—aspects of our character, personality traits, and behavior. Each of us, as it has been said, sees "through a glass darkly," viewing the world through our own filter.

Stage Two: Minimization

As our blindness about an area of weakness dissipates, we often transition into minimization. We have begun to accept that we have a weakness or a situation that must change in our lives, but we minimize its importance because we are not quite ready, able, or willing to do so.

Sadly, many people spend most of their adult lives in this stage of awareness and its accompanying emotional pain.

For example, Nancy is an oncology nurse who steps out for regular smoking breaks throughout her twelve-hour shift. Obviously, her nursing training has made her well aware of the dangers of smoking, not to mention her daily interaction with patients suffering from smoking-related cancers. Yet she tells herself she does not smoke that much and that there are many smokers who do not develop cancer. She likes to defend her position by mentioning a neighbor who smoked like a chimney and lived to be ninety-six.

Stage Three: Shame

Shame—once exposed to the air, so to speak—can be incredibly painful and embarrassing. For this reason, it must be carefully and compassionately addressed, or the behavior you hope to resolve will head far underground where it does the most damage to our souls and relationships.

If a person is unable to deal with shame, invariably, he or she will return to a state of pretend blindness and again engage in the self-destructive behavior as a way of blocking the pain. This is especially true when struggling with compulsive behaviors such as sexual addiction, gambling, or substance abuse.

Ultimately, shame is not only painful and unhealthy; it literally kills, either by fork, drink, disease, avoidance of treatment, suicide, or slowly via a broken heart. In many other cases, if shame doesn't kill outright, it robs us of fruitful years that could be experienced in close community with others. We have observed that shame tends to be more an issue for men than women, but there are exceptions.

Meet Charles, a department manager, who is addicted to a narcotic painkiller. Originally prescribed this medication for debilitating back pain, Charles is now dependent on it and lying to several doctors to receive more. His job is at risk, his health is compromised, and after several attempts to get him to seek treatment for his addiction, his wife moves out with their children. Finally, he participates in an inpatient program and begins recovery, but his teenage children, now living with their mother, refuse to visit him. While in recovery, he is confronted with a litany of losses that plunge him into deep grief and shame. His addiction has cost him nearly everything, and after becoming sober, he feels the full impact of these losses. One month after finishing his treatment program, Charles returns to his addiction because he cannot bear facing the shame of his losses alone. The pain is just too intense. He will need much support from others if he is to finally break free.

If we keep our shame a secret, we will remain stuck in our pain. As the well-known Alcoholics Anonymous saying goes: "We are only as sick as our secrets." Yet, it is often not easy to confess our failures to others, especially if we have failed time and again. Depending on the severity of our weaknesses, we need support to feel genuine remorse without also getting mired in the emotional purgatory that is shame.

There are many weaknesses that cannot be overcome by mere willpower or by trying harder on our own. The answer is found in the next stage.

Stage Four: Grace

Have you ever had someone give you grace? For example, I (Bill) was in a tourist shop in Mexico, just south of the border. My coat caught the ear of a large plaster leopard and the statue crashed to the cement floor. Its head became a pile of crushed plaster and the body was cracked and splintered. The shocked look on my face told every vendor within 200 yards that there was "blood in the water"—obviously this clumsy gringo would pay hard U.S. currency for his clumsiness.

I will never forget the words of the gracious shopkeeper. "*Está bien, Señor*," he said simply, freeing me to return to my friends and make my way across the border without paying a significant sum. I had received grace.

The word *grace* is often defined as "unmerited favor." When we are given grace, we are given a break that we did not expect or believe we deserved. Grace can be both transforming and unsettling. When we are confronted with our weaknesses, grace is something we can either accept or push away. When we accept grace, we can step into a better, healthier way of living. When we reject grace, we slip back into denial, self-hate, or even death in the case of some addictions and health habits.

One of the most well-known literary examples of grace is found in Victor Hugo's classic novel, *Les Miserables*,[7] also a Broadway musical hit and the subject of at least two motion pictures. The main storyline is the lifelong pursuit of Jean Valjean, a reformed convict, by Javert, a heartless policeman and parole officer.

Jean Valjean is first imprisoned for stealing bread for his starving sister and her family. After his release from prison 19 years later, the kindly Bishop Myriel gives him food and shelter, but in the night, the desperate Valjean steals the silverware and flees. In the morning he is captured and brought to the bishop to verify guilt. Instead of confirming the robbery, the bishop shows Valjean amazing grace and covers for him, telling the arresting officers that the silverware was a gift. After the officers are gone, the bishop tells Valjean that he must now become an honest man and do good to others. This act of grace begins the transformation process in Valjean, but not before one additional moral lapse— he steals a coin from a child. The authorities learn about the incident, and Valjean is pursued as a repeat offender by the legalistic and relentless Javert.

Despite his rough beginning, the remainder of Valjean's life is a study in goodness. He becomes wealthy, provides for the poor, and performs courageous acts of kindness toward others. Unfortunately, he is always looking over his shoulder for Officer Javert.

In marked contrast to Valjean, Javert also receives grace but he is unable to accept it. As Javert closes in on him, Valjean has the unexpected opportunity to save Javert's life. He does so even though it means Javert will likely arrest him. Javert now feels he owes Valjean a favor, a man he has hated and pursued all his life. Javert, however, simply cannot accept the grace he received from Valjean. Having been shown conclusively to be the lesser man, he takes his own life.

We are all like Valjean and Javert at different times in our lives and have experienced the consequences of either accepting or rejecting grace. What do you need to admit so that you can experience freedom and accept the grace of others? What weaknesses, moral lapses, or compulsive behaviors do you need to address right now?

While the *Grace* stage is the turning point of the awareness and growth cycle, it is not the final one. Two more remain. The next step is pivotal in dealing with our weaknesses.

Stage Five: Acceptance

The idea that we must accept our weaknesses is caustic to many who strive for excellence in every area of life. But denying weaknesses not only blinds us to those areas we need to fix, it also sets us up to be judgmental and naive, and likely to fail repeatedly.

It must be said that acceptance does not mean inviting your weakness to move into the proverbial spare bedroom. Nor does it mean that tolerating a weakness, particularly one that can destroy a career or a relationship, is acceptable. Acknowledging that you have diabetes doesn't mean there's nothing that can be done. Acceptance simply means recognizing that you have a weakness. It requires patience as you go about seeking out the resources needed to lessen its impact or to overcome it.

In a video interview,[8] blind mountain climber Erik Weihenmayer maintained that the secret of his success has not been in beating or overcoming his blindness but in accepting it. As he puts it: "You learn to accept the 'what is' in your life."

The whole notion of accepting our weaknesses runs counter to our "you can do anything you want to if you try hard enough" Western mindset. Ironically, it is precisely the inability to see and accept weaknesses that robs us of any chance of accomplishing what we desire to do in life. Persistent habits laugh in the face of new resolutions and seasonal attempts to eradicate them. They are as effective as bringing a slingshot to the Battle of the Bulge.

Picture a team of horses all pulling together. Your weak areas are like those horses in the team that are lame or for other reasons unable to pull at full strength. What happens if you try to drag a suffering horse along while it is still attached to the team? You will get nowhere, or worse, the rest of the team will stumble and fall as well. Ignoring important weaknesses in your life has the same limiting and destructive effect.

Here's an example. Tamara is a department head for a Fortune 500 technology company. She is bright and articulate, but her most recent performance evaluation reveals that her productivity "needs improvement." She is hurt and angry, and she rejects this feedback for several months, blaming it on unrealistic expectations on the part of her superiors. After all, she puts in more than ten hours each day and often fields emergency calls on weekends.

On a recent holiday, Tamara was planning to host a barbeque for close family friends. She was frazzled, short-tempered, and exhausted, even though her husband attempted to help. An hour before the party, her best friend, Nancy, arrived to help with the final preparations. As the party wound down, they had their first moment to catch a breath. It was then that Nancy turned to her and said: "Tamara, what a great party! Why didn't you call me earlier? We could have called a few of our friends and made it a lot easier on you."

It is only then that Tamara remembered the words of her supervisor during her last performance evaluation: "Tamara is a hard worker but has much difficulty delegating." She now realizes that this is a significant weakness and it has robbed her of a much-needed raise at work. It is a weakness she has finally come to accept.

The Final Stage—Stage Six: Healing

Healing usually comes only after we have worked through the *Acceptance* stage. If you are fortunate enough to be able to eradicate your weaknesses with minimal effort, you are blessed indeed. Many of our weaknesses, especially compulsive behaviors, require much more than a quick fix. Others, like severe arthritis, will not be resolvable but must be tolerated, treated if possible, and worked around.

Sadly, many are simply unwilling to do the work that addressing lifelong habits and weaknesses often requires. Working with others in recovery, we know that it is a frequent recommendation to attend ninety meetings in the first ninety days to make a strong start to achieving sobriety. Those who continue to use are often unwilling to pay such a high price and quibble over attending one meeting a week. Similarly, many of us who have dealt with less obvious habits have quietly given up all hope of change.

Cindy is different. A struggling student who, until high school graduation, was put in classes that lowered her academic expectations, she all but ruled out further education. Fortunately, her parents did not agree, and with much encouragement, she enrolled in college. During her first semester, she was quickly identified as having a reading problem and was assessed as being dyslexic. It was the feedback that she had needed throughout her education but had not received. It transformed her.

EXCUSE GAMECHANGER
Those who best know their blind spots have mirrors that talk.

The first time Cindy was introduced to an audio book, she was hooked. She found she had an above-average ability to absorb and retain the information she learned by listening. Cindy has grown from a person who spent most of her time in secondary school in a less challenging class to someone who can easily debate complex business principles she has learned from audio formats of such scholarly sources as the *Harvard Business Review*. A career in sales has turned out to be the perfect fit for her. It requires great verbal and auditory skills but not a lot of reading.

Your Moment with the Mirror

To address our weaknesses, we must first have the insight or feedback to see them. List three people in your life who would give you honest feedback about your blind spots and weaknesses:

1. _____

2. _____

3. _____

Action Step

Ask each of these individuals the following two questions. We know they are not easy to ask, and the answers provided may be hard to hear. But the feedback you receive will be invaluable. Feel free to choose other individuals if you think the above three people cannot speak to all of the questions below. For example, your sister in Iowa may not know enough about the career side of your life to answer Question 1.

Question 1: "What weaknesses or blind spots do I need to address in order to continue to grow in my career? I give you permission to tell me even if it is hard to say and you don't want to hurt my feelings. I really value your feedback."

Example Answer: "Janet, you are great at what you do. I sometimes get the feeling, right or wrong, that you are too busy to connect with others and would rather not be interrupted. I think your air of efficiency will hurt you in the long run as you will miss out on important formal and informal networking activities."

Question 2: "What three habits or personality quirks in my personal life should I also address?"

Example Answer: "Steve, you have traveled a lot and done many things. At a party you have a tendency to trump people when they talk about their latest adventures. Do you remember last week when Martha was talking about her recent trip to Paris? I happen to know that she has waited forty-seven years to go there and only could afford to go with the money she received when her mother died last year. You have been there many times, and I think when you started asking where she went and telling her what to see next time, you really stole her thunder. Did you notice how people stopped listening and left the couch for more food?"

If you took the above challenge, congratulations! You are a person who takes the risk of seeking out honest feedback about yourself, not someone who shies away from hearing the truth about your blind spots and weaknesses.

While we all have blind spots, it is even more common for us to not know how to fix our *known* weaknesses. Fortunately, most weaknesses can be greatly improved by performing just a few key actions.

Walking the "Last Mile of Denial"

After decades of weight-loss research, the results are in: We lose weight when we consume fewer calories than our body needs each day! If you consume a few calories less than you need, you *will* lose weight. The key is determining your unique calorie needs, given your activity level and metabolism, and sticking to it.

Many of the so-called revolutionary (in other words, *fad*) diets are little more than a glitzy repackaging of this simple principle—eat fewer calories than your body needs. One popular commercial,

> **ADDRESS YOUR WEAKNESSES WITH POWERFUL INTERVENTIONS**
> Working on or around your weaknesses is surprisingly *simple* but it is not *easy*. The bad news is that you will likely need outside help to address lifelong weaknesses. The good news is with help, most weaknesses can be addressed with a very short list of powerful, straightforward, but often neglected, interventions.

for example, pushes a "special clinically proven weight loss pill," but in the finest of small print it also mentions that subjects lost 3.8 pounds over eight weeks while taking their "secret formula," eating a sensible diet and exercising. Incredible! Nearly anyone could lose 3.8 pounds if he or she exercised frequently and ate healthy for two straight months!

But if weight loss is so simple, where do we all go wrong? It is in execution and discipline, of course. We find it difficult to accept and even more difficult to follow the math of calorie intake. We tend to get part of the formula right—maybe exercise or nutrition—but ignore the other part, usually our calorie count.

Think for a moment about the effect of doing several important things right but ignoring a critical action needed for success. The results, especially if you have put in a lot of effort to get things right, might be very disappointing and costly.

For example, imagine going on a long awaited summer vacation, and 1) locking the front door, 2) locking the back door, but 3) leaving a basement entrance unlocked. Despite your efforts, you could still be robbed blind.

We call these "number three" actions—whether locking that final door or window, or taking that final step toward living within a written budget or diet—*walking the last mile of denial*.

> **It is only when we are willing to 'walk the last mile of denial' and face up to our remaining 'hold-out' actions and oversights that we can hope to achieve lasting, permanent change.**
> **– Dr. Bill Dyment**

Walking the Last Mile in Real Life

Here are just a few examples of *walking the last mile of denial*.

Financial Honesty

You take the "final step" to address your financial excuses by ...

- Investing $35 for a simple accounting software program so you can finally track your spending.

- Sitting down with a financial planner or tax accountant, hiding nothing and asking for help.

- Creating and following a budget using your new software.

Medical Issues

You take the "final step" to address your health excuses by ...

- Calling your specialist to schedule that scary follow-up test, the one you've been putting off.

- Deciding you will no longer buy large amounts of sweets "for the kids." You know you're the one who raids the kitchen for ice cream or cookies after others are asleep.

Compulsive Behaviors

You take the "final step" into full recovery by ...

- Seeking out a weekly meeting to address a compulsive behavior you have not been able to eradicate on your own.

- Breaking the silence by telling someone close to you that you need help with a secret struggle.

Emotional Issues

You take the "final step" needed to resolve your emotional hurts and avoidant behavior by ...

- Investing in some long overdue counseling to address what your friends have been pointing out for years— your tendency to shy away from closeness because of past hurts.

- Joining a small group of supportive peers because you know it will help with your mood, motivation, or a tendency to isolate under stress.

Spiritual Growth Areas

You take the "final step" in exploring your spirituality by ...

- Admitting that you have been running away from your spiritual roots by using excuses that don't really hold up to scrutiny. You make arrangements to reconnect by accepting the invitation of a friend to attend a retreat in two weeks.

- Realizing that you haven't been a part of a service organization for over five years, you finally decide to volunteer for at least one serving opportunity this month.

If you have been unable to make progress toward a coveted goal, there's a good chance a blind spot or known weakness is holding you back. We encourage you to reach out and receive the help you need. We can help you with professional coaching, you can get into counseling or a group, or begin to reach out to those you trust. The last mile is the mile that changes everything.

Tracy heads a division of a small pharmaceutical company. Her job depends on taking a new medicine from discovery to market. She has neither the sufficient scientific knowledge nor the personal time to complete such daunting projects, yet she is responsible for getting it done. Fortunately, that's why she has a team. Her skill in putting together a department of people who can get things accomplished has enabled her to land the job she currently has and all the perks that go with it.

We are all like Tracy when it comes to our weaknesses, especially medical, emotional, and compulsive ones. In many cases we cannot fix ourselves but we are responsible to manage our "project" and to seek out the help we need to eradicate our weaknesses or illnesses. The fact is that by the age of 40, most people have at least one chronic health or emotional concern.

> ### THE WASTED YEARS
> Many people who struggle with addictive or compulsive behaviors spend years trying to prove to themselves and others that they can change on their own. Attempts to find more self-discipline invariably lead to an endless cycle of short-term success followed by failure. One man we knew in recovery spent ten years like this until, in desperation, he finally shared his struggle in the safety of a weekly accountability group. Within one month, he had broken the relapse cycle of his compulsive behavior. Today he looks back on his independent efforts as "the wasted years."

Medical and emotional illnesses are *real* and must be courageously addressed with the help of a professional. In many cases, we are not responsible for the onset of these illnesses. We are, however, responsible for our response to these challenges. This means getting the help needed to address them immediately. Like Tracy, you are the project manager. You can't do it alone but you are ultimately responsible for your success in life.

Your challenge might be a nagging thyroid problem, a mood-related issue, a bad back, compulsive eating, or even difficulty sleeping. Dealing with your weaknesses will enable you to achieve a far better outcome than the average person who lives up to only a portion of his or her potential.

Here are a few examples of some of the challenges you may be facing:

Chronic Medical Issues

- Allergies
- Arthritis
- Back pain

- Cancer
- Diabetes or hypoglycemia
- Fibromyalgia
- Gastrointestinal illnesses
- Heart disease
- High blood pressure
- High cholesterol
- Migraines
- PMS or menopause
- Sexual dysfunction
- Sleep disorders
- Substance abuse and other physical addictions
- Thyroid disorder

Emotional Illnesses, Compulsive Behaviors, and Destructive Habits

- Anger
- Attention disorders, including ADD and ADHD
- Bipolar and psychotic disorders
- Chronic anxiety
- Communication difficulties
- Compulsive, non-physical, addictions (for example, pornography, excessive video gaming, gambling, and shopping)
- Depression, mild to severe
- Hoarding and cluttering
- Overeating
- Panic attacks
- Post-traumatic stress disorder
- Reactions to past abuse
- Social phobias and other fears

One of the biggest killers of dreams is untreated depression. Those who suffer from it, at the very least, will need to adjust their lifestyle to include more one-on-one support. In most cases, counseling will be essential along with sufficient social activity, proper nutrition, and exercise. For some, medication will be an important part of their recovery.

Weaknesses:
Genetics, Environment and Our Part

In 2003, The Human Genome Project[9] achieved a milestone in scientific history by publishing the first complete sequence of human DNA. Its impact on science cannot be overestimated. We now have the beginnings of a standard of comparison, a genetic yardstick, if you will, that enables us to look at the genetics of many common illnesses. As a result, new treatments based on genetic findings have been developed to treat diseases, such as breast cancer, with treatments more tailored to a patient's specific genetic code.

What has been learned so far is that most medical and emotional disorders have some genetic component, usually a predisposition based on a few genes that differ from the rest of the human population. The encouraging news is that, in many cases, we are finding that the genetic factors, while almost universally present, account for only 30 to 40 percent of the story. In other words, your lifestyle, diet, environment, and self-care contribute 60 percent of the likelihood that you will develop a certain illness, and your parents' genetics contribute only 40 percent.

Further, even if we have a genetic predisposition to a certain illness, we can often do much to limit its severity by our choices. For example,

FREE *BLIND SPOTS AND WEAKNESSES* EXCUSESTOPPER
To help you answer the question, "Has my behavior crossed the line into an addiction?" go to www.FireYourExcuses.com, register if you are not yet part of the Fire Your Excuses Community, and type in the keyword: BLINDSPOTS

a person who is genetically prone to high cholesterol but eats a healthy diet might do better than a person without a predisposition but eats whatever he or she wants.

We always do better in life when we assume that we have more control over a weakness or medical issue and seek out proper help. Two researchers, Wayne Sotile and Robin Cantor-Cooke, found that more optimistic heart patients are more likely to 1) follow-up with the doctor, 2) eat healthy, and 3) exercise.[10] They are also more likely to live longer, as the following Harvard University School of Public Health study reveals:

> In 1986, a group of male volunteers were asked to complete a questionnaire that judged whether they were optimistic or pessimistic. They all were healthy individuals with no known chronic medical conditions when the study began. The men were followed for an average of 10 years after filling out the questionnaire. Study participants with the highest levels of optimism accounted for less than half the number of cases of angina, and nonfatal and fatal heart attacks during the course of the study when compared to pessimistic men.[11]

When the final chapter of your life is written, will your weaknesses be your "Waterloo," or what you have used to inspire others?

Immediate Steps to Take

Here are a few steps you can take immediately to live your life well in spite of your weaknesses.

"Don't go dark." What you are running from will eventually be found out in time. Follow up with your doctor regularly for all routine physical exams, and especially for any chronic illnesses or concerns. Don't operate from an out-of-date understanding of what treatments and options are available to you.

"Don't remain uninformed." Seek out the perspective of trusted

mentors and friends to help you identify any weaknesses that might be hindering you as well as your areas of strength.

"Don't keep trying to resolve things on your own." Get serious about tackling your known weaknesses. Chances are, it has been years since you have known about a certain weakness. Are you still minimizing it and stuck in the "I can do it myself if I really try" stage?

"Don't let what you can't do, keep you from doing what you can." Remember, and, more importantly, live by John Wooden's famous quote. Surround yourself with stories of those who have overcome and worked around their weaknesses, not those who have used their weaknesses to remain a victim.

Not Limited by What We Can't Do

Finally, we would like to introduce you to Brigadier General Joshua L. Chamberlain. For many readers, he is likely an unfamiliar name but one you should know.

A true American hero, this former college professor left everything and volunteered to serve in the Union Army. This man of letters, who spoke nine languages, left behind his comfortable academic and family life and soon led the most decisive action of the pivotal battle of the Civil War—the struggle for control of Little Round Top that took place in the midst of the Battle of Gettysburg. For this victory, he had the honor of leading the Union troops at the surrender of General Lee and the Confederate Army two years later. Had Chamberlain's 20th Maine Infantry not held Little Round Top's ridge and had they permitted the Confederate soldiers to outflank them, the whole history of our country may have been written in a profoundly different way.

Chamberlain's involvement in the war, however, did not come without great personal cost. Wounded six times, he spent the next 49 years cruelly tethered to a primitive catheter, which he required after being shot at the Battle of Petersburg in 1864 by a bullet that ripped through his hip and groin. Yet, whereas a lesser man might have drawn a pension and felt sorry for himself, Chamberlain became the president of Bowdoin College, and served four terms as Governor of Maine before finally succumbing to his war wounds in 1914.[12]

Truly, Joshua Chamberlain lived out his life as a great man despite his obvious physical disabilities. He embodied John Wooden's challenge by never letting what he couldn't do keep him from doing what he could. What was he doing when he grew weak with the final illness that would lead to his death? He was busily planning the 50th anniversary of the Battle of Gettysburg.[13]

TAKE THE 30-DAY BLIND SPOTS AND WEAKNESSES CHALLENGE

1. Ask three people who know both your work and personal life to answer the following question honestly: "What weaknesses or blind spots are important for me to address in order to continue to grow in my career?"

2. Ask these same people a second question: "What three habits or personality quirks, in my life in general, should I also address?"

3. List any habits or issues you haven't been able to overcome on your own, even though you have tried for some time. It is crucial to be honest with yourself about whether another attempt on your own will achieve different results. It is likely time to reach out for help.

4. Pick the most troublesome issue from Question #3 and make an appointment with a professional or attend at least one group meeting to begin the process of addressing it, this time with help.

FIRE YOUR EXCUSES

CHAPTER TWO:

HEALTH AND WELLNESSES

CHAPTER 2

HEALTH AND WELLNESS

You can't solve a problem with the same kind of thinking that created it.
—*ALBERT EINSTEIN*

WITNESSING A DEATH IS SOMETHING YOU NEVER FORGET. LESSONS taken from such an experience are also forever memorable, as I (Bill) learned five years ago.

Approaching the entrance of a coffee shop with a friend, I nearly stumbled over a man lying face up in the doorway. He had collapsed there just seconds before. Inside the café were two medical doctors, whom I happened to know, who began CPR. But the rattle in his breath told them he was leaving this world. The cause of death: A heart attack and brain hemorrhage. He was only 46.

One of the doctors later told me that she had found the goals he had written for the day tucked in the book he was carrying. I couldn't help wondering if he had any premonition that "today" would be his last as he was writing them.

All of us must face the fact that one of our days will be our last. When will that day come for you? Of course, there's no way of knowing. But ask yourself, do your own lifestyle and health practices suggest that you will live a long and healthy life?

Typically, the average person grossly overestimates the number of years he or she is likely to live. Many believe they will live eighty, ninety or even a hundred years, when their behaviors and medical data strongly suggest decades otherwise. Sure, there are exceptions, but thinking "maybe I'll win the health lottery" is like taking out your retirement savings and trying to double it in Vegas.

People who make permanent healthy lifestyle changes are usually mobilized by some type of emotional awakening, a powerful event that inspires change. Your emotional awakening might be a frightening doctor's report. Or perhaps it is a conversation with your concerned daughter, a strong desire to continue to do what you love, or simply wanting to feel good again about the way you look.

What motivates you? Take a moment to answer the following important questions as if your life depends on it. It does!

My emotional awakenings are _____

_____

_____

_____.

I plan on living until the age of _____.

The reasons I wish to live this long are _____

_____

_____.

I believe I will make it to this age because I am _____

_____

_____

(i.e, list healthy choices being practiced.)

A Cultural Shift

Recently, we had the opportunity to speak to employees at a well-known Fortune 500 company. Lining one prominent hallway was a series of framed photos chronicling corporate gatherings attended by the organization's executives beginning in the 1940s.

When we studied the first photo closely, we were stunned. Clearly visible in the large, black-and-white photo were the smiling faces of the entire executive team filling a banquet hall. Not one of them was even slightly overweight. As we walked down the row of photos, the faces smiling back at us grew fuller and fuller. By the time we reached the photos of the present decade, there were many heavy executives sitting around the tables.

There are at least two explanations, of course. Either the organization now intentionally hires and promotes more obese executives, or executives sixty years ago were simply less rotund. The second hypothesis seemed far more likely, but we needed concrete evidence that we were not reading into things. It was not hard to find.

America's waistline has increased tremendously, and disturbingly, over the past twenty years. In 1990, ten states had an obesity rate of less than 10 percent, and no states had a prevalence equal to or greater than 15 percent.[1] By 2010, at least 20 percent of the residents of every state, except Colorado, were obese. In twelve states, 30 percent of their residents were obese.[2]

Preventable illnesses make up approximately 75 percent of all healthcare costs and account for eight of the nine leading causes of death.[3] We have allowed excuses to shorten our lives and to limit our ability to achieve great things because of our poor health practices.

To see anything else as more important is, as the saying goes, as silly as "rearranging deck chairs on the Titanic." Sadly, this is precisely what otherwise smart people do every day.

Achieving a Balanced Lifestyle
of Health and Wellness

The four most critical aspects of health maintenance are nutrition, exercise, rest and stress management. Our health is foundational. It determines how long we each have to pursue our highest calling and deepest interests.

For some who are reading this right now, your fundamental challenge in establishing a healthy lifestyle is not being confused about what to do in the gym, how many calories to eat, or what to buy in the grocery store. It is to finally have the courage and humility to seek out a strong support system. We wish it were as simple as deciding on a new attitude, but often people need much more than a fresh start, new gear, or a new diet to break a lifetime of poor health habits.

If you have battled weight and health issues related to your own lifestyle choices for a number of years, a new diet, exercise program, machine, or gadget will not be sufficient to achieve permanent change. In the long term, you will fail. This is not said to discourage you but to recommend what will give you the very best chance for success.

Permanent lifestyle change can only be sustained by addressing long-standing behaviors that have deep emotional roots. Yes, dramatic changes can be sustained for short three- to six-month periods, but unless the root causes are also dealt with, we invariably return to our previous weight and fitness. Eventually, many simply give up and begin to rationalize or ignore their extra weight and poor health choices.

In our Fire Your Excuses Coaching Programs, clients make the commitment to connect with at least two strong accountability partners before attempting big behavioral changes, and also to seek out the assistance of a supportive group of friends. We hope that you too will give yourself the very best chance of success by doing the same. Know that as you take action, the amount of support to which you commit will be as important as your new knowledge and techniques.

Nutrition—Is There a "Right Plan"?

A high-fat, fast-food love affair does devastating damage to our health over time, but the problem is, it takes a while. A "devil-may-care drive-through" lifestyle may work in your teens and twenties, but as we age, our lab work and yearly physicals begin to tell a very different story.

Is it the message of this book to never enjoy a burger with fries? No, it is that these immensely high-fat foods should be enjoyed no more than once a week. It is long past time for most of us to slow down, assess what we are putting in our bodies, and make better choices.

Is one diet plan really better than another? If you are catching on, we had you at "diet," always a word that should raise concerns if not red flags. Early in my EAP profession, I (Marcus) took on the assignment of assessing the most popular diet and nutritional programs for our client organizations. I was to formulate an opinion about which program would be most helpful to employees. I examined several well-known weight loss and diet programs. I concluded that all had merit and the results of following one program versus another varied only slightly. Everyone I interviewed who was consistently following one of these programs said they were experiencing significant benefits. Interestingly, they were equally vocal about other programs they had tried without success.

Each reputable program has its strengths and weaknesses, but if after talking to your doctor and nutritionist you choose one you like and follow it closely, you will see results. The challenge is not discovering a new diet plan that will get you into shape for your sister's wedding or your high school reunion, but a way of caring for your physical self that is sensible, permanent, and based on sane science.

The FYE Nutritional Plan is a summary of the best current guidelines from top nutritionists, trainers, and health scientists. It consists of eight deceptively simple guidelines to reach and maintain a healthy balance of nutritional wellness.

FYE's Eight-Step Nutrition Plan

1. Eat four to five moderately sized meals each day to regulate sugar levels, increase metabolism, and avoid excessive and binge eating.

2. Balance protein and carbohydrates with every meal to sustain energy, maintain and build healthy muscle mass, and stabilize insulin levels. Have a fist-size portion of each.

3. Plan your meals ahead of time to avoid junk food snacking. Keeping healthy snacks with you at all times—at home, in the car, at work, in your purse or gym bag, will greatly assist you in taking control of what you eat.

4. Drink at least five glasses of water daily to stay hydrated and to dilute sugar and caffeinated drinks. Not only does it flush out toxins and hydrate our bodies, water is essential for our digestion.

5. Until you achieve your goals and maintain them for at least six months, keep a food diary or use any of the many phone applications to monitor food intake and daily calorie count.

6. Make it your new lifelong habit to weigh yourself and measure your waist over your navel at least once a week. Your waist measurement should be no more than half your height, in inches.

7. Know your ideal daily calorie intake based on your weight. The USDA and many other online sites can also help you calculate this important number based on your age and activity level.

8. Talk to your doctor to determine if vitamins or other supplements are necessary to make up for any nutritional deficiencies.

Additional Tips

Eat more healthy fats. Recent government guidelines have been adjusted upward from a suggestion that we receive 10 percent of our calories from healthy fats to 20 to 25 percent. Great sources of healthy fats include olive oil, nuts, and fish, which are high in Omega 3. These foods have also been shown to be a good way of regulating healthy cholesterol levels.

FULL NUTRITIONAL DISCLOSURE: A TREND WHOSE TIME HAS COME The federal healthcare bill that passed in 2010 requires "chain restaurants with more than 20 locations to post calories and nutrition information next to items on the restaurant menu and menu at the drive-through."[4] Between the online calorie counters, blogs, and these recent menu changes, it is now easy to have a fairly accurate idea of how many calories we are consuming each day.

Focus on increasing your fiber intake. Most Americans get far less fiber than actually needed. If this is you, consider topping your cereal with wheat germ or a similar healthy fiber addition.

Rethink your soft drink habit. Try a "soda fast" for a week and see how you feel. Diet soda has zero calories but, for some people, it can really upset their stomach. Enjoy your favorite soft drink on special occasions. One soda a week makes for a refreshing treat. Try the gourmet ones, they are great.

Break the caffeine addiction. If you get a "caffeine headache" whenever you miss your next dosage of caffeine, it's time to admit you are an addict. Admitting it is the first step! Try cutting back, drinking more decaffeinated coffee, or eliminating it altogether.

Additional considerations. Recent studies at the Amen Clinics have shed new light on the relationship between the brain and our diet. Certain foods seem to help in the prevention and treatment of brain disorders, anxiety, depression, anger, and impulsiveness. It is suggested that we avoid or reduce the consumption of artificial food coloring, sugar substitutes, alcohol and cigarettes. It is also recommended that we consume more protein and less simple carbohydrates, i.e., sugar, candy, white flour, rice, and pasta, and instead eat more complex carbo-hydrates found in many fruits and vegetables.[5]

SAL'S SUCCESS STORY

We'd like to introduce you to someone who has undergone an extraordinary, permanent health change. Sixteen years ago, Sal Fazio weighed 310 pounds. In our interview, he explained that he was raised in a Mexican-Italian family where great food in great qualities was always available, and others around him struggled with health issues too. Nevertheless, he made a radical decision to change his life and never looked back. He lost 140 pounds and has kept it off ever since. Sal became a Certified Personal Trainer for the exclusive Sports Club Los Angeles in Irvine, California. If you would like to hear more about his journey and his secrets, you can hear his powerful story at www.15MinuteAdvantage.com.[6] Like the old Sal, we too can succumb to poor lifestyle and health habits and choose to remain a victim to denial, excuses, and a sabotaging support network. Sal was at a huge risk for sudden death; now he spends his time helping others make better health choices.

Exercise and Fitness

Doctors commonly report that just a brisk walk for twenty minutes each day can greatly reduce the risk of a variety of cardiovascular and heart problems. The critical question is, what realistic and reasonable exercise activity can you commit to weekly to elevate your heart rate for a consistent period of time?

Calories, Calories, Calories

Jillian Michaels,[7] celebrity fitness trainer for the popular *The Biggest Loser* television show, reminds us that weight management is all about the calories. Undoubtedly, some exercise programs are more effective than others, but the bottom line is this: If you burn more calories than you consume, creating a calorie deficit, you will lose weight.

Jillian recommends a daily target of 1500-1800 calories a day for healthy weight loss for men and 1200-1500 calories a day for healthy weight loss for women. Remember, though, there are

TIP:
"Bring your own snacks that are portion controlled," Jillian Michaels, fitness trainer on *The Biggest Loser* advises. She allows herself "a couple hundred calories a day of treat food."[8] The problem is most servings of cake or ice cream are far more than that. Some can top 700 calories.

exceptions based on your health and age. Be sure to talk to your doctor or nutritionist about what target goal is right for you.

Resistance Training Is Key

The secret weapon for brisk, healthy weight loss is resistance or weight training. If you only do aerobics, you will burn calories and raise your metabolism, but by skipping the resistance training, you will be missing out on the second half of the equation: using your body's natural repair cycle to not only tone up, but to burn additional calories in the process.

Involve large muscle groups, such as chest, leg, and back areas. By exercising them twice a week, your body will have to work overtime to repair and rebuild itself, adding new muscle development and greater tone. The results achieved by combining aerobics with strength training can be dramatic. We find that we lose weight much faster and are far more pleased with the results when we use free weights or do circuit resistance training using machines. You will too. Aerobic exercise is essential, but for great body tone, it is simply not enough.

Some women are concerned that if they lift weights they will build up too much muscle mass. The fact is, it is very difficult, even for men who lift weights consistently, to bulk up after age thirty due to hormonal changes.

Becoming "too husky" is not a realistic fear. It is, however, a charter member of the "exercise excuses hall of fame."

"Hey, you're at your ideal weight, too!"

"Prune" or "Lean Beef"?

Gary, 38, played varsity football in high school. He kept active in college, working out regularly and playing basketball with his friends. He's now married and has kids. He bought a treadmill and let his gym membership lapse, telling himself that he had a set of weights in the garage and would just work out at home.

The truth is that he has worked out only sporadically for the past decade. Every couple of years his weight creeps up and his wife chides him about his extra fifteen or twenty pounds. He jumps back into a diet routine, but the weights continue to gather dust and he does little or no exercise. In three months, usually after the holidays, his weight is back up again and the cycle repeats itself. The problem is each time he diets down to 195 pounds, he looks a little flabbier when he gets there.

Yo-yo dieting is not only tough on us psychologically, it also destroys our much needed muscle mass, condemning us to more and more difficulty in maintaining our healthy weight. For this reason, it is not uncommon to see people gain more weight each time they start and stop a weight maintenance program. Eventually, some just give up and begin to rationalize that being heavier is just part of being older. This, of course, is not true. As one fitness expert put it: "If you are a *plum* and you just lose weight, you will become a *prune*." The goal is not to shrivel up or to become thin-but-spongy, it is to slim up and tone up at the same time.

"But I Have a Slow Metabolism!"

Many people point to a slow metabolism or a thyroid issue to explain their struggles with weight. Hypothyroidism *is* associated with a slower metabolism, but exercise is well known to increase it. If you believe you have a thyroid issue or metabolic problem, make sure you have been tested to confirm this and you are receiving the proper treatment. If not, it's time to see a doctor. Thyroid disease is a real disorder and is not an excuse. Not doing anything about it is.

Efficient Aerobic Exercise

Make no mistake, aerobic exercise is an essential part of our health maintenance program. Fortunately, for those who have bad knees and backs, there are many other aerobic options besides high impact aerobic activities like jogging and running. What are the best aerobic machines in the gym? The VersaClimber and the StepMill, according to Jillian Michaels.[9] If you have never used a VersaClimber, the vertical motion you perform is a little like climbing a tree. The StepMill is more familiar to most gym members. It looks and acts like a rolling staircase that simulates climbing up an endless flight of steps. Both are excellent, high-intensity, cardio machines. If these machines are not available in your gym, other good low impact options are the elliptical trainer, the treadmill, and the StairMaster.

Before You Begin

- *Check with your doctor.* Always consult with your medical doctor before starting on any major exercise and diet plan. Any weight loss plan that results in losing more than two pounds a week is generally too aggressive to be healthy and maintained. Take it slow and you will give yourself time to adjust to the new you. Your goal is permanent lifestyle change, not fitting into your swimsuit because the summer months are just around the corner.

> **TIP:**
> As a reward for your first three months of consistent exercise, consider treating yourself to a Polar or Garmin heart rate monitor. They also make a great gift. This device features a thin elastic strap that wraps around your chest and a watch that wirelessly records your heart rate and the number of calories consumed during your workouts, yard work, or long walks. Many gym machines automatically display Polar's heart rate information on the screen as you train. Some models even allow you to download your workout data onto your computer.

- *Do short workouts.* Notice that the program below features very short workouts—just 30 minutes a session. You will see far better results, and it will be much easier to stay motivated if you exercise more often for less time.

- *Adjust to setbacks.* You will certainly experience obstacles on the way to better health. A torn knee ligament does not mean you can't do upper body resistance training while you heal or wait for surgery. An injured shoulder doesn't mean you can't ride a bike or use leg machines. Those who are in great shape continue to exercise even when they are injured. They simply work around the affected area. Exercise excuses are always available. It is our choice if we use them.

The simple exercise plan below has been approved by several of our fitness experts. If you follow it consistently, and eat the right amount of calories for your height, weight, and activity level, not only will you lose the weight you want to lose, you will be very happy with your muscle tone when you get there.

FYE FitWeek Plan: Exercise Schedule

Day 1. Aerobic workout. Keep your heart rate elevated and stay within your heart-rate training range for thirty minutes. Note: Your heart-rate training range will vary depending on your age and fitness level.

Day 2. Weight training. Upper body workout: chest/shoulders/triceps/back/biceps.

Day 3. Aerobic workout.

Day 4. Weight training. Lower body workout: abdominals/quads/hamstrings/calves.

Day 5. Aerobic workout.

Day 6. Weight training. Upper body workout: chest/shoulders/triceps/back/biceps.

Day 7. Rest or light walk.

Aerobic Training Tips

- As much as possible, keep your heart rate up continuously for at least thirty minutes. Know your target heart rate for your age and health.

- Change things up. As your body will adapt to your aerobic routine over time, change your speed and the machine's resistance often to keep your body guessing. Best-selling author, Bill Phillips, recommends interval training, where you sprint and jog alternately, to bring the heart rate up and down throughout your exercise session. This technique burns fat more effectively during your workout and keeps your metabolism high for a longer period afterward.[10]

Weight Training Tips

- Rotate your upper and lower body workouts two times per week. Keep working each area evenly by scheduling two upper body workouts one week and two lower body workouts the following week.

- Change your weight routine in some way every two weeks for maximum results.

- There are various ways to conduct weight training, depending on your individual goals. To maintain current muscle mass or to tone, start with a light set of 8-10 reps for the first set and then do 4-5 more sets of 8-10 reps, increasing the weights slightly. If you wish to increase your muscle mass, start with a light set of 6-8 reps, then increase the weight steadily over 4-5 sets doing 6-8 reps each.

- Give yourself a one-minute rest between reps but keep the workout moving to maintain your heart rate.

Final Exercise Tips

- Most injuries, especially those sustained in weight training, come from not stretching properly—at least five minutes, before and after your workout—and making quick jerky movements during repetitions. Pay attention to your body for any signs of increased pain, sharp sudden pain, or muscle exhaustion. This usually means you need to stop momentarily or completely.

- For both aerobic and weight-training workouts, always schedule your workout times into your calendar just like any other appointment. This will keep you on track and less likely to cancel your exercise session for another meeting.

- Tell family and friends about your standing workout appointments ahead of time. This will reduce surprise and random requests, such as errands, drop-offs, and other distractions that can sabotage your workout goals.

- While working out at home can be great, fitness centers help keep the focus on your workout and serve as a place of refuge.

- Get a trainer to help you, even for a single session or two, if you start to feel as if you are struggling with the last few inches or are no longer making progress.

- Keep an activities chart to set specific goals, monitor progress, and keep yourself accountable. Use the **FYE FitWeek Plan** as an aid.

> **WAIST NOT, WANT NOT**
> Cardiac surgeon and host of *The Dr. Oz Show,* Dr. Mehmet Oz, maintains that your waist size must be no more than half your height. Take the measurement around your belly button.[11]

FYE FitWeek Plan

To help you keep track of your fitness progress, we recommend you use the following chart for at least the first 90 days. Please consult with your doctor before beginning any fitness program.

FYE FitWeek Plan **for the week of** _____

Day of the Week	Exercise (Alternate Strength Training Days between Upper Body and Lower Body)	Column A Daily Calorie Target	Column B Calories Eaten	Column C Calories Burned in Exercise	Column D Net Calories (Col. B minus Col. C)
Sunday	Rest Day				
Monday	Upper Body or Lower Body Strength Training (circle one)				
Tuesday	Cardio Training				
Wednesday	Upper Body or Lower Body Strength Training (circle one)				
Thursday	Cardio Training				
Friday	Upper Body or Lower Body Strength Training (circle one)				
Saturday	Cardio Training				
		Comments, observations, insights about week:			
Weekly Calorie Summary	Sum of Column D				
Weekly Weigh in	Same time, method and day each week				
Weekly Waist Measure- ment	Measure around your waist and over your belly button				

Rest Hygiene

Many individuals minimize the importance of proper sleep and rest. *Rest hygiene* can be defined as the degree of attention we give to our sleep and relaxation needs.

Rest hygiene not only refers to how many hours of sleep we get at night but also to how we use weekends and vacation time. In our counseling practices, we cringe when we hear people comment that they cannot remember the last time they have taken a vacation. Some unconsciously feel as if they are not important enough to take care of themselves, even as they sacrifice for others. Caring for the needs of children, family, or your boss can be a legitimate challenge to your rest hygiene or it can be the perfect excuse. Self-care habits run very deep, and have profound emotional and familial roots. If everyone around you performs marginal self-care, an unhealthy lifestyle can begin to feel very "normal."

A recent Carnegie Mellon University study reported that those who received fewer than seven hours of sleep per night were three times more likely to suffer from cold and flu than those who received eight hours or more.[12] In another study, a professor at the University of California Berkeley reported that sleep-deprived subjects shown a series of increasingly disturbing images manifested a 60 percent greater amygdala response than those who had adequate rest. The amygdala, which is the part of our brain that acts as an emotional switchboard, was severely overheating. As the researcher, Dr. Matt Walker, explained, "...when you're sleep deprived you're all accelerator and no brakes. You don't have control over your emotions."[13]

It is estimated that 70 percent of all Americans experience some form of sleep disorder, and many more go undiagnosed. According to the National Sleep Foundation's 2008 Sleep in America Poll, 65 percent of Americans reported some type of sleep problem at least a few nights a week, and 44 percent admitted to sleeping poorly almost every night.[14] Eighteen million Americans suffer from sleep apnea—brief interruption of breathing during sleep—and 12 million Americans have restless leg syndrome.[15] Sleep-related symptoms can also be life threatening. Amazingly, 37 percent report having dozed off while driving this past year.[16]

Many couples avoid dealing with sleep issues, like snoring and apnea, and instead opt for sleeping in separate rooms. This doesn't solve the underlying medical problem and, inevitably, it leads to less emotional and physical intimacy. A medical sleep condition is not your fault; ignoring it is. Firing your sleep-related excuses may mean seeing your medical doctor to request a sleep assessment or making an appointment at a sleep clinic to explore possible treatments.

Napping Facts[18]

- Within 20 minutes of falling asleep, we experience Stage II sleep, which is needed to achieve alertness and improve motor skills.

- A 90-minute nap is necessary to increase creativity and enjoy deep REM-stage sleep.

- The afternoon period between 1 p.m. and 3 p.m. is the prime nap time, as this is when our alertness dips.

FAMOUS NAPPERS[19]
Napoleon Bonaparte
Winston Churchill
Leonardo daVinci
Thomas Edison
Albert Einstein
John F. Kennedy
Ronald Reagan
John D. Rockefeller
Eleanor Roosevelt

> ## THE SECRET WEAPON OF NAPPING
> **A memory study at the University of California Berkeley found that those who slept 90 minutes after learning the names and faces of 100 individuals actually improved their memory retention score by 10 percent when retested. In contrast, those who did not sleep actually did 10 percent poorer when retested.[17]**

Healthy Sleep Habits

How well do you respect your own sleep and rest needs? We endorse the following sleep guidelines.

- *Consistent schedule:* Maintain a consistent bedtime and wake time, including weekends, when the temptation is to sleep in. This practice strengthens our brains' circadian (sleep rhythm) cycles and can help greatly with sleep onset.

- *Wind-down routine:* Develop a relaxing winding-down ritual right before bedtime and conduct it away from bright lights. It will tell your body and mind you are getting ready for bed.

- *Sleep-friendly setting:* Create a sleep-conducive environment that is dark, quiet, comfortable, and cool.

- *Optimum mattress:* Make sure your mattress is comfortable and supportive. The one you have been using for years may have exceeded its life expectancy—about nine or ten years for most good quality mattresses.

- *Natural sleep aids:* If you have a difficult time falling asleep, ask your doctor if a natural sleep supplement such as Kava, Valerian, or Melatonin would be beneficial.

Vacation Deprivation in America—Our "No Vacation Nation"

Proper rest hygiene not only requires careful attention to our sleep, it also demands that we reevaluate our use of vacation.

"Not only are we putting in longer hours on the job now than we did in the 1950s," reports Take Back Your Time, a vacation advocacy group, "we are working more than medieval peasants did and more than the citizens of any other industrialized country."[20] Expedia.com's 2009 International Vacation Deprivation™ Survey reported that American workers receive an average of 13 vacation days per year and 35 percent don't use all this time.[21]

Not taking vacation can be deadly, reports travel writer Rob Lovitt: "Men who don't take regular vacations are 32 percent more likely to die of heart attacks. It's even worse for workaholic women, who have a 50 percent higher risk—and are more than twice as likely to suffer from depression—than their vacationing counterparts."[22] The problem is so widespread, Lovitt pronounces, that we are the "no vacation nation." For the person who wants to live a long, healthy life, regular vacations are not optional. They are "doctor's orders."

"Taking our vacations" begins by building rest into our weekly schedule. Start by deliberately planning one night of the week to be a vacation night, then move on to planning a vacation or "staycation" weekend once every two months. Next, plan at least one week a year, not around the holidays, where you really get away. Beware of simply tacking on a day here or there around

---

A 24-HOUR CHALLENGE

Try this for thirty days: Take the risk of setting aside one 24-hour period each week in which you do not perform any significant chores, errands, paperwork, or prepare for the week ahead. Instead, spend the day reconnecting with family, friends, faith, or nature, and work as much as you like on the other six days. You will find you get more done in the remaining six days than you do by working all seven days.

a Monday holiday, a business trip, or family gathering. Cancel your getaway plans only for true emergencies. If money is an issue, choose a cheaper, not shorter, vacation, rather than delaying or giving it up. Your vacation time is your rejuvenation time.

To get in the vacation mood, consider renting the inspiring film, *The Bucket List,*[23] starring Jack Nicholson and Morgan Freeman. They play two dying hospital roommates who share their lists of the forty things they want to do and places they wish to visit before they die. After seeing this movie you will want to create your own list. Two other great references for vacation ideas are Patricia Schultz's *1,000 Places to See Before You Die,*[24] an international directory of the most amazing places on the planet, as well as *1,000 Places to See in the U.S.A. and Canada Before You Die.*[25]

Stress Management

Our most requested seminar topic, overwhelmingly, has been "stress management." Stress-related illnesses have emerged as one of the key health challenges of our era, and for this reason we must address this topic in a comprehensive way.

Our modern understanding of stress was introduced by Hans Selye, MD, who in 1936 began researching the effects of stress on the body.[26] When we feel stress, a powerful sequence of physiological reactions immediately occurs within us. Those amazing stories you have heard are true. In a traumatic stressful crisis, mothers have been known to experience almost superhuman strength, lifting up a car to free their injured children. Under stress, our brain signals to the rest of us that a "fight or flight" response is needed, and our bodies almost instantaneously ready for either option. Muscles strengthen and our heart rate, breathing, blood sugar, and blood pressure all increase. In past centuries, it was more common that the stress we were experiencing would be a physical threat. Today, our bodies are more likely to be alerting us to an emotional assault in which response options are far less clear. It is no wonder many suffer an ill-defined sense of anxiety and worry by day and insomnia by night.

It is important to realize that stress is not the enemy of health.

Without it, for example, our muscles would atrophy and life would not be exciting. We would also stop growing personally and professionally. Further, what may be relaxing to one person may be stressful to another. Many factors come into play when considering the likely impact of certain stressors, including our genetic makeup, other stress we may be experiencing at the time, our support system, and our emotional health. *Unmanaged* stress is the real danger, and it is epidemic in America.

When "Stress" Becomes "Distress"

Many clients have appeared at our offices on Monday morning because they were rushed to the hospital over the weekend experiencing frightening symptoms. What they had feared was a heart attack fortunately proved to only be symptoms of severe stress. We are glad they erred on the side of caution. Our first meeting always reveals some area of their lives where stress is being badly mismanaged or not managed at all. In many instances, it does take a medical emergency or our bodies "shouting at us" to take action. Here are the most common symptoms of stress.

Stress Warning Signs and Symptoms

Cognitive Symptoms

Memory problems

Indecisiveness

Inability to concentrate

Trouble thinking clearly

Poor judgment

Seeing only the negative

Anxious or racing thoughts

Constant worrying

Loss of objectivity

Fearful anticipation

Physical Symptoms

Headaches or backaches

Muscle tension and stiffness

Digestive problems

Nausea, dizziness

Insomnia

Chest pain, rapid heartbeat

High blood pressure

Stomach and esophageal acid

Weight gain or loss

Skin eruptions (hives, shingles)

Loss of sex drive

Lowered immunity and frequent colds

Emotional Symptoms

Moodiness

Agitation

Restlessness

Short temper

Irritability, impatience

Inability to relax

Feeling tense and "on edge"

Feeling overwhelmed

Sense of loneliness and isolation

Depression or general
  unhappiness

Behavioral Symptoms

Eating more or less

Sleeping too much or too little

Isolating yourself from others

Procrastination, neglecting
  responsibilities

Using alcohol, cigarettes, or drugs
  to relax

Nervous habits (e.g. nail biting,
  pacing)

Teeth grinding or jaw clenching

Overdoing activities (e.g.,
  exercising, shopping)

Overreacting to unexpected
  problems

Lashing out at others

Over time, persistent, unmanaged stress begins to break down the organs of the body that regulate stress including the adrenal glands. Distress can seriously affect our wellbeing, causing or worsening physical illnesses including high blood pressure, ulcers, and heart disease. It limits the body's natural ability to heal itself, and unaddressed, can significantly shorten our lifespan.

Although many stressors are external, others are internal, psychological, and self-generated. These may include self-criticism, obsessive thinking, chronic worry, a pessimistic attitude, unrealistic beliefs, low self-esteem, unexpressed anger, passivity, and perfectionism.

Stress is a silent and not-

> **STRESS FACT:**
> People with uncontrolled stress do not take on additional challenges. Those who ignore their stress miss out on thousands of dollars of added pay each year because they avoid the more difficult but financially rewarding opportunities and the job promotions and perks they bring.

so-silent partner in many mental illnesses, including anxiety, depression, bipolar, and psychotic disorders. In many cases, counseling and medical intervention are essential in addressing the symptoms brought on by severe stress. Each year one fails to manage stress adequately is a year of strain on the body and mind, which, over time, results in a stream of diagnosed illnesses, lost income, career stagnation, damaged relationships, passivity and, ultimately, disability.

Preventing a Systems Crash

If you have never had a serious computer problem, you are lucky indeed. While booting up your system and seeing the dreaded blue screen of hard-drive death may represent one of the most catastrophic types of computer crashes, your laptop or home computer can begin to malfunction in many other ways long before that time. There are a number of interconnected systems that must be maintained to keep a computer running smoothly, including regular updates and the use of good anti-virus and anti-spyware programs.

Managing stress is similar to keeping a computer running smoothly. Several interconnected "operating systems" must be properly maintained to prevent a "systems crash," bringing our ability to function to a grinding halt. It's amazing how many people simply ignore one or more health areas, then are surprised by their inevitable system slow down.

The best way to avoid such events is, of course, conscientious scheduled maintenance. How about you? Can you honestly say you take as good care of your body as you do your automobile? If not, why not?

When we are young, we feel invincible. While many individuals in their twenties and thirties who own a newer, more powerful "operating system" seemingly get away with ignoring such maintenance, inevitably reality sets in as we age and one or more systems

EXCUSE GAMECHANGER
Our health issues usually have less to do with genetics than with lifestyle, environment, and stress management.

begins to fail—in undeniable and sometimes dramatic ways. Maybe you've heard this thought: We spend the first half of our lives spending our health to make money, and the second half spending our money to restore our health. Our task, therefore, must be to monitor and maintain our operating systems, whether our "computer" is a newer or older model.

What systems are we referring to? Familiar areas of our being fall neatly into four categories: the physical, mental, emotional and spiritual. Together, these four systems enable us to remain fully functional in our daily lives. When we are functioning at our best we not only can complete basic tasks, but we also have the power to process stressful and challenging projects that require the input of our entire system. This allows us to live beyond survival and to pursue success.

Do you know friends who are intelligent and knowledgeable but never seem to have the resources available for more than recovering after work or over the weekend? Most likely, they are ignoring one of their four primary operating systems.

Our Four Resource Areas

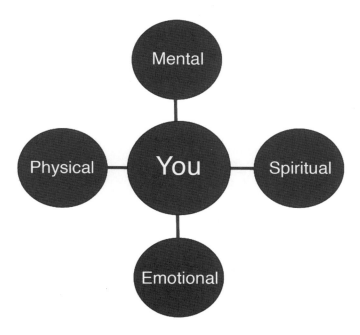

Although these four systems might seem timeless and obvious at first, in practice they often are altogether neglected. It's like a person who plans to make a back-up of computer data but never does. Many of us know better, but have pushed off needed self-care tasks, simply hoping for the best. Those who carefully attend to all four systems are different from the rest. As it has been said, common sense is far from common. No one living with perpetually slowed resources enjoys any serious prospect for personal development or career success.

Stop and think. In this past week have you caught yourself saying statements like "I'm wiped out," "I feel like I'm in a rut," or "I can't focus"? If so, one or more of your operating systems needs immediate attention.

Operating Systems: Core Components

1. All of our systems must function at or near capacity for the proper performance of our entire being.
2. Stress-related symptoms usually manifest first in our most resource-depleted system.
3. Negative energy in its various forms is the greatest challenge to maintaining system resources.
4. Regular maintenance is essential to sustain and speed up our operating systems.
5. Although each operating system requires specific attention, cleaning up one area often speeds up the entire computer.
6. We must frequently monitor each operating system to ensure proper functioning.
7. Carefully monitoring our feelings and using objective feedback from others are the primary means of assessing our system's health.

Maintaining Speed and Power with Regular Maintenance

With careful attention and practice, we can learn to accurately assess the functioning of each of our four operating systems. Once we pinpoint the likely source of our slowdown or crash, we can then immediately apply the appropriate maintenance steps to free up system memory. These steps consist of activities that are critical to keeping our operating systems functioning at maximum levels.

Some action steps we must perform habitually. Others, like reformatting our entire computer, are infrequent and drastic actions brought on by crises or neglect. Maintenance actions can be as simple as eating an antioxidant-loaded bowl of fresh fruit and cereal, reading a book before bedtime, scheduling a weekend vacation, or going to a weekly support group. Big or small, they serve important roles in preserving our computing power. The following sections highlight some of the key steps in maintaining each of our operating systems.

Our Physical System

Fire Your Excuses Self-Assessment Snapshot: John, 43

Scale	Score	Range
Total Excuse Scale	233	Below Average
Potential for Change Scale	48	Average
Health and Wellness Scale	17	Low
Offense Scale	105	Average
Defense Scale	86	Below Average

John, 43, came to us several years ago with a laundry list of life stressors. He was fifty pounds overweight, working long hours, and lacked energy, concentration, and motivation. In addition, not surprisingly, he struggled with low self-esteem. John was experiencing a classic case of generalized anxiety with depressed features. It was obvious that several of John's operating systems needed attention, and the first step was for us to find out why.

We began by assessing his health practices. Our conversation easily verified John's neglect of his physical system as evidenced by poor eating habits and no significant exercise. We challenged John to start with the obvious. We talked frankly about his bulging stomach and honestly explored what was in his control. In most cases, with proper attention, a man John's age continues to enjoy abundant physical resources. In contrast, John's unhealthy physical practices were slowing down his entire system. His extra pounds were just the most obvious result.

John's FYE assessment shed additional light on his current struggles and potential for change. Health concerns were not the only area in which John was struggling, as reflected by his Below Average Total Excuse Score. Nevertheless, his Health Score, which fell within the Low range, was the lowest of all his scores and needed immediate attention. John's Average Potential for Change Score suggested that he was the type of person who, while stressed, was not likely to blame anyone for his problems but generally saw solving them as his responsibility. This made it easier to work with him than with others we had seen with similar challenges. Not surprisingly, his Average Offense Score was offset with a Below Average Defense Score. Lacking motivation, John was using whatever energy he had for others, not for self-care.

John followed our recommendation to get checked out by his physician for any underlying physical conditions that would prevent him from taking action. As we agreed, he started with weekly exercise, was careful to get proper rest, and enrolled in a weight maintenance program. Each of these steps quickly served to speed up his physical operating system.

While his physical system was not the only area needing attention, it proved to be a critical component in dealing with his anxiety and self-confidence. As John started to become more physically fit, he felt better about himself and less depressed. These changes gave him an estimated 40 percent more physical energy.

In the end, John's physical system was a key factor in rehabilitating his life in all areas. This is not surprising. The proper functioning of our physical system is foundational, as it provides us with many of the resources needed to run all other operating systems.

What *physical maintenance activities* have you completed today to keep yourself operating smoothly?

_____

_____

_____

_____

Physical Maintenance Activities

Start with what is obvious as you seek to increase the quality of your health practices.

Think of daily health and fitness activities, especially those that address the Big Three—diet, exercise, and rest hygiene. Here are just a few easy examples.

- Take a walk

- Eat a healthy breakfast

- Get to bed early

- Take a quick nap

- Snack on healthy foods

- Hydrate throughout the day

- Cut down on caffeine

- Get in an aerobic or strength training workout

- Stretch to avoid injury

- Get a massage

- Schedule a medical, dental, vision, or chiropractic appointment

- Take your vitamins

Physical maintenance activities can be obvious and easy, yet they are often some of the most neglected of all.

Our Emotional System

Jan is an extremely intelligent and giving person. After twenty-three years of professional teaching and taking care of family at home, she had begun to experience symptoms of burnout and depression.

"I just don't feel like I have anything left these days," she explained. "I continue to work hard but I'm getting less and less done. It's like I am hitting the wall," she added, in frustration.

The more she explored her lifestyle, the more she discovered just how emotionally drained she had let herself become. Unaware of the true state of her emotional operating system, she would experience sudden, frightening crashes.

In counseling, we explained to Jan that paying attention to her emotions in real-time could help her identify when she needed to take care of herself. She also needed someone to tell her that she was emotionally and physically exhausted and currently functioning on "auxiliary life support." She had to immediately stop playing "teacher of the year" in every area of her life and putting everyone else's needs above her own. Going forward, it would be essential for her to carve out some "Jan time" for renewal and reflection.

Our emotional system gives us the ability and passion to be aware of others and ourselves, and to live our lives to the fullest. Without self-awareness, we are in danger of losing our very humanity. Many emotionally depleted individuals can no longer feel all their emotions.

Knowing what we feel, be it joy or pain, is a huge part of what makes us human and aware. It also provides us with creativity and the vital ability to experience empathy, intimacy, and trusting relation-ships with others. Taking special care of your emotional system is a top priority.

What *emotional maintenance activities* have you performed today to help you become self-aware and available for life's challenges and joys?

_____

_____

_____

_____

Emotional Maintenance Activities

• Initiate new friendships

• Grieve unresolved losses

• Forgive

• Strengthen friend and family ties

• Get professional support

• Explore beloved hobbies and ambitions

• Express gratitude toward co-workers or business partners

• Identify daily feelings (you may need to keep a log at first)

• Listen to a variety of music

• Sing or whistle in the shower

• Give and receive hugs

• Watch feel-good movies

Our Mental System

Tomas was struggling to move on after surviving a horrific car accident in which the driver, his friend of twenty years, was killed.

Three years after the trauma, Tomas was still plagued by periods of anxiety and depression. Like many others who have sustained a traumatic loss, Tomas was suffering with thoughts of guilt and self-punishment.

As we helped him work through the irrational thoughts and painful memories of the past, he began to open up to others and use self-affirming statements. He was able to forgive himself and move on toward recovery.

In many cases, our negative thoughts and attitudes represent our greatest challenge to maintaining and rebuilding our mental operating system. Our mental system helps us to keep our lives centered and enables us to view our circumstances accurately. The brain's continued ability to test reality, achieve clarity, and remain focused on our goals is critically important to experiencing success.

What *mental maintenance activities* have you performed today to keep yourself mentally healthy and fit?

_____

_____

_____

_____

Mental Maintenance Activities

- Read a chapter of an inspirational or business book each week
- Change weekly routines
- Learn to play a musical instrument
- Keep a journal
- Plan out your schedule
- Listen to downloadable podcasts, audio books, or CDs
- Engage in professional development activities

- Play board games and outdoor sports that challenge your thinking
- Minimize negative messages
- Have a daily 15-minute quiet time
- Reflect on peaceful images and memories
- Repeat calming words or quotes daily
- Challenge your negative self-talk with positive statements

Our Spiritual System

Mona was raised in a traditional religious family and had always been taught that if she did the right thing, life would always work out. After experiencing a bitter divorce and getting laid off from her job of twenty years, she was left feeling rejected, disillusioned, and spiritually empty.

Many like Mona wrestle with existential questions about their life's purpose and meaning. Formative life events such as death, illness, career setbacks, financial issues, and negative religious experiences, can severely test the strength of our "anchors." Eventually we all come to that place in life where we face questions about our own mortality, the existence of God, our purpose, and our values. Faith communities can play an important role in our need for spiritual refueling.

Given proper care, a fully functioning spiritual operating system positions us to find answers to these questions. It also provides a renewed sense of identity, thankfulness, and a willingness to contribute to the lives of others who may be struggling.

What *spiritual maintenance activities* have you performed today to keep yourself spiritually connected?

_____

_____

_____

_____

Spiritual Maintenance Activities

- Participate in art activities
- Forgive someone
- Play or listen to music
- Give purposefully
- Participate in prayer and meditation
- Volunteer; serve others
- Reconnect or connect with a faith community
- Explore nature
- Join a spiritual growth group or class
- Deliberately seek God's purpose for you
- Rethink what is "owed to you," and what you can expect
- Keep things simple
- Cultivate an "attitude of gratitude"

Summary

Whether our main challenge is managing stress, balancing work and family, cultivating a love relationship, or finding purpose in life, giving careful attention to each of our four operating systems is critical to our success. Make the decision to start giving each area the daily attention it deserves. It's time.

TAKE THE 30-DAY
HEALTH AND WELLNESS CHALLENGE

1. For the next two weeks, create a sleep diary. Record hours slept per night, difficulty falling or staying asleep, and issues related to poor sleep. With six to eight hours of quality sleep per night as your goal, address any identified problem areas and seek outside help if necessary.

2. Take a three-day "getaway" weekend. Limit any distractions so that you may enjoy two fully relaxing days. Upon your return, explore ideas and dates for a week-long vacation within the next twelve months.

3. Commit to the Fire Your Excuses FitWeek Plan for thirty days. Weigh yourself at the beginning of each week. Enlist two friends to be your accountability partners, checking in with them weekly.

4. Take two ten-minute rest breaks daily to assess your physical, emotional, mental and spiritual systems and the maintenance steps needed to keep each of them functioning efficiently.

FIRE YOUR EXCUSES

CHAPTER THREE:

SOCIAL CONNECTIONS

Blind Spots
and
Weaknesses

Health
and
Wellness

Social
Connections

Communication

Time
Management

Finances

Career

Serving

CHAPTER 3

SOCIAL CONNECTIONS

If we have no peace, it is because we have forgotten
that we belong to each other.
—MOTHER TERESA

We cannot live for ourselves alone.
Our lives are connected by a thousand invisible threads.
—HERMAN MELVILLE

ON A MARCH DAY IN 1974, SECOND LT. HIROO ONODA SURRENDERED
to his commanding officer, ending one of the most bizarre tales of
World War II. Onoda was one of the last two Japanese soldiers living in
the jungles of the Pacific Islands following the war.

A Japanese army intelligence officer, Onoda was assigned to Lubang
Island in December 1944. In February 1945, the Americans overran the
island, and within a short time all but Onoda and three other soldiers
had either died or surrendered. Eventually, through desertion and
death, Onoda was left alone. Three decades later, a Japanese college
dropout, Norio Suzuki, went looking for Onoda on a lark and found
him in February 1974. Still, Onoda refused to surrender, saying that he
would only lay down his arms to his superior officer, Major Taniguchi.

Located with the help of the Japanese government, Taniguchi, now
a bookseller, flew to Lubang. On March 9, 1974, he informed Onoda
of the defeat of Japan and ordered him to lay down his arms. Onoda
immediately emerged from the jungle in his uniform, bearing his sword,

Arisaka Type 99 rifle (still in operating condition), 500 rounds of ammunition, and several hand grenades.

Arriving in Japan, he returned to a hero's welcome. When questioned, Onoda said he had heard announcements broadcast over a public address system that the war was over, but he feared that it was just a trick. He also ignored several attempts to contact him by leaflet, concluding that they were just Allied propaganda. In 1952, letters and family pictures were dropped from an aircraft urging him to surrender, but Onoda concluded that this too was a hoax.

However mystifying or paranoid Onoda's actions might appear, a careful reading of the account adds some important details often omitted in the retelling of this amazing story. First, two fellow soldiers had been killed by outsiders, including those who made up an alleged rescue party. Years of isolation would have made anyone wary of strangers, especially strangers who had shown they were willing to kill. Furthermore, Onoda also had been given strict orders to surrender to no one but his commanding officer. Finally, his particular unit was commissioned for battle with the repurposed ancient Samurai code of "death before dishonor." In fact, according to historians, only five percent of Japanese WWII soldiers so bound by this code ever returned alive. In truth, his unwillingness to come out of hiding may have had as much to do with shame as it did with fear.[1,2]

Why People Avoid Connections

It is easy to understand why someone like Onoda who has been through traumatic events would isolate themselves from others, but what about the rest of us? It could be argued that the inability to make deep social connections is not an irregular peculiarity of a few in our culture but one of the most distressing characteristics of modern society. A closer look at our changing demographics hints at part of the answer.

- From 1900 to 1999, the U.S. population grew nearly four times larger, from 76 million to 273 million.[3] Over the same period, even adjusting for the increase in population, the divorce rate exploded. It increased to 21 times the 1900 rate for women by the year 2000, and 28 times the 1900 rate for men.[4] According to a report issued by The National Marriage Project at the University of Virginia, in 2009, 40.6 percent of all U.S. births were to unmarried mothers, up from 10.7 percent in 1970, an increase of nearly 400 percent.[5] Just 61 percent of American children grow up with both biological parents.[6]

- About 1 in every 6.6 children in the United States is exposed to alcohol abuse or dependence in his or her home, according to Bridget Grant's exhaustive analysis issued in 2000. Over the course of a lifetime, this figure swells to an estimated 1 in every 2.3 individuals. This percentage does not include those exposed to similarly affected biological or nonbiological family who do not reside in the same household, nor does it account for any exposure to drug addiction or abuse.[7]

- Among substantiated reports of abuse investigated by Child Protective Services (CPS) throughout the United States, 60 percent of victims experienced neglect, meaning a caretaker failed to provide for the child's basic needs. Nearly 20 percent experienced physical abuse, and 10 percent suffered from sexual abuse. Seven percent involved emotional abuse, which includes criticizing, rejecting, or refusing to nurture a child.[8]

- The estimate commonly cited in the mental health field for sexual abuse alone is that 1 in 3 women will endure some form of sexual abuse growing up, and the prevalence of sexual abuse against men, less discussed and reported, has been estimated at 1 in 5 to 1 in 7.

As we can see, few of us arrive at adulthood unscathed by exposure to a caretaker wrestling with some type of significant impairment.

People who have been traumatized or have had to fend for themselves emotionally in one way or the other often learn that it is better to go it alone. Community and connection can be messy and one has to risk being known and possibly hurt again.

Sometimes our reluctance to connect is based on our perception that others are not worth our time or that we will be exposed to unwanted experiences. It reminds us of the story of the man who invited his neighbor to go to church with him. His neighbor refused by saying: "You know, Joe, I will never go to your church because everyone there is a hypocrite!" To this, the man replied: "No problem, we can always make room for one more."

Loneliness, the "Disease Epidemic of the 21st Century"

We are also growing into a far more mobile, anonymous, and urban society. In 1900, 40 percent of Americans lived in suburban or urban areas;[9] today this number stands at 79 percent.[10] A large majority of the audience members we talk to each week admit that, unlike their childhood years, today they do not know even their nearest neighbors.

These days it is not uncommon to endure commutes to the workplace of an hour or more each way, leaving little time for connecting until the weekend. Long commutes have also been linked with cardiac disease. Dr. Kim Connelly, an Australian cardiologist, cites that "studies have shown that the rate of heart attack increases with the length of time you are stuck in traffic."[11]

What are the effects of limited authentic, heart-to-heart social connection? They are depressed mood, higher levels of anxiety, stubborn addictions, emptiness, and the chronic lack of direction and motivation.

Prominent cardiologist Dean Ornish, in his book, *Love and Survival*, writes:

> The real epidemic in our culture is not only physical heart disease, but also what I call emotional and spiritual heart disease—that is the profound feelings of loneliness, isolation, alienation, and depression that are so prevalent in our culture with the breakdown of the social structures that used to provide us with a sense of connection and community. [12]

His analysis rings true with many in our society who are speeding along the information super highway, often passing up needed support.

Author Robert Holden calls loneliness a "'disease' epidemic of the 21st century." He argues convincingly that the "me decade," the prosperous post-war 1950s, gave rise to the baby boomer's "me generation" and its excessive individualism. What was the result? It is our almost universal sense of loneliness, which is the core of many medical and emotional problems.[13] Being connected with others is an essential building block for our health but one that often receives little recognition.

SINGLE BEST THING
Increasing one's connections is the emotional equivalent of getting adequate physical exercise. It is, by far, the single best thing you can do to increase the mood and motivation needed to pursue your dreams.

Mike, age 34, a manager at an IT firm, fidgets in his chair. Tears well up in his eyes as he describes the persistent emptiness inside and wonders out loud if others ever feel it too. "Will it ever go away?" he asks.

Raised by parents who eventually divorced after years of rancor, long business trips, and mutual affairs, Mike and his sisters, emotionally speaking, raised themselves. Their emotionally shattered mother simply was not able to bounce back from the end of her marriage, let alone rally to provide the children a stable, nurturing home.

Fire Your Excuses Self-Assessment Snapshot: Mike, 34

Scale	Score	Range
Total Excuse Scale	309	Above Average
Potential for Change Scale	56	Above Average
Social Connections Scale	26	Below Average
Offense Scale	105	Average
Defense Scale	128	Superior

Mike's FYE Self Assessment scores are not unlike other individuals who have had to overcome early obstacles to be successful. Most striking is his Superior Score on the Defense Scale. Five minutes with Mike and you know he is the type of person who leaves nothing to chance. His finances, health, and career each receive careful attention. Few are better at the maintenance aspects of daily living.

His pain comes from his lifestyle of isolation as reflected by his Below Average Social Connections Score. His Above Average Potential for Change Score strongly suggests that he will aggressively address his isolation once he fully understands its impact and learns what will help the most. His Average Offense Score indicates that he needs to put more energy into other life-affirming activities.

Mike knows he needs to rebuild his social network, which is now limited to work associates and a few left-over friends from high school and college, but he is reluctant to do so. At the same time, he is puzzled over why he feels "stuck" and unable to move up in his career or to land a great relationship.

While Mike's upbringing may appear less than typical, his presenting situation is all too common. "Underconnected" individuals struggle with self-destructive health issues or have stalled out in an unsatisfying, unstable relationship. A number are underemployed and know they need to make a change, but lack the energy to do so. Though the level of impairment varies, the common denominator for all is that they are isolated and highly resistant to the idea of reaching out for additional social and emotional connection.

We have observed clinically that healthy socialization requires several one-on-one contacts a week, outside of a spouse or roommates. Such contacts must be with those with whom we can talk openly and deeply. For many, this simply does not happen in any significant way. Those who experience such additional support are able to greatly reduce the risk of slipping into low-grade depression, a mood state where individuals chronically suffer from lowered job performance and impaired social functioning. People can live with these symptoms for years.

In contrast, we seldom counsel those with depression or anxiety who have three or more, one hour, meaningful contacts a week with others. Yet, people continually ask us: "What difference does talking to others make? You still have the same problems." Our answer is that, in terms of lowered blood pressure, better stress management, improved relationships, enhanced focus, new ideas, elevated mood, and lowered anxiety, social contact is a "game changer."

The "Mirroring" Effect of Connection

Connection serves another key purpose in addition to raising our mood and motivation. It provides us with the critical feedback we need to clarify our values, abilities, and skills.

We only see who we really are in the reflection of community and in connection with others. In essence, this is one of the core functions of therapy—to "hold up a mirror" so that others can accurately see who they are in the world. Yes, there are times for reflection in solitude, but as a general rule, it is in community that we learn what we like and what we do not, and whom we prefer to make part of our lives. This simply doesn't happen by reading a book, even ours, or by engaging in extended periods of time away from others.

Consider a room with a light switch panel on one of its four walls. If you are "in the dark" or "blind," you can spend three or four decades looking for the light switch on any of the other three walls. No matter how hard you look and how many years you suffer looking, your search will be fruitless until you search the correct wall. Connections represent the "fourth wall," the place where the light switch resides. There are things we can only learn through our connections with others.

It does not matter how long you search in isolation or how much you suffer in the process, you will never find what you need to succeed while searching alone. Every year we meet people who are trying to find the "light switch" on walls where they will never be successful. Many are quite adamant that they should be able to find success without changing walls.

Over the past few years a virtual tidal wave of research has confirmed the critical role connection plays in all aspects of our health. Isolation will not only rob you of your dreams, it will rob you of your years.

> **EXCUSE GAMECHANGER**
> Just as you can't find a light switch in the dark if you are looking for it on the wrong wall, isolation is the wrong place to look for what you can only find in community.

In his book, *Outliers*,[14] Malcolm Gladwell introduces readers to the classic study of the inhabitants of Roseto, Pennsylvania. Roseto was once a community entirely made up of immigrants from a small village in Italy who moved almost *en masse* to the New World. Medical researchers were shocked to find that although these new citizens ate a heavy diet, many smoked, and a significant number did risky work in the quarry, they defied all longevity statistics. In fact, they had half the heart attack deaths of the rest of America. The question was, "Why?"

To find the answer, researchers began to study the small community intensely. In time, the surprising answer emerged. The strength of the connections and community within Roseto, which had been a relatively insular place for decades, had an amazing effect on health. Their socialization was literally keeping them alive much longer than would otherwise be expected. Sure enough, once the next generation began moving away to find work and the town grew, connections weakened and death and disease rates began to mirror the rest of the state.

In 2006, a study conducted at Rush University Medical Center in Chicago examined the relationship between Alzheimer's disease and the quality of our social connections.[15] They reported the following.

- Having close friends and staying in contact with family members offers protection against the damaging effects of Alzheimer's disease. To determine social network, participants were asked about the amount of contacts with children, relatives, and friends they feel close to and see monthly.[16]

- "Many elderly people who have the tangles and plaques associated with Alzheimer's disease don't clinically experience cognitive impairment or dementia," said Bennett. "Our findings suggest that social networks are related to something that offers a 'protective reserve' capacity that spares them the clinical manifestations of Alzheimer's disease." As the amount of pathology in the brain increases, the size of your social network matters even more.[17]

- The effect was evident across different kinds of cognitive abilities, but was most associated with semantic memory, which is related to your knowledge about the world and your language abilities.[18]

We can now conclude that not only do healthy and frequent interactions with friends and family lift our mood, they have a positive neurological impact on brain function.

REBUILDING YOUR SOCIAL NETWORK
Rebuilding your social contacts may not feel "right" at first if you have become accustomed to a more isolated lifestyle. Instead, reconnecting may actually be accompanied by some degree of anxiety.

If you are used to being alone, there are many times when, initially, the right action of reconnection will feel very wrong. After years of ignoring the need for connection, becoming a joiner, reaching out for help, and consistently doing life with others can feel very uncomfortable, even scary. These unpleasant feelings will eventually subside. We become accustomed to how we are living, even if the way we are living is unhealthy and non-productive. How about you? What is your excuse for not connecting with others?

"If a person does not make new acquaintances as he advances through life, he will soon find himself alone."
—Samuel Johnson[19]

"We Get It. Now, Where Do We Meet New People?"

Have you ever moved to a new city where you knew only one or two people at most? Maybe you have even moved to a place where you knew no one. Did you know that there is a way to "take a city," a way to build your social network from scratch quickly? If you find yourself in this situation, it is important to meet people of quality and character early in your networking.

Question: Where do you find new, quality friends?

Answer: You become a joiner and you volunteer.

Carolyn and Julie work for the same insurance company. In August, each of them takes advantage of a moving bonus to transfer to Chicago and work in the home office. They know each other at work casually, but there the similarities between their lives end.

Carolyn spends the first three months "getting settled," furnishing her apartment, working long hours at her new position, and going to the gym. At Christmas time, she catches a flight back to Dallas for the holidays and tells her friends and family how hard it is to make friends in Chicago.

Before she left Phoenix, Julie, a single parent of a 10-year-old, asked a Breast Cancer Association colleague for the name of a few contacts in the Chicago chapter. Five days after her arrival in Chicago, Julie and her daughter dig out their casual clothes and volunteer to help out at a cancer walk along Lake Michigan. She figures it will be a great way to meet other single parents and for her daughter to meet new friends. She's right. The following Sunday they decide to check out a new church. Julie also joins a biking club that rides every Saturday morning while her daughter attends Girl Scouts. By the time Christmas comes, she has been invited to a number of holiday gatherings sponsored by her new organizations and has met three or four promising new friends. Julie is torn because she would like to see her old friends in Phoenix, but there is so much going on in Chicago. She decides to fly home for five days at Christmas but jets back in time to celebrate New Year's Eve with her new friends in Chicago.

Julie's willingness to reach out made all the difference in adjusting to a new city and feeling connected and supported again. Whether you spend a day, serve over a weekend, or go on a longer trip to help the less fortunate, these are all great ways to become acquainted with new friends. Also, there are some extraordinarily positive, creative volunteers out there, and they are some of the best people you will ever meet in your new city, or in the one you reside in right now!

Online Connection, Physical Isolation

"Open sourcing" refers to the recent phenomenon of millions of individuals uploading their creative contributions and collaborating on online projects. Examples include "open source software," blogs, network sites such as Facebook, LinkedIn, Twitter, and of course, Wikipedia, the first encyclopedia assembled entirely from the free contributions of thousands of "editors." Thomas Friedman, in his illuminating book, *The World Is Flat*,[20] cited the open source phenomenon as the most profound shift in our way of connecting in decades.

But there are dangers. As we move toward more technological connectivity and express ourselves in a very public fashion, we can become more shallow, narcissistic, and ego-driven. Few are likely to use any of these new communication platforms to express the deepest of feelings. Instead, we will tend to present ourselves as more entertaining, hip, and social than we really are. As technological communication increases, face-to-face contact may actually decrease. As one of our colleagues recently remarked: "I have 503 friends on Facebook, but I spend more nights alone than ever!"

As an adjunct to connection, social networking sites like Facebook can actually enhance our sense of community, but as a substitute for face-to-face socialization and touch, they are a very poor counterfeit indeed.

What Is Your "Network Quotient"?

In other parts of this book we have stressed the importance of EQ, your emotional intelligence quotient. When speaking of our connections, our NQ, or Network Quotient, a term first introduced by Tom Boyle of British Telecom, is the key competency needed for 21st century socialization. NQ is defined as "the capacity to form connections with one another." [21]

People high in NQ are continuously identifying useful resources and building helpful alliances with others. They reach out to others for help before they are in dire need. They place very little importance on looking as if they have all the answers themselves.

This is not only true in our personal lives but equally important in the business world. Henry Ford is an example. The founder of the

Ford Motor Company, he is also considered the father of the modern assembly line. His introduction of the Model T automobile revolutionized transportation and American industry. Born on a farm in 1863 in what is now Dearborn, Michigan,[22] Ford became one of the richest, best-known people in the world and is often held up as an iconic self-made man. In actuality, this incredible inventor, the recipient of 161 U.S. patents, was a master connector.

Early in his career, his job as chief engineer at Edison Illuminating Company gave him enough money to spend time on his passion—gasoline engines. His experiments eventually led in 1896 to the Ford Quadricycle, a light weight forerunner to the first automobile. [23] He had the chance to meet Edison himself at a meeting of Edison executives. The great inventor encouraged him to continue his experimentation.[24] Eventually, the investment of Detroit lumber baron, William H. Murphy, enabled him to resign from Edison, and found Detroit Automobile Company in 1899. The sale of his second automobile was weak, and the young company dissolved in 1901.

Again, he sought financial help, on this occasion from C. Harold Wills. This time Ford designed, built, and successfully raced a 26-horsepower automobile in the fall of 1901. In October 1902, Ford received the backing of a third investor, Alexander Y. Malcomson, a Detroit coal dealer.[25] A partnership was formed to produce automobiles, and this time Ford focused on producing an inexpensive vehicle. Ford sought out the help of John and Horace E. Dodge to produce the needed parts. When Ford and Malcomson could not make payment on over $160,000 in parts, Malcomson brought in additional investors and gave the Dodge brothers part ownership. The new backers, which soon grew to include Ford's uncle, John S. Gray, Horace Rackham, and James Couzens, reincorporated as Ford Motor Company. The company produced what is widely regarded as the first affordable automobile in 1908, the Model T. Sales were slow at first but took off once the assembly line process made mass production feasible.[26] By 1914, they had sold 250,000 cars. In 1916, when the price dropped to $360, total sales surpassed 472,000. [27]

Henry Ford was truly a genius, but he relied on a team every step of the way. It was his connections that breathed life into his ideas and inventions.

Are You a Connector?

Which people are the best at social networking? Malcolm Gladwell, in his book, *The Tipping Point*,[28] calls them Connectors. Connectors are people who know a number of key individuals in many groups. Those who are not connectors may know a lot of people but they are predominantly from just one group, organization, or subculture. Is your social circle limited to one main group? Or are you a part of many groups?

Some of the best networkers we know "make an appearance in a number of organizations." Take Ali, a chiropractor. He seems to instinctively sense just the right amount of involvement needed to connect with the key members in several associations. Each group feels as if Ali is one of their own but, in actuality, he is a part of a number of groups. While this may not be the best strategy to follow in our love life, Ali's networking techniques work very well socially and in business.

> **STUDY:**
> Twenty-five percent of Americans have no one in whom they can confide.[29]

Your Social Network—a Reality Check

According to research conducted at the University of Chicago, the circle of friends for the average American decreased by a third between 1985 and 2004.[30] In the mid-1980s, the average American adult had three close friends. By the middle of the first decade of the 21st century, this number had decreased to two. Most disturbing, one in four reported having no close confidants at all.

As the number of friendships wane, people are leaning more on their families. The percentage of people who only confide in a family member rose from 57 to 80 percent, and those who depend solely on a spouse climbed from five to nine percent.[31] As the study's co-author, Lynn Smith-Lovin, observed, "If something happens to that spouse or partner, you may have lost your safety net."[32]

Our Shrinking Social Network

Year	U.S. Residents: Average Number of Close Friends[33]
1985	3
2004	2

In our FYE seminars, we often begin by conducting an exercise that illustrates the amount of untapped resources in our audience. Participants are asked to write down as many things as they can think of that are edible and white in color within a three-minute time limit. The highest number of edible food and non-food items ever generated by an attendee is 33. In contrast, together, our audience members often come up with 50 to 75 unique answers. This simple exercise illustrates that no matter how creative and experienced you may be, you will always do better by taking advantage of the added contribution of others.

Take a moment to answer the following questions about your own social network:

Who makes up your core social network?

_____

_____

In what ways and how often do you meet with your network?

_____

_____

What could you do to strengthen and increase the size of your existing network?

_____

_____

Rating Your Support Network

The people with whom we surround ourselves can have a tremendous influence upon our success or failure. Here's an example.

Throughout the years we have worked with many individuals wrestling with substance abuse. As a part of our initial assessment, we always ask about the network of people that surround our new clients. It is critical to know who is a part of their circle of influence, with an eye to assessing who may be supporting their drug or alcohol habit. A careful exploration of their social network invariably reveals those who are negative influencers, e.g., other users, and those who might not be supportive of their recovery efforts. For sobriety to be maintained, our clients will need to be firm about their new direction and limit their interactions with those who might sabotage their efforts. Our progress truly has much to do with "the company we keep."

Consider your own social network. Does your network provide you with more positive or negative energy? Let's return to our social inventory one more time:

Who are the eight most influential people in your life right now?

_____

_____

_____

How would you rate each one on a scale of 1-10, 10 being most positive?

_____

_____

What steps might you take to limit the impact of those who negatively influence you?

_____

_____

Choose a Generous Social Network— Social Behavior Is Contagious

Nicholas Christakis and James Fowler, researchers at Harvard University and the University of California at San Diego, respectively, are some of the first scientists to prove in the laboratory that acts of kindness and generosity are contagious. They found that positive behaviors spread as easily as negative ones.[34] Other studies had looked at related phenomenon but had investigated groups who were comprised of similar individuals or ones who know each other. In this case, subjects were complete strangers.

Christakis and Fowler found that participants who were given money by their peers in a simulated philanthropy game were more likely to give away their own money in future games. Further, there was a domino effect in this "pay it forward" type scenario. Givers often gave to two others, and the effect was felt to the third degree of separation as the chart below illustrates.

When you become more generous, Fowler observes, "you don't go back to being your 'old selfish self.'"[35] We continue to help others. "Personally it's very exciting to learn that kindness spreads to people I don't know or have never met," says Fowler. "We have direct experience of giving and seeing people's immediate reactions, but we don't typically see how our generosity cascades through the social network to affect the lives of dozens or maybe hundreds of other people."[36]

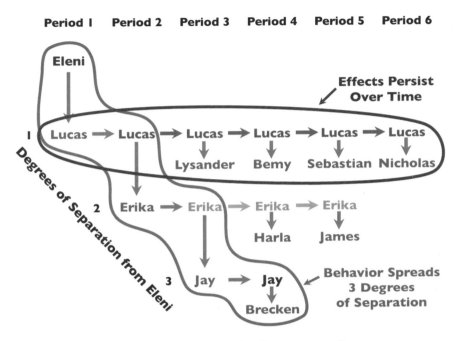

This diagram illustrates how a single act of kindness can spread between individuals and across time.

Credit: Courtesy James Fowler, UC San Diego

Your Personal Board of Directors

Our friends in Hollywood tell us that the average feature film takes at least five years from idea to screen. This is evident watching the Academy Awards and hearing the acceptance speeches of those who worked tirelessly behind the scenes. Few winners are tongue-tied. Most struggle to thank the long list of colleagues, family, friends, coaches, and mentors who were in some way responsible for their success before the music rises, signaling it is time to relinquish the microphone. What they are really telling us are the names of their "personal board of directors"—those without whom they would never have achieved their goals.

You will need the accountability and support of your own personal board of directors to achieve your goals and overcome challenges. Have you made an executive decision about who you will invite to be on your board? Are each of your closest mentors and wisest friends aware of your vision, challenges, and goals? If not, why not?

The following is an example of how your personal board of directors might look:

Board Member Title	Name	Relationship	Credential/ Business Title
President/CEO	You	Self	Business professional
Vice-President	Joseph	Neighbor	Marketing director of software company
Senior Advisor	Larry	Former business colleague	Local politician
Advisor	Tom	Son's baseball coach	Medical center vice-president
Advisor	Mary	Wife's best friend	President of daughter's school PTA
Secretary	Susan	Sister's best friend	Freelance writer
Treasurer	Tammy	Wife of son's piano teacher	Accountant
Legal Counsel	Bob	Uncle	Business attorney
Spiritual Advisor	Dr. Jones	Golf buddy	Pastor

FREE *SOCIAL CONNECTIONS* EXCUSESTOPPER
For help in building your own board of directors, go to www.FireYourExcuses.com, register if you are not yet part of the Fire Your Excuses Community, and type in the keyword: DIRECTORS

EXCUSE STOPPER

Personal Mentoring and Coaching

Best-selling author Charles Swindoll has said that to progress rapidly in our goals, we need more than just "life experience," we need "guided experience." There is, of course, the school of hard-knocks, but this method of learning is often unnecessarily painful, and its curriculum inadequate and spotty. In contrast, thinking back on our lives, most of us would have to admit that we were never in better physical shape than when we played on a team and had a coach. Similarly, we were never more disciplined in learning a subject than when we had a teacher.

The words *mentoring* and *coaching* are often used interchangeably when we speak about one-on-one experiences with someone we have sought out for guidance. In practice, they are actually a bit different. A mentor may be your boss, a respected relative, or a pastor. In mentoring, you may or may not meet together formally but you can learn much from his or her wisdom and life experience. We were especially impacted by the informal mentorship of Lawson Sanders, the senior custodian at our *alma mater*, Eastern Nazarene College. "The Colonel," as he was affectionately known, was far more than a janitor to hundreds of young students. He embodied one that offered wise counsel and a listening ear—core attributes of a great mentor. Like "The Colonel," there are potential mentors all around us.

Coaching relationships, in contrast, tend to be far more formal. Here the focus is on setting specific goals and timelines and having regular, structured meetings

---

Maya Angelou, Poet and Author, on Her Own Mentoring

"Mrs. Flowers took me to the library in the black school. The library was probably as large as a telephone booth. It may have had 110 books in it, maybe. She said. 'I want you to read every book in this room.' And I found poetry. And I loved it, I just loved it. I had no idea what it would sound like since I had never heard any recited, but I loved it. And I was able to translate it at eight, at nine, at 10. I consider that a lifeline, because finally, when I was about 12-and-a-half, almost 13, Mrs. Flowers—who would allow me to come to her house and she would read to me—when I was almost 13, she said, you will never really love poetry until you speak it, feel it come across your tongue, over your lips."[37]

---

that include discussions of obstacles. Most people have at least one mentor in their lives but very few have any formal coaches who lend specific help in goal setting, obstacle identification, and accountability.

In truth, we need both. Consider working with a coach to help you push through that one area that has left you feeling defeated or immobilized. There is information at the end of this book about our own Fire Your Excuses Coaching Programs.

Peer Support and Accountability

We have just explored many ways to make connections, but what if you are dealing with a significant challenge at this time? One of the best ways to break the isolation trap and to get adequate support and accountability is by connecting with one of the thousands of groups available worldwide. Although, at first it may feel intimidating to get connected, the return investment can be life changing. The following are suggested ways to begin.

- Ask your doctor, counselor, or other health professional for suggestions.

- Ask your religious leader or organization.

- Ask your family, friends and colleagues.

- Ask people who have the same goals or challenges.

- Contact a city, state, or national association. Your library, community center, or government agencies will have a list of these groups.

- Search the Internet. Forums, e-mail lists, and chat rooms can be informative, provide encouragement and support, and allow you to ask questions and get answers.

In our recent search of support and social groups, we found hundreds of online and face-to-face associations, blogs, and forums addressing every challenge imaginable. It is amazing how many people really want to help, serve as mutual accountability partners, and connect with others experiencing the same medical, emotional, spiritual, or business interests. Nearly all of these groups are free of charge.

We encourage you to do your own search and connect not only online but face-to-face, keeping in mind one of the *Fire Your Excuses* principles: "If you don't have the answer to your problem, your immediate goal is to find someone who does."

TAKE THE 30-DAY
SOCIAL CONNECTIONS CHALLENGE

1. Make a list of the 10 people with whom you have the most contact, including friends, family and work associates. Beside each name, write a number between one and 10 indicating how positive or negative their influence is in your life. A score of one represents the most negative and 10 the most positive.

2. This month, do two things:

   First, limit or avoid contact with anyone scoring a three or less and spend extra time with those who scored eight or above.

   Second, seek out one new person who could eventually be a nine or 10.

3. Get together at least once a week with someone, other than your spouse or significant other, with whom you can be completely honest about your challenges and goals.

4. Attend at least two events this month that foster spiritual and emotional growth.

FIRE YOUR EXCUSES

CHAPTER FOUR:

COMMUNICATION

CHAPTER 4

COMMUNICATION

Who you are speaks so loudly I can't hear what you're saying.
—*RALPH WALDO EMERSON*

IN THE MOVIE *JERRY MAGUIRE*, JERRY IS A SPORTS AGENT PLAYED BY Tom Cruise. One night, confronted by the questionable morality of his own work, Jerry labors feverishly until morning, writing an inspiring mission statement about how his business ought to function.

```
INT. MIAMI HOTEL ROOM -- NIGHT
Jerry types, a pot of coffee and tray of
room service nearby.

We watch his face, alive now ... His
fingers fly. Even his eyes grow moist.

JERRY'S VOICE: What started out as one page
became 25. Suddenly I was my father's son.
I was remembering the simple pleasures of
this job, how I ended up here out of law
school, the way a stadium sounds when one
of my players performs well on the field[1]
```

When Jerry, bleary-eyed but buoyant, is finished with his *magnum opus,* he rushes off to Kinko's in the wee hours of the morning, makes enough copies for his entire company, and has them stuffed in everyone's mail box. As he descends the stairs later in the morning, everyone claps, but within a few hours he is fired. Ironically, the best Jerry has ever communicated in his life results in him losing his job.

In the movie, Jerry's written communication initiates an entrepreneurial adventure that eventually brings him new friendships, marriage, fatherhood, career success, and a deep sense of accomplishment. In real life, it is not uncommon for our strongest communications to ruin our relationships, derail our career advancement, and needlessly hurt others. We have all winced as scores of otherwise intelligent, caring leaders have been unable to communicate effectively when it mattered most. Communication difficulties are among the top causes of relationship break-up, divorce, and poor family relationships. They are frequently "the smoking gun" when we seek to understand the loss of important clients, key management and staff, lowered consumer perception, and a sea of unnecessary lawsuits.

It is critical that we are truthful with ourselves about this essential interpersonal and career competency. The tough truth is this: While we would like to believe we are excellent communicators, when we honestly look at how we typically handle our most difficult conversations, unfortunately most of us are average at best.

> **LIMIT YOUR SPEECH IN PROPORTION TO GROUP SIZE.**
> Note how many people are in your group and limit your talking time accordingly. If there are four of you and you are talking more than 25 percent of the time because you feel what you are saying is important or interesting, you need a second opinion.

If you already consider yourself a great communicator, you will find techniques and concepts within these pages that will help you communicate even better. Excellent communication can be readily learned if it is valued and practiced. Even a 10 percent improvement in your communication skills is enough to make a significant difference in your success. We invite you to think of this level of improvement as your minimum target goal, knowing that you will likely find yourself improving much more. Let's get started.

The Great Communication Paradox

If we live in the greatest information age in all of history, why is it still so hard to communicate effectively with our neighbors, colleagues, friends, and families? On a weekly basis we hear the phrases, "We just don't talk anymore." "We cannot seem to connect with our kids." Or, "My boss yells at me in front of everyone." How well do you communicate? Would others agree with your assessment?

The Three Most Common Communication Problems

Three themes emerge whenever communication breaks down. They are 1) difficulties in our "outbound" communication, most importantly, how we form our messages; 2) deficits in listening skills; and 3) the inability to communicate effectively in confrontational situations.

"This is the nicest conversation we've had in weeks. Let's not spoil it by talking."

©2004 by Randy Glasbergen. www.RandyGlasbergen.com [2]

Improving Our Outbound Messages

Fire Your Excuses Self-Assessment Snapshot: Maria and Felipe

	Communications Score	Range
Maria	26	Below Average
Felipe	25	Below Average

Maria and Felipe came in for marriage counseling. Despite twenty-five years together, they had not had a meaningful conversation for months. Each reported feeling very alone and not sure how to get back on track. "I can't take this any longer, I would rather be by myself than to live together like roommates," Maria said in frustration.

The problem began five months ago over dinner. Their conversation became heated as they discussed plans now that their last child had "left the nest." At one point, Felipe told Maria, in a commanding, loud voice, that it was time for her to go back to work. The tone Felipe used embarrassed Maria and she felt as if she'd been treated like a child. In response, she withdrew and refused to tell him how she felt. Felipe, not feeling as if he had done anything wrong, decided to wait her out. The result, with the occasional exception of statements such as "I paid the electric bill today," was five months of deafening silence. Sadly, this period came at a time when they both needed each other's help to redefine their lives as "empty nesters."

When we looked at their assessment scores, certainly no clear winner emerged. This was not a couple where one spouse had a significant communication weakness and the other, a much better communicator, was struggling with this reality. Rather, both their Communication Scores fell within the Below Average range and the rest of their assessment scores were unremarkable. Each had stronger and weaker areas, but when it came to their presenting issue, both seemed to play an equal part in the standoff they had experienced over the past weeks.

Did Felipe and Maria stop communicating five months ago? No, they communicated volumes to each other during their prolonged silence. Their problem, of course, had to do with *how* they communicated. The "how" of communication is largely nonverbal and, in most cases, far more important than the actual words we use.

In a classic, oft-cited study, Albert Mehrabian[3] investigated this critical facet of communication by measuring the impact of our messages. His study suggested that only seven percent of our communication's impact has to do with our words. Amazingly, tone and other nonverbal expressions account for 93 percent of how our message is received and interpreted. A striking example of this truth is found in observing interpersonal communication within the deaf community. The deaf not only use sign language but also highly animated facial expressions to communicate with one another. Yes, our words matter, but we must conclude that in terms of our message's impact, *how* we communicate is by far the most crucial factor.

How aware are you of your tone and nonverbal expressions when communicating?

COMMUNICATION IMPACT[4]
Words: 7 percent
Voice Tone: 38 percent
Nonverbal Expression: 55 percent

Four Types of Communication

Our daily communications with others typically fall into one of four categories.

Aggressive communication: Denies respect for others.

This type of communication says, in effect: "I don't really care what you say, think, or feel. It is more important that you hear what I need to say." Aggressive communicators will forcefully tend to speak in a menacing, controlling, and insensitive manner. If their words do not show disrespect, their volume, tone, facial expression, or posture often do.

Passive communication: Denies self respect.

When we communicate in a passive manner, we appear to be in agreement or compliance. We may either not know what to say or refrain from saying what we feel out of fear or politeness. In the end, this method of communication always minimizes one's own value. It is not uncommon for a passive communicator to eventually blow up or even end a relationship for no apparent reason. These outcomes could have been avoided if the communicator had been willing to speak more honestly and assertively in "real time."

Passive-aggressive communication: Denies or hides one's true feelings and does not respect others.

In this type of communication, the communicator appears to be in agreement or compliance but is also communicating in a more aggressive and resistant fashion. This pattern of confused communication can be conscious or unconscious, verbal or nonverbal. For example, Jordan, who repeatedly tells his boss that he will finish his weekly report by Friday at five p.m. but always seems to forget, is communicating in an unconscious passive-aggressive way. In contrast, Ashley, who agrees with her mother that she needs to finish her homework before going to the movies but has no intention of doing so, is communicating in a conscious passive-aggressive manner.

Assertive communication: Allows for all to feel valued and respected

When we communicate assertively, words and actions are delivered in a way that values all parties.

In our previous example, Felipe communicated with Maria in an "aggressive," parental way. In turn, Maria communicated her anger and hurt in a "passive-aggressive" manner, which Felipe soon adopted himself. If each had chosen to communicate in an "assertive" style, they may have avoided five needless months of lost connection that they will never get back.

Communicating our concerns, requests, and questions in an assertive, adult manner means that they will have the maximum chance to be fully understood. Delivering our messages with maximum effect does not mean all our assertive communications will be well-received. What it does mean is that communicating in this way always safeguards the respect of all parties and honors others with the most accurate, truthful information.

Communicating as Equals

In the 1950s, psychotherapist Eric Berne presented his iconic theory of Transactional Analysis (TA) arguing that all our communication is sent and received differently depending on how we are feeling at the time. [5] Whenever communication takes place, communicator and hearer take on one of three alter egos, or what Berne calls "ego states." We either communicate or hear from the perspective of a *Parent*, *Adult* or *Child*. How we communicate in the real world, however, is not always so simple. In actuality, the way we communicate can be deeply influenced by our upbringing, past experiences, and memories.

To see these ego states in action, we return again to Felipe and Maria. Their conflict began when Maria perceived that Felipe was talking down to her. According to TA, it is likely that Felipe was speaking from the Parent state instead of his Adult state. In turn, Maria was not able to respond from her Adult state and to confront him assertively but instead distanced herself for months relying on her Child state. To be a healthy and functional person who wishes to be respected and respects others, we need to make sure we communicate on a consistently Adult-to-Adult level.

Excellent Communicators Make Use of Multiple Senses

The best communicators do not rely on the sense of hearing alone. They make sure the listener is able to hear what is communicated (auditorily), see what is communicated (visually), and feel what is communicated (kinesthetically). Excellent communicators consider which sense is most preferred and thus likely to be the most effective in communicating with their intended audience.

In America, our school systems favor the visual learner—one who can read well and keep up in a highly visual environment. As educators learn more about the diverse ways students process and absorb information, alternative teaching styles are being incorporated to meet the needs of nonvisual learners. With this in mind, try to incorporate a visual, auditory, and experiential (kinesthetic) component whenever communicating.

FREE *COMMUNICATIONS* EXCUSESTOPPER

To learn how to be more impactful in your expressions of thanks, go to www.FireYourExcuses.com, register if you are not yet part of the Fire Your Excuses Community, and type in the keyword:

THANKER to download *"How to Become a Memorable Thanker."*

Emotional Intelligence and Our Communication

Earlier, we looked at the role our emotional intelligence plays in recognizing the areas of our lives which need attention. The study of emotional intelligence also offers us many considerations as we seek to improve the "how" of communication. The foundational trait of being emotionally intelligent is to "be aware of our self." Truly, communicators who are not self-aware are sadly the last to know.

Daniel Goleman, in his research[6] into what makes us "emotionally intelligent," highlights five core skills:

1. **Self-Awareness:** Knowing what we feel "in real time." This keeps us from saying things that are unnecessarily hurtful to others or emotionally inaccurate.

2. **Emotion Management:** Controlling the outward expression of our feelings, even in times of crisis.

3. **Motivating Oneself:** The ability to use self-control to curb impulsivity and distraction in order to remain attentive and engaged in conversation.

4. **Empathy:** Recognizing the impact of our communication, and sensing when our listener needs affirmation, compassion, or patience.

5. **Managing Relationships:** Handling difficult interpersonal interactions, conflicts, and negotiations with ease. Practicing the Golden Rule—treating others how we wish to be treated and looking for win-win outcomes whenever possible.

Other Critical Elements— Why, When, Where, and What We Communicate

Why

On the wall of one company board room we visited hung a striking plaque that stated, "NO AGENDA, NO GOALS, NO MEETING." How true. If we don't know *why* we are meeting we are likely to waste time, communicate ineffectively, and irritate others. The "why" is critical because it helps to clarify goals and increase our motivation.

> **TIPS TO IMPROVE YOUR COMMUNICATION INSTANTLY:**
> *Steer your conversation to topics that are important or interesting to all.*
> **When communicating in a group, continually steer the conversation back toward topics about which everyone can comfortably speak. For example, it is rude to leave the group behind by talking about technology if only**

one other person in the group understands what you are saying. Politely steer the conversation back to a topic of general interest.

When and Where

The "when" and "where" of our communication must be addressed next after we have settled on the "why" of our message. For example, if you have determined your communication "why" is to discuss an out-of-state job offer with your wife, the "when" might be over dinner and the "where," at a nice restaurant.

Discussions of delicate topics should take place in an appropriate location that allows for animated dialogue and passionate disagreement. Mark may or may not want to ask his girlfriend, Lori, to marry him on the JumboTron in front of 43,000 sports fans, or, alternately, break up with her inside of a library. The right "when" and "where" are crucial elements in communicating effectively when the stakes are high.

What

Arguably the centerpiece of communication is "what" we wish to communicate. As reported by the Mehrabian study,[7] there are several important elements that make up the "what" of communication. What we communicate is inseparable from how we communicate. Our body language, tone, facial expressions, and even our clothing and grooming are all parts of what we communicate. Human resource recruiters tell us many stories of potential candidates who were not hired because their dress, grooming, or mannerisms spoke louder and more negatively than their carefully chosen words. Think about yourself. Does your physical presentation match your words?

The wrong takeaway from any discussion of Mehrabian's percentage breakdown of verbal versus nonverbal communication would be to think that the words we use are an afterthought. One only has to look at politics to see how elections are won or lost based on a poorly chosen phrase, regardless of how masterfully executed the nonverbal communication and how carefully chosen the setting. All of us remember that oft-repeated childhood phrase: "Sticks and stones may break my bones, but names will never hurt me." No statement could be more inaccurate. Poorly chosen words bring hurt and devastation.

TIPS TO IMPROVE YOUR COMMUNICATION INSTANTLY:
End your gossip habit.

Refuse to gossip or to listen to it. We are amazed at how many employees feel that it is fine to listen to gossip as long as they don't repeat it. We all need to "blow off steam" sometimes. Gossip does not have to be the result.

The solution is easy but rarely chosen: Find a person who does not know the individual with whom you are having a conflict, use no names, and get all the feedback you need. Imagine how you will stand out if you become known as someone who has never been heard to say anything negative about anyone else and refuses to listen to the same.

Our words are critical. The best communicators are masters of the "perfect phrase," continually incorporating the best examples of word choice and phraseology into their own speech and writing. Ask yourself: "Do I study the best speakers and take careful note when I am moved, motivated, or pleased by a certain phrase or illustration?"

Words can brighten an entire room with their grace and elegance, or they can cut like a knife with their bitterness and hatred. They can also get you fired. Many employees are terminated because they have shown poor judgment in the words they used in a heated discussion with a co-worker or supervisor. On one occasion, we sat with a recently terminated employee who admitted using profanity toward his supervisor but tried to maintain that it was said in a professional manner. Needless to say, his employer had found his argument unconvincing.

Studies suggest that the words you use can determine how you are viewed by others, influence whether or not you are hired, and even correlate with your income level. In some legal, criminal, and warfare situations, poor word choice can determine if you live or die. In our high-tech communication age, the words we use can have a much wider impact. Today, more people communicate their words electronically than ever before. During the Revolutionary War it could take six weeks or more for London to learn what was happening on the American battlefields; today it takes just seconds for information to travel the same distance!

Light-speed communication has its dangers. It is best to assume that everything you send electronically might one day become public. It can mean that we often fail to take a few extra moments to ensure that we are communicating in the right way. One top executive said it this way: "Email errors in grammar and spelling tell the world you either don't care or you're not the smartest person in the room!" So before you press *Send,* take a minute to run the spell check, which can still miss some errors. Then, reread your e-mail carefully.

Finally, make building your vocabulary a life-long endeavor. Practicing your vocabulary daily, by doing crossword puzzles, for example, can help keep the mind sharp and the neurons growing. There are many language-building programs available today to assist you.

TIPS TO IMPROVE YOUR COMMUNICATION INSTANTLY:
Avoid the "curse phrases" of communication.
Refrain from using the following words or phrases when talking to or about someone else. Though we have all been guilty of using them, they will immediately peg you as an amateur communicator.

- **"Always"** – as in: "You *always* **act as if you are right."**
- **"Never"** – as in: "You *never* **say anything nice."**
- **"You make me feel"** – as in: "*You make me feel* **so angry!"**

"All-or-nothing" words, like *"always"* and *"never,"* have the effect of shutting people down and eliminate the

opportunity for honest dialogue. Rarely is anyone *"always"* anything and, even if they are, you will spend your time debating exceptions.

What is wrong with, *"You make me feel?"* It is a blaming phrase and, in addition, it is inaccurate. First, no one likes to be attacked. Second, no one has the power to *make* you feel anything. We are responsible for our own feelings.

Improving Our Listening Skills

Great listening skills are as important to great speaking as fuel is to an automobile. Possessing one without the other will get you nowhere. People tend to be far less aware of their listening skill deficits than their speaking ones. The most common complaint we hear in counseling wives is, "I don't feel heard." No one is ever chastised for being too good a listener, but we are often irritated when others talk too much. The greatest listeners may or may not be quoted in the history books but they are heroes in the eyes of those they bless with their skills.

> **TIPS TO IMPROVE YOUR COMMUNICATION INSTANTLY:**
> *Giving 100 percent of your attention for a short time is better than offering 60 percent for much longer.*
> Give others your full attention for as long as you can, then politely end the conversation. Which communicates that you are of value: having someone "half-listen" for ten minutes while they are multi-tasking, or having someone listen 100 percent for five minutes before politely breaking away to get back to work? When you find yourself in a similar situation, respond to the communication request with: "Sure, I have a few minutes. You have my 100 percent attention."

There's an old story of a young lady who was taken to dinner one evening by William Gladstone and then the following evening by

Benjamin Disraeli, both eminent British statesmen in the late nineteenth century. Asked what impression these two celebrated men had made upon her, she replied:

"When I left the dining room after sitting next to Mr. Gladstone, I thought he was the cleverest man in England," she said. "But after sitting next to Mr. Disraeli, I thought I was the cleverest woman in England."[8]

Which man do you think was the better listener?

TIPS TO IMPROVE YOUR COMMUNICATION INSTANTLY:
Learn to listen like an ambassador.
Omar Sharif, the famous actor, built a long movie career around his civility and class. He exudes the kind of kingly aura of someone you would expect to extend to you impeccable hospitality, no matter how much he may disagree with your message.

Learn to listen with civility, patience, and class to those with whom you strongly disagree. Have you noticed that fewer and fewer in the broadcast media are able to debate with elegance and conviction? Usually, such debates degenerate into a shouting match where opposing sides interrupt and talk over one another.

How about you? Can you listen to someone whose opinions you find noxious, wait patiently until they are finished, and then politely paraphrase and debate what they have said? Be a statesman or stateswoman in your office, home, or social circle and "watch your stock rise."

HD Listening

HD Listening, which we define in our FYE programs as "listening in high definition," is a level of listening that requires full engagement in the conversation. It involves the fine tuning of one's skills for 100 percent clarity (understanding) and brightness (engagement). Just as great HD programming captures and displays image details that viewers have never seen before, the HD listener "captures" and "reflects back" to speakers new insights about their message.

Skills Critical for HD Listening

- **Listening without interruption**. We often underestimate the value of just letting someone debrief, or speak his or her mind. Many escalating problems, including lawsuits, originate from the feeling that one is not being heard.

- **Listening with empathy**. Listening attentively and reflecting the emotions expressed communicates that you care and are in sync with the speaker. If you want to immediately boost your communication skills, be quick to respond to any strong emotions expressed. It is easy to try to fix a negative emotion rather than understand and reflect back just how intense the feeling appears to be for the speaker.

- **Listening with your whole body**. Having a sense of "body awareness" enables us to respond physically to what is being said. As a general rule, mirroring the body position of the speaker and consistent eye contact is an effective start.

- **Listening with openness**. Being aware of common communication barriers, including our own mental filters, helps us minimize their intrusive effects and frees us to listen more openly. One of the biggest challenges is to avoid obvious changes in facial expressions and body language when we are hearing others state a view with which we strongly disagree.

- **Listening with feedback**. We honor our speaker whenever we show we were actively listening by paraphrasing, making sure we understood correctly, and offering opinions and suggestions only when asked.

Listening Barriers

All of us struggle to listen openly as we contend with communication barriers. Anyone who has ever taken an important call just before getting on a plane knows how difficult it can be to give one's full attention to such a conversation. If we are aware of these barriers and our own response to them, we can minimize their effect.

> **EXCUSE GAMECHANGER**
> Sometimes the conversation of others hides needs and interests seeking to be discovered. Be willing to pursue them.

Common Barriers to Listening

- **Mental Preoccupation:** Being distracted by concerns other than the immediate situation.

- **Mental Filtering**: Being unable to hear accurately because of your own internal agenda or prejudices. These include the following:

    Mind Reading: Believing you know what the speaker is really thinking or feeling.

    Rehearsing: Trying to mentally prepare a response before you have clearly heard what is being said.

    Prejudging: Making an assumption about the person or their message before they have finished speaking.

    Evaluating: Judging what the speaker is saying limits the hearer's ability to listen openly.

    Advising: Preoccupation with fixing the problem being presented makes it difficult to hear the whole message.

- **Poor Feedback Skills:** Being unable to provide appropriate verbal responses to what is being communicated:

  Derailing: Steering the conversation off topic because the content of the message is uncomfortable, you lack sufficient listening skills, or you would like to talk about something you feel is more interesting.

  Interrupting: Constant intruding into the flow of what is being said for any number of reasons, including unnecessary questions and personal anecdotes.

  Fixing: Giving advice when help is not requested.

  Placating: Feigned agreement or support for the statements communicated for the purpose of being liked or to appear "on the same page" as the speaker.

- **Environmental Distractions:** Location constraints, distracting activity or interruptions that make it difficult to maintain focus.

- **Personal History:** Unresolved conflicts within the listener make it difficult to stay "in the moment." For example, the topic being discussed triggers painful memories or past conflicts with the speaker.

- **Power/Control:** The hearer is unable to listen openly due to real or imagined authority concerns. For example, the speaker is attempting to exert unnecessary power or control, or the listener perceives the speaker does not have the credentials to deliver his or her message.

- **Physical Well-being:** There may be a physical concern that prevents the listener from maintaining full attention. For example, the listener may be tired or struggling with a migraine headache and unable to fully track what is being said.[9]

Review the list of barriers. Which ones do you find the most challenging?

TIPS TO IMPROVE YOUR COMMUNICATION INSTANTLY:
Quickly, but politely, set limits on abusive speech.
Sadly, unchecked abusive speech can result in the ending of an otherwise salvageable relationship. How do you respond when your boss, spouse, child, or friend begins to speak to you in an abusive way? We have found that in 90 percent of all cases where abusive language begins, firm limit setting will prevent such communication in the future. For example: "I respect you as my boss and I want to hear what you have to say about my job performance, but calling me lazy is not appropriate."

Improving Our Ability to Communicate in Conflict Situations

Dr. Steve is one of the most influential ER doctors to ever work at Famous American Medical Center. He is responsible for admitting more patients to the facility than any other consulting physician. He is also among the most respected doctors in the state for his area of specialty, and he socializes with a large network of politicians, celebrities, and business leaders.

Those who work alongside of Dr. Steve, however, tell a very different story. His communication style is aggressive, Napoleonic, and downright rude. Many believe that he is the biggest reason why FAMC has four times the national average of nursing turnover in the ER.

The hospital contacted us in a quandary: Should they confront their most economically valued physician and risk him leaving the organization and taking his patients elsewhere? Or, should they look the other way and allow him to continue to verbally abuse his co-workers, risking even more staff turnover?

Perhaps you are dealing with a "difficult person" and a delicate situation of your own. Whether you are an H.R. professional who must confront a "Dr. Steve," or an individual dealing with a personal relationship, effective intervention takes planning and courage. In some cases we may need outside assistance, including the help of a professional.

Eight Ways to Successfully Handle Confrontation

The following recommendations have been proven to be helpful in resolving conflict:

1. *Whenever possible, plan before you meet with a difficult person.*
   Taking a few minutes to plan or get some outside support helps us cool down and gain objective, anonymous, feedback.

2. *Seek first to understand, then to be understood.*
   Try to see the conflict as a source of information, not just as a threat. First, ask yourself: "What's going on for this person right now? What's important to them? What do they want from this interchange? What might they be feeling?" In many instances, hostility can be reduced when others know you are making an effort to hear them out, whether you agree or not.

3. *Make statements that show you anticipate a positive outcome.*
   There may be a variety of reasons why someone may appear to be difficult or say something confrontational. However, having a positive attitude and making statements such as: "I know we can find a solution to this problem," or "I want to help," may be the most important thing you can say. Carefully chosen words can rapidly de-escalate a conflict and move it toward a positive outcome.

4. *Focus more attention on the truth of the message than on how it was delivered.*

    Sometimes we must admit there are "bits of truth" that need to be acknowledged, even within a message that was poorly communicated. Start your next communication with an acknowledgement of that fact, regardless of your feelings about what the other party should have said or done better.

    TIPS TO IMPROVE YOUR COMMUNICATION INSTANTLY:
    Initiate a follow-up conversation whenever possible to gain closure.
    It is easy to avoid difficult conversations. Innumerable marriages and jobs have needlessly ended because the parties involved refused, out of pride or discomfort, to meet again. In so doing they missed a critical opportunity to negotiate further, express difficult feelings, and to validate the relationship in spite of the conflict. You will set yourself apart if you consistently initiate uncomfortable but important conversations, if only to say a proper farewell. Great communicators always initiate the follow-up conversation, even if they feel they are in the right!

5. *Acknowledge your mutual concerns and restate the conflict in terms of interests and options.*

    Focusing on the interests of the person initiating the conflict will often eliminate any further personal attacks and will be instrumental in reaching common ground. For example, you might say: "I know you are very angry. I want to fully understand why you are so upset and to make things right if at all possible."

6. *Don't go at it alone.*

    There are many times when we need social support to help

us calm down and see things from a different perspective. Again, to avoid gossip and to get the most objective feedback, seek outside help from someone who does not know the other person.

7. *Know when to retreat.*

    When a confrontational person is not willing to communicate in a reasonable manner, you may need to take a time out or get away from the situation indefinitely. As with any relationship, if there are signs of abuse or potential violence, retreat from the situation and call for assistance immediately. Sometimes cutting your losses in the short term is crucial to de-escalating the conflict so that you can return to the discussion at a better time.

8. *Be sure to debrief after the conflict.*

    Reassessing what happened can be invaluable for either brainstorming ways to resolve the conflict later or to prepare for continued conflict. Give proper consideration to your emotional and physical needs after the conflict. Get additional help if too much time passes and you are still feeling shaken, angry, depressed, or "stuck."[10]

TAKE THE 30-DAY
COMMUNICATIONS CHALLENGE

1. Find two people who have an opposite view on a topic very important to you. Ask them to describe in detail why they believe the way they do. Your goal is to listen as graciously as possible, paraphrasing their statements to show you understand. Do not challenge them at any point to change their views.

2. Learn one new word every day this month and use at least fifteen in conversation, crossing them off your list when you do. Don't tell anyone what you are doing. Your goal is to insert new vocabulary naturally into your conversations.

3. Research and tell a motivating story when communicating in the following three settings: With a family member(s), at work, and with a friend.

4. Optional: If the opportunity arises, gently confront at least one individual who attempts to share negative information about another person you know.

FIRE YOUR EXCUSES

CHAPTER FIVE:

TIME MANAGEMENT

Blind Spots and Weaknesses

Health and Wellness

Social Connections

Communication

Time Management

Finances

Career

Serving

CHAPTER 5

TIME MANAGEMENT

Nine-tenths of wisdom is being wise in time.
—THEODORE ROOSEVELT

JENNY MASCHE[1] OF ARIZONA NEARLY DIED OF HEART FAILURE IN 2007. Just twenty-four hours before surgery to deliver her sextuplets, she learned she had a blood clot. She survived and delivered six healthy children. Jenny, then thirty-two, immediately lost 42 pounds of baby weight and, in time, began to regain her health. Six months later, still recovering, she set the goal of running a marathon by the time of her children's first birthday. At first, she took it very slowly, but as she began to run, her strength grew. In June 2008, she finished all 26.2 miles of the Rock 'n' Roll San Diego Marathon, alongside her husband.

How did she find the time? Jenny responds: "There are always going to be chores. There will always be something to do."[2] In other words, she *makes* the time. She either runs at 5:00 a.m. before the kids are up, after 8:00 p.m. when they have been put to bed, or she calls a friend to babysit in the afternoon during nap time. She also has an accountability partner, who often runs with her. It's "girl time,"[3] she adds. Jenny hopes her motivation will be an inspiration for her children. "It is best to lead by example."[4] At the time of this writing, Jenny is already gearing up for another race, the Surf City USA Marathon in Huntington Beach, California.

What causes a person like Jenny, against great obstacles, to do whatever it takes to make an incredible dream possible? As we shall see, while her dreams do depend on careful time management, there is much more at play than the number of minutes available in her day. The following story illustrates that several far deeper factors are at work that, if ignored, will doom any plan to failure.

Joel works forty-five hours a week and has a ninety-minute round-trip commute to work. His wife, Trisha, has been nagging him for the past three months to keep his promise to re-stain the deck and clear out the brush left over from last fall's tree-trimming project. Joel knows he agreed to do it months ago. In fact, he feels guilty whenever he steps into the backyard. Trisha works very hard too. She takes care of the kids and also manages their growing Internet-based business from their home.

One Wednesday morning, as Joel is leaving for work, he notices a flyer in the mail for an outdoor theater production that Friday night. He tells his wife that evening that he is taking her out on a date on Friday and the kids will be taken care of by their uncle and aunt. At first his wife is resistant. She has had a tough week and she has lots to do on Saturday morning to prepare for a baby shower that afternoon. Joel lovingly insists, and on Friday night he surprises her with a casual, romantic picnic. Both have a great evening enjoying one of Trisha's favorite musicals under the stars.

The next morning, Trisha awakens to the aroma of coffee brewing, the long-neglected brush neatly stacked in their truck, and Joel already well into re-staining the deck. Needless to say, Trisha is both shocked and delighted.

What motivated Joel to finish his backyard projects after months of avoidance? The answer is simple but paradoxical. Ironically, by adding a restorative event to his already busy week, Joel was able to finish the projects he had been avoiding. It would have been easy for Joel and Trisha to do what they normally do on a Friday night—feed and entertain the children then collapse in front of the TV after a tough week of work. Instead, they addressed the emotional side of their week and it made all the difference in Joel's avoidance pattern.

Fire Your Excuses Self-Assessment Snapshot: Joel

Scale	Score	Range
Total Excuse Scale	339	Above Average
Potential for Change Scale	55	Above Average
Time Management Scale	29	Average
Offense Scale	106	Average
Defense Scale	99	Average

Joel's assessment scores indicate that he is generally a hard-working man of action rather than excuses. Even his Average Score for Time Management is respectable. His Potential for Change Score confirms that he was ready for a change. His situation illustrates that several areas of our lives, as measured by the assessment, can have a strong positive or negative effect on each other and must often be considered together. In Joel's case, engaging in offensive, life-affirming action—going on a romantic picnic—had an immediate effect on his time management.

We are not unfeeling machines. Motivation, mood, and rest play a huge part in whether or not we get to those tasks we promised we would tackle in a given time slot. If you have ever said: "I wish I could be as productive as I am the day before a big trip," you also know that having something to look forward to significantly increases our motivation and focus.

A Different Approach to Time Management

Much has been written about time management. What is unique about the FYE approach? It is its focus on mood and motivation management. Your success does not lie in purchasing the newest exercise video, electronic gadget, or tool. These products may offer some help, but they are unable to provide you with motivation that is not there already.

Time Management Principle 1:
Time Management without Emotional Management is Unsustainable

Maintaining consistent time management begins, not with the intro-duction of a number of great techniques, but with an unflinching exam-ination of the emotional and motivational components of managing our time. This includes our hope, mood, ability to delay gratification, and the power of incremental effort. Without careful attention to these important factors, your time management plans will always unravel. Our problem is often follow-through—the challenge of remaining disciplined over a long period of time.

When our emotional needs are not addressed, we "go on strike." We get bored, become emotionally overwhelmed, and need consistent breaks and an adequate number of emotionally refilling events. For some, such activities involve socializing with friends and family; for others who are bombarded with people all day, it may be time alone. Are you working long hours and skipping restorative experiences because you "don't have time?" We challenge you to take that time anyway and see if you don't get more done with the time you have left in your schedule. In this section we will explore some of the core reasons behind our struggles with time management and then share a list of helpful techniques to greatly increase your efficiency.

Time Management Principle 2:
Choose Your Pain

A key tenet of our approach is encouraging our clients to "choose their pain." Each of our choices has a cost. There is pain or discomfort in completing a certain task or goal, and there is pain in avoiding or aban-doning the project. When we clearly know the pain involved in each of our options, the motivation to manage time in support of our dreams is enhanced.

Consider the pain of time, stress, and debt in returning to school to finish a four-year degree. This must be weighed against the pain of the income lost by not having obtained the degree. According to 2008 data from the U.S. Census Bureau,[5] the average 25 or older, full-time worker in the U.S. with a four-year degree earned $63,277 per year. This amount is 105 percent more than the $30,879 earned by the average full-time worker whose highest degree is a high school diploma. Multiply this average $32,398 per year difference over a lifetime of work, i.e., forty years, and the difference (without earning a penny of interest) is $1,295,920. This is an immense sum; even considering the spiraling costs of attending college today.

Focusing on the pain of not succeeding in a given endeavor can be a powerful motivator. Andy Stanley,[6] a popular leadership speaker and writer, likes to challenge leaders to soberly consider the costs of inaction. We would like to extend his leadership challenge to you by asking the following question: "What won't happen in the world if you don't do what you feel called to do?"

Thoughtfully consider your response and write your answer below to better remember it in the future.

_____

_____

_____

_____

Time Management Principle 3:
Choose Your Joy!

Pain avoidance is not the *most* effective motivator. We all know people who have been told by their doctor that they will die if they don't lose weight or stop drinking. Sadly, this sobering confrontation has had only a temporary impact on their health habits. A far more powerful and permanent motivator is one that is positive, life-affirming, and joyful. Hearing your granddaughter say, "I love you, Grandpa and I want you to be there at my wedding one day," can be far more motivating than a frightening lecture from your doctor.

It is important to be crystal clear about the anticipated joys of achieving your goals. These might include the continued pleasure of enjoying your favorite sport, still feeling good about going swimming in the summer, or having the energy to play with your son or daughter.

Consider two women, age forty-five, both who wish to lose twenty pounds and who have roughly the same starting weight and height. The first woman, Cheryl, says she feels "fat" and would like to look better in her favorite jeans. The second woman, Christine, would like to drop the weight so that she can run a half marathon to raise money for breast cancer in honor of her sister who recently passed away. Which of the two women do you think is more likely to push through the inevitable setbacks and reach her goal?

Think of your top three goals, and answer the following questions about each one:

1. *Is the motivation for your goal joyous and compelling? Or, is your primary motivation fear-based, i.e., mainly to avoid negative consequences if you don't act?*

2. *What will you need to give up and for how long?*

3. *Are you really willing to make these sacrifices at this time?*

If your answers reveal the truth that your goals are not a priority right now, that's okay. Just be honest with yourself and re-label your *goals* as *wishes*. What is the difference between a goal and wish? A *goal* without a date is actually a "pre-goal," better known as a *wish.*

It's essential to remember the difference between the two. Don't shame yourself if you realize you have other more pressing priorities that make sense to address first. This can be the right choice depending on the situation.

Two Phrases We Will No Longer Utter

What is the deadliest weapon in our arsenal of life-limiting, dream-killing excuses? It is the phrase: "I just don't have enough time." Time is rarely the *primary* reason we fail to achieve our goals. As we have explored above, the most essential factors are our ability to maintain our hope, motivation, and discipline, even when it feels emotionally and physically painful.

All of us struggle daily against intrusions into our time. Some are used as convenient excuses; others represent real obstacles in our lives. Phrases like "I'm just a procrastinator," or "I don't have enough time," usually give us a "hall pass" just when we need to be taking our "final exam." Instead, we must each strive to identify the *real* reason for not working on our task—be it fear, mood, lack of self-esteem, or an unwillingness to pay the price needed.

> **The explosive popularity of *Facebook* proves the point that our failure to achieve our goals is not due to lack of time.**

Commit to expunge from your speech these and similar phrases! Instead, say: "X is not yet one of my top time priorities." This is a far more honest statement. That said, it might make sense to delay your goal at this time in your life. You just need to be clear about your current priorities.

The Role of Hope and Motivation in Time Management

Most of us grew up believing that Thomas Edison invented the light bulb. The truth is, he didn't. What he did do was invent the first long-lasting light bulb, greatly improving on the work of others, and making it a commercial success.

One thing that can be observed in all of the men who helped bring us electricity was their dogged determination. Joseph Wilson Swan was one of Edison's predecessors and is credited with inventing the world's first workable electric bulb. Beginning in 1840, he toiled for twenty years until, in 1860, he created and patented the first electric bulb, which only burned briefly. Returning to his project in 1875, he achieved a better result—a bulb that burned for thirteen hours. Edison and his assistants tried 6,000 different types of filament before, in 1879, they surpassed Swan's result. They designed a longer-lasting oxygen-less bulb with a carbon filament that burned *fourteen* hours. A year later, in 1880, Edison's team came up with a vastly improved bulb that burned between 1,200 to 1,500 hours, which they took to market. As they say, the rest is history.[7]

We can certainly admire such celebrated determination and spectacular results, but what about you? Would you try anything 6,000 times before you gave up? How about 2,000? How about twenty?

What's the *most* number of times you have tried anything before you finally succeeded?

_____

What did you attempt? _____

How many times did you try? _____

In truth, our motivation varies greatly based on our perception of the following:

- Our ability
- Likelihood of success
- Self-confidence
- Fear of failure/resiliency

One example of how the perception of opportunity can transform our lives is found in the following story.

A young, newly-married Asian couple immigrated to California in 1993. Upon arrival, the two immediately began working fifty hours a week in an uncle's dry cleaning business. The first year was a difficult one. They missed home terribly and struggled with the new language and customs, and the much higher cost of basic necessities. However, on the advice of relatives who had made a successful transition to American life, the couple made a critical decision. They decided not to rent an apartment or buy a car. Instead, they slept in the back of the store and washed up after hours in the shopping mall's public restroom for their first two years. This enabled them to bank nearly all of their income. In their first year, they managed to save $25,000. In five years they invested $130,000 they had saved up, and with an additional loan from their uncle, they bought a store of their own. Now, ten years after their arrival in the U.S., they are millionaires.

EXCUSE GAMECHANGER
If achieving time management goals becomes difficult, put extra focus on elevating your motivation level.

What does this inspiring, but surprisingly commonplace, Southern California story have to do with time management? Everything! It highlights the "hope" factor in the persistence, sacrifice and focus needed to change one's life.

Our immigrant couple sincerely believes America is the land of opportunity, having lived in a culture where upward mobility was far more difficult. We must admit few American-born adults would be willing to make the same sacrifices so they could then buy a business of their own. Hope is an amazingly powerful force. We will do almost anything if we have hope. For your dreams to succeed, you will need to maintain a great deal of hope over a number of years—hope that your small incremental efforts will add up to something much bigger.

How Do You Find the Hope You Need to Stick with Your Goals?

Unless you have a regular infusion of hope in your life, you will most likely not have the discipline you need to keep striving, especially when you sense your goal may require some severe lifestyle choices like the ones our millionaires made. Without hope and the motivation it offers, you will find any number of activities to pursue instead, even necessary ones, to avoid spending time on a scarier but potentially more rewarding project.

What can you do to increase your hope and motivation as you set your goals? Surround yourself with optimistic, hopeful people.

The Role of Self-Esteem and Support in Time Management and Perseverance

There is a great irony in the pursuit of a difficult goal. If too much of your self-esteem is on the line, you may feel too stressed to pursue your goal or unwittingly sabotage your own progress.

Those who have hope have a well-honed ability to fail and keep on trying. Like a top football team, they know sometimes you have to punt and hope that you will get the ball back soon enough to have another shot at a touchdown.

Pretend for a moment that the amount of hope you have could be measured as water in a sports bottle. When we look at your bottle we see your hope level is very low. Does swirling the water around in the sealed plastic bottle do anything to raise your hope level permanently? Sadly, it does nothing. This is where one of our favorite commercial slogans, "Just Do It," has its limits. Unless you have a lot of "internal water" already, a Just Do It-style pep talk is not going to do it.

Bottom line, for permanent change, you will need to surround yourself with people who can add to the level of water in your bottle. These will need to be individuals who have consistent motivation and discipline in the areas you lack. Stay in close contact with them until their strengths become part of your emotional DNA.

It is hard for most of us to accept this need for outside assistance. While we all want change, we often would rather skip the "inner work"— the emotional and social restructuring necessary to change permanently. We prefer a pep-talk, a new diet, or a quick-fix. In contrast, permanent change is more often caught than taught.

In psychology, we use a technical term called "receiving positive introjects." What is an *introject*? It is a new way of seeing ourselves and behaving in the world. It is something that must be absorbed by osmosis from others, over time. You just can't read it in a book. Not even this one. Without new introjects, we simply slip back into our default mode, the thoughts and behaviors that have kept us where we are for years.

If you can't find such a group of people, you will need to create a mastermind/goal setting group of your own. Or, better yet, join one through the burgeoning Fire Your Excuses Community. If you have a dream but it is not in an area where you have shown consistent discipline or strength, you will need support and accountability from others. This will mean regular contact and inter-action over time, until your emotions and behaviors are rewired and you are ready to solo.

> **MYTH AND TRUTH.**
> **Myth: "I just need to try harder this time."**
> **Truth: You will be far more successful in six months if you reach out to a coach or a group than you will be after twenty years of "trying harder."**

The great surprise is this: High levels of motivation and hope do not have to be sustained for as long as you may think. Every driver knows that idling and getting up to speed from a dead-stop burns a lot more fuel than cruising at highway speed. In an identical way, we know that starting on your projects and goals and building the momentum in the early phases of a project requires much more motivational energy than when you're well into your task. The key is not to give up before you experience the breakthrough to cruising speed.

We have all experienced this "zone." Have you ever gone ahead and completed all of your grocery shopping even though you went into the store just for a few necessities? Why? Because once you were in the store, it was easy, even exhilarating, to toss a few more needed items into your basket. You found the zone. In just a short time, you realized you were more than half-way done. Like a long distance runner, once you saw the finish line, you experienced a surge of energy no matter how tired you felt in the middle of the race.

Depressed Mood—The Silent Slayer of Our Dreams

According to the National Institute of Health, twenty million Americans suffer from depression.[8] Millions more experience what is called "sub-clinical" depression. This is the experience of a number of depressive symptoms—not enough to be diagnosed with major depression but certainly enough to rob you of your motivation and dreams.

> **GET THE HELP AND SUPPORT YOU NEED**
> Trying to fire your excuses about any goal when you are depressed is as silly as kicking yourself for not running a six-minute mile when you've just had knee surgery. Get the help and support you need.

Mood matters tremendously in the management of time. If you have ever blocked out three hours to tackle a neglected chore, but when that time arrived you just didn't feel up to it, you know that your mood can be a huge help or hindrance. Statistically, we know that a certain percentage of those reading this book right now are dealing with some level of unaddressed depression. It can be especially difficult for men to admit to a depressed mood, let alone seek treatment for this medical condition. Fortunately, as the shame surrounding depression fades, more and more men are getting the help they deserve. We hope if your mood is robbing you of your potential and your dreams, you will seek out the help that is readily available for this highly treatable illness.

Eleven Time Management Techniques that Will Add a Half-Day to Your Week

Before we explore some specific techniques to help you add hours to your week, it is important to underscore that having a system, whether low tech or high tech, beats having no system every time! In fact, a wealthy friend of ours just carries a 3x5 spiral notebook. Every appointment, phone number, and "to do" is written on that pad and nowhere else. That's his low-tech but highly effective system. What does matter is your ability to consistently apply your chosen system while maintaining your mood, motivation, and hope. If you have not been able to stick with your time management goals, you will need to seek out additional support.

We challenge you to try a few of the techniques below to see how they will add several more hours to your week. If you believe your main problem is too little time, your first assignment is to keep a time log charting how you spend every fifteen-minute increment of your day for two weeks. Begin your time management plan by reviewing your completed log for "time leaks" you may not have noticed.

1. Schedule in Thinking Time.

People who handle time well set aside a few minutes each day just to think. A current business trend is to give top executives short company-paid vacations just to go away and think. If you want to live your life in a proactive rather than reactive way, you need to do so too, even if on a smaller scale.

You may need to be a little creative to find a place where you can think uninterruptedly. If you have a big dream or need to make a radical change, it may call for some thinking sessions. Take something to write with to a quiet location and try not to leave until you have some fresh ideas. You'll find that the time you spend will be made up by being more efficient during the rest of the week.

On Monday mornings, resist the urge to just "jump in" and respond to pressing calls, chores, or emails. Whether you work in the corporate world or at home, try setting aside an hour at the beginning of each week to think strategically about the big projects you want to begin or push forward. If you cannot take this time at work, do it over the weekend on your own. It is that important.

2. Take-in, Take-out.

Never wait in line again at your favorite take-out restaurant. Pick up a take-out menu next time, and *always* call in your order ahead, even if you plan to eat there. You'll often gain an extra fifteen minutes over lunch, and you'll save time if you are swinging by to pick up dinner on the way home after work.

3. The 1-31 File Folder System.

This is the immediate antidote to searching for important paper-work. If you're tired of searching for your latest bill or wedding invitation, try this: Set up 31 hanging file folders and number them from

"Organized people are just people who are too lazy to look for things!"

© *Randy Glasbergen. www.RandyGlasbergen.com* [9]

1 to 31. Now you have a number for each day of the month. When a birthday invitation or bill arrives in the mail, put the information in the folder that corresponds to the event's date of the month or due date.

It doesn't matter if your event or payment date is in February, October, or December; if it falls on the tenth, drop it in file folder #10. Use the 1-31 system, and you'll never have a stack of bills, applications, renewal notices, or invitations left on your desk again, nor will you ever spend time searching for them.

4. Tame Your Television Time.

Do you subscribe to cable or satellite TV? If so, get your provider's digital recorder service and commit to *never* watching live TV again. Why? Because fast-forwarding through the commercials shaves more than fifteen minutes off of each one-hour program.

If the average cost of a digital video recorder (DVR) is approximately $16/month and you watch four hours of TV a week, you save four hours a month by not watching commercials. That means you've bought back a morning of your life at the cost of $16, each and every month. By the end of the year you have saved six working days, or forty-eight hours.

What could you do with that time? You could exercise ninety-six times for a half-hour! You could get together with neglected friends, or volunteer every other week for two hours. You get the idea.

5. Split the Time Difference.

When we speak, people often come up afterwards to ask us for small follow-up favors. For example, they may ask for the name of the best book for an issue they are wrestling with, or for our thoughts on a difficult problem. While we do our best to respond to each question at the time, the volume of requests can sometimes be overwhelming.

One approach that works well in such cases is to answer briefly and ask the person with a more involved request to contact us by email. This saves the time of sorting through piles of handwritten requests and enables us to respond more quickly. Can you think of any situations in your own life, business or volunteering, where you are doing all the follow-up or preparation? Consider small adjustments that would enable you to still be helpful but where the time load could be shared more equally among all participants.

6. Time Your Tasks.

Using a simple timer can help to move along chores that take longer than they should to complete. Yes, it sounds a bit obsessive-compulsive, but it works like a charm. All microwave ovens and most cell phones now come with an alarm. Your mind will like the challenge and your body will appreciate the workout.

Can you tidy up the house in thirty minutes instead of forty-five? We especially like to time ourselves in the gym when doing circuit training. Limiting your rest between sets adds an aerobic component to the workout, gets you out of the gym quickly, and makes you more likely to come back a day or so later.

7. Use the "O-H-I-O" Method.

This one has been around for years. The OHIO method stands for "Only Handle It Once." You can tell how efficient you are at using the OHIO method by making a tiny pen mark on the corner of each document every time you pick it up. You know the ones we mean—that invitation, form, memo, and so on. If you look at your paper multiple times without taking the appropriate action, you need the OHIO method.

8. Partition, Partition, Partition!

Can you remember back to your kindergarten and grade school days? In many of our brightly-colored classrooms there was a wall of cubby holes near the entrance where we stored our lunch boxes, book bags, and, for some, our cold weather clothing. These individual shelving spaces made it easy for everyone to keep track of their belongings.

Well, guess what? Your mind is the same way. It still yearns to go back to those early years. When you got older, that cubbyhole became a locker, then a briefcase, and eventually a storage locker, but the idea is the same: Keep all your things in their own space and life is a lot easier. That's what the time management concept of partitioning is all about. Separate all the items, tasks, or projects in your life into very clear, discreet "boxes," and your productivity will increase dramatically.

How can you build your partitions? It's best to build up your fortress walls when you are not "under siege." But, you can and must still build, even if more slowly, when you are in the pressure cooker of life.

Here are just a few simple ways to add partitions and save hours of time.

Partition financially. Enter every purchase, check, and withdrawal into a computer-based accounting system. It takes just five minutes a day, but it makes tax time a breeze and you can just click a button to see what you've spent on every item. Additionally, 90 percent of your bills can now be paid online. This will save at least two hours a month. These programs are simple to learn and will help you immensely in your budgeting.

Partition your projects. David Allen, author of *Getting Things Done*,[10] said this in a recent podcast interview[11] with us: Your goal is to "get everything out of your head." In other words, why waste the biggest supercomputer ever created—your brain—to remember to pick up an extra ream of paper at your local office supply store? Don't waste your valuable neurons. Get those to-do's out of your head immediately.

How do you organize your emails, project to-do's, etc? Keep it simple. Consider keeping two lists on your computer, your smartphone, or on paper to keep track of your projects. Allen urges us to title one of them "To-do's," a kitchen-sink listing of all possible projects, to-do's, and leads. Title the other "Open Projects," where each of your working projects is broken down into very doable, small next steps.

By having these two lists, you do not have to keep your desk piled up with working folders or Post-It notes. Your two lists are a way of partitioning all the to-do's and projects you have to complete, and to keep from being overwhelmed. As an added benefit, you will not be wasting any more time looking for missing information.

If you are not techie, that's fine; just buy a small spiral notepad you can carry in your pocket or purse. It doesn't have to be fancy, just effective.

Another low-tech solution is to pick up a $4 package of yellow pads from your local office supply store. Number each yellow pad at the cardboard top, and write out the date you begin, e.g., March 1, 2012. When you fill up the pad, add the ending date, i.e., March 1, 2012-April 3, 2012.

Use these pads to record phone numbers, meetings notes and anything else that is important and not stored digitally. When you finish one pad and have filed away the pages that need to go into their respective folders, put the pad with its remaining pages into a hanging file for easy reference. Then take out a fresh second pad and write the date at the top and you are good to go. If you know that your friend called and she gave you the name of a great lead some time back in March but you are not sure when, you'll know it must be on March's yellow pad. You'll never be searching for information again.

Here's another crucial step. Buy a cheap back-up hard-drive and set up an online or off-site back-up system as double protection for your data, just in case of fire, theft, earthquake, or storm. Once you have your secure back-up system in place, you no longer need to mindlessly print out everything.

Your goal: No papers on your desk. Everything is either filed electronically or placed in a file folder or envelope—no exceptions.

Partition your spring cleaning. One sort a week is all we ask! For most people, a disorganized, cluttered environment is the antithesis of a calm, relaxing place to work, entertain, or rest. Here's a deep cleaning trick that will work for all but the most cluttered homes and offices:

In addition to your routine cleaning, tackle one space in your world each week that needs serious attention and clean it. If you do, you will never have to clean all day or weekend. Divide your deep cleaning activities into a hundred or so small tasks, then just do one, two, or three a week. Never use up a whole day to clean the garage unless you find the change of pace exhilarating. Instead, sort through two or three boxes a week, and no more. You can also use this technique to clean your house—clean out just one shelf, drawer or closet a week.

Partition your clutter. There are times when it is best to remove everything from your trunk, closet, garage, or filing cabinet to jump start your progress. That doesn't mean you must deal with all your clutter the same day. Use the technique of partitioning to work on some of your piles, boxes, paperwork, or shelves each day. It's less overwhelming that way.

For example, do you have a file cabinet at home that is in dire need of attention? Begin by taking out all of your files and setting them on the floor. Emotionally speaking, your job is more than halfway done. Now, sort through a few inches of files each day. In two short weeks, taking just ten to fifteen minutes a day, you can completely dispose of unnecessary papers and files with no measurable loss of day-to-day productivity.

9. Use Time Redirection.

Most of us fail to achieve our goals, not because the road is difficult, but because it is long. The trick is to fool your psyche—to make your initial changes so small that they hardly feel like changes at all. Like coffee and lunches out? Give up five lattes a month ($15/month) and eating lunch out twice a week ($60/month) and you could be sipping lattes in Italy every three years or taking a great vacation in the U.S. yearly. It's easy to think travel is for others but for most it is a matter of *redirection*, in this case, of your cash.

You can redirect time in exactly the same way with profound results. What do you consistently do with that spare fifteen minutes? Are you writing, walking, or calling friends you have long neglected? It is in these small, fifteen-minute windows that excellence is achieved.

We will never forget a Monster.com executive's response when we asked how he landed his enviable position flying all over the country introducing executives to his online recruitment services. He said: "I was the guy who made just one more phone call after everyone else went home."

What are you willing to do for fifteen minutes each day after everyone else has gone home or to bed? This will likely be the laser-focused activity that will change your life.

10. Protect Your Time.

Did you know the latest research has challenged the efficiency of multi-tasking? Constant project switching has been shown to be deadly to the flow of thought needed for complex tasks that often require some warm up time. Tim Ferris, in his inspiring book, *The Four-Hour Work-week,*[12] suggests that for most people the world doesn't stop if we answer our email and voicemail a little less often. If you are constantly inter-rupted, it may be time to disappear, or at least be a little less reachable.

Try it. Experiment with the amount of time you can go without responding to outside requests or being physically available to others. You'll be surprised in most cases how well the world can do without you.

While many of us pride ourselves on being great multi-taskers and responding in real-time, these activities can come at too high a price in our productivity. What could you group together to save time? "Task grouping" is a powerful way to save time, even gas. For example, group all your calls together. It is easy to call ten people back if you are prepared to do so and you can leave a voicemail message for eight of them. In fact, business people appreciate a short, cordial conversation during a busy day.

11. Use Transition Time.

Waiting time is really *bonus time*, especially if you insist on leaving at the time you planned. Efficient people never show up for a meeting or travel to a destination without reading material or having paperwork to do if they arrive early. Transition time can be used in a number of strategic ways. Here are just a few.

- *Initiating*: Making that first call to a business contact.

- *Scheduling*: Writing out the "very next steps" for each project you have open.

- *Connecting*: Calling family and friends just to say, "I miss talking with you" or "What's going on?"

- *Outlining or brainstorming*: Highlighting the main points of a project, article, or presentation.

- *Reviewing:* Updating your goals, to-do's and projects.

- *Recording ideas*: Writing down useful ideas before you forget them.

- *Refilling:* Reading an inspirational book, praying, meditating, or listening to some of your favorite music.

- *Resting:* If a short "power nap" worked for John D. Rockefeller; it can work for you too!

Are You Playing Good Offense and Defense?

Finally, we would like to go a little deeper in our discussion of *offensive* and *defensive* activities. These two actions, measured by the assessment, are especially relevant when we speak of time management. Good strategic planning requires focusing on both offensive and defensive activities. It is important to be clear about what we mean when we speak of these terms.

First, our use of the word *defensive* is not referring to someone who is closed to hearing the truth, or who is acting stubbornly. Nor are we talking about negative actions. We are using the word in a positive way. For example, there are a number of defensive actions we take every day that are critically important to minimize loss and pain and to keep things running smoothly for ourselves, our family, and our workplace. We cannot ignore the defensive tasks of our day or week.

What are some of these defensive actions? They include paying our bills, picking up a wedding gift, seeing our doctors regularly, cleaning our houses, and mowing our lawns. You could certainly add many more things to this list. Yet, by definition, to borrow a sports example, these defensive actions, however important, do not move the ball further up the field when it comes to our dreams or our career, nor do they leverage our influence.

In contrast, *offensive* actions do just that. They expand the scope of our influence; they capture new territory; they have the effect of improving our lives and those we serve by growing more crops rather than by thinning the soup. What are some examples? Offensive actions include: going back to school, selling your highly praised salsa on the Internet, taking the initiative to plan a simple but meaningful gathering, or reading the five best books on a subject of interest.

HERE ARE TWO SIMPLE DEFINITIONS:
Offensive actions: Actions that *enhance* our current environment, career, or social life and serve to expand our sphere of influence.

Defensive actions: Actions that *maintain* our current environment, career, or social life, and serve to prevent loss.

Your FYE Self-Assessment measures your offensive and defensive activity. As you review your scores, it is important to remember our definition of defensive activities. A high Defensive Score is great, but having a high Offensive Score is equally important. In other words, ideally, you should be actively engaged in both defending your territory and taking new turf.

Consider the four possible outcomes:

1. Your Offensive Score is high but your Defensive Score is low.

This is a good start. You are proactive and future-focused but you are "leaving the door open" in a number of important areas that challenge your quality of life.

Example: Despite a number of personal challenges, Elena

has seen the importance of being more competitive in the marketplace in this economy. She has returned to school, is now halfway through completing her bachelor's degree online, and has begun working out consistently. When stressed she tends to buy a few extras for herself and her family, yet she has no life insurance nor is she putting away anything at all for retirement, telling herself she will start when she finishes school and gets a better job.

2. Your Defensive Score is high but your Offensive Score is low.

You have done well to maintain your current situation and avoid many of the common pitfalls that erode or destroy your quality of life. You are to be commended for your considerable wisdom and sensibility. Yet, you lack forward motion as you progress toward your dreams. You may not be experiencing the growth and influence you desire.

Example: Kevin's home office computer and filing system is a sight to behold. It is run with the efficiency of an air traffic controller's console. His financial affairs are organized and his yard is equally well cared for. His career planning is another story. While Kevin's job performance is consistent, he is stuck in a lower management position with no prospects for advancement.

3. Your Offensive and Defensive Scores are both low.

You are experiencing loss in both spheres. You are struggling to maintain your current situation and you are having difficulty creating opportunities for growth. Strong support in the form of groups, coaching, or counseling may be needed as you review both what you can do to take care of important daily activities and still make room for offensive growth actions.

Example: Catherine has been a single mom for the last six years. Since that time it has all been about her eight-year-old daughter, Michelle. She continues to struggle paying the bills, keeping up with her car's maintenance, and working at her current position. She is feeling overwhelmed and has been for some time. Despite being a talented photographer, she has set aside her camera for the past five years. The truth is, agreeing to just one local photo shoot a month would provide much "breathing room" for herself and her daughter.

4. *Your Offensive and Defensive Scores are both high.*

Congratulations! You are currently engaged in a good balance of maintenance and building activities. You are not getting mired in looking only toward sustaining what you have created, nor are you pushing toward the future but leaving the "back door" of your life open to the possibility of great loss.

Example: Three years ago, Pam recognized that she was ignoring several areas in her personal life, including her finances and her health. Between her work and her family, she was giving 120 percent. She knew she needed help and set up a number of appointments with friends and professionals who could assist her. Not doing anything was costing her a lot more than any consultation fee. Today, her Offen-

---

FREE *TIME MANAGEMENT* EXCUSESTOPPER
For help in achieving a better offensive and defensive balance, download, "Living an Offensive Day." Go to www.FireYourExcuses.com, register if you are not yet part of the Fire Your Excuses Community, and type in the keyword: OFFENSE

EXCUSE STOPPER

sive and Defensive Scores reflect the "new Pam." Not only has she addressed a number of defensive areas she had been ignoring, but she is also engaged in two or three important career and charity activities that have transformed her life.

TAKE THE 30-DAY
TIME MANAGEMENT CHALLENGE

1. Keep a time log for two weeks listing every activity you perform in 15-minute increments. You will be amazed at the "time leaks" that exist even in your busy, "efficient" schedule.

2. Once a week, hold a personal business meeting with yourself for 30 minutes. Review your weekly plan at least twice a week for 10-15 minutes.

3. Complete one noteworthy project every week, i.e., change insurance, send a proposal, clean your closet.

4. Pick a major goal that you have been putting off until you have more time and begin working toward it in short 15-minute sessions, several times a week.

FIRE YOUR EXCUSES

CHAPTER SIX:

FINANCES

Blind Spots and Weaknesses

Health and Wellness

Social Connections

Communication

Time Management

Finances

Career

Serving

CHAPTER 6

FINANCES

It's not your salary that makes you rich, it's your spending habits.
—*CHARLES A. JAFFE*

*The real measure of your wealth is how much you'd be worth
if you lost all your money.*
—*Anonymous*

TOM WAS A SERIOUS YOUNG MAN. AS A COLLEGE STUDENT HIS STRICT
schedule was fifteen hours of study, three hours of violin practice, and six
hours of sleep. Widely read, he was shy by nature but grew to be a great
lawyer and a brilliant writer. Still in his twenties, he began construction
on a lavish mansion. Later, he lived in Europe for five years as a trade
negotiator. He remained active throughout his life. In his final years, he
started a university.

Sadly, Tom also had a dark secret, which over time became increasingly public and humiliating for him and his family. For decades, he
had been living in deep debt and spending far beyond his means. In
truth, some debt he took on was from his wife's father, but most of his
misery was his own making. In deep denial he spent lavishly on expensive home remodeling and in extravagant tastes. His debt grew so large
he couldn't even keep up with the interest payments. When he died, it
is estimated that he owed several million dollars.

Immediately after his death, his large home and every stick of furni-
ture in it was auctioned off to pay his creditors, leaving his daughter,

now his sole heir, penniless and relegated to living off the charity of others. We have spoken of him casually but the world knows him as Thomas Jefferson, our third president and author of the Declaration of Independence.[1]

The trajectory of Thomas Jefferson's financial woes is, tragically, far from unique. There are millions of intelligent, creative, loving, and well-meaning individuals who find themselves hopelessly mired in debt. While some arrive at a financial crisis through little fault of their own—illness, abandonment, fraud, etc.—too many others languish there because of their inability to properly handle money. As we shall see, money affects us in surprising and powerful ways, and the small financial decisions we make day-to-day have dramatic consequences over time.

"Money Changes Everything" – Cyndi Lauper

In 2008, a fascinating international study was conducted at Sun Yat-Sen University in China.[2] Subjects were randomly assigned to two groups. One group was asked to count out eighty $100 bills, the other 80 slips of paper. All participants were then asked to play a computer-simulated ball-tossing game in which some players were deliberately excluded and others were not. Those who had counted out the money but had been excluded in the tossing game reported feeling significantly less social distress than those who had counted out the paper and had also been excluded from the game. Simply handling a large sum of money for a few minutes had a strong effect on how distressing it felt to be socially rejected!

In another part of the experiment, participants were asked to put their hands into water of varying temperatures. Those who had counted out cash reported significantly less physical pain than those who had counted out slips of paper. These findings, concluded the researchers, "indicate that the mere idea of money has considerable psychological power, enough to alter reactions to social exclusion and even to physical pain."[3]

Lest we think that these effects are not true of those of us who live in the United States, the above study was actually a further investigation of similar findings reported the year before by Kathleen Vohs and her American colleagues conducted in the States.[4] If our feelings have been shown to be so affected by handling money that is not even our own, imagine how we are influenced by dealing with our own finances and by having or not having sufficient funds. As we shall see, the way we deal with money has as much to do with psychology as it does with math skills.

A Different Conversation About Money

We have all sadly watched the unfolding of the tragic financial crisis gripping our world. Each of us likely has duly noted the consequences that occur when financial denial and excuses run our country and our own spending. It is time to re-evaluate, regroup and rebuild. Like the recovering heart patient who narrowly escapes death, we may find the first months and years of our recovery to be especially austere, painful,

---

FROM THE FINANCIAL FILES: A TALE OF TWO CITIES

Two California couples saw their financial dreams slipping away. Both wanted a better standard of living, which included buying a home. The first couple hoped that their construction business would turn around so that they could have children and buy a home. They are still waiting. The second couple, also in the housing industry, moved out of state and rented a cheaper apartment. They spent two years taking online courses at night to transition into a new profession so that they could buy a home. Their California friends felt sorry for them when they left and even sorrier when they visited during those early years. They too felt a bit as if they had failed. They are now proud homeowners in a nearby state and visit California often—to see their still-renting friends.

---

and sobering. It is time for more realistic priorities and a radical shift in behavior.

The financial tsunami that struck Wall Street, then the rest of the world, was not unexpected. We all knew if we continued with our voracious appetite for consumption, there would come a day of reckoning. It has arrived. Many financial experts tried to warn us, but we needed more than a counseling session—we needed an intervention. Intoxicated with artificial prosperity based on credit and a huge real estate bubble, we were not interested in listening to any "designated drivers."

Two such advisers, Thomas Stanley and William Danko, authors of *The Millionaire Next Door*,[5] challenged us with the facts of what it takes to achieve and maintain wealth years before the current economic downturn. They published the results of their landmark research into the spending habits of hundreds of millionaires in 1998. They found that the "true millionaire," not just one with a big house (and an even bigger mortgage), lived far below their means. Typically they:

- Lived in a middle-class suburb, not in the best house on the street.
- Bought a sensible, well-maintained, three-year old car.
- Saved for purchases instead of using credit.
- Made very few luxury purchases.
- Would be considered "extremely frugal."
- Went to "normal" instead of "high priced" restaurants.
- Were long-term investors who rarely moved around their assets.
- Were more interested in high financial independence than high social status.

In contrast, those who lived in the richest neighborhoods typically:

- Had high income but little in emergency savings.

- Had low net worth or much debt.

- Spent much of their income purchasing and maintaining expensive "toys."

- Enjoyed spending for high priced entertainment.

- Were committed to monthly spending for a number of luxury services.

- Kept up with the "Joneses," who, by living on an expensive street, made that challenge costly.

More than a decade ago, almost prophetically, Stanley and Danko radically challenged their readers by saying: "If you're not yet wealthy but want to be some day, never purchase a home that requires a mortgage more than twice your annual income." Such counsel seemed laughable and unrealistic back then, but has proven surprisingly prescient advice today.

Firing our Financial Excuses

Martin and Sarah came to see us for marital problems. It soon became evident that they were facing an immediate financial crisis. After years in which Martin dispersed small amounts of money to his wife for incidentals, Sarah's anger about feeling treated like a child took an ugly turn. Her resentment led to secret spending binges revealed only when creditors began calling for payments not received. When Martin found out the truth, he was enraged and threatened divorce.

It was easy to see that their financial and emotional problems were rooted in distrust, anger, and miscommunication. Over the next several sessions we confronted the long-standing relational and personality issues leading up to the current crisis, helping them to vet their financial and communication issues in a respectful, healthy, and transparent manner.

Sarah learned to speak up when she felt like she was not being treated as an equal partner. Martin agreed to give up the tight control he had been exercising over their finances. Both committed to strict spending procedures, which included providing a receipt for every expense no matter how small. The days of secret spending and surprise bills were over. In time, they forgave each other, learned to trust again, and developed a workable plan to retire their debts.

As we can see from the above story, our financial health touches upon a number of emotional and relational factors. We will explore them in the section below.

**"I'm wealthy beyond my wildest dreams!
Unfortunately, my dreams were never very wild."**

©2001 by Randy Glasbergen. www.RandyGlasbergen.com [6]

Thoughts on Financial Fitness

Thought 1:
Faulty thinking is responsible for financial breakdown.

Here in the West, our self-esteem is strongly rooted in our net worth. It is important to observe that this is not the case in the developing world. Whether one travels to South America, Africa, India, or Asia, in each region you will meet many people who have very few material possessions, yet who carry themselves with dignity and believe they are people of great value and worth.

Here at home, even our queries about others are telling. We ask such questions as "What does she do?" and "How well do you think he does?" mainly to size up one's status and wealth. In many corners of the globe, these questions would be considered rude and absurd.

Psychologically speaking, we know that our feelings are greatly influenced by what we think and say. So the very fact we routinely ask the above questions is revealing. Even if we intellectually know there is much more to our worth than our finances, the repeated use of these phrases has a profound emotional impact on all of us. We actually begin to believe that those who have acquired more things have more worth, and, even more disturbing, we are somehow worth more than others who have less.

If we do buy into the idea that our worth equals our wealth, it is no wonder we will do almost anything to look prosperous to others. This includes living far above our means and not having any significant savings for emergencies. After all, our very self-worth is on the line!

It is plain to see that how we think about our finances matters a great deal. In fact, it determines how much we need to spend to feel good about ourselves. If we are not extremely vigilant, we can allow our neighborhood to dictate to us how successful and worthy we should feel.

"What are you

> **MOOD, SELF-ESTEEM AND SPENDING**
> The relationship between our spending, mood, and self-esteem are highly interrelated. Negative moods and low self-image can start a financial excuse cycle that initiates the slow but steady downward slide to financial ruin. For too many, spending is like a drug abused to medicate unpleasant feelings but whose long-term effect is severe financial stress, even bankruptcy. If the financial messages we received growing up were dysfunctional, it is possible our own habits will be as well.

worth?" If we can answer this question more broadly, recognizing the true source of our worth, then this will immediately impact our financial behavior. We will be less likely to spend beyond our means and take dangerous financial risks to keep up with the Joneses.

What are your thoughts about money? Do you give mere money the power to make you feel good, depressed, empowered, deflated, or secure? Does your income define who you are or how you feel about yourself? If your response to "What are you worth?" immediately causes you to think about your savings balance, your 401K, or how much you owe, then we challenge you to think deeper about what is necessary to feel good about yourself.

Thought 2:
Our relationship with money is the key concern.

Money, in itself, is not the issue. Its use and our relationship to it is the real concern. While some struggle with wanting too much, others have been brought up to think that an impoverished lifestyle is a badge of courage, or a lifelong struggle with money is all they can expect. Maybe the message you received growing up was "life is difficult." The best you could hope for would be to become a hard-working survivor and not to be prosperous.

We must be very honest with ourselves and our situation. The person who has experienced years of financial misery because of legitimate setbacks is very different indeed from the person who has never dared to strive for more, is unwilling to work hard, or continues to make poor choices. One who subscribes to a full array of cable television stations while receiving government assistance functions at a far different level of financial honesty than someone who has lost a job and has cut out all extras but still needs help. Relating to money responsibly and dealing realistically with life's unforeseen setbacks are keys to making wise decisions and not being enslaved to debt.

Question: What is your relationship with money? Does it enslave you? Does your life feel controlled by it? Are you completely honest with yourself about the difference between your "needs" and "wants?"

Thought 3:
There are no excuses for living beyond our means.

In 1284, the small village of Hamelin, Germany, was overrun with rats. A man dressed in motley or "pied" clothing appeared, offering a solution to help rid the town of the rodents. A deal was struck for a certain sum of gold and the man used a musical tune played on his pipe to draw the rats into the river, where they promptly drowned. Even though the man fulfilled his end of the bargain, the town officials refused to pay him. He left angrily vowing revenge.

Some time later, on a religious holiday while everyone was in church, the piper returned again and began to play his pipe. This time he drew away not rats but 130 boys and girls who followed him hypnotically out of town. In one version of the story, the children were never seen again; in another, he returned them only after the townspeople paid him several times the original amount due.

The story above is, of course, the tale of the Pied Piper,[7] which circulated in Europe for centuries before the Brothers Grimm wrote it down for posterity. It is a brutal story, actually. It's one that many of us vaguely know, and whose disturbing ending is rarely discussed. But today we stand at the midpoint of our own national and personal "Pied Piper tale." In a very real sense, millions of us who live in the West have been freed from poverty, but we have also collectively refused to "pay the piper." We have enjoyed services for which payment is now due, and the piper has appeared to collect it. As in the story, our piper has been ignored. He is still willing to be paid, but his price has gone up considerably and the stakes are very high. If we refuse to pay him, we will never see our precious standard of living again.

No matter how we may try to sell it, there's no free handout, and, at some point, the piper knocks, first politely, then incessantly. The question of our time is, who will pay him? And is the piper knocking at your door?

Thought 4:
We reap what we sow.

Michael came to our office with a gambling problem. He always thought if he could just hit it big some day that he could take care of all his bills. His gambling had caused major rifts in his marriage and he was on the verge of bankruptcy.

Thankfully, Michael was able to see how he was "planting the wrong seed," and though he would have to endure a hard season of "crop failure," there was hope for him to "replant" in the new year. It would not be easy. He would have to get some serious help for his compulsive gambling and start on a financial path called "hard honest work" but he was willing to do so to save his home and marriage.

There is an old proverb that says, "We reap what we sow."[8] In Spanish there is a saying: *"Lo que empieza mal, termina mal,"* or 'that which begins poorly, ends poorly." If we plant nothing in life, we will get nothing. If we plant foolishly, in the end we lose our crop. It's amazing how some people really expect a "bumper crop," even though they spent minimal energy planting or researching the best seed. By not confronting our debt or planning our financial future, we are really saying to our family and ourselves: "I am sowing some real seeds of financial pain and suffering for all of us. So get ready, everyone will have to pay for my irresponsibility."

Suze Orman, well-known financial expert and author, strongly feels that we must be responsible to those we love. She bluntly says: "It's not okay when you get sick, or when you die, to leave financial chaos behind you for everyone else to clean up." At minimum, she urges us to "make sure you have a will, including a testamentary trust, adequate life insurance, income protection insurance, and health insurance."[9]

How people perceive the value of things and the difference between "wants" and "needs" can be stunning. Perhaps you too have listened to a friend describe a period of financial hardship, knowing that they recently returned from a Hawaiian cruise. Think about your larger expenditures over the last year. Have you talked yourself into any purchases that were irresponsible?

It's time to plant good seed. Remember, the wise farmer begins to plant even when the weather is still quite cold. What financial fields are you currently sowing? Do you have unrealistic expectations about what you will reap? Do you need a better plan to plant the right seed? Do you need to swallow your pride and tell someone the *entire* story of your crop failure—your complete financial picture? Not being honest about even 10 percent of your financial situation can eventually result in catastrophic ruin. What loved one, friend, or financial advisor knows *every* detail about your finances? If you still haven't shared the complete truth about your financial situation, it is time to break the silence.

Thought 5:
"Where your treasure is, that is where your heart is also."

We firmly believe that true wealth is not defined by what is in your bank account but what is in your "people account." As the Good Book states: "Where your treasure is, that is where your heart is also."[10]

When we began Fire Your Excuses, we decided that our giving would start from day one, not just after things "took off." Being fortunate to make numerous trips to Africa and other parts of the developing world, we had seen the effects of war, poverty, malaria, tuberculosis, and AIDS. We noticed an obvious need that would be easy for all of our readers to understand— millions around the world drink filthy water every day. Surely we could help others rally around providing the most critical element we need to live—free, adequate, clean water.

Our current service partner is World Vision's project to dig new wells. It is thrilling to redirect some of our treasure into a cause that is close to our heart—helping those who have so little. (For those who wish to learn more, information about this program is highlighted on our website, www.FireYourExcuses.com.)

Where is your heart? What do you treasure? Are you investing your treasure in the areas that are closest to your heart?

Financial Matters: First Things First

Before we get into the specific "do's and don'ts" of personal finance, we need to pause briefly to propose an honest assessment of two primary money-related addictions: compulsive gambling and compulsive spending. We assure you that following the other steps in this chapter without addressing any financial addictions that may be present is like building a gleaming skyscraper out of balsa wood. You will need to first address the emotional issues that frame your spending habits.

It is estimated that "2.5 million adults in America are pathological gamblers and another 3 million of them should be considered problem gamblers. Fifteen million adults are at a risk for problem gambling and about 148 million are low-risk gamblers."[11] Amazingly, according to a 2008 Gallup poll, two-thirds of Americans placed some type of bet last year.[12]

The problem of overspending affects both genders at the same rate. Compulsive spenders make up about six percent of both sexes, according to Dr. Lorrin Koran, a Stanford University emeritus professor of psychiatry and lead author of a study on spending habits.[13]

Some could say that we are a nation of gamblers. Consider the following questions:

- Have your purchases or lifestyle made it impossible for you to save up at least six months of income in case of an emergency?

- Have you invested money in any real estate deals that you "couldn't afford to lose?"

- Have you put any money into stock investments that were too aggressive but promised bigger returns?

- Have you invested money on a business venture that would make you go bankrupt if it didn't work out?

- Are any of your credit cards currently at more than 80 percent of their spending limit?

If two or more of these are true of you, whether you ever go to the track or spend time in a casino, you may be a "gambler." In fact, you stand far more to lose than if you spent a few hundred dollars at a gaming table every few months.

Millions in the Western world turn to shopping and gambling to escape their problems and deal with other negative emotional issues. Is this you?

Consider the following questions:

- Do you shop or gamble when you are feeling depressed?

- Do you lie to others or yourself about how much you actually spend or bet?

- Do you buy things you do not need or don't end up wearing or using?

- Have your purchases or gambling debts harmed your personal relationships?

- Do you spend or bet more than you can afford or planned?

If you need assistance, seek professional help. If you truly have a spending addiction you will need more than a new resolution to "keep a budget." You can find online support at gamblersanon.com or overspending.com.

Taking Care of Debt

We have just explored how faulty thinking and other underlying emotional concerns often contribute to financial problems. In these cases, psychological help is a critical first step. You don't need to carry the weight of financial stress by yourself. Things are much bigger in the dark. As they say in the recovery world: "You are only as sick as your secrets." Your next task will be to assess your personal debt and develop a solid strategy to eliminate it.

Who should you talk to first? Begin with your spouse, significant other, caring family member, or close friend. Then seek out the help of a qualified accountant or financial advisor. It is especially important that you seek out someone who is an objective professional. Meet with them on a pay-for-service basis. This is not the time to try to save $100 by meeting with someone for free but is really there to sell you a product that may not be right for you.

Depending on the severity of your debt situation, you may benefit from the services of a professional debt counselor. This person will be able provide you with a personalized debt management program to repay your creditors and get you back on track with your finances. Notice that we did not mention a professional debt counselor first. Why? Because this contact should be your last resort. Some such services will help you, but they may also severely damage your credit for years to come, limiting your purchasing options as much as a bankruptcy.

If your accountant or financial advisor can't help you, we personally recommend that you get debt counseling advice from an organization like David Ramsey's Financial Peace University (DaveRamsey.com) before considering any professional debt consolidation organization. His group of advisors is strictly fee-for-time.

Ramsey's book, *Total Money Makeover*,[14] is a must-read for any who feels as if getting out of debt is nearly impossible. His book is as much a book of hope as it is of financial strategy. In it he outlines seven "baby steps" to take along the road to financial freedom. They are listed below:

Seven Steps from *Total Money Makeover*

1. Before you do anything else, set aside $1,000 as your emergency fund.

2. Get out of debt—starting with the smallest debt first, regardless of interest rate.

3. Build a six-month emergency fund.

4. Start a retirement fund.

5. Set up a college fund for your children, if applicable.

6. Pay off your mortgage.

7. Build wealth.

There is an old saying: "The best way to get out of a hole is to stop digging!" What can you do today to stop incurring more debt and start improving your financial situation? The first step is to take a complete financial inventory and set a budget.

Setting a Budget

One of the most damaging financial excuses we use is rationalizing why we don't have a monthly budget. Without one, we have no accountability for our money management. A budget is just as important for those who have plenty as those who have little.

It is not uncommon to hear: "I don't have a budget, nor do I balance my accounts, I just know I have extra every month." Such individuals certainly miss many opportunities to put their money to more strategic purposes. Regardless of income, without a budget we all spend more than we realize.

In the nineteenth century, a wealthy man from Asia had the opportunity to travel to the United States. There, for the first time, he learned of the microscope and had the opportunity to witness its incredible powers of observation. Amazed, he bought one and brought it back to his spacious home. Over dinner, he decided to surprise his guests by revealing his purchase and put a grain of rice, grown on one of his own farms, on a slide for all to see. To his horror, it was then that he noticed hordes of microscopic organisms swarming over the rice they had just been eating. Confronted with this terrible reality, what did he do? He took the microscope outside and smashed it to pieces.

The man in this story had two clear choices. Either he could have found a way to better sanitize his rice or he could destroy the evidence that his diet was not as healthy as he had hoped. When it comes to our finances, not having a budget is much like smashing the microscope.

Instead of working on improving the health of our financial diet, we eliminate evidence of the contrary. Is your microscope alive and well?

The Answer to Hidden Expenses

Many are unaware that they actually need to save more each month to fully cover all their debt and savings goals. For example, some simply ignore a critical category, such as life insurance. Others avoid honestly looking at just how much they are actually spending on known expenses such as clothing or entertainment.

Ramsey observes that those who use credit cards spend 12 to 18 percent more than those who use cash for the same transactions.[15] Drazen Prelec and Duncan Simester,[16] researchers at MIT's Sloan School of Management, discovered this credit versus cash difference can be much larger when we are purchasing big ticket items. In their research, they found the willingness to pay can be increased when customers are instructed to use a credit card rather than cash. The effect may be large, up to 100 percent. Why? When we use plastic, we do not feel and see the cash leaving our possession.

Take the critical first step if you haven't already, whether you have plenty or are in debt, set up a budget and stick to it. Budgets are necessary. They are the only practical way to get a grip on your spending.

Budgeting Essentials

Creating a budget generally requires three steps. First, identify what you have been spending on average in recent months. This can be done by keeping a spending log for at least one month. Second, set new spending goals that take into account your long-term financial objectives. Be sure to include your spouse and family. Third, track your spending to make sure it stays within those guidelines.

Use financial software to save you time and effort. Even a simple personal-finance program has built-in budget-making tools. They provide instant feedback on expenditures and save hours of accounting time.

Plug all cash leaks. Grab a receipt for your day-to-day purchases and give every penny spent and received a "home," placing it within a budget category so that you can see exactly where your money is going. Resist the temptation of hiding frivolous purchases in the miscellaneous category.

The best financial gurus all say the same thing: Set aside 10 percent for savings, give away 10 percent to the charity of your choice, and live off the 80 percent that is left. This may require some lifestyle "surgery," but you will eventually recover and be glad you did.

Don't count on windfalls. When projecting your budget, never include dollars that you can't be sure you'll receive, such as year-end bonuses, tax refunds, or investment gains.

Don't wait to start. Have a retirement fund and a savings account even if you fund it with only a dollar a month to start. The important thing is that you begin!

Consider inflation when planning out your savings and budget. When projecting future spending, always consider inflationary increases to accurately predict what you will need.

Whenever making a purchase, ask yourself: "Is this purchase moving me closer or further away from my financial goals?"

Use a cash display to build excitement for a large recreational purchase. Example: Do you and your family like eating out but want to save for a cherished trip? Each time you eat in, prominently deposit the cash just saved in a glass jar. This shows everyone that their sacrifice has brought them a little closer to their vacation goal.

Print out your savings goals for all to see. Review them regularly.

An Important Word for Those Who Have Variable Income

Just as having a job in which you are constantly being interrupted is not an adequate reason to abandon carefully planning your day, having variable income is not a sufficient reason to forego a written budget.

Many today have variable monthly incomes, including the self-employed, small business owners, and those who have second businesses. You too can and must create a budget. In fact, it is even more critical that you do so to avoid unnecessary hoarding in lean months, overspending in windfall periods and terrible surprises at tax time.

FREE *FINANCIAL* EXCUSESTOPPER
To obtain printable copies of the Sample Monthly Budget, go to www.FireYourExcuses.com, register if you haven't yet, and type in the keyword: **BUDGET**

Not sure how much will be coming in next month? Just calculate your budget using your average monthly income. Better yet, set up your budget based on one of the leaner months of the last few years. Adjust your budget as needed. In a few months, you'll have a realistic one that works for you. Download this chapter's *ExcuseStopper*; a detailed and customizable sample budget, to take action today.

For expenses incurred more or less often than monthly, convert the payment to a monthly amount when calculating your monthly budget. For instance, if your auto insurance is billed every six months, convert that amount to six monthly payments for budgetary purposes. Then, set aside this money so that it is available when the six-month premium is due.

You Might Need to Hire Professional Help

Kyle and his wife, Terri, had always lived large on their middle-class income. You could always count on them for a great party on game day and during the holidays. As a result, they paid their bills but had considerable credit card debt and very little in savings. They kept up because Kyle had a great job and Terri worked part time while also taking care of their two children.

When Kyle lost his job, their meager savings was gone in a matter of weeks. Suddenly they were in dire straits. They were able to pay their mortgage but fell behind on their taxes. Eventually, a stream of certified letters began to arrive from Uncle Sam. Unable to pay what they owed in taxes, they panicked and, as they say in the business, "went dark." They didn't answer the phone or respond to any of the letters. They hoped that Kyle would soon land a job and they would be able to pay back their taxes then.

One day, they received a notification from their mortgage lender that their automatic monthly payment had bounced. Shocked, they checked with their bank to find that the IRS had taken everything out of their account two days before as payment toward their debt.

Kyle and Terri were eventually able to make a plan to pay back their debt, but not before many sleepless nights and a ruined credit score. Further, they were humiliated as they learned that their employers, past and present, were notified about their plight. It was a brutal experience for both of them. This may all have been avoided if Kyle had immediately reached out to his college buddy, a CPA, and learned that making payment arrangements was a relatively simple procedure. Because of their shame and fear, they did not seek outside help and suffered needlessly, a mistake that nearly cost them their home.

> **EXCUSE GAMECHANGER**
> The secret to financial fitness greatly depends on managing our emotional spending and seeking immediate and periodic assistance.

One of the biggest principles of this book is this: Just because *you* do not see the answer to your problem does not mean that there *is* no solution. The Fire Your Excuses mindset is to reach out immediately to find solutions to any problem you cannot quickly solve on your own. To do so, this may require that you humble yourself and admit to a weakness in some area of your life.

A good, objective financial advisor will be essential. Many have lost thousands of dollars letting a relative do their taxes each year because they did not want to hurt someone's feelings by switching to a professional as their financial situation became more complex. Ideally, your financial planner should be the most objective and knowledgeable person you can find. Interview at least three of them before you make a decision.

Your most important question after asking about their credentials is, "How are you paid?" There are three ways:

- A flat consultation fee is paid for counsel and advice but no investing is done.

- Your consultation is free and the professional is paid a commission for each product sold to you. Be careful, as this can mean more pressure to buy certain investment products and to frequently change your investment portfolio.

- Your consultation is free and the professional is paid a percentage of all gains on the money he or she invests for you.

Never forget choosing a financial advisor is a very personal decision and that everyone's financial goals are unique. In the end, it is your responsibility to do your homework and to make sure you choose wise counsel.

Your Investments

Knowing whom to trust with your investments is the $64,000 question. While specific advice is beyond the scope of this book, we can say that simply ignoring things is never the best strategy and may be particularly perilous in these economic times.

Suze Orman agrees: "You cannot sit this one out, hoping the storm will pass and everything will be just fine. If you do nothing, I am sorry to say you may be in deeper trouble … The fact is, the new reality requires new strategies ... I know many of you are thinking there is no point in continuing to invest for retirement as long as the markets are down. Big, big mistake."[17]

While riding things out with your current investment portfolio may prove, in the end, to be a smart decision, it must be one that is arrived at after careful review of your own situation. Continually assessing how to make your money work best for you is an important next step.

The words of John Wooden also ring true for our finances: "Don't let what you can't do keep you from doing what you can." Knowledge is power. It is important to look at the excuses you may have about saving, investment, and retirement planning. Do you have a college degree in your chosen profession but a grade school degree in investing? You are not alone, but it is important to catch up, look after your finances, and get into the game. When it comes to saving for your future, as the saying goes: "It is never too late to begin doing the right thing."

Tax Truths

Each year we see many who are experiencing deep emotional distress due to tax-related issues. Garnished wages, levied property and limited cash flow are but a few of the miseries incurred by ignoring one's tax issues. As long as we work, and even in our retirement, we will be faced with the harsh reality of paying taxes. Best-selling author Robert Kiosaki suggests that to exercise your financial IQ means paying your taxes in an up front, well-strategized manner that safeguards your income as much as possible.[18]

Making excuses about taxes leads to grave consequences and can even land you in jail. Any CPA or tax attorney will tell you that you can provide them with any profit and loss numbers you wish, but if audited, you will be held responsible.

There are a variety of excellent resources and assistance available to help you with your taxes. One good resource is *Ernst and Young Tax*

Saver's Guide.[19] Each year this book has a wealth of information and strategies to help you keep money that is rightfully yours.

Remember, it is easy to let convenience, fear, and denial keep you from getting a second, even a third opinion about your taxes and investments. When one considers how many thousands can be lost because your money is parked in the wrong investment or a significant tax savings has been missed, such unwillingness to pay for another perspective is the height of folly.

Even well-meaning advisors, trusted friends, and family members can misinform you on critical financial matters. Don't let friendship and family ties keep you from double-checking what is best for your situation. Misplaced loyalty can literally cost you thousands of dollars over a few short years. A wise advisor will never feel insulted or threatened by your decision to get a second opinion. The ones that are should make you very nervous.

Retirement

Although we have covered financial planning from many different angles, we conclude with a poignant reminder about the importance of saving for retirement. In a 2007 *Market Watch* article, Robert Powell cites this alarming statistic: "Roughly half of all working Americans don't participate in a retirement plan or don't have an employer-sponsored plan in which to participate. It also means that a huge number of adult Americans—by my estimate 150 million of a potential 200 million—aren't saving for retirement in any meaningful way, if at all."[20]

Even the word *retirement* can create a sense of stress for many people. With this in mind, we want to look at some specific measures to add to your retirement plan:

- *Needless to say, "the cavalry is not coming."* You will need to provide for yourself.

Consider making it a goal before retirement to develop a small, simple home business that can provide you with extra income during your retirement years. It has never been easier to use the Internet to make additional income. Some of you who are reading this right now have two or three decades to come up with a viable idea you can use to supplement your income. It might be one as simple as sharing your secret barbeque sauce with the world or your own handcrafted jewelry.

- *Working part-time in retirement can be a big help.* It can mean the difference between being on an austerity budget and having some extra income to enjoy. It will also keep you engaged in life.

- *Save!* If you haven't started or are way behind on your savings for the future, don't fall for the doomed strategy that you will make up for neglected savings when you have more. Each month you wait will make it harder for you to catch up.

- *Think about what is most important to you.* If you are willing to move to a cheaper area or cut overhead on things that don't matter to you, you can have a much better quality of life.

- *Max out any "matching-funds" retirement plan your employer offers.* You can't beat it. Putting two dollars into savings is always better than putting one.

- *Know your savings goals* and what type of portfolio investments make sense for your current and expected age of retirement. Every situation is different. You need to play it safe, but not so much that inflation robs you of all your interest gains.

A Tale of Two Retirements: A Case Study

Fire Your Excuses Self-Assessment Snapshot: Jim and Rick

Scale	Jim's Score	Range	Rick's Score	Range
Total Excuse Scale	239	Below Average	327	Above Average
Potential for Change Scale	57	Above Average	46	Average
Finances Scale	25	Below Average	33	Above Average
Offense Scale	122	Above Average	95	Below Average
Defense Scale	85	Below Average	121	Above Average

Consider Jim and Rick. They have been best friends since college days and work in similar professions. Jim and his wife, Linda, would not be considered crazy spenders by any means. They are simply a little bit in denial about their actual needs and how much they spend. On average, they have been spending about $84 more than they make each month and have been doing so for several years. If this slow-leak spending pattern persists for fifteen years, but their growing debt is hidden in credit cards or in a second mortgage, their little problem will balloon to a whopping $30,000 of debt. And this is assuming their debt is at an eight percent interest rate, much lower than most credit card rates.

In contrast, Rick and his wife, Sandy, manage to save an extra $84 and deposit it into their retirement account, which also yields an interest rate of eight percent. In fifteen years, they have earned an extra $30,000 in savings, but in comparison they are now $60,000 wealthier than their friends. Upon retirement the difference between the two couple's spending and saving habits will be evident.

As close friends, Jim and Rick share much in common, but a look at their assessments quickly illustrates how much they diverge in their abilities and lifestyle habits. First, Rick tends to use fewer excuses in most areas of his life. Finances are not just one strong point for him. His Total Excuse Score is considerably higher than his friend Jim's.

Notice, too, that Jim is not without his stronger areas. His Offense Score is higher than his friend Rick's. It may be that Rick admires Jim's ability to pursue life and career-affirming activities. On the other hand, not surprisingly, Jim's Defense Score is not a strong area for him. A good portion of financial planning is characterized by the consistent defensive (maintenance) actions that Jim does not execute as well as Rick. What is encouraging is that if we had to guess who would be most likely to make a big change, it would be Jim. In contrast, Rick's Potential for Change Score suggests someone who may be more likely to play it safe. It has worked well for him financially, but there may be other areas where it has not.

Finally, we are reminded of the words of George S. Clason, author of *The Richest Man in Babylon*, a classic parable on saving: "Gold cometh gladly and in increasing quantities to any man who will put by not less than one-tenth of his earnings to create an estate for his future and that of his family."[21]

TAKE THE 30-DAY FINANCES CHALLENGE

1. Research and list all debts. Create a written plan and timeline to retire them.

2. Make a list of two- and five-year financial goals and a specific plan of how you will achieve them.

3. Take a "heart inventory" of how much of your income you are giving to help those outside of your family and yourself.

4. Make a retirement plan and include how much of your income you should start saving. Also, draw up a "will" and any other legal documents that you may need to clarify family concerns, health directives, and wishes.

FIRE YOUR EXCUSES

CHAPTER SEVEN:

CAREER

CHAPTER 7

CAREER

The mass of men live lives of quiet desperation.
—HENRY DAVID THOREAU

A Barrier to Be Broken

ON MAY 6, 1954, ROGER BANNISTER BECAME THE FIRST TO BREAK the four-minute mile at Oxford University's Iffley Road Track by running the race at 3:59.4. Years later, *Forbes* magazine would declare Bannister's four-minute mile "the greatest athletic achievement of all time."[1]

Prior to that historic day, it had been thought that running a four-minute mile might be physically impossible. For the nine years leading up to 1954, the mile record had been stuck at 4:01.3. Once Bannister broke the record, four other runners joined him over the next decade. The fastest mile is now 3:43.13, sixteen seconds faster than Bannister's record, set in Rome by Hicham El Guerrouj of Morocco in 1999.

Many of the highest barriers you will face on your way to an excuseless life will appear insurmountable. What career goal feels like your four-minute barrier? What "impossible" barrier looms between you and your own career breakthrough? Whether a barrier is external or self-imposed, it cannot be taken lightly. For example, dismantling a barrier erected deep within your own heart where it has lived undisturbed for decades is not a trite undertaking. It is a task that may garner very little support from friends, colleagues, and family. Even those who care can become accustomed to you attempting or avoiding the usual things and may have difficulty, consciously or not, with you changing your lifestyle in a permanent way.

There are a number of great books on the market that outline the most effective strategies to find and succeed in your career in these challenging times. Techniques that once worked well have grown passé, and economic forces have altered the workforce demands of entire industries. Keeping up-to-date with the most effective strategies will be a critical part of your career success.

However, equally important to your professional development are the excuses that hold you back in your career advancement. With a clearer understanding of how to work around your career fears and obstacles, you will be in a far better position to either succeed in your current vocation or astutely maneuver into another career pathway. Now let us turn our attention to some of the most destructive, but most common, career excuses.

The Career Excuses We Love the Most

You have probably heard of eHarmony.com, but did you know its founder, Neil Clark Warren, began the hugely successful online dating service when he was age sixty-six? Anna May Robertson Moses, known best as "Grandma Moses," became an accomplished painter in her seventies when she could no longer do embroidery due to her arthritis. When she was seventy-eight, a collector discovered her paintings in a drugstore window and soon exhibited her work at a New York art gallery. This brought her fame around the world. In fact, she enjoyed many more fruitful decades. She lived to be one hundred and one![2]

Harland Sanders, better known as "Colonel Sanders," was sixty-five when he decided to franchise his fried chicken restaurant located in Corbin, Kentucky. Not content to live off of his meager $105.00 a month Social Security check and armed only with his now-famous secret recipe, he set out around the country in search of restaurants that would carry his chicken. It has been reported that only after 1,008 rejections did someone invest in his product. Colonel Sanders sold the Kentucky

Fried Chicken Corporation nine years later, in 1964, but remained its corporate spokesman until his death at age ninety in 1980.[3]

"I'm too old" is one of the most common excuses we hear. We believe that being old is when you have decided to stop learning. Old age can come upon you whether you are thirty-five or eighty; much of it depends on you. The moment you say: "I will sit out this next ride," you begin to become old. We've seen "very old" twenty-eight-year-olds whose main after-work pursuit is drinking with their friends, and who are now stuck in dead-end jobs. We've also seen career professionals in their sixties and seventies, who have an insatiable desire to learn and grow and are still "cutting edge."

Here are some of the most common excuses we hear:

"I don't have the money."

"I would have to go back to school."

"I'm a single parent."

"I can't leave. I need the benefits."

"What else could I do?"

"I'm not what they're looking for."

"Jobs are going overseas."

"The economy is terrible right now."

"No one is hiring."

"My job is close to home."

"I would have to move."

"It would take X number of years to do that."

"I have a learning disability."

"I have a medical condition."

"I'm too old."

What are your career excuses? Take a moment and finish the following statement.

The barriers I usually use to convince myself and others that I can't advance in my career are:

_____

_____

_____

_____

CAL RIPKEN, JR.: A STUDY IN PERSEVERANCE[4]

Former Baltimore Orioles shortstop Cal Ripken, Jr., is known to baseball fans everywhere as "The Iron Man." He will always be remembered for his consistency and longevity in a baseball career that spanned nineteen years.

On September 20, 1998, at age thirty-eight, he played in his 2,632th consecutive game before taking a well-deserved "day off." He had not missed a game since May 30, 1982! Three years earlier, on September 6, 1995, he had shattered the long-standing record set by Lou Gehrig of 2,130 consecutive outings. Cal finished his career at the end of the 2000-2001 season, after appearing in his last All-Star game in July of that year and winning the MVP award. He has not only played more consecutive games than any other major leaguer in history, he also holds the record for ninety-five errorless games as a short-stop, and a number of Orioles records, including the most doubles, homers, and runs batted in (RBIs).

How persevering are you willing to be to achieve excellence in your career or calling?

Moving Beyond Linear Career Thinking:
Three Steps Forward, Two Steps Back

It seems part of the unwritten American success code that every new purchase, career move, or big change must be immediately recognized as an improvement of one's social, career, or material status. Whether it's acquiring a new cell phone or new home, few people ever buy anything that is smaller, less powerful, or has fewer features. Is there anything else in life that progresses in such a linear fashion?

Linear thinking can rob you of your dreams and adds an unnecessary burden on your cash flow. It is likely that you will, at some point, have to take a step backward to move forward again. Your career is very much like a game of football. There is gained and lost yardage, and there is offense and defense.

We challenge you to consider your career much like you would an investment portfolio—a balanced approach of low-, medium- and higher-risk strategies. We call this "career partitioning." To use a baseball metaphor, some part of your work activities must be reserved for "swinging for the fences," other portions must fall squarely into the "base hit" category.

Counting the Cost: What Are You Willing to Give Up?

If you are going to move ahead and design a life and career based on your purpose, family goals, and core values, it may well cost you something financially and socially. Fortunately, your social circle will adjust itself. Those who were unimpressed with your choices eventually will no longer be part of your inner circle. Others will take a step closer, intrigued and inspired by your new journey.

Maintaining the right perspective throughout our careers means embracing the seasonal nature of work and the temporary nature of today's career success. Many successful people experience waves of setbacks and victories in their career endeavors. The present is not permanent. Both tough times and good times change and we must change with them.

We know many who have made difficult choices to nurture their career dreams. Here's a sampling. They have...

- Sold an impressive car or truck.

- Sold their home and rented for a few years.

- Moved out of state to afford a home or to continue their dream.

- Skipped their daily coffee.

- Eaten every meal at home for weeks, even months.

- Let their friends know they could no longer attend those $30 birthday dinners or arrived later, for coffee, with a card and small gift.

- Let people know that they were unable to reciprocate with gifts but performed acts of service instead.

- Gave up their gym membership.

- Shopped at a bargain store instead of their favorite department store.

- Enjoyed "staycations" instead of "vacations."

- Got an inexpensive online movie subscription instead of going out to movies.

These strategic decisions can all be part of the life of the career transitioner, entrepreneur, artist, newly divorced, and returning student, to name just a few. And, if you have a big dream, they may need to become part of your life too. Just be prepared to be misunderstood at times; it is a frequent part of the life of those who pursue their dreams.

Considering the feelings of your family is also immensely important. We are always surprised at how little family dialogue centers on important career decisions. If you are a parent, be sure to sit down and talk to your children, spouse or both, if applicable, about the likely impact of any new job. If you are single without children, sit down with some trusted peers, or better yet, a mentor.

What is important to you? What are you willing to sacrifice, at least for now, to achieve your career goals?

Your Work Is Not Your Worth

Fire Your Excuses Self-Assessment Snapshot: Gene, Engineer

Scale	Score	Range
Total Excuse Scale	303	Average
Potential for Change Scale	53	Above Average
Career Scale	29	Average
Offense Scale	107	Average
Defense Scale	115	Above Average

Gene came to us seeking vocational direction. We measured his interests, weaknesses and strengths using various assessment instruments, then held a series of follow-up interviews. It became apparent that Gene, an engineer, had drifted far from his original career interests, activities and strengths. However, he was one of the rare individuals who not only noticed his career shift, but, more importantly, had the courage to steer back on course as soon as it became evident.

As Marcus Buckingham observes in *Go Put Your Strengths to Work,*[5] it is tempting, indeed, to allow the siren call of more income to woo you away from your areas of career strengths. If you are not continually pruning off work responsibilities and projects that take you away from your strengths, you may experience the biggest missed opportunity seen among those who are already moderately successful and fulfilled.

It is rare to meet people like Gene, who seek out career assistance and whose score falls within the Average range. It is likely that his well-honed maintenance activities, as evidenced by his Above Average Defense Score, brought his professional drift to his attention sooner rather than later. His proactive mindset, aided by a high potential for change, suggests that whatever changes he needs to make will be rapidly executed and permanent.

Buckingham[6] also asserted that each of us has at least one area in life where we have the *potential* to be world class. All of us have career weaknesses we must avoid and strengths needing cultivation. Like Gene, most of us have only a fuzzy idea of what they are. If you do not have an acute understanding of your top areas of competency, there's an excellent chance you are focusing in areas where you are not your best or simply wasting time. Discovering your interests and abilities may require the use of career assessments. Think of this as the most important class you never took. Once you find that intersection of passion and natural competence, your goal is to shift your time so that you spend an increasing amount of your work life in this area.

Within six months, Gene found a position in a different company. His former colleagues were stunned that he was leaving to take a job that paid $15,000 less and offered him less prestige. But these days he is able to come home by 6:00 p.m. instead of 8:00 p.m. He is sleeping much better and is happier doing tasks that he enjoys. Rarely, if ever, does he need to work on Saturday mornings or stay late to catch up as he used to. He now has time to run in the evenings with his boys as they train for a charity race in the fall. And on top of it, working on projects that call upon his strengths, Gene now is earning more than he did at his old organization.

Fears about the current job market and economic climate are perfect excuses for many to simply acquiesce and say: "I should just be happy to have a job." You owe it to yourself and your employer to be grateful and give your job 100 percent or take action if your strengths and interests are not a fit. Yes, it will require great courage, dedication and investment to identify and work toward using more of your strengths each year, but it can and must be done.

Career Secret #1

Pay and Worth Are Not Commensurate with the Amount of Effort or Time Spent at Work

During the height of the real estate craze, I (Bill) was shocked to learn why my friend had no trouble buying dinner out. A mortgage broker, he made three percent on every loan he closed. It didn't take me long to do the math. In many cases, he was making $1,000 per hour for each of the five hours it took to close a typical loan. Some months he closed ten loans. Times have certainly changed, but the principle of this section has not: Your pay often has little to do with how hard you are working. It has much more to do with two important principles:

First, you can charge a considerable amount for your services or product if it saves your customer even more time or money. People who are looking for a loan won't mind giving you $4,000 for four hours work if they know they are saving $20,000. This is just good business.

Second, if you can perform a service that others cannot, you can charge handsomely for your work. The trick is to always be one step ahead of what other people know! Website design and other technology-related jobs are a good example. While it is easier than ever to design your own site, there will always be new features that the average person does not know how to add.

Generating Passive Income

Many people make a great living selling their "forty hours a week." Those in the service professions have no other choice. Just know that this arrangement is not the only way to earn your income. Everything changes the minute you begin to get paid even when you are not physically working, either by creating some passive income stream or by having people work for you and receiving a percentage of what they generate.

For a fascinating read on moving away from the "nine to five" mindset, pick up a copy of Tim Ferris's inspiring book, *The Four-Hour Workweek.*[7] It will challenge, irritate, and make you jealous at times, but you will never again say, "I have no options." To help you think about this possibility, we challenge you with the following assignment.

Exercise: The $100 challenge.

Within the next two weeks, find a way to earn or save $100 without working more hours at your current job. Here are a few ideas:

- Sell no longer needed items such as electronic gadgets or baby clothes online.

- Hold a garage sale.

- Negotiate a raise.

- Participate in a paid research study or focus group.

- Complete online surveys.

- Sell your great digital photos online. (Check out istock-photo.com, for an example of how this works.)

- Rent out a room.

- Sell your proofreading, editing, writing, or other services online on a website such as elance.com.

- Barter your skills instead of paying for services.

- Swap for what you need—check out uswapit.com and swaptree.com.

- Clip coupons.

- Donate your old clothes, books, or unused gear to a charity and enjoy a tax savings.

- Resell your old books on Amazon.com.

Career Secret #2

Resources Trump Ability

Those who do well in their career endeavors in the twenty-first century follow one simple but critical maxim. Their philosophy is: "Just because I don't know the answer doesn't mean there is no answer." In contrast, unsuccessful people rarely ask for help and rapidly give up. Amazingly, they reason that if they don't know the answer, then there is no answer or it's simply too hard to find. Successful people ask for answers online, ask their friends and colleagues, and eventually, through connection after connection, get the answers they need.

Keith Ferrazzi, author of the best-selling book on networking, *Never Eat Alone,*[8] confesses that he has never been to a formal networking event. He argues that there are much better ways to get to know others. He prefers to meet his contacts face-to-face but more indirectly— before or after a presentation, by volunteering to drive the speaker to the airport, even helping to set up the room.

If there is one common trait among those who are stuck in their careers, it is that they suffer from a poorly developed network. Most of us have a healthy network of friends upon graduation from school, but like a garden left untended, our network becomes a patchy, uneven group of names you may remember fondly but have not reached out to in years.

Collaborating with others is no longer optional. Long gone are the days where a smart person could do quite well on his or her own. Success is now the single mother in Tennessee who has a great homemade chili recipe reaching out to a designer in Florida to help her come up with a first-rate logo and packaging. It's using a webmaster in Romania to create an online storefront.

Your Online Life Matters to Prospective Employers

Job Applicant Information Found on Social Media Sites that Helped Employers Decide to Hire[9]	%
Candidate's (online) personality would likely fit within the organization	50
Corroboration of candidate's professional qualifications	39
Candidate's creativity	38
Solid communication skills	35
Candidate appeared to be well-rounded	33
Other good references about the candidate	19
Awards and accolades received by the candidate	15

Job Applicant Information Found on Social Media Sites that Led to Employers Deciding Not to Hire	%
Provocative or inappropriate photographs or information	53
Posts about drinking or using drugs	44
Negative posts about previous employers, co-workers, or clients	35
Poor communication skills	29
Discriminatory comments	26
Lying about qualifications	24
Sharing confidential information about a previous employer	20

A new generation has joined the workforce. They are fluent in the use of online social networking and invested in connecting with others in an unprecedented way. Social media sites are now not only a growing way employees find jobs, they are also where would-be employers go to screen out potential hires. Refusing to learn the nuances of this new language is like hoping to make it big in America without learning English.

Sites like Facebook, LinkedIn, and Twitter point to the way connecting with others is evolving, even among those well beyond their college years. Without a sufficient network, we simply fade into the woodwork, drowned out by those who are far more adept at personal branding. A good network is like money in the bank. It is the new "social capital" needed to succeed. Those who think joining online networking sites is beneath them will be at a distinct disadvantage.

In today's world, an above-average, well-connected professional will do far better in his or her career than a brilliant, isolated genius with decades of experience. The good news is that one does not need to attend an endless series of meetings to network. There is much you can do right from your own home via the Internet. For a great read on just how to get into the new networking game, consider picking up a copy of Ferrazzi's *Never Eat Alone*,[10] or *The Little Black Book of Connections*[11] by Jeff Gitomer.

EXCUSE GAMECHANGER
Much of career success flows from investing heavily in your network and prudently asking them for "a little bit more."

Downsizing Your "Anti-Network":
Side-stepping Victims and "Frenemies"

Our own mind can be our greatest enemy as we move forward. We must not only be careful what we tell ourselves but also what we allow others to tell us. Those who will stand as obstacles to our goals, we call our "anti-network."

You will need to quarantine the highly contagious career victim—

a person who has given up the hope of his or her career progression. Every office, family, and organization has one. You don't have to be rude or avoid them altogether—they may be a relative—but you must dilute their negative impact on your goals and dreams. Many actually are trying to be helpful; others are downright jealous of your plans and consciously or unconsciously hope you fail.

There are other times when you must avoid such people like the plague. Your nascent dreams just don't have the strength to fight off the doubts these people will engender. Unsolicited "advice" can extinguish your dreams, setting you back for months, even years. Toxic and demoralizing counsel often seems to be offered during those dark times when you are struggling to "keep the faith."

"Frenemies" are another story. *The Online Urban Dictionary*[12] defines *frenemy* as "an enemy disguised as a friend." Frenemies seem to come out of the woodwork, offering left-handed, negative advice liberally lacquered with a lot of concern and interest. Do not be fooled. They can be very kind until you start to move ahead of them professionally or socially in some perceived fashion. Ironically, just when you must muster all the courage you can manage, they tell you that you probably will not succeed.

The attacks of frenemies come from three flanks:

1. *Assaults on your character:* Disbelief that you have the personality, drive, or professionalism to succeed.

2. *Assaults on your abilities*: Disbelief in your skills, intelligence, and the likelihood you have the ability to pull off your project.

3. *Assaults on your goals:* They imply that your goals are misguided, silly, or even worse, will yield very little benefit even if accomplished.

"Frenemies" are not benign, well-meaning family, friends, and colleagues who question your ideas at times. With frenemies you get the distinct sense that they are finally telling you just how they really see you, rather than expressing what they feel are legitimate concerns. When you realize that someone really does not hold you in high esteem, you have little choice but to back away and surround yourself with others who believe in you and your dreams.

Career Secret #3

The Top 10 Percent in Every Field Enjoy Most of the Benefits

In every profession, the top 10 percent are well paid and get to perform very interesting work. Our field, the world of clinical and corporate psychology, is no exception. Though it is true that insurance reimbursements are less these days for individual counseling services, we can easily cite five or ten psychologists in our area who have thriving private pay practices, a significant media presence, and a busy speaking schedule.

The big question is, if you are unhappy with your current job, do you have the potential of being a "10 percenter" in another part of your industry? Have you identified who these 10 percenters are? If you have, do you know any personally? If not, you are probably spending your time with people who cannot mentor you in the way that could be transformational for your career.

It's time to make the acquaintance of the top 10 percent in your field. Some of the best ways to meet are at conferences, by email, and by writing an article about them. You might offer to help them (even for free), or seek to be introduced through mutual friends and colleagues. Joining the organization to which they belong and becoming an active member is also an excellent way to make their acquaintance.

Career Secret #4

The First to Know Get All the Deals

Ten years ago, Spencer Johnson and Ken Blanchard delighted and challenged the business world with a fun little book entitled, *Who Moved*

My Cheese?[13] Perhaps you have read it too. The essential message of this short fable is that there are times when the "cheese," the good stuff we enjoy, disappears, never to return. It is important to be observant and take action when you first see this happening.

If ever there was a time in the world when the "cheese is on the move," it is today. Old paradigms, the time-honored ways we have always done things, are falling like dominos and there will be winners and losers in many industries. The rules are changing and the way we have lived and worked for decades are likely to be done differently or not at all in the very near future.

Are you a keen observer of the profound changes shaping your field? If so, what action steps, besides hand-wringing or circling the wagons, are you currently taking?

Just as the DVD and music CD industries have forever been impacted by downloadable digital content, the automobile industry is also undergoing a tremendous shift. It is likely that your industry is not far behind. As we look at these changes, we can have two reactions. We can act like Chicken Little and nervously announce "the sky is falling" but do little else, or we can look for new opportunities that await those flexible enough to "move with the cheese."

This is, of course, what this book is all about. Welcome to the revolution! Don't sleep through it even if you can't hear the tumult from your sector of the city. It is likely headed your way too. Stay prepared, in shape, and ready for action.

When it comes to your career and industry, be the first to know and act on that information, not the last. If you are, you can expect to enjoy many of the first fruits of your new venture long before others arrive. This is precisely what movie rental powerhouse Netflix did when it recognized that people would prefer to rent or stream videos from home if given an option. Can you see what is happening in your career? Do you have a Plan B, or even C?

On Not Giving Up

"We shall not flag or fail. We shall go on to the end. We shall fight in France, we shall fight on the seas and oceans; we shall fight with growing confidence and growing strength in the air. We shall defend our island, whatever the cost may be. We shall fight on the beaches, we shall fight on the landing-grounds, we shall fight in the fields and in the streets, we shall fight in the hills. We shall never surrender!"

—Winston Churchill, June 4, 1940, speech before the House of Commons following the evacuation of British and French armies from Dunkirk.[14]

What does it take for you to surrender, to give in to despair, discouragement, or defeatism? For some, sadly, the answer is "not a whole lot."

Those who succeed often have a markedly higher tolerance for failure. Did you know that half of all self-made, non-real estate millionaires have once been bankrupt?[15] Walt Disney, Larry King, Henry Ford, Milton S. Hershey (of Hershey's Chocolate), and Henry J. Heinz (of Heinz Ketchup) all filed for bankruptcy before making their millions. So has Mark Victor Hansen, co-author of the *Chicken Soup for the Soul* series, which has sold over 140 million copies!

Lim Tow Yong headed Emporium Group Holdings. He went bankrupt in 1996, at age seventy-two, after once having $300 million in sales revenue. He lost everything due to the recession in the mid-eighties and to fierce competition. Did he feel sorry for himself? Did he retire in shame? Did he destroy himself with alcohol or take his life? No, a dinner given for him by eight hundred of his former employees gave him the motivation to go on. He said: "It just touched my heart and I have never forgotten it. I've thought about it every day for the last ten years and I told myself that I must work harder and one day pay them back."[16] And pay them back he did! At a time of life when many are winding down, he worked harder than ever. He used the next ten years to rebuild his wealth, sold a series of seventeen stores and supermarkets, and by 2006, at age eighty-two he had acquired over $4.2 million. Lim Tow Yong is definitely a man who fired his career excuses. We salute him.

What is the worst thing that could happen to your career? Would you let the shame of failure shorten your life or put you on the sidelines? The choice is yours.

Write Your Own Story

Remember, this is the only life story you will ever write. The best stories all contain some amazing twists and turns and moments of cliff-hanging drama. Maybe this is where you are at right now. Perhaps you are in the middle of your story. There are others watching your life to see how it will turn out. You can either be an inspiration or a cautionary tale for your children, your friends, and your colleagues.

FREE *CAREER* EXCUSESTOPPER
If it is time to "reboot" your career, go to www.FireYourExcuses.com, register if you are not yet part of the Fire Your Excuses Community, and type in the keyword: ADVANCE to download "Seven Questions to Help You Strategize Your Career Advancement."

Reach out to get the help you need; you are walking the dark valley where many great people have walked before. Your adventure is not over unless you decide it is.

Guidelines for an Excuse-Free Career

Volunteer to Find a Better Job

Monty Python's Flying Circus, the hugely popular 1970s British comedy show, reported a 2,300 percent increase in DVD sales when they began posting generous amounts of their past series on *YouTube* for free.[17]

"Free" is the way to go in the twenty-first century. Those who stingily insist on getting paid for every service they offer will simply be left behind. Will some people take advantage of your generosity? The answer is "absolutely," but volunteering your services, especially when you are trying to break into a new career or market, is very wise indeed.

In the speaking profession, there is a name for that time when you must speak for free to build a business. It is called "doing the rubber chicken circuit," meaning that your only pay is an unexceptional chicken lunch or dinner—if you are lucky. We still volunteer regularly. It is the right thing to do.

Build Your Own "Board of Directors"

As mentioned in the chapter on social connections, one of the least used career-building strategies is creating your own "board of directors." A board of directors isn't just for the big business, it's for you too. The smart person puts together a team of people who are fully in his or her corner for those key career moments. People enjoy helping others, and the more fun and organized you are, the better. Few will turn you down if you communicate passionately how much you value their advice and input into your life.

Barbara Sher and Annie Gottlieb, in their classic book, *Wishcraft: How to Get What You Really Want*,[18] offer some timeless instructions on possible agendas for these board meetings. Your board of directors can help you in two ways: They can help you "brainstorm," or determine what steps you should take next, and they can help you "barn-raise," or help you identify people and resources to enable you to perform the steps you have already identified.

Why is the "personal board of directors" strategy so powerful? Because no one ever does it! A person who is purposeful enough to build his or her own "executive team" is a person who has already taken a big step and will be viewed seriously. Such focus and organization is unusual. Unusual is memorable, and memorable is hirable.

What to Do When Career Fears Begin to Get the Best of You

When it comes to the job market, there is no shortage of scary stories in circulation. Maybe you have lost your job due to economic factors and are deeply worried about your prospects of being rehired. There are plenty of people willing to tell you their frightening tales about the perils of making a change or starting again. In truth, the most "convincing" stories are anecdotal—they describe one powerful, unfortunate incident, not necessarily a whole industry trend.

It is not uncommon to feel lost and a bit fearful when it comes to the next step in your career. Informational interviewing, talking to others without the purpose of finding a job, is the antidote when you find yourself paralyzed by fear or lost as to what to do next. The longer you stay isolated, the less accurate will be your understanding of what waits for you in the dark. Be careful where you get your information. Talk to those who have made a successful transition themselves. Differences in compensation can vary widely, even within the same industry. Once a wise person starts looking around, the secret is out.

Infuse Others with Optimism, Hope and Enthusiasm

What happens to the temperature of the room when you walk in? Whether you are currently employed or interviewing for a job, does the energy take a noticeable dip or does your presence spark a heightened sense of excitement and fun? Research has shown that the most influential person in the room is the one with the best attitude—in other words, the most hopeful and optimistic. If ever there was a time for optimism, it is today! What can you bring to your new setting? Do others see this or something else?

Exercise: Ask three friends who will give you honest feedback the following questions:

1. *When you talk with me face-to-face these days, what energy do I give off?* (e.g., positive, negative, etc.)

2. *How likely would you be to ask me to take on a big task to lighten your own load?*

3. *Is there any issue, attitude, or mood you feel I am trying to mask but my body language says otherwise?*

What did you learn? It is truly amazing how our attitude and body language can communicate even those things we wish to keep concealed. What are you saying without words?

Beware of Dumb Loyalty

Vince Lombardi once said: "Winners never quit and quitters never win." Do winners really "never quit?" Hardly!

According to Seth Godin, author of the *The Dip*,[19] it is critical to know the difference between a career "dip," a career "cul-de-sac," and a career "cliff." In fact, career winners quit all the time and so should you. There is an old saying in the Southwest: "If the horse is dead, get off it!" There is such a thing as loyalty. There is also such a thing as dumb loyalty.

If you find yourself in a career cul-de-sac or, worse, about to walk off a "cliff," get the encouragement and support you need to execute a well-thought-out exit strategy. Don't stay in your current situation out of pride, obligation, or fear.

Ask, Ask, Ask

A delightful friend of ours has absolutely no shame whatsoever in asking for anything, and we mean *anything*. You know her type. She is someone who has gotten out of mountains of speeding tickets, been invited on yacht trips, and convinced her boss and customers to give her the impossible. One thing is certain, if she is looking for a job, she will get hired months before you do.

There is no shame in asking for what you like, but be prepared, there are many who will try to make you feel small or even insubordinate for doing so. Truth be told, not asking is one of the biggest mistakes we make in our careers. Often, we don't ask our best contacts and clients for additional business, nor do we reach out to those we know well socially for business help.

ASK "THE MAGIC QUESTION."

When seeking to expand our careers or to find a new job, we often fail to ask "the magic question."

Always Ask: "Who do you know who _____."

This exact wording of the question encourages your friend or contact to think deeply about your request.

Never Ask: "Do you know anyone who _____."

While only slightly different in wording, this form of the question can quickly be answered "Yes" or "No" and is easily dodged and dismissed.

If your friend or contact "can't think of anyone at the moment," ask: "Can I call you in a week or two after you have had a chance to think about it?"

Every barbeque, Christmas party, and volunteer group has a "Good Ole Jack," the guy who always makes the coffee and is also a top executive for a well-known company. Sadly, few ever ask him for anything other than more cream and sugar. Be different, ask Jack the magic question: "Who do you know who [someone who represents a key contact or lead]?" If you suspect "Jack" may know some people but seems a little unwilling to give you a name or two, don't be discouraged. Continue to build your friendship and see what develops later. If you called us out of the blue and asked us to share the name of our best lead, it is very unlikely we would do so. But, hey, you can always ask!

Continually Communicate Your Specific Career Interests to Others

News flash: There are plenty of people you know that could introduce you to an important career contact but mistakenly think you wouldn't be interested. How sad to later hear someone say: "Really, you are interested in that type of work? I thought you only did [what you told them you were interested in three years ago]? I wish I had known that!" Do your best contacts know *exactly* what work you are *currently* doing or seeking?

It's Time to Move Beyond Your Fear of Partnering

Good partners assume that their joint venture will eventually end and have drawn up the details at the very beginning on how to do so fairly and amicably. When you think about it, all traditional jobs are partnerships. If you are an employee, you are in partnership with the organization for which you work.

New creative partnerships can be a great way to grow your bottom line. The best thing about small partnerships is that together you determine the rules. As co-authors, we each enjoy business partnerships with others. Some of our partnerships are very formal, others are loose, but all contribute to our careers or are quickly renegotiated or ended. Don't be afraid to partner up. Just do your legal homework to ensure there are clear boundaries.

Ask Friends What They See You Doing

It is easy to get sidetracked in the wrong career, even for decades, for reasons other than interest and ability. It could be the money, it could be your fear, but it is often just garden variety inertia. Your true friends will be able to cut through all of this and tell you what they see you doing.

Honest friends and family have an amazing way of telling you like it is. Sometimes they are right! Ask three insightful friends the following question: *"You know I have been doing [current business activity] for a while now. If you could picture me in any other company or career, what would you see me doing next?"* Listen closely. You may learn volumes about where you should be heading in the future.

TAKE THE 30-DAY CAREER CHALLENGE

1. Invest in yourself by taking one emotional intelligence or career assessment. Consider taking either the BarOn Emotional Intelligence Inventory, which we offer, or the popular, StrengthsFinder.

2. Seek out a one-on-one meeting with a business professional who can help you evaluate the steps you need to take to address the biggest obstacles to your career advancement. They might include education, finances, personal or health issues.

3. Make a list of any current business mentors. Commit to growing this list by identifying, contacting and setting up a meeting with at least one potential new mentor.

4. Read two books on the latest ways to grow your career or develop that big idea.

FIRE YOUR EXCUSES

CHAPTER EIGHT:

SERVING

SERVING

Do not wait for leaders; do it alone, person to person.
—MOTHER TERESA

*There is nothing wrong with dedication and goals,
but if you focus on yourself, all the lights fade away
and you become a fleeting moment in life.*
—PETE MARAVICH

CAUTION!
We have tried our best in this book to offend everyone at least once, but have saved the best attempt for last! Keep reading with an open mind. You will notice that this chapter is a bit more personal. We hope you will know why by the time you have finished and it will change your life and shift your priorities, at least a little. If so, we would love to hear from you. You can email us at: MyStory@FireYourExcuses.com

CARLY ZALENSKI[1] WAS ALREADY A VETERAN OF SERVICE ACTIVITIES when she hit upon her big idea. She had participated in a winter coat drive in her hometown of Clintonville, Ohio, volunteered at a soup kitchen, and filled food baskets for delivery to needy individuals on Thanksgiving. Then, in April 2006, she founded *Kids Building Hope* to help with her new dream. Eighteen months later, with the support of family and friends, she had raised $50,000, a sum matched by the Vietnamese Children's Fund, for a total of $100,000. Just the funding needed to build Hoa Lac School in Vietnam. What is more remarkable was that Carly was fourteen years old.

Over the past decade it has been our privilege to serve in a number of churches and charitable organizations and to research the best practices of nonprofits here and in the developing world. We know many of our readers, from all faiths and philosophies, share our passion for service. Personally, as Christians, we believe serving others is central to our faith and what Christ called us to do when He said, "Love one another." Some we meet have never truly experienced the joy and fulfillment of serving others in a significant way. Or, they have served in the past but have been uninvolved for a number of years.

Susan tells us her work leaves her with little energy, resources, and time for much else. Paul and his wife, Toni, parents of two teens, make a familiar but unconvincing case that they can do nothing until their kids are grown and out of the house. We know they are missing out. Serving others lifts one's mood, decreases loneliness, and offers a deep sense of satisfaction found nowhere else. It is not coincidental that serving others is also the final step for those who are in a 12-step recovery program.

If you wonder why you feel aimless, lonely, empty, or sad, and serving others is not currently a prominent part of your life, we urge you to begin now. Even a slight shift in your use of time and budget can have a dramatic impact on the world around you and in your own happiness. There are hundreds of adventures in serving awaiting those of every age and interest. To do so, however, requires a change of heart. You will need to look at a number of excuses that the average person uses to delay or avoid this shift in lifestyle. Let's start with the most common ones.

Serving Excuse #1:
Not Enough Money

Most people immediately equate helping with giving money. While it is an important part of giving, it is just one aspect of what it means to serve. Let's assume for a moment that money is a legitimate obstacle for you, especially in these tough economic times.

Financial pressure is very real, but as we see below, there are at least three main ways to give "money":

1. Give your own money.
2. Highlight the need so that others will give.
3. Give away your services for free.

Financial Giving Method #1:
Give Away Your Own Money

To give of your resources you must first be convinced that there are people who are worthy to receive what you have to give. This, of course, also applies to giving your time and skills as we will talk about later. Determining the "worthiness factor" of a particular need can be a big hurdle. If you sense that those who are requesting help are largely responsible for their difficult circumstances, you will naturally feel far less inclined to give. One person we knew who received a number of government services spoke often about waiting for the economy to improve before looking for a job.

The worthiness issue raised in the example above touches upon a fascinating psychological and emotional phenomenon. It affects each of us as we try to absorb the

---

**"JUST WORLD HYPOTHESIS"
—A DEFINITION**

It is human nature to want to believe that the world for the most part is just, and "if we play by the rules," we will be okay. In contrast, we would like to believe that those who suffer, in some way, have brought their misfortunes upon themselves.

---

overwhelming needs and disturbing tragedies of our world. It is called the "Just World Hypothesis."

Here's an example most drivers can relate to: On your way home, you hear on the radio that there was a fatal accident on a local freeway. You listen closer and learn that the fatality involved a drunk driver who was speeding, drove off the road, and over an embankment.

You feel minimally affected. You didn't know the speeding driver and, after all, he was intoxicated. Everyone knows if you are driving while drunk there's a good chance you could have an accident and kill yourself or someone else. While you wouldn't say it out loud, you think that he knew the risk but still did something very unwise and suffered for it.

Now, let's change the scenario a bit: What if, instead, you learned of a fatality involving a mother and her children who were randomly struck by a semi-truck who couldn't stop in time—a tragically true story that happened in our area recently. You also learn that they were driving a Volvo, wearing seatbelts, going the speed limit, and had the latest air bag system but still died.

Now this news is far more disturbing. This family could have been you! Your "just world" has been shaken. It is suddenly harder to believe that if you do the right thing, drive the right car, take all the necessary precautions, you will be safe. Clearly, you and your loved ones may not.

What does the just world hypothesis have to do with serving? It is this: We look for information that helps us to feel like the world is fair and safe for those who play by the rules. When we are confronted with information that challenges our hope for a just world, we tend to become very unsettled. In the case above, knowing that the mother took every precaution and still died is disturbing indeed and we don't like to spend much time thinking about sad, frightening things. So, psychologically, we look for evidence around us that supports the conclusion we much prefer. We grab onto information that quietly reassures us, that as sad as the tragedy may be, those involved are very different from us on some level, e.g., culturally, morally, or geographically, or at least made some very unwise decisions.

The more you look around the world, you will find that it is far from just, predictable, and safe. As we know, sometimes bad things happen to good people. Yet, it is our natural desire to believe in a just world. This can blind us to the needs of others and keep us from reaching out. Once we do shift into a serving perspective, we delightfully discover that there is no purchase that brings us as much joy as adding another plate to the table even if it means thinning the soup. By the way, if you have never tried it, the taste of "thinned soup," especially enjoyed with someone who would have had no soup, is delicious.

Those who learn to be wise givers will, in some way, be entrusted with more to give. It is hard to fully explain, but it seems that those who are astute in giving to others, over time, end up in the position where they can give more and more away. We are, of course, talking about more than money here, as some of the most giving people we know are not the richest, just the richest of heart. Will giving make you wealthy? There is no such promise of financial riches. Although, without a doubt, you are sure to become wealthy in every way that really matters: rich in heart, friendships, and wisdom.

If you agree with these principles, then the key is to begin to give even very small amounts. If you are not used to giving away a dime of every dollar, we can almost guarantee you won't have the heart to give away $10,000 if you make $100,000 a year. An extra $10,000 in your pocket makes the mind wander. There are so many good reasons to hang on to your money. You can't expect that you will become more generous when you earn more. It just doesn't happen that way.

You see, while those who are wealthy do give away more than their poorer neighbors in overall dollars, study after study reports that the rich give away far less as a percentage of their total income. "According to the Social Capital Community Benchmark Survey, people at the lower end of the income scale give almost 30 percent more of their income."[2] That's an astounding difference in generosity!

Quick question: Which state is the poorest in the United States?

Answer: Mississippi.

Second question: Which state gives away more, per capita, than any other state?

Answer: If you said "Mississippi," again you would be correct!

If you want to become a great giver, start before you have a lot to spare. A few dollars given away wisely, especially in secret, can be far more satisfying than that frozen yogurt or coffee.

Financial Giving Method #2: Highlight the Need So that Others Will Give

It is simple but true: People don't give to causes they know nothing about. For any of us to consider giving to help others we must first be made aware of the need. When we truly see poverty, here or abroad, and get our hands dirty helping others, we are generally forever changed by the experience. For a long time afterward you will think about those images whenever you consider getting that latest gadget or designer purse. It will become a new part of what you consider when you make future financial decisions.

One way to begin is by volunteering to help out at fundraisers and other service events. Then you can spread your newfound awareness to others around you. Eventually, you will be ready for the second way of giving—hosting small events of your own where others can give to the cause that you have identified and want to support.

Hosting Your Own Charitable Event

Planning a themed event is easier than you think. Charge a small admission. Families with children can do this together. Ask local businesses who want to receive some great PR to provide the food and beverages. Here's the key part: Sell raffle tickets for donated items, events, and "getaways" people would enjoy. For example, you could raffle off "acts of service," a dinner for four or an evening on a boat. Many people will buy raffle tickets even if they can't come to your event.

It's okay to start small and host the gathering in your own home or that of a friend. If need be, decorate your garage and use it as additional space. The important step is to reach out for help. The more people you have on your "advance team," the easier it will be for you and the more people will attend your event. Of course, because it is a fundraiser your helpers will want to pay too. Don't worry about asking for a small admission fee and kindly refuse to negotiate with those who balk at the price.

The key is to create a team of people who have the skills and connections you lack. If you are not a connector, team up with someone in sales who loves to meet new people. He or she won't mind approaching local restaurants or hotels for a raffle giveaway item or for help in catering the event. If at least thirty people attend, invariably someone will surprise you with a larger donation. Often that someone won't even be able to attend your event. It may even be one of your restaurant sponsors.

You can do this! Start small and watch your event grow every year.

Financial Giving Method #3:
Give Away Your Services For Free

Many who cannot afford to write a check due to their own financial challenges can easily give financially in another way—by providing their services for free to those individuals or groups that could otherwise never afford them.

Here are but a few skills and services that can be offered for a reduced fee or for free: Auto repair, catering, counseling, tax preparation, beauty salon, computer/IT, legal, construction, tutoring, babysitting, and music lessons. The list is endless. Without a doubt, you have some skills that could be offered to a needy individual or agency.

The practice of giving away your time rather than your financial resources has been called a "time tithe." Just as many individuals give away a financial tithe, a tenth of their income, we can also consider giving away a tenth or a portion of our time. Nations like Switzerland and Israel have formalized this time-tithe concept in the form of compulsory military service. Every young person must serve time in the military in these countries as part of their "national service." It works amazingly well.

Serving Excuse #2:
Not Enough Time

How many years do you think you have left? Recently we were sent a fascinating online assessment that calculates the number of days one has left to live. While not a perfect prediction of longevity, the results were spellbinding, motivating, and sobering. It seems human nature to avoid thinking much about the end of life or at least overestimating the time we have left—to love, to enjoy and to serve.

If you are interested in how long you might be expected to live given your current lifestyle and health practices, you can find many such calculators by simply Googling the phrase, "life expectancy calculator."

Combine Service with Fun

It can be extremely difficult to weave in service activities with an already busy family calendar. The trick is to make serving others a significant part of how you already have fun, socialize, and celebrate. Here are some examples:

For years I (Bill) hosted a Christmas Crepe Breakfast on a Saturday morning in early December. The cost of admission was $5 and an unwrapped toy. The night before, our advance team enjoyed a pizza party and made two hundred crepes for the next morning's big event. It was the most fun serving I had all year. It didn't cost much and brought a lot of joy to the needy children of our community.

Another simple idea is to host a beach party, picnic or barbeque and charge $10 for admission. One particular event we held was in support of a little girl sponsored through Horizon International[3] whose mom was dying with AIDS in South Africa. Our little party raised $550 dollars—enough to support her for a year and a half—all because we spent a few hours on the beach together.

Take the Long View

Malcolm Gladwell, in his intriguing book, *The Tipping Point*,[4] observes that in most worthy projects the early days and years yield no perceivable return on investment. You need to overcome a lot of inertia at the beginning to see results in any endeavor. This breakthrough Gladwell calls "the tipping point."

Recently, we learned that conditions are finally improving in the South Africa township where we have been working with various mission teams for eight years. It can take years, even decades, to fully see the impact of our life and our service activities. Rick Warren, author of the mega best-seller, *The Purpose Driven Life*,[5] likes to say: "We tend to overestimate the impact we can have in ten years and underestimate the impact we can have in thirty years." Do you have a thirty-year plan to help anyone or any cause? Have you given up on causes because you have invested a couple years and seen little fruit?

Don't expect to see immediate results when you serve others. Keep planting seeds. If you are fortunate, you will be around for the harvest. If not, you are in good company. Mozart never made much money from his compositions. Da Vinci was never able to give up his day job and support himself with his artwork. Amazingly, he was one of the most gifted artists of all time yet never made a full-time living with his art. Are you telling yourself that you have nothing to share because you must fuel your dreams with a regular job or because the giving you can do now represents very little time or money? Take the long view. Some of the best stories of your impact you will never hear. Trust that they are out there, and pursue your calling to serve others.

Volunteering in America—Quick Facts[6]

Between September 2009 and September 2010:

- About 62.8 million people, or 26.3 percent of the American population, over age sixteen, volunteered at least once during the twelve months studied.

- The average volunteer donated fifty-two hours per year or about one hour a week.

- Women volunteered more than men. The volunteer rate of women was 29.3 percent in 2009. The volunteer rate for men was 23.3 percent.

- Married people volunteered more than singles. 32.0 percent of married, 20.3 percent of those who had never married, and 20.9 percent of those with other marital statuses volunteered in 2009.

- Among those over age twenty-five, college graduates were more likely to volunteer (42.3 percent), than high school graduates (17.9 percent), and those without a high school diploma (8.8 percent).

- Employed people (29.2 percent) volunteered more than those who were not employed (23.8 percent), and part-timers (33.2 percent) volunteered more than full-time employees (28.2 percent).

- People were most likely to volunteer for religious organizations (33.8 percent), followed by educational and youth services institutions (26.5 percent), and social community services (13.6 percent).

- About 43 percent of volunteers were asked to serve, usually by someone in the organization. Forty-two percent became involved after approaching the organization on their own.

Serving Excuse #3
I'd Like to Serve, but Where?

In the 1986 movie, *Crocodile Dundee*,[7] Australian actor Paul Hogan abruptly tells his co-star that he's leaving to go on a "walkabout," to clear his head. A *walkabout* can be defined as a time to look around, investigate needs, and clarify options. When you don't know where to serve, it is time for a walkabout of your own.

There are plenty of people who need help right in your own backyard. Even if you don't connect with the cause itself, you can still learn a great deal about "best-practices" by observing a well-run organization. We like to attend events just to see how people do things. Much of what we've learned about fundraising, we've learned by observing. Can't afford the price of admission? Volunteer so you can go for free, meet great people, and learn from them. Eventually, if you put yourself

"Some men are born great, some achieve greatness, and some have greatness thrust upon them by a friend who knows how to use Wikipedia."

© Randy Glasbergen. www.RandyGlasbergen.com [8]

out there, you will find an area that really touches you and resonates with your abilities and interests. Don't allow any organization to guilt you into performing a role you know is not the best use of your abilities.

You may find that you go through an informal "apprenticeship period" where you volunteer for one organization, learn the important aspects and challenges surrounding the need, and discover their best practices. Then, you can intelligently decide whether to invest further, find a more suitable group, or even start your own organization. Time serving is never wasted time. Just keep moving the ship and you will eventually find the right heading and the most favorable wind.

Serving Excuse #4
How Do You Know If You Are Really Making a Difference?

It is easy to find the flaws within any charitable organization. Some are run by well-meaning individuals with no business sense. Others feature an unacceptable lack of financial accountability, or worse, they exist largely for the needs of the leader. It's all there if you look closely.

Government-run organizations are the easiest targets. Yet, did you know that the U.S. government gives away five times as much in foreign aid than all of the nonprofit organizations in America combined? Certainly, where this money goes and what it goes for is a fair question, but it is difficult to say that a lot of good has not been done by Uncle Sam.

Smaller organizations are more nimble and targeted in their giving but each organization has its own personality, foibles, and red-tape— enough for any business-minded person to ask uncomfortable questions. That is where personal relationships and trusted contacts are so important to cultivate.

You can easily become very cynical until you meet an actual AIDS sufferer using her last days without any medicine to visit school children in the classrooms of Malawi, Africa, like we did. You can think your gift of a book bag goes to no one in particular unless you volunteer to pass them out one Christmas in a poorer neighborhood just minutes from your own. You can think that there are plenty of others who are caring for the elderly until you find out from the staff at a local skilled nursing facility that the sweet old woman you just met in Room 103 hasn't had a visitor in six months.

Meeting the people you are helping face-to-face is critical. It cuts like a healing knife through the heart of the most jaded professional and cocky teenager.

You will need to find a way to maintain your heart-connection or you will experience what is commonly called "compassion burnout"— too many walkathons, too many fund-raising letters, too many pictures of desperate children from faraway lands. You will need to meet the people you are trying to help in a personal way, even if through the first-hand accounts of others who see them regularly.

Sometimes, your role can be blessing someone who is involved in a helping venture such as an American working for a charitable group overseas, or a foreign worker visiting the states. You might invite them over for dinner, give them a ride to the airport, or let them stay for a short time in your home. Either way, you will get to hear, first-hand, the work they are doing, and it will bond you and soften your heart.

Serving Excuse #5
I'd Like to Help but My Family Is My Top Priority These Days

Serving the less fortunate and taking care of our own families is a difficult balancing act indeed. Many singles, single parents, and married adults are currently caring for members of their family even as they contemplate how they might also help others. Some are dealing with their own economic difficulties. Yet with the right strategy and focus, serving can be something that is done *as* a family.

Think your children will really be scarred for life if they don't have the latest athletic shoes, video game, smartphone, or lavish Christmas gift? Think again. You can have a lasting impact on the values and life of your children by involving them in significant acts of service very early in their young lives. Both of us were raised by parents who sacrificed so that we could experience life in the third world during our formative years.

Consider the words of Don Schoendorfer, President and CEO of the Free Wheelchair Mission:[9] "I used to think that I would make sure my family was all settled then I would give back in a big way, now I know that thinking is wrong." Who is Don you might ask? This is his story:

Don Schoendorfer is an unassuming suburban engineer from Irvine, California, who had an idea for a low-cost wheelchair and built one in his garage. He had been shaken by what he had seen on a trip to Morocco with his wife in the 1970s, where they encountered a disabled woman who was unable to walk, literally crawling across the street on all fours. She would be the first of thousands Don would notice around the world who had no hope of a standard wheelchair, which in the U.S. can cost up to $1,000. His idea was to build a cheap, easy-to-repair wheelchair out of Huffy bicycle tires and the standard-issue white plastic lawn chair. As of this writing, his experiment has lifted over 636,405 of the world's poorest people from a life in the dirt to one of dignity.

Don was recently presented with the "Above and Beyond" award, which is given to three civilians each year who have performed extraordinary acts of service. The award is chosen by another group of extraordinary individuals—those who themselves received the Congressional Medal of Honor for acts of bravery defending our country on the battlefield.

Don's ultimate goal is to distribute 20 million wheelchairs, 20 percent of the estimated world need. To see the impact of his efforts, visit his website: www.FreeWheelChairMission.org. To hear our interview with Don, please visit www.15MinuteAdvantage.com.[10]

"The person who has the vision has the job!" says our friend Dave Coen, head of *Threads Africa*,[11] a nonprofit that reaches out to those who live in the shantytowns of South Africa. He believes that whoever has the passion for a need may just be the one called to do something about it.

Looking for a place for you and your family to serve? What really angers or touches you? What obvious need should be met about which nothing is being done? What group is "falling through the cracks" or being oppressed that needs your support, advocacy, or protection?

Even with the best intentions, it is easy for you and your family to get distracted. There's finishing school, paying off student loans, buying your first house, mortgages, kids, sports, careers, and health concerns. Then there is saving for college, weddings, remodels, and retirement. It is quite possible to be distracted the rest of your life!

Experience the "Helper's High"

Fire Your Excuses Self-Assessment Snapshot: Steve, 32

Scale	Score	Range
Total Excuse Scale	323	Above Average
Potential for Change Scale	56	Above Average
Serving Scale	25	Below Average
Offense Scale	136	Superior
Defense Scale	129	Superior

Steve, 32, a salesman, tells us he feels empty and can't say why. Steve is a go-getter with Offense and Defense Scores to match. He works hard and plays hard. Not surprising, after our first meeting, we later discover his Serving Score could use some improvement, falling in the Below Average range. He is used to pressure and enjoys a challenge, which is confirmed by his Above Average Potential for Change Score.

The key will be Steve's interest in changing. If the salesman can be sold, he is likely to tackle improving his Serving Score with gusto, just like he does everything else. A look at his Blind Spot and Weaknesses Score would be helpful too. It would show how open he might be to hearing challenging information about his lifestyle and career skills. His Total Excuse Score is high indicating that he tends to make few excuses.

As we begin to meet, he comes to realize that serving has always been the missing piece in his life. Finding the right cause and organization proved to be a challenging assignment. But as his history had shown, when Steve locks on, he attacks any new challenge with a vengeance. In this case, once he located the right fit, he jumped in immediately. He would experience for himself the added benefit of serving others, what is known as "the helper's high."

"THE HELPER'S HIGH"—A DEFINITION
The term first used by Arizona State University psychologist Robert Cialdini to describe the euphoria reported by frequent givers. These good feelings may cause the lowering of the output of stress hormones, which improve cardiovascular health and strengthen the immune system.[12]

Older adults who live by the adage, "It is more blessed to give than to receive," enjoy longer life spans than people still focused on material acquisition, suggests a pioneering study on altruism. The University of Michigan study followed 423 couples for five years. All of the men were at least age sixty-five.

At the start, participants were asked if they had given or received emotional or practical help in the past year. Five years later, those who said they had helped others were half as likely to have died.[13] In another study, a group of subjects were given $20 and told to spend it any way they wished. When assessed afterward, the subjects who gave away at least $5 of the $20 were rated as far happier than those who spent the gift on themselves.[14]

EXCUSE GAMECHANGER
It is in service to others you will find the most happiness in life. Don't allow any obstacle or distraction to deny you this fulfillment—not your career aspirations, finances, time, or even your own cynicism.

In the same spirit, try the following experiment: Go to your bank and take out a cashier's check for any amount you wish to give. Make it out in the name of a person you know who really needs the money. Cashier's checks are great because they let you give to someone anonymously. Drop the check in the mail with a note, if you like, saying something encouraging, but don't sign your name. Be sure to mail your letter from a different town than the one where you live or work so you can maintain your secret identity. Wasn't that a lot more fun than a dinner for yourself, a new shirt, or gadget?

If You Feel Misunderstood by Others, You Are Probably Doing Something Right!

When you start to make some lifestyle changes so that you can serve, expect some opposition. People who live a bit counter-culturally so that they can give to others can receive a lot of flack from friends, even family. Those who serve others in a significant way make their friends who don't serve a little nervous. It is difficult to brag about your new car to someone who could have afforded one, too, but made a different lifestyle choice. This is especially true if that person decided to drive an older car a little longer so he or she could invest the extra few hundred dollars a month in the lives of others.

You will be changed by the process of serving in ways you may not initially expect. There is a difference between writing a quick check and helping from a safe distance versus investing face-to-face time with people in need. Certainly financial giving is important but if we are not careful our generosity can simply become a nice tip that lets us continue our comfortable way of living.

Serving changes children too. There is nothing like a trip to an orphanage, crisis center, or soup kitchen to help an entitled teenager see how good he or she has it. If you don't have children but hope to one day, your challenge might be to sponsor as many children as you wish to have in the future.

Serving can be a natural extension of what you already love. If you love pets, why not share them with others? One group in our area holds birthday parties at a local motel where needy families stay long-term. Some helpers bring their dogs for the children to pet—a rare treat indeed. Investing in others, be it your time or income, changes people, yourself included!

Join the Cause

You are essential to the war effort.
—OSCAR SCHINDLER, FROM SCHINDLER'S LIST

The Academy Award winning film, *Schindler's List*,[15] a story about the Holocaust, ends with a gripping, emotional message. Oscar Schindler has built a factory and staffed it entirely with Jews who would otherwise be destined for extermination. Month after month, Schindler convinces the Nazis in command that his workers are "essential to the war effort." For each worker hired by Schindler to supply the Nazis with war materials, it is, ironically, the difference between their life and death.

When the war is over and the factory is shut down, Schindler is immediately surrounded by a throng of grateful workers. Overcome with emotion and regret that he has not hired and saved more laborers, he breaks down. Though he has rescued so many, he is tortured by his calculation of how many other lives his Nazi lapel pin and his big car would have purchased. Like Oscar Schindler, we can't save the world but we can do something and all are needed for "the cause."

In 2003, a group of us toured the devastation that is modern day Congo. Death and misery seemed to hang in the air—from AIDS, starvation, and the still smoldering war that had divided the country essentially in two. One of the few encouraging moments we experienced there was seeing first-hand the impact of *World Vision's*[16] child sponsorship program that had transformed several impoverished villages.

What did we learn that memorable week? In most helping and serving situations it takes so little to do so much. Helping in a developing country is a lot like shooting at the ground. It's highly unlikely that you are going to miss! Further, those we partner with in the developing world or hire around the corner to perform a needed part-time service, we invite to "join us in the war effort." In the process of serving we can be profoundly changed as well.

Quiana Childress, of Arkansas, grew up in poverty, the second of ten children. When she was sixteen, her mother announced that she was leaving and that Quiana would have to find a place to live. That "place to live" turned out to be in a late model Pontiac.

Despite fighting anxiety and depression, she continued to plan for her dream of becoming a doctor by working as a nurse's assistant and even took on a second job to survive. To keep up her grades, she often woke at 3:00 a.m. to finish her homework. Eventually, she called relatives she seldom saw to ask if she could live with them in Little Rock. With their support, she was able to rededicate herself fully toward finishing school.

Last spring, Quiana graduated not only first in her biology class, but first in the School of Arts and Sciences at the University of Arkansas. She plans on attending medical school. Reflecting on her remarkable journey, Quiana observes: "If you focus on helping others then you can make it through. I think helping people heals us."[17]

FREE *SERVING* EXCUSESTOPPER
For help in deciding where to serve, go to www.FireYourExcuses.com, register if you are not yet part of the Fire Your Excuses Community, and type in the keyword: SERVING

EXCUSE STOPPER

A Final Challenge

Today America is experiencing the most difficult financial days it has seen in years. It would be easy to say: "Yes, serving others is great, but after I get on my *own* feet." We believe there has never been a better time to serve others than right now when we ourselves feel a bit of the suffering that others *always* feel. Will these economic times turn your attention inward or outward?

We hope you will join us in serving others. If you have been challenged to take the next step in serving, we want to hear from you.

If I am not for myself, then who will be for me?
And if I am only for myself, then what am I? And if not now, when?
—RABBI HILLEL

The greatest use of life is to spend it for something that will outlast it.
—WILLIAM JAMES

 TAKE THE 30-DAY SERVING CHALLENGE

1. Volunteer to help out with a fundraiser of your choice. Consider involving your family, if appropriate.

2. Anonymously, give $20, $50 or $100 to an individual you know personally who is in need, along with a note of encouragement.

3. Pick up the phone and "interview" three service organizations that might interest you.

4. Sponsor a child from your community or the country of your choice. You might even consider a second child if you are already a sponsor. (World Vision is our favorite but there are several other excellent child sponsorship organizations.)

CONCLUSION

WE WOULD LIKE TO CONGRATULATE YOU ON FINISHING THIS BOOK. You are now armed with many new insights and techniques to help you "fire your excuses." It is our hope that the stories and concepts discussed have challenged you to a deeper sense of personal ownership and, with this rekindled resolve, you will address the areas of your life that are currently holding you back.

At the beginning of the book, we introduced you to the FYE Excuse Cycle. Now we would like to reveal the rest of the model: The FYE Change Cycle.

Just as there is a downward spiral that leads to an endless loop of excuses and negative actions, there is an upward spiral that leads to permanent change. The shift from being caught in an excuse cycle to experiencing the freedom and growth of the change cycle is made by crossing the bridge between these two lifestyles.

The bridge that makes this shift possible is held up by two important pylons: First, is a willingness to accept the need for additional accountability and support. Second, is a willingness to take action, to do whatever it takes, not just what you have been willing to do in the past. If either of these pillars is missing, permanent change will not be achievable.

The level of support you need to achieve permanent change will likely be considerably more than you have had in the past. In turn, your actions will need to include the use of the stronger, more effective strategies such as the ones provided in this book. Once you cross over this bridge, permanent change is almost inevitable.

The Fire Your Excuses Change Cycle

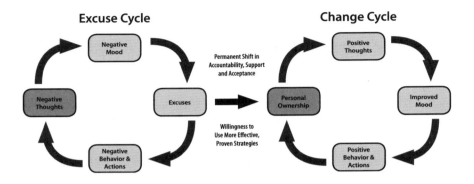

Life in the Change Lane

The starting point for lasting change is a deeper sense of personal ownership. This shift in perspective leads to more positive, useful and realistic thought patterns. As we choose to think differently, we, in turn, begin to feel more hopeful about our ability to change. It is with this improved mood, that we are able to take positive steps that confirm and support our commitment to an excuse-free lifestyle.

Stronger Medicine

Permanent changers anticipate that they will tend to deny, minimize, and justify their actions. They have immense respect for their own capacity for self-deception. Having experienced repeated cycles of relapse, they continually reach out for the needed answers, accountability, and support to break free and stay that way. Ralph Waldo Emerson said it well: "Every man I meet is my superior in some way, and in that I learn from him."[1]

Eventually we, too, must come to the place where we realize that we could fool ourselves into believing that next month or year will be different—for the rest of our lives! The decision to fire your excuses for good is based on the realization that what you have been doing to address your area of weakness has not been enough and never will. As much as it may be inconvenient, taxing, or a bit embarrassing, we must admit we will need to seek out stronger medicine.

Past behavior, as it is said in our field, is the best predictor of future behavior. If you believe that you just need to "get serious" to achieve permanent change in a desired area, we offer you this challenge: Write down what you will change by what date. Sit down with a trusted friend and commit on paper to your ultimate "serious attempt." Reconnect on your due date to reassess your promise to yourself. If, *for any reason*, you have not achieved your goal, you have your final answer and it's time to seek out additional help. We all have a tendency to say: "We would have been successful this time but..." Remember, this is how excuses work.

Let Us Help

We are very optimistic about your ability to change permanently, beginning the moment you get the level of accountability and support you need. *Fire Your Excuses* is much more than a philosophy, a set of techniques, or a book. It is first and foremost a community of like-minded individuals who help each other and serve their neighbors and their world.

We invite you to join us on your journey to permanent, sustainable change. On our website you will find many free resources, including a community blog, short audio programs, videos, articles, a newsletter, and practical tips that work. We also offer public and web-based seminars. *Fire Your Excuses* keynote and team presentations are offered live and via the web. Our Fire Your Excuses Coaching Program consists of single-session, 30-day, and 90-day programs. In addition, each of our team members has expertise in one of the life domain areas explored. There is more information about each of these offerings in the back of this book. We also look forward to hearing your story and hope for you that...

"It's Time!"

INTRODUCTION

1. K. Khan, "How Does Your Debt Compare?" *MSN Money,* http://moneycentral.msn.com/content/SavingandDebt/P70581.asp.

2. M. B. Reinsdorf, "Saving, Wealth, Investment, and the Current-Account Deficit," Bureau of Economic Analysis, U.S. Department of Commerce, http://www.bea.gov/scb/pdf/2005/04April/PersonalSavingBox.pdf.

3. L. Streib, "World's Fattest Countries," *Forbes: Health,* February 8, 2007, http://www.forbes.com/2007/02/07/worlds-fattest-countries-forbeslife-cx_ls_0208worldfat.html.

4. Centers for Disease Control and Prevention, "U.S. Obesity Trends 1985-2008," http://www.cdc.gov/obesity/data/trends.html#State.

5. L. Baertlein, "Mississippi Most Obese State, Colorado Least," *Reuters,* July 7, 2011, http://www.reuters.com/article/2011/07/07/us-usa-obesity-idUSTRE7663JD20110707.

6. Bureau of Labor Statistics, Economic News Release, "Table 1. Time Spent in Primary Activities (1) and Percent of the Civilian Population Engaging in Each Activity, Averages Per Day by Sex, 2010 Annual Averages," U.S. Department of Labor, http://www.bls.gov/news.release/atus.t01.htm

7. J. S. Atherton, "Piaget," Learning and Teaching, http://www.learningandteaching.info/learning/piaget.htm.

CHAPTER ONE

1. J. H. Burnett III, "Technology Has Redefined What It Means to Be 'Disabled'," *Erik Weihenmayer-Blind Adventurer,* online newsletter, June 17, 2009. http://www.touchthetop.com/newsletters/2009/headline.php?No-Barriers-Wraps-Up-Spectacular-Festival-at-Shake-A-Leg-Miami-12#skip2.

2. P. Gavin, "The Blitz," *The History Place: World War II in Europe,* webpage essay, http://www.historyplace.com/worldwar2/timeline/about-blitz.htm.

3. *Merriam-Webster Online* , http://www.merriam-webster.com/dictionary/blind%20spot.

4. D. Goleman, *Vital Lies, Simple Truths: The Psychology of Self-Deception* (New York: Simon & Schuster, 1996).

5. D. Goleman, *Emotional Intelligence: Why It Can Matter More than IQ* (New York: Bantam, 1995).

6. R. Bar-On, *Bar-On Emotional Quotient Inventory* (EQ-i) (Toronto: Multi-Health Systems) 1997.

7. V. Hugo, *Les Miserables* (New York: Signet Classics, 1987).

8. A. Andrews, "Andy Andrews Interview Blind Climber, Erik Weihenmayer," video clip, 2008, http://www.youtube.com/watch?v=pg57G9Lsxu8.

9. U.S. Department of Energy Genome Programs, "Human Genome Project Information," http://www.ornl.gov/sci/techresources/Human_Genome/home.shtml.

10. W. M. Sotile and R. Cantor-Cooke, *Thriving With Heart Disease: A Unique Program for You and Your Family / Live Happier, Healthier, Longer.* (New York: Free Press, 2003).

11. "Research Suggests Optimistic Attitude Can Reduce Risk of Heart Disease in Older Men," *Harvard University Gazette*, online periodical, Wednesday, November 21, 2001. http://news.harvard.edu/gazette/story/2001/11/research-suggests-optimistic-attitude-can-reduce-risk-of-heart-disease-in-older-men/.

12. "Joshua Chamberlain," National Park Service, Petersburg National Battlefield, http://www.nps.gov/pete/historyculture/joshua-chamberlain.htm.

13. Gettysburg 50th Reunion, Joshua Lawrence Chamberlain: Biographical Map, Bowdoin College, http://learn.bowdoin.edu/joshua-lawrence-chamberlain/map/.

CHAPTER TWO

1. Centers for Disease Control and Prevention, "U.S. Obesity Trends 1985-2008," http://www.cdc.gov/obesity/data/trends.html#State.

2. L. Baertlein, "Mississippi Most Obese State, Colorado Least," *Reuters,* July 7, 2011, http://www.reuters.com/article/2011/07/07/us-usa-obesity-idUSTRE7663JD20110707.

3. "Preventable Illnesses Account for Eight of the Nine Leading Causes of Death in the U.S.," news release, American College of Preventative Medicine, *Reuters.com,* February 2, 2009, http://www.reuters.com/article/pressRelease/idUS173975+02-Feb-2009+PRN20090202.

4. S. Wasu and D. Hatcher, "Restaurants Required to List Calories: The New Law Applied to Chain Restaurants," WDTN2.com, March 25, 2010, http://www.wdtn.com/dpp/health/Restaurants-required-to-list-calories.

5. D. G. Amen, *Change Your Brain, Change Your Life: The Breakthrough Program for Conquering Anxiety, Depression, Obsessiveness, Anger, and Impulsiveness* (New York: Three Rivers Press, 1998).

6. B. Dyment, "Making Big Changes Permanent: An Interview with Sal Fazio," podcast, *15 Minute Advantage,* June 29, 2006, http://www.drbillspeaks.com/15minuteadv.htm.

7. J. Michaels, "Lose Weight Online with Jillian Michaels," JillianMichaels.com, http://www.jillianmichaels.com/publicsite/funnel/v2/weightloss.aspx.

8. J. Michaels, "Jillian Michaels' Fitness Secrets! Jillian Answers Your Burning Workout Questions Now!" http://www.projectwedding.com/wedding-ideas/jillian-michaels-fitness-secrets.

9. J. Michaels, *Jillian Michaels Sunday Radio Show.* KFI 640-FM, Burbank, CA, 2009.

10. B. Phillips and M. D'Orso, *Body for Life: 12 Weeks to Mental and Physical Strength* (New York: William Morrow, 1999), 65.

11. M. Oz, "Dr. Mehmet Oz—Healthy Tip," http://www.youtube.com/watch?v=60uPoA6JB3g.

12. T. Thomas, "Missing Out on Your 40 Winks? You May Wind Up With a Cold, Carnegie Mellon Study Says," news release, Jan. 12, 2009, http://www.cmu.edu/news/archive/2009/January/jan12_coldstudy.shtml.

13. F. MacDonald, "Can Sleep Deprivation Be the Cause of Mental Illness?" March 2, 2009, *The Telegraph*, http://www.telegraph.co.uk/health/4862280/Can-sleep-deprivation-be-the-cause-of-mental-illness.html.

14. National Sleep Foundation, "2008 Sleep in America Poll," Summary of Findings, http://www.sleepfoundation.org/sites/default/files/2008%20POLL%20SOF.PDF.

15. National Sleep Foundation, "Women and Sleep," http://www.sleepfoundation.org/article/sleep-topics/women-and-sleep.

16. National Sleep Foundation, "Drowsy Driving," http://www.sleepfoundation.org/article/sleep-topics/drowsy-driving.

17. R. C. Rabin, "Behavior: Napping Can Prime the Brain for Learning," February 22, 2010, *The New York Times*, http://www.nytimes.com/2010/02/23/health/research/23beha.html.

18. S. Mednick, *Take a Nap! Change Your Life* (New York: Workman, 2006).

19. "Famous Nappers: Historical Figures Known for Napping, January 14, 2010, *The Huffington Post*, http://www.huffingtonpost.com/2010/01/14/famous-nappers-historical_n_423279.html?slidenumber=zpY%2FMIbZKZc%3D&&&&&&&&&&,.

20. Take Back Your Time, http://www.timeday.org/.

21. "Expedia.com–2009 International Vacation Deprivation™ Survey Results," Expedia, annual survey, http://media.expedia.com/media/content/expus/graphics/promos/vacations/Expedia_International_Vacation_Deprivation_Survey_2009.pdf.

22. R. Lovitt, "Only You Can Prevent Vacation Deprivation: You Deserve a Break Today—Now Get Out There and Take It!" May 26, 2009, *MSNBC.com/Travel*, http://www.msnbc.msn.com/id/30947066/ns/travel-rob_lovitt_columns/.

23. C. Zadan, producer, and Rob Reiner, director, *The Bucket List*, motion picture (Burbank, CA: Warner Bros. Home Entertainment Group, 2007).

24. P. Schultz, *1,000 Places to See Before You Die: A Traveler's Life List*, (New York: Workman, 2003).

25. P. Schultz, *1,000 Places to See in the U.S.A. & Canada Before You Die* (New York: Workman, 2007).

26. "Hans Selye," Encyclopædia Britannica Online, http://www.britannica. com/EBchecked/topic/533770/Hans-Selye.

CHAPTER THREE

1. H. Onoda, *No Surrender: My Thirty-Year War,* (Annapolis, MD: U.S. Naval Institute Press, 1999).

2. C. Gibson, and J. McGrath, "Why Were Some Japanese Soldiers Still Fighting Decades after World War II?" *Stuff You Missed in History Class Podcast.* January 1, 2009, http://www.howstuffworks.com/ podcasts/stuff-you-missed-in-history-class.rss.

3. U.S. Census Bureau, "Historical National Population Estimates: July 1, 1900 to July 1, 1999," April 11, 2000, http://www.census.gov/popest/ archives/1990s/popclockest.txt.

4. U.S. Census Bureau, "Marital Status of the Population by Sex: 1900 to 2002 (Table No. HS-11)," Statistical Abstract of the United States, 2003, http://www.census.gov/statab/hist/HS-11.pdf.

5. University of Virginia, The National Marriage Project, "The State of Our Unions 2010: The New Middle America," http://www.virginia.edu/ marriageproject/pdfs/Union_11_12_10.pdf.

6. U.S. Census Bureau, "Majority of Children Live with Two Biological Parents," news release, February 20, 2008, http://www.census.gov/ newsroom/releases/archives/children/cb08-30.html.

7. B.F. Grant, "Estimates of US Children Exposed to Alcohol Abuse and Dependence in the Family," *American Journal of Public Health*, 90(1), 114, http://www.ncbi.nlm.nih.gov/pmc/articles/PMC1446111/ pdf/10630147.pdf.

8. V. Ianelli, *Child Abuse Statistics,* About.com: Pediatrics, July 15, 2007, http://pediatrics.about.com/od/childabuse/a/05_abuse_stats.htm.

9. U.S. Census Bureau, "Urban and Rural Population: 1900 to 1990 (Table 1)," http://www.census.gov/population/censusdata/urpop0090.txt.

10. U.S. Census Bureau, "Urban and Rural, Farm and Non-Farm - Universe: Total Population. (Table P5)," April 30, 2007, http://ceic.mt.gov/ C2000/UA_UC/urban_rural_us_sf3.pdf.

11. K. Flaxman, "Are the Suburbs a Health Hazard?" *Globe and Mail Update,* January 4, 2008, http://www.theglobeandmail.com/real-estate/ are-the-suburbs-a-health-hazard/article658534/.

12. D. Ornish, *Love and Survival: 8 Pathways to Intimacy and Health* (New York: Harper Collins, 1998) 12-13.

13. R. Holden, *Success Intelligence: Essential Lessons and Practices from the World's Leading Coaching Program on Authentic Success* (Carlsbad, CA: Hay House, 2008) 134-145, 155.

14. M. Gladwell, *Outliers: The Story of Success* (New York: Little, Brown and Company, 2008).

15. D. A. Bennett, J. A. Schneider, T. Tang, S. E. Arnold, and R. S. Wilson, "The Effect of Social Networks on the Relation Between Alzheimer's Disease Pathology and Level of Cognitive Function in Old People: A Longitudinal Cohort Study," *The Lancet Neurology*, 5(5), 406 – 412.

16. *Ibid.*

17. *Ibid.*

18. *Ibid.*

19. S. Johnson, *World of Quotes.com*, http://www.worldofquotes.com/topic/Friendship/2/index.html.

20. T. Friedman, *The World Is Flat 3.0: A Brief History of the Twenty-first Century* (New York: Picador, 2007).

21. D. Cohen and L. Prusak, *In Good Company: How Social Capital Makes Organizations Work.* (Boston: Harvard Business School Press, 2007) 1,171.

22. The Henry Ford Museum, "The Life of Henry Ford," *The Henry Ford*, http://www.hfmgv.org/exhibits/hf/default.asp.

23. The Henry Ford Museum, "The Showroom of Automotive History: 1896 Quadricycle," The Henry Ford, http://www.hfmgv.org/exhibits/showroom/1896/quad.html.

24. F. R. Bryan, *The Birth of Ford Motor Company*, Henry Ford Heritage Association, http://www.hfha.org/HenryFord.htm#FordMotorCo.

25. *Ibid.*

26. *Ibid.*

27. D. I. Lewis, *The Public Image of Henry Ford: An American Folk Hero and His Company.* (Wayne, IN: Wayne State University Press, 1976).

28. M. Gladwell, *The Tipping Point: How Little Things Can Make a Big Difference* (New York: Little Brown & Company, 2002).

29. J. Kornblum, June 22, 2006, "Study: 25% of Americans have no one in whom they can confide," *USAToday.com*, June 22, 2006, http://www. usatoday.com/news/nation/2006-06-22-friendship_x.htm.

30. *Ibid.*

31. *Ibid.*

32. *Ibid.*

33. *Ibid.*

34. I. Kiderra, "'Pay It Forward' Pays Off—UC San Diego and Harvard Deliver First Experimental Findings on Spread of Cooperation in a Social Network," news release, March 8, 2010, http://www.eurekalert. org/pub_releases/2010-03/uoc--if030510.php.

35. *Ibid.*

36. *Ibid.*

37. Harvard Mentoring Project, "Who Mentored You: Who Mentored Maya Angelou?" Center for Health Communication, Harvard School of Public Health, http://www.hsph.harvard.edu/chc/wmy/Celebrities/ maya_angelou.html.

CHAPTER FOUR

1. C. Crowe, *Jerry Maguire,* movie script, http://www.imsdb.com/scripts/ Jerry-Maguire.html, 7.

2. R. Glasbergen, http://www.glasbergen.com/marriage-love-dating-relationship-cartoons/?nggpage=2); used by permission.

3. A. Mehrabian, *Silent Messages: Implicit Communication of Emotions and Attitudes,* 2nd ed. (Belmont, CA: Wadsworth, 1981).

4. *Ibid.*

5. E. Berne, *Games People Play: The Basic Handbook of Transactional Analysis* (New York: Ballantine, 1964-1992).

6. D. Goleman, *Emotional Intelligence: Why It Can Matter More than IQ,* 10th anniversary ed. (New York: Bantam Books, 2005) 43.

7. A. Mehrabian, *Silent Messages: Implicit Communication of Emotions and Attitudes,* 2nd ed. (Belmont, CA: Wadsworth, 1981).

8. C. Fadiman and A. Bernard, *Bartlett's Book of Anecdotes* (New York: Little, Brown, 2000) 169.

9. M. McKay, M. Davis, and P. Fanning, *How to Communicate: The Ultimate Guide to Improving Your Personal and Professional Relationships*, 2d ed. (New York: MJF Books, 1995).

10. A. Bell, and D. Smith, *Difficult People at Work: How to Cope, How to Win* (New York: MJF Books, 2004).

CHAPTER FIVE

1. L. Connelly, "The Mother of All Runners," *The Orange County Register*, January 29, 2009 http://www.ocregister.com/articles/run-six-kids-2292977-marathon-masche.

2. *Ibid.*

3. *Ibid.*

4. *Ibid.*

5. U.S. Census Bureau, "Money Income of People—Selected Characteristics by Income Level: 2008 (Table 701)," http://www.census.gov/compendia/statab/2011/tables/11s0701.pdf.

6. A. Stanley, "High Performance Teams," *Andy Stanley Leadership Podcast*, podcast, January 27, 2009, http://www.itunes.com.

7. M. Jacks, "The History of the Light Bulb – An Electric Dawn," article, TheHistoryOf.com, September 11, 2008, http://www.thehistoryof.net/the-history-of-the-light-bulb.html.

8. U.S. National Library of Medicine, "Depression," Medline Plus, a service of the National Institutes of Health, http://www.nlm.nih.gov/medlineplus/depression.html.

9. R. Glasbergen, http://www.glasbergen.com/business-computer-cartoons/?album=1&gallery=3; used by permission.

10. D. Allen, *Getting Things Done: The Art of Stress-Free Productivity* (New York: Penguin, 2002).

11. B. Dyment, "Getting Things Done: An Interview with Best-Selling Author, David Allen," *15-Minute Advantage*, podcast #2, January 23, 2007, http://www.drbillspeaks.com/15minuteadv.htm.

12. T. Ferris, *The Four-Hour Workweek: Escape 9-5, Live Anywhere, and Join the New Rich* (New York: Crown, 2007).

CHAPTER SIX

1. J. J. Ellis, "Thomas Jefferson," *Biography.com*, http://www.biography.com/articles/Thomas-Jefferson-9353715.

2. Z. Zhoul, K.D. Vohs, and R. F. Baumeister, "The Symbolic Power of Money: Reminders of Money Alter Social Distress and Physical Pain," *Psychological Science*, (20), 6, 700-706.

3. *Ibid.*

4. K. Vohs, N. L. Mead, and M.R. Goode, "Merely Activating the Concept of Money Changes Personal and Interpersonal Behavior," *Current Directions in Psychological Science* (17) 3, 208-212.

5. T. Stanley and W. Danko, *The Millionaire Next Door* (New York: Pocket Books).

6. R. Glasbergen, http://www.glasbergen.com/?s=wealthy; used by permission.

7. D. L. Ashliman, "The Pied Piper of Hameln and Related Legends from Other Towns: The Children of Hameln by Jacob and Wilhelm Grimm," *Folklore and Mythology*, University of Pittsburgh, http://www.pitt.edu/~dash/hameln.html#grimm245.

8. Galatians 6:7, *The Holy Bible: New International Version*. Carlisle, UK: Authentic Media.

9. S. Orman, "Suze Orman's 9 Steps to Financial Freedom," *Raising Entrepreneurs.org*, http://raisingentrepreneurs.org/blog/2008/03/31/suze-ormans-9-steps-to-financial-freedom/3.

10. Luke 12:34, *The Holy Bible: New International Version*. Carlisle, UK: Authentic Media.

11. "Gambling addiction - Gambling Addiction Statistics," *The ClearLead Directory*, http://www.clearleadinc.com/site/gambling-addiction.html.

12. J. Jones, "One in Six Americans Gamble on Sports," *Gallup.com*, http://www.gallup.com/poll/104086/one-six-americans-gamble-sports.aspx.

13. M. Hitti, "Compulsive Spending: Both Sexes Buying Study: About 6% of U.S. Men and Women are Compulsive Buyers," *WebMD Health News*, http://www.webmd.com/balance/guide/20070201/compulsive-spending-both-sexes-buying.

14. D. Ramsey, *Total Money Makeover* (Nashville, TN: Thomas Nelson, 2004).

15. D. Ramsey, *The Truth about Credit Card Debt. Life, Hope and Money*, DaveRamsey.com, http://www.daveramsey.com/the_truth_about/credit_card_debt_3478.html.cfm, 1.

16. D. Prelec and D. Simester, "Always Leave Home Without It: A Further Investigation of the Credit-Card Effect on Willingness to Pay." *Marketing Letters* (Netherlands: Springer, 12 (1), 5-12).

17. S. Orman, *Suze Orman's 2009 Action Plan* (New York: Spiegel and Grau, 2008), 4.

18. R. T. Kiyosaki, *Rich Dad's Increase Your Financial IQ: Getting Richer by Getting Smarter.* (New York: Business Plus, 2008).

19. P. W. Bernstein, (2007). *Ernst and Young Tax Guide 2008.* New York: Vanguard Press.

20. R. Powell, "Lies, Damn Lies and (Retirement) Statistics: Reluctant Retirement Savers May Be Scared Straight by These Data," *Market Watch*, http://www.marketwatch.com/story/reluctant-retirement-savers-may-be-scared-straight-by-these-stats.

21. G. S. Clason, *The Richest Man in Babylon* (New York: Signet, 1955) 65.

CHAPTER SEVEN

1. "Mile Run World Record Progression," Answers.com, http://www.answers.com/topic/world-record-progression-for-the-mile-run.

2. S. Esaak, "Artists in 60 Second: Grandma Moses," About.com: Art History http://arthistory.about.com/cs/namesmm/p/moses_grandma.htm.

3. "Colonel Sanders—Story of Perseverance & Entrepreneurship." ArticlesBase.com, http://www.articlesbase.com/entrepreneurship-articles/colonel-sanders-story-of-perseverance-entrepreneurship-100394.html.

4. "Cal Ripken Jr. Biography," *Encyclopedia of World Biography*, http://www.notablebiographies.com/Pu-Ro/Ripken-Jr-Cal.html.

5. M. Buckingham, *Go Put Your Strengths to Work: 6 Powerful Steps to Achieve Outstanding Performance* (New York: Free Press, 2007).

6. M. Buckingham, *Now Discover Your Strengths* (New York: Free Press, 2001).

7. T. Ferris, *The 4-Hour Workweek: Escape 9-5, Live Anywhere, and Join the New Rich* (New York: Crown, 2009).

8. K. Ferrazzi, *Never Eat Alone: And Other Secrets to Success, One Relationship at a Time.* (New York: Broadway Business, 2005).

9. R. Haefner, "More Employers Screening Candidates via Social Networking Sites: Five Tips for Creating a Positive Online Image, *Careerbuilder.com,* http://www.careerbuilder.com/Article/CB-1337-Getting-Hired-More-Employers-Screening-Candidates-via-Social-Networking-Sites/.

10. K. Ferrazzi, *Never Eat Alone.*

11. J. Gitomer, *Little Black Book of Connections: 6.5 Assets for Networking Your Way to Rich Relationships* (Austin, TX: Bard Books, 2006).

12. *Online Urban Dictionary,* http://www.urbandictionary.com/define.php?term=frenemy.

13. S. Johnson and K. Blanchard, *Who Moved My Cheese? An Amazing Way to Deal with Change in Your Work and in Your Life* (New York: G. P. Putnam's Sons, 1996).

14. W. Churchill, "We Shall Fight on the Beaches," June 4, 1940, House of Commons Speech," The Winston Churchill Centre and Museum at the Cabinet War Rooms, http://www.winstonchurchill.org/learn/speeches/speeches-of-winston-churchill/128-we-shall-fight-on-the-beaches.

15. K. Phillips, "Financial Failure: The Dark before the Dawn," April 12, 2009, The Garden of Plenty weblog, http://totalwealthcoaching.com/wp/?p=776.

16. A. Khoo, "Bankrupt at 72 Years Old, Millionaire Again at 82!" November 4, 2006, Adam-Khoo.com, http://www.adam-khoo.com/41/bankrupt-at-72-years-old-millionaire-again-at-82/.

17. L. LaPorte, *The Tech Guy Radio Show, Episode 530,* January 25, 2009, KFI-FM, Los Angeles, CA.

18. B. Sher and A. Gottlieb, *Wishcraft: How to Get What You Really Want* (New York: Ballantine, 2003).

19. S. Godin, *The Dip: A Little Book that Teaches You When to Quit (and When to Stick).* (Portfolio Hardcover, 2007).

CHAPTER EIGHT

1. K. Joy, "Reaching Out to Vietnam: Ohio Girl Raises Thousands to Build School for Poor," *The Columbus Dispatch*. March 12, 2008, http://www.dispatch.com/live/content/life/stories/2008/03/12/1_VIETNAM_SCHOOL.ART_ART_03-12-08_D1_NO9I8G8.html.

2. J. Stossel and K. Kendall, "Who Gives and Who Doesn't? Putting the Stereotypes to the Test," November 28, 2006, *ABC News 20/20*, http://abcnews.go.com/2020/story?id=2682730&page=1.

3. For more information about Horizon International, Inc. go to http://www.horizoninternationalinc.com/.

4. M. Gladwell, *The Tipping Point: How Little Things Can Make a Big Difference* (New York: Little Brown & Company, 2002).

5. R. Warren, *The Purpose Driven Life: What on Earth Am I Here For?* (Grand Rapids, MI: Zondervan, 2007).

6. Bureau of Labor Statistics, "Volunteering in the United States, 2010" news release, January 26, 2010, U.S. Department of Labor, http://www.bls.gov/news.release/volun.nr0.htm.

7. J. Scott, J. Cornell, and W. Young, producers, and P. Faiman, director, *Crocodile Dundee*, a motion picture, 1986. Los Angeles, CA: Paramount Studios.

8. R. Glasbergen, http://www.glasbergen.com/?s=greatness; used by permission.

9. For more information about *Free Wheelchair Mission* go to http://www.freewheelchairmission.org.

10. B. Dyment, "Counting the Cost, Experiencing the Joy: An interview with Don Schoendorfer, FreeWheelchairMission.org," *15-Minute Advantage, Podcast #5,* September 3, 2008, http://www.drbillspeaks.com/15minuteadv.htm.

11. For more information about *Threads Africa,* go to http://www.threadsafrica.org/.

12. M. Elias, "Generous Spirit May Yield Generous Life Span," *USA Today: Health and Behavior,* November 13, 2002, http://www.usatoday.com/news/health/2002-11-13-long-life-usat_x.htm.

13. L. Dye, "Giving Can Save Your Life: Researcher Finds Evidence Why It's Truly Better to Give than Receive," *ABC News: Technology and Science,* December 19, http://abcnews.go.com/Technology/Story?id=97792&page=1.

14. S. J. Gilbert, "Spending on Happiness," interview with Michael I. Norton, *Working Knowledge,* Harvard Business School, June 2, 2008, http://hbswk.hbs.edu/item/5944.html.

15. B. Lustig, G. R. Molen, I. Glovin, K. Kennedy, and L. Rywin, producers, and S. Spielberg, director, *Schindler's List,* motion picture, 1993, Universal City, CA: Universal Studios.

16. For more information about *World Vision* child sponsorship go to http://www.worldvision.org.

17. S. Aasen, "Person of the Week: Quiana Childress," *ABC News with Diane Sawyer,* May 14, 2010, http://abcnews.go.com/WN/person-week-quiana-childress-homeless-16-college-graduate/story?id=10652350.

CONCLUSION

1. Quote by Ralph Waldo Emerson, http://www.goodreads.com/quotes/show/8468.

GLOSSARY

30-Day Challenge: A coaching "dare" that appears at the end of each chapter, consisting of four action items designed to be accomplished within one month. Successfully completing the *30-Day Challenge* will help you make significant progress toward the elimination of your excuses for that domain.

Accommodation: The process of making room. When we use this term in the context of the *Fire Your Excuses* change model, we are affirming that permanent change will require "breaking the mold" to make room for a new way of living. Permanent change will not be achievable if you insist on staying within your comfort zone. The accommodation process takes courage, time, and effort, but yields permanent benefits.

Anti-Network: Those in your social circle who stand in the way of your goals.

Assimilation: The process of incorporating something into one's existing framework. Assimilation is being willing to do only those things that are achievable within our comfort zone or existing lifestyle. In contrast to accommodation, assimilation promises a much easier route—minimal investment and little, or only short-term, change to one's lifestyle. It is a surface-cleaning approach that will not produce the permanent change desired.

Barn-raising: A formal or informal gathering held to share the names of people and resources to enable you to perform the steps you have already identified (from Barbara Sher and Annie Gottlieb, *Wishcraft: How to Get What You Really Want.*)

Brainstorming: A formal or informal gathering held to assist you in identifying what steps you should take next.

Bridge to Change: The transition one must make to leave behind the *Excuse Cycle* and enter into the *Change Cycle.* Crossing this bridge requires 1) a permanent shift in accountability and support, 2) an acceptance that one has been caught in excuses and blame, and 3) a willingness to try stronger medicine.

Choose Your Pain, Choose Your Joy: These two parallel concepts are used frequently in the FYE Coaching Program to help participants weigh the cost/benefit of continuing in a negative behavior. Validating that we all have the right to choose our pain as well as our joy helps us decide when it is time to get serious about change.

Compassion Burnout: The natural dip in empathy and the tendency to detach as one reaches his or her saturation point of involvement in service activities or exposure to significant needs. For example, one may experience these feelings after participating in too many fundraisers, watching too much disaster coverage, or receiving an endless stream of support letters.

Compulsive Behaviors: Actions in our lives that have taken on an addictive, self-destructive quality. They are performed as a way of blocking pain and include such behaviors as chronic overeating, sexual addiction, gambling, and substance abuse.

Connector: A well-networked person who has significant contacts in many groups, versus someone who knows many people within just one or two groups.

Conscious Denial: A state of being, where we have been confronted with evidence of our weakness but still refuse to believe it. For example, a man who is told he has terminal cancer but never mentions it and continues to talk about what he will be doing in the next ten years.

Contacts: Those with whom we can talk openly and deeply. According to a UCLA wellness study, we need three to four, one-hour contacts per week, not including the connections we have with those with whom we live. Face-to-face contacts are best but, more recently, webcam conversations have surpassed phone conversations as the next best way to connect.

Curse Words of Communication: The following words and phrases should be considered off-limits in your difficult conversations with others: "always," "never," and "you make me feel."

Defensive Actions: Actions that maintain our current environment, career, or social life, and serve to prevent loss, for example, scheduling your yearly physical.

Emotional Management: The unflinching examination of the emotional and motivational components of managing our time—including issues of hope, mood, delayed gratification, and the incredible power of incremental effort.

Excuse GameChanger: A key strategy for defeating the excuse highlighted in each chapter.

ExcuseStopper: A supplemental resource offered in each chapter that is available on the Fire Your Excuses website, which has been created to help you tackle the excuse explored.

Fire Your Excuses Community: An online network of individuals who gather for support, accountability, and to share new ideas surrounding the foundational FYE principles of personal ownership, permanent lifestyle change, and service to others.

Fire Your Excuses Self-Assessment: An 82-item inventory included with the purchase of this book, which measures the impact of excuses on our life and goals. The assessment generates a Total Excuse Score, eight life excuse scores, and a Potential for Change Score.

Frenemies: An enemy disguised as a friend who assaults your character, abilities, or goals.

FYE Change Cycle: The process beginning with personal ownership and leading to permanent change. A deeper sense of personal ownership results in better choices and positive actions. As we begin to think more hopefully about our ability to change, we feel better about ourselves (improved mood), and make better choices. We, in turn, are less likely to use excuses and the positive upward cycle of change continues.

FYE Coaching Program: The distinctive feature of the coaching program is a focus on personal ownership and the abandonment of excuses. Current program offerings include single-session mastermind consultations, a 30-day program, and a 90-day program. Goals are set, and, equally important, obstacles and their solutions are pre-identified, increasing the likelihood of success.

FYE Excuse Cycle: The road to seeing oneself as a victim and unable to change begins with our thoughts. How we think about ourselves and the world can be influenced by several factors—our upbringing, experiences, and even genetics. Left unchecked and unchallenged, negative thoughts invariably lead to negative feelings. Eventually, we begin to overlook the true options available to us and to fall into denial and excuse-making. Finally, our behaviors reflect our excuses in our actions or inactions, and the cycle repeats itself.

FYE FitWeek Plan: This seven-day fitness program combines exercise, attention to daily fuel (calories), and nutritional planning.

HD (High Definition) Listening: An advanced form of active listening, which requires full commitment to the conversation and the fine tuning of one's listening skills. The result is 100 percent clarity (understanding) and brightness (engagement).

Helper's High: The euphoria reported by those who frequently engage in serving others.

Just World Hypothesis: The belief that the world is, for the most part, just, and if we play by the rules we will be okay. Those who suffer have brought their misfortunes upon themselves in some way.

Lean Beef: Someone who is not only at his or her normal weight but has maintained or built healthy muscle tone and mass through resistance and strength training. (For the opposite, see "Prune.")

Life Coaching: The formal process of contracting with individuals who desire specific help in goal setting, obstacle identification, and accountability. Different from therapy, the focus of life coaching is on the future and presumes that deeper emotional issues have already been addressed.

Magic Question: In networking settings it is asking, "Who do you know who ...?" This query encourages the listener to think more deeply about who might be able to help you in your job search or dream development. Using the exact word order of the magic question is critical. For example, the phrase, "Do you know anyone who ...?" can easily be answered by a quick "Yes" or "No," and is less effective.

Mirroring Effect: The healthy feedback we receive which reflects who we are, what we like, our strengths and weaknesses, and whose company we enjoy.

NQ—Network Quotient: The capacity to form important connections with others.

Offensive Actions: Actions that enhance our current environment, career, or social life and serve to expand our sphere of influence. Example: looking for a new job or joining a new group.

Operating Systems: The four main interdependent areas of our lives that need to be maintained, and malfunction when resources run low. They are the physical, mental, emotional, and spiritual dimensions of our being.

Partitioning: A time-management technique that involves separating all the items, tasks, or projects in your life into very clear, discreet spaces. This increases productivity and helps us avoid the feeling of being overwhelmed. Just as it was reassuring to have your own cubby hole in your preschool classroom, it can be gratifying as an adult to know that you have a clearly labeled bin in the garage where all of your holiday decorations are stored.

People Account: The idea that it is better to measure your net worth by how much you have invested in helping others rather than how much you have in your bank account.

Personal Board of Directors: A formal or informal executive team who support your personal goals, provide wise counsel, and keep you accountable.

Potential for Change: One of the scales of the Fire Your Excuses Self-Assessment. It measures our hardiness under stressful conditions and the degree to which we feel as if the power to change lies within. Those who score higher on this scale are likely to have a greater ability to address their negative habits even if their Total Excuse Score suggests they currently have much work to do.

Prune: Someone who has dieted down to his or her optimal weight but has lost muscle tone or mass because resistance/strength training has been neglected. (For the opposite, see "Lean Beef.")

Rest Hygiene: The degree of attention we give to our sleep and relaxation needs. Rest hygiene not only refers to how many hours of sleep we get at night but also to how we use weekends and vacation time.

Self-Monitoring Technique: Keeping a time, food, or spending log to see what patterns are present. This technique is based on the finding that what is observed invariably changes. For example, keeping a log of exactly what you spend during a two-week period will raise awareness as to where your money actually goes.

Slow Leak Scenario: A modest but continual habit of overspending. An example would be a couple who spends slightly more than they make each month. Unchecked, this spending pattern eventually leads to significant debt.

Stages of Awareness: Each of us passes through a series of emotional and behavioral responses as we grapple with a newfound weakness. Some stages we may skip, e.g., jumping from denial to acceptance, but usually we follow the trajectory of the following six stages: 1) Blindness, 2) Minimization, 3) Shame, 4) Grace, 5) Acceptance, and 6) Healing.

Stronger Medicine: A metaphor for more effective strategies, e.g., being willing to try new, more radical steps, or those that are less familiar but more likely to achieve the desired results.

Systems Crash: Using a computer metaphor, this term refers to our functioning ability coming to a grinding halt. This is brought on by neglecting one of our four life systems, which can result in a highly disruptive or catastrophic life crisis, e.g., medical, emotional, spiritual, etc.

"The Millionaire Next Door" **Lifestyle**: The conservative strategy of living well below one's financial means practiced by many wise millionaires, from the book by the same name.

Thinking Time: A period of time that we set aside just to think creatively.

Time Tithe: The practice of donating a portion of time, just as we might our financial resources.

Tipping Point: The moment in time in which significant growth is now obvious. Coined by Malcolm Gladwell, in his book by the same name, the term is based on the observation that, in most endeavors, the early days yield no perceivable return on investment. It is only until one overcomes inertia or achieves critical mass that a breakthrough is seen. The challenge is to be persistent in one's efforts, sometimes without much outward evidence of progress, until that point is reached.

Transition Time: The time between scheduled events. Those who manage their time make the most of these moments, never being caught without something to do when this opportunity presents itself. Unexpected transition time often occurs when others run late or when we arrive early.

Unconscious Blindness: A state of being where we have no awareness of our blind spots nor have we ever been confronted with them. For example, a high school basketball star from a small town believes he is destined for greatness because he has never competed against someone at his level.

Vacation Deprivation: This term refers to the fact that many Americans receive fewer vacation days than the rest of the industrialized world. Further, 35 percent of us fail to use the vacation days we have accrued. This deficit has been shown to have profound health and social consequences.

"Very Next Steps" Technique: The strategy of writing down the very next action for each project on your list. This technique, described by David Allen in *Getting Things Done*, prevents us from avoiding projects because we don't know what to do next or don't have time to finish the entire project at the moment.

Walk the Last Mile of Denial: The willingness to face up to *any* and *all* neglected information and to finally do whatever it takes in order to fully address the weaknesses that still remain in our lives.

Walkabout: A term made popular by the movie *Crocodile Dundee*. It refers to taking some time to look around in order to get perspective when you are not sure what to do next. It can also refer to the process of trying any number of volunteer activities, social groups, or career paths to see which one feels right.

You as "Project Manager": The acceptance that you are ultimately responsible for your success in life but that you cannot complete all aspects of this task alone and must reach out for help.

The 12 Scales of the Fire Your Excuses Self-Assessment

Total Excuse Scale

The Total Excuse Scale is a summary score for all areas measured by the assessment. The higher your Total Excuse Score, the better. A high Total Excuse Score indicates that you are less likely to rely on excuses in your life. Keep in mind, however, that any two Total Excuse Scores falling within the same range—Average, Above Average, etc.—rarely reflect an identical excuse profile.

For example, Mark's and Jeff's Total Excuse Scores both fall within the Average range. But here is where their similarities end. Mark scored Superior in a number of his individual excuse scores and Low in several others, while Jeff received an Average Total Excuse Score because he scored in the Average range on all of his individual scores. Clearly, what Mark and Jeff need to do to improve their scores will be radically different. Mark might have some areas that require critical and immediate attention, whereas Jeff may not.

Keep in mind as you review your results, that it is important to be on the lookout for excuse areas that are particularly low and therefore likely to jeopardize your quality of life and success in other areas.

The Eight Individual Excuse Scales

Blind Spots and Weaknesses Scale: This scale examines excuses about our weaknesses and areas we do not see. It also looks at our willingness to seek out feedback that we need to hear but that may not be pleasant.

Health and Wellness Scale: This scale examines excuses about the way we take care of our physical, mental, emotional, and spiritual health as we pursue our career and personal goals. It also looks at our stress management habits.

Social Connections Scale: This scale examines excuses about our connections with friends, family, colleagues, and community.

Communication Scale: This scale examines excuses about the way we communicate with others in every domain of life.

Time Management Scale: This scale examines excuses about the way we use time, especially time needed for our most important personal and career pursuits.

Finances Scale: This scale examines excuses about the way we handle our debts, income, budget, investments, and retirement.

Career Scale: This scale examines excuses about our career goals, planning, and "calling."

Serving Scale: This scale examines excuses related to how we serve others.

Three Additional Scales of the Fire Your Excuses Self-Assessment

Potential for Change Scale: This scale measures the likelihood you will make significant changes in the excuse areas that need attention. Knowing your potential for change is as important as how well you scored on the individual excuse scales. The Potential for Change Scale is based on research that indicates who is most likely to make *significant* and, equally important, *permanent* changes.

Offense Scale: This scale measures the amount of career- and life-enhancing actions currently part of one's daily life.

Ideally, your assessment will show a high score on both the Offense and Defense Scale. There are those who are all offense but neglect critical defense activities; likewise, there are those who are all defense and are stuck in a protective holding pattern.

Defense Scale: This scale measures critically important maintenance activities. Be careful not to confuse these set of questions with a measurement of negativity, defensiveness, or denial. Instead, this scale measures *positive* traits, such as how well we take care of the important fundamentals of day-to day living. A good score will be a high score on this scale.

INDEX

B

C

F

N

O

P

T

T

W

Y

Z

FireYourExcuses.com
Log on and make this your year!

You know you have waited long enough to make those changes and fulfill your calling. You are not alone. Log on and get all the support and tools you need to finally keep those promises, to yourself and to others.

Is Your Team or Organization Being Held Back By *Excuses?*

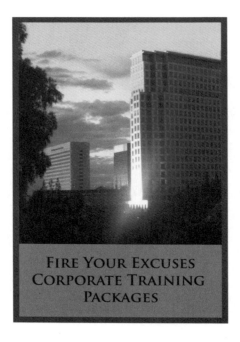

**FIRE YOUR EXCUSES
CORPORATE TRAINING
PACKAGES**

Did you know we deliver more than 250 corporate seminars each year?

If you are interested in exploring a *Fire Your Excuses* seminar that addresses your team's specific leadership, customer service, sales or team-building needs, please contact us at:

info@fireyourexcuses.com

At our website you can order bulk copies of Fire Your Excuses for your team or organization at a discounted price, sign up for our newsletter, and take advantage of our free video and audio tips, interviews and articles. Visit us at:

www.FireYourExcuses.com

Aim Higher...

Introducing the

Fire Your Excuses Coaching Programs

Are you living the life you promised yourself you would be living by now? How much longer do you think it will take to break through on your own? Let us cut years off that timeline by helping you create a challenging, workable and exciting plan of attack.

Unlike traditional goal-setting activities, we will also identify likely obstacles, develop effective responses ahead of time, and provide the necessary support to keep you motivated and on track.

Three Programs to Meet Every Need and Budget

- Level One: Our Single Session: Fire Your Excuses Mastermind Meetings
- Level Two: Our 30-Day Coaching Program
- Level Three: Our 90-Day Coaching Program

For questions about our programs visit:

www.FireYourExcuses.com

"It's Time!"